J. G. Hayes

This Thing Called Courage
South Boston Stories

More pre-publication
REVIEWS, COMMENTARIES, EVALUATIONS . . .

"**T**his *Thing Called Courage* marks the arrival of a major new talent on the gay literary scene. Brutally honest and skillfully crafted, the stories of Hayes' debut collection show us the mean streets of South Boston as we've never seen them before. His young protagonists seek safe haven and succor, some brief respite from the soul-destroying violence of the world around them. Again and again, Hayes strips his characters of their defenses, offering us their longing and confusion, their pain and powerlessness, in prose both lean and lyrical. With an exceptionally sharp eye, and an equally keen ear, Hayes brings to life his embattled Southie boys in all their rough-edged complexity. These are young men hardened by bitter experience, yet Hayes is able to capture, with exquisite precision, the delicate and terrifying beauty of their masculinity, the agonizing tension of their desire.

There is much sadness here, to be sure, but also radiant glimmers of hope, no matter how fleeting or costly. *This Thing Called Courage* is an extraordinary and beautifully written book. Hayes' prose shimmers with life, its rhythms and images luminous with the passion of his young protagonists, boys and men searching, desperately, for some small measure of tenderness in a world determined to deny and destroy it."

Karl Woelz
Co-editor,
Men on Men 2000

Southern Tier Editions
Harrington Park Press®
An Imprint of The Haworth Press, Inc.
New York • London • Oxford

This Thing Called Courage
South Boston Stories

HARRINGTON PARK PRESS
Southern Tier Editions
Gay Men's Fiction
Jay Quinn, Executive Editor

Love, the Magician by Brian Bouldrey

Distortion by Stephen Beachy

The City Kid by Paul Reidinger

Rebel Yell: Stories by Contemporary Southern Gay Authors
edited by Jay Quinn

Rebel Yell 2: More Stories of Contemporary Southern Gay Men
edited by Jay Quinn

Metes and Bounds by Jay Quinn

The Limits of Pleasure by Daniel M. Jaffe

The Big Book of Misunderstanding by Jim Gladstone

This Thing Called Courage: South Boston Stories by J. G. Hayes

Trio Sonata by Juliet Sarkessian

This Thing Called Courage
South Boston Stories

J. G. Hayes

Southern Tier Editions
Harrington Park Press®
An Imprint of The Haworth Press, Inc.
New York • London • Oxford

Published by

Southern Tier Editions, Harrington Park Press®, an imprint of The Haworth Press, Inc., 10 Alice Street, Binghamton, NY 13904-1580.

PUBLISHER'S NOTE
This is a work of fiction. Names, characters, places, and incidents either are the products of the author's imagination or are used fictitiously, and any resemblance to actual persons, living or dead, business establishments, events, or locales is entirely coincidental.

For more information, please visit <www.thisthingcalledcourage.com>.

Cover design concept by Gary Ragaglia.

Photograph by Bernard Lynch.

Library of Congress Cataloging-in-Publication Data

Hayes, J. G. (Joseph George), 1965-
    This thing called courage : South Boston stories / J. G. Hayes.
        p. cm.
    ISBN 1-56023-380-X (alk. paper)—ISBN 1-56023-381-8 (alk. paper)
    1. South Boston (Boston, Mass.)—Fiction I. Title.

PS3608.A93 T48 2001
813'.6—dc21

                                                                    2001039706

For my father

CONTENTS

Acknowledgments

The author wishes to thank all those who inspired, encouraged, and supported this work, but invariably some are forgotten, and I would like to thank those first.

Those I can always remember include Dan Jaffe, who first encouraged me when I was starting out; my two favorite teachers in the world, Roger Mulford and Bill Brotchie, who trekked to New York for another reading, and have always given me laughter, support, and joy; my soul mate in California, Chris Reidy; Vonn "Brett" Moore, who has lovingly kept me fed; my first fan, Johnny O, wherever you are; Jay Quinn, without whom this book would not have been possible, and the best editor a writer could hope for; Susan Abrahms, my client, dear friend, and endless supporter; and my brothers, Bob and Mike, and sisters, Peggy and Maureen, whose love and support have been the few constants in a sometimes crazy life. And a special thank-you to the newest member of the family, Big John, in Florida, whose kindness and support will never be forgotten.

I must also mention my eternal gratitude for the great tale-tellers whose stories filled my head as a child: my late father Franky; and the late Ahern Sisters: Hanorah, Bride, and (especially) Molly and Margaret, who once began a story in Medford, Massachusetts, and didn't come up for air until we had reached our destination somewhere in Upstate New York; and to the greatest listener and supporter of all, my mother, an unflagging beacon of support and love for as long as I can remember.

To all of you, and to the Great Creator who fills our heads with the music of Stories, I will always be grateful.

Regular Flattop

I can't deal with being in this stinking cemetery—

So I close my eyes and see a field of green, the greenest field you've ever seen. There's a boy moving across this field, running in slow motion . . .

There.

That's better.

I feel The Crazies subside.

Audrey Hepburn called them The Mean Reds in *Breakfast at Tiffany's,* and oh I know what she meant but we always call them The Crazies and our names for whatdya whatdya are as good as anybody's.

Now you might be asking what's a kid from the Projects doing knowing Audrey Hepburn movies, but see Ms. Loomis Sophomore year Social Studies made us watch movies once a week, it was pretty cool and once we watched *Breakfast at Tiffany's* though you couldn't really concentrate, Wacko Gibbons had taken a leak in a squirt gun and every now and then was shooting kiss-ass "Straight A" Francis McKay with it two seats in front of him. Francis kept whining that the ceiling was leaking, which was funny, but the best part was when finally Ms. Loomis said, "Francis, just *SHUT UP!*"

Course we took the squirt gun away from Wacko at lunchtime, me and some of the other D Street Boys, we're kinda The Law at school and you can't really have that kinda shit going on. Especially when we hadn't . . . sanctioned Wacko's actions. You know?

So like I was saying I close my eyes and see a field of green—the greenest field you've ever seen. The grass is perfect, mowed to a regulation three-eighths of an inch, flawless. There's a boy moving across this field, moving in slow motion like it's time for the broadcasters to be thanking the sponsors and they're replaying highlights from the game to swelling music, he's moving in slow motion, muscles working beneath the smooth uniform, he's flowing like slow electricity, his face full of quiet intent, the eyes steady, full of purpose, meaning, the chin square, and he's reaching, running, and soon we see for what, a spiraling ball enters the circle of blue above him, it's to catch this ball that he's yearning, toward which the muscles are swirling beneath the clean uniform.

And I feel The Crazies subside as I see all this, as I occupy my mind with trying to see if this is a day game or a night game I'm playing in.

Listen, I do this all the time. Some of us boys drink and some of us do a little drugging ("Scooby Snacks") and some of us do a little of both. But the only thing that really helps me any lately is my field of green.

Calmer now, I open my eyes. Maybe I can handle this now—

Before me is a field of green. But it's not my field of green. This field's bumpy and the early summer sun's already desecrated the grass with these browned-out splotches like oil spills, only dry, because this ain't the ocean, see, it's Gate of Heaven Cemetery. A hungry hole gapes at my feet, even the June sun won't go down there, though Dad's flowered, flagged (of course he's a veteran, who do you think fights all these wars, we do) coffin does go down there, four fat guys from Ryans' Funeral Parlor are huffing puffing getting red-faced as they fight with the screeching pulleys. And the coffin lowers before my eyes.

Ma goes into a flop and The Girls more or less catch her. The Girls are Dad's two unmarried sisters, about fiftyish, they own the Hair Say Salon down on West Broadway. They're twins, they got identical jet-black beehives and matching black moustaches and huge jiggly triceps the size of Cincinnati. And moles, that's the only way you can tell them apart, Claire's is on the right side of her mouth and Shirley's is on the left, and sometimes when I'm weird in the head I think of them in Grandma Donovan's womb, like they started out not as an egg but as a mole, and as they grew they were face to face, mole to mole, floating in fluidy inner space, they were like Siamese twins joined at the mole until the mole split and they were born.

"Don't say mole, you retard, say Beauty Mark," Ma corrected me one time in her very own way when The Girls were over to our house for Friday Night Cards.

"Whatdya whatdya," I said back to her, I always say that we always say that, The Boys and me. I mean, what the hell else you gonna say sometimes, I'd like to know.

The Girls kind of prop Ma up. A wave of satisfied sympathy wiggles through the crowd, "God Help Us" and "The Poor Thing" run through the gathered mourners like the first flu bug of the school year, quick like that. People like Ma's display of grief, it's what they came here for.

But I just stand there.

I know she's just drunk again.

I remind myself not to look East, toward the ocean three blocks away, Bib's buried down that end of the cemetery somewheres, I try to find his grave once in a while but I get all fucked up, that's Crazies Turf big time down there, all those dead people, too many, who would've thought there was so many dead people in the world and I start sweating and running crazy like in a dream.

Fuckin' Bib, man. People always say We Don't Know Why, We Don't Know Why—

But I know why.

Tommy puts his arm around my shoulder and squeezes my right delt. This relaxes me a bit. I'd maybe be flopping too if Tommy wasn't here with me, all six feet of muscle and bone and blue eyes of him. He's my best friend, Tommy Flaherty, always has been, one of my best friends, him and me and Bib, and also Sean and Kevin and Brian. We're part of The Boys, The Project Boys, The D Street Boys, you can tell who we are, we got the shamrock tattoo on the right delt and the DSBF (D Street Boys Forever) on the left, and we got the certain way of dressing and the certain way of walking—light, like—and we got smooth skin (I wish mine was hairier) and we tan it down at Castle Island playing ball or just hanging out. Though me and Bib and Tommy decided at the last minute to get a heart around the DSBF. The other Boys were a little pissed but didn't say nothing.

"You need a haircut," Tommy whispers in my ear. I've let my flattop grow out a little since I promised Dad I'd get the fuck outta here, this is the first sign and Tommy knows it.

"You still thinkin' o' leavin'?" he mumbles.

I squeeze my eyes bite my lip I didn't even know I was crying The Boys don't really ever cry but I feel an embarrassing tear squirming down my cheek. Tommy takes one long finger from his hand on my delt, and wipes it away.

"Fuck," he says. "You can't leave."

We're back at the house now for the Back to the House, there's a
million people in the kitchen but not Tommy, he had to go back to
work, his brother gets him this job every summer roofin'. You wouldn't
think Tommy this big strong kid would have stuffed animals but he
does, there's five or six of them on his bed, Teddy, Fuzzy, What's Up
With That? But when he was twelve I'll tell you all about it his father
ran off with his own second cousin Rita Flaherty (remember her?)
and Tommy was playing in the Babe Ruth Championship Game the
next day, and before they started they had like this father-son game
for the players and their dads and they had these pre-game introduc-
tions with a real microphone and they kept calling and calling
Tommy's father. But no. And everyone knew why. On the biggest day
of his kid's life. Tommy was standing out there on the third-base line
all alone wind blowing his uniform with everyone else, except everyone else had a father beside him or at least an uncle or something.
Tommy didn't talk for weeks after that, no not a word, even the nuns
at school couldn't get him to talk ("Defiant! March Yourself Down to
the Principal, Mr. Defiant!'). Then one day we were up to Woolworth's and Tommy pulled this Teddy Bear out of a bin, he was buried beneath the others and all mushed and dusty, he stole him and
brought him home and every year close to the anniversary of that
Babe Ruth game he goes out and does the same, gets this really sad-
looking Teddy Bear and adds him to his collection.

I asked him about it one night we were fifteen, "What's Up With
Those Bears?" and he looked at me but didn't say nothing then about
a week later we were playing in a game and right in the middle of the
third inning he called Time and walked over to me and said, "They
Don't Go Back on You, That's Why."

Whatdya whatdya. We all got our thing and it ain't for me to say. I
got my Field of Green, Tommy's got his bears, and Bib—

I don't know, I guess maybe Bib figured he had me.

These losers from Dot High one time after a game jumped Tommy
and insulted his bears, I don't know how they heard and Tommy
kicked the shit out of them all but at the last second one of them
pulled a knife and sliced Tommy's face open. He's got this scar that
runs from his eyebrow all the way down to his chin, like the Master
Hand that carved his chiseled face oopsed at the last second.

I wish he was here back to the house with me now but he's not, I
think of him up on a roof a couple of blocks away banging nails with

his shirt off dangling tool belt and something goes click inside me. Me, I still got my paper route even though I'm going into Senior Year, what the hell, I'm free by six every morning and then I can go back to bed or whatdya whatdya then go play ball.

Baseball's really the only game worth playing. There's this beauty about it, the flow of the game's like Life, it can be as nice and easy as a summer sky or as crazy and intense as a Fellini movie on Scooby Snacks (Ms. Loomis made us watch one of them too) and there's no such thing as a regulation size outfield (that's where I play) it goes on and on forever, even if you jumped over the left-field fence and caught a ball a mile from the stadium it would still be an out. It goes on, is what I'm saying. Man, nothing like a neon-green ballpark on a summer's night, Excitement, Stretching, Sweat, The Crowds, Sweet Summer Smell, Boys in Clean Uniforms, Anything Can Happen (but within reason, you know?) Your Best Nine Against Ours. *You* try hitting a ball coming at you ninety miles an hour with a piece of wood three inches in diameter. It's Art, man.

Bib always dreamed of going to Art school.

Bib played left field next to me, Tommy still plays right, I'm in the middle, the center fielder, always been. I'm sitting at the kitchen table at Back to the House, my father was buried today but I'm thinking about something Bib said about a month ago, right before he died. We were playing rich kids from some prep school way the fuck out in the suburbs somewhere. There was trouble of course, two of the rich kids were talking before the game and one of them said to the other Is Your Pater Coming Today, I Just E-Mailed Mine With Directions, and Tommy behind them thought they were talking over his head on purpose so he said Who the Fuck's Pater and gave one of them a wedgie and chucked the kid's laptop into these bushes. Coach benched Tommy, told us all You Embarrassed Yourselves, but hey they're gonna have everything and us the shit end of the stick so for once, plus they won the game that day you wonder why does God let shit like that happen you'd think just once, but I wouldn't trade places, they're geeks and we're cool and it must really suck being a geek even if you do have everything.

Plus what the fuck was that kid doing bringing a laptop to a baseball game for?

Bib of course didn't get involved, he never would in that kind of thing unless someone was about to hurt me.

He'd been quiet that day, more than usual I mean, then he yelled over to me from left field when there was a lull in the game and said, "Timmy. You can't go nowhere no more."

I turned to look at him. Someone hit a ball toward Bib just then and I guided him like we always did for each other, Back Back Left Now Stay and he caught it, carefully like he always did, both hands clutched softly like he was catching a bird you wouldn't want to hurt. Then he'd take the ball—always—out of his glove and look at, like he was surprised such a thing as a baseball was in his glove, his head would like jump back a little. Then he'd throw the ball in.

And turn and look at me.

"You can't go nowhere," he repeated, his eyes like open wounds. Bib was the redhead in our group but he had the same Regular Boys Flattop we all did, that's another way you can tell we're The Boys. Except I'm letting mine grow out a little, I promised Dad I'd get the fuck outta here.

Someone made the last out and we trotted in together.

Bib put his arm around me, you could get away with that in a game. Bib was always careful about when he touched me, looking around even when we were alone. Just funny things you notice.

"In the olden days you could go off to the woods, the frontier or something," he said lowly, holding me back as we got near the bench, "you could start a new life. Say we lived a hunnert years ago, if you and me wanted to—I mean, as an example, I mean—we could just get the fuck outta here and be smelling pines by the end of the day and just . . . just squat on some land and start a farm."

I got that sizzle again, the one I got whenever he talked about me and him. But these talks about our future only went so far with Bib. Maybe, I think now, that's as far as he could go without me meeting him halfway, which I was always afraid to do. But that sizzle, it started in my mouth like you just had Novocaine, then shot down to your stomach and settled where your protective cup goes, right there and behind.

Tommy was sitting on the bench, he didn't like not to be included when it was just me and Bib and when Bib got up to bat Tommy slid over to me and said, "What was you and Bib talking about?"

"Just Bib shit," I answered, sometimes Bib said weird stuff.

"Whatdya whatdya," Tommy said, kicking his left cleat forward, raising a mini-dust storm, that meant Okay Don't Tell Me I Don't Give a Fuck.

I had to wait for us to get back to the outfield for Bib to finish what he was driving at.

"You can't do that no more, go somewheres," he called over from left. "The . . . see, the whole world's been snatched and deeded and clicked off and turned into . . . into Windermere, An Exclusive Executive Community By The Sea. Architect Designed, and Gated for Your Protection." He was quoting the sign down at the new condos for rich people where the skating rink used to be.

He didn't say nothing more went right home after the bus trip back to town.

I think of Bib's words today at my father's funeral party. But then I'm always thinking of Bib's words lately. Trying not to really.

I'm sitting at the kitchen table and Uncle Joe's latest girlfriend, I think her name's Sally, she's sitting next to me and she's listening to a Ma harangue across the table from us and I want to tell this Sally lady Look, You Don't Have To Try and Impress Ma, She's Going to Forget Everything Later Anyway, and the one thing I like about Ma, the thing I hate about her the most is She Just Don't Give a Fuck.

About anything. Or anyone.

And you can't go nowhere no more.

Whatdya whatdya.

"He wahs a saint," Ma's blurring now, her plastic cup has a butt floating in it but she has her red hand in a vice grip around it like she's going to drink from it and I sit here hoping she will, wondering if she will. "And let me tell you something, Missy!" she rasps, changing tack, and now her finger is in this Sally's face and I know trouble's about to start and Uncle Joe sails over from the getting-moldy cold cuts on the counter where he's been having a race I think with some yellow-toothed fat guy to see who can cram the most sandwiches down their gullet. He pulls Sally up from the table and leads her to less troubled waters, Hey Cousin Pat, Have You Met Sally, and I look up and notice one of The Girls is eyeing me rather ill-humoredly, I think it's Shirley but I'm confused today, they just buried my father.

My mistake is—see, you want to hate us, The Boys, cuz we're cocky and maybe beautiful some of us, but we always make mistakes and we crash and burn just as you others are getting ready for Grad

School, Thanks Pater—my mistake is I make eye contact with Shirley (I think) and she springs to life like she's a Disney animatron pro-
grammed to come alive once someone makes eye contact with her.
She dumps her hairy forearms onto the table, leans toward me and
rasps, "Your mother's gonna need a lot more help around the house
Mister now that your father's . . . G-G-GONE!" This last word comes
out like a hippopotamus precharge warning bellow I saw once on one
of those nature shows they got on Cable at three in the morning when
no one's watching, and now all eyes are on me which I hate except on
the ballfield. Ma and The Girls light up fresh cigarettes of grief at this
latest display, adding to the pall that's stuck just below the ceiling like
incense Heaven doesn't want. Oh, I forgot to say that Ma and The
Girls are still wearing their sunglasses from the graveside service an
hour ago, which makes them look like The Furies we read about in
Greek Mythology, only like postmodern, burned-out versions, all
fucked up at what they've done but compelled nevertheless to Do It
Again Do It Again Harder, Harder.

Ma jerks to life at Shirley's words.

"What, him?" she snorts, jerking her rat's nest hair in my general
direction. "Oh, forget it, brother! Goddamn paperboy! Thinks he'sh
gonna be another Ted Williams, the stupid dreamer!"

The Girls shake their beehives in collective sympathy. Relations I
haven't seen in years and strangers I've never met before stare at me
as if Ma's appraisal is the definitive one.

"Whatdya whatdya," I mumble back, downing the last of my beer
in one gulp, but I close my eyes and see a field of green, the greenest
field you've ever seen, and there's order here, there's, okay, symme-
try, beauty, as a boy with my smooth face, my eyes, black smudges
beneath the too-long-for-a-boy lashes moves in slow motion across
this field. Above, a sky of blue arches over me like a gymnast stretching before a meet at a track, or maybe out in woods still undeeded
where you could go start a farm with a friend.

But Bib died a month ago.

I lift myself up from the table, excuse myself through the crowd
that seems to part for me and climb the stairs knees shaking to my attic bedroom. The walls are covered with my heroes, baseball players
all, I like the full-length posters best, that way I can compare my body
alone at night with my heroes', I'm catching up to them here in the bi-
ceps, there in the shoulders but beneath my belt down there you know

my pants aren't quite as full but when I think about that The Crazies come so I try to come quick and not tell myself what I'm thinking about. I have Thoughts. But I have to be careful of these Thoughts or Mr. Cozy will get me again and then they'll be no stopping anything.

Like before.

I told the priest once. I talked about It. I had to or I would have imploded with The Crazies. It was two years ago I was sixteen, I went to Confession and picked the priest visiting from Ireland he's blind so you could see his eyes open all the time that he was kind and not looking at you like some of the others sniffing out Thoughts. The New Curriculum brought these Thoughts to a head. Let me explain.

They'd given certain ones of us a special curriculum at school, *Urban Youth at Risk* they called it, new teachers, skinny angry guys with long hair, sour-faced women pickled in patchouli that seemed to have a thing against white boys How Do You Feel, Tell Us How Does That Make You Feel they'd constantly ask us, but we could tell they looked down on us Projects Kids, Aggressive White Males they said, but they couldn't see how scared living in The Projects made us dirty needles wife beating husband beating kid beating dick beating to try and forget broken glass grass won't grow it tries but dead by May that's when my birthday is Ma forgot this year so we'd just say Whatdya Whatdya, That's How I Fuckin' Feel, and then they'd send you to the principal just like any other teacher. One of these new courses was Processing Feelings and one time the teacher wanted us to talk about our dreams and Tommy said deadpan he had one recurring that he couldn't figure none, a hot dog was chasing a doughnut down Broadway. We all laughed but the teacher turned red instead Go to the Principal You yeah funny but the important thing was, that night wet I dreamt of a hot dog chasing another hot dog down Broadway then catching up rubbing against each other sweating and then Tommy was there with a hot dog dangling from his mouth it was mine.

I thought I'd go crazy every night these dreams came back but different so I went to see the blind priest from Ireland Bless Me Father For I Have Sinned.

"I have Thoughts," I whispered through the screen, Mrs. McGillicuddy was right outside the Confessional booth and she's a gossip with Mother Ears you gotta be careful.

"And what are these thoughts, my son?"

One-billionth of these Thoughts are Bib in the locker room drying off one foot up on the bench open up like that and I could see standing behind it was hanging there and I want to catch it soft like a bird you wouldn't want to hurt and Tommy the way his neck looks after a regular boy's flattop there's a ribbon of white flesh where the sun hasn't tanned it yet and I want to take his Teddy Bears' place at night and hold him and tell him everything will be okay and that I'll always go to his games, all of them, and I want to climb on top of him I'm a hard drill there's never been nothing in the universe half so hard and drill into him till I strike oil but I don't know how and this is the worst thing a nightmare of yes and no at the same time and you can't ever tell anyone—

"And what are these thoughts?" the priest asks again.

"Whatdya whatdya," I whisper. I start to get up.

"Don't go," he says. "Don't be afraid."

I kneel back down. I think I'm gonna puke.

"Is it . . . is it other boys?" he asks.

I panic, it must show. "How the—how did you—"

"I can feel your despair," he says. "I can tell. Everyone thinks it's the worst. It isn't. It's what you've been given."

I feel sweat running down my sides. The Crazies have entered the Church and they're sniffing getting closer, they know I'm here but they don't know exactly where yet—

"I can't go on," I say. It's odd—the words come out casually like I'm saying Bismarck is the capital of North Dakota instead of relating suicidal thoughts.

"You're not alone," he says. "Try . . . try thinking of this as a blessing, instead of a curse. A blessing. That's a good start. Can you do that?"

"Thank you," I say. I have to leave. I think I might faint or scream or puke so I lurch to the front of the church and kneel before the altar. I like the smell of churches when there's hardly anyone here beeswax candles furniture polish oak benches wet wool brought in from the rain altar flowers incense.

A Blessing. I've been given a Blessing. Actually I was hoping for a Longinnes. Then I think of something. I raise my eyes up to the statue of Jesus before me, he's pointing to his open heart like he's down at the Free Clinic describing his symptoms.

"God," I pray, "bless Bib and Tommy."

Up in my room I hear the voices from Back to the House down-stairs the laughing the crying the shrieking the yelling the singing the arguing the tale-telling, they don't hear me but The Crazies do, they bound up the stairs merciless motherfuckers two at a time after me. The Crazies: they are a jumbo size anxiety attack a baker's dozen of anxiety attacks a battalion of anxiety attacks and finally they catch up to me in my room, I'm sitting on the floor in a corner of my bedroom with my fingers jammed into my ears and they find me and finally at last I must think of Bib. My father was buried today but thoughts of Bib finally get me. They lay me low. I lay down flat and let them wash over me like acid rain or the terrible coming of God I have no choice I start dry heaving I haven't eaten yet today.

My whole body begins to shake. My mind hits the turbo-charge button and I hear those engines hum. Weird thoughts come at me like obstacles in a road to me the speeding car and I crash into them over and over. I think: somewhere in this city at this moment there is a woman, and she's trying to decide whether to do her afternoon shop-ping at Neiman Marcus or Talbots. Somewhere downtown, there's a man moving vast amounts of imaginary money from Singapore to Sydney for his banking firm, identifying all the while with the corpo-rate careerist ads scrolling away at the top of his computer screen while two feet away from him, separated by a wall, lurks the Upper Management Rest Room and its porcelain heart, where today's power lunch will eventually make its way. Close by, I think also, there's someone else working for an ad agency, and they're airbrushing a platinum-toothed model so that this model will look even more per-fect. But perhaps, I think, this airbrusher has a child with Down's syn-drome. Who will never be in an ad. Meanwhile, while they are doing all that, I'm lying here on the floor wondering if I can stand up. I try but I can't. But maybe I can crawl. I do crawl. I crawl to the opposite corner of my bedroom. There's a shrine here. There's a Shrine to Bib here. Dusty baseball trophies I pulled from his mother's trash a week after he died how could she the sweatshirt that Oh God still smells of him I borrowed and never got to return soft against my face like a bird you wouldn't want to hurt ever some photos: First Holy Communion Day, some times at Fenway Park, flexing down at the beach when no one was looking I bring these things to my chest I think I might be dying or giving birth something inside like *Aliens* I'm wracked by sobs like knives I double over Oh Bib I'm So Sorry,

So So Sorry, Can You Come Back I'll Tell You, I Swear Bib I'll Tell
You Everything, I Should Have Told You That Night Bib But I Couldn't,
I Couldn't . . .

And more. Private though.

After a while I think—
I have to get to Tommy's. Or die.

This thought hits me quick. I have to get to Tommy. I wonder if
he's home from work yet and I wonder if he's . . . okay. He'd never do
what Bib did would he?

Would he?

There's this game at the arcade we used to play Save the Princess a
video game (they got rid of it), you could push either button once you
put your quarters in, Save the Princess or Save the Prince. If you were
a boy, you were supposed to push the Save the Princess button and
your character was this Big Stud who kicked ass for ten screens then
finally rescued The Princess in this temple or something on the very
last screen, she was lying there on this fancy purple couch with this
look on her face like she wanted to do something she'd have to go to
Confession for later. If you were a girl you were supposed to push the
Save the Prince button and your character was this very pissed-off
Amazon who kicked ass for ten screens and then finally rescued The
Prince in his castle but just standing there like he was waiting for the
Broadway Bus not like he wanted to do something. But this one time
it must have been broken cuz I was the Big Stud but when I got to the
final screen I was pretty good at this there was The Prince there by ac-
cident not The Princess, I guess the machine was broken once, it
never happened again. But for once I was the Big Stud and I rescued
The Prince and hot dogs chased each other around the castle all afternoon.

It was broken, defective.

That's not why they got rid of it. It had an ending that's why, you
could win this game, see, now all the games have no ending but the
screens just get harder and harder and they used psychology I guess
they know how to drive you crazy and I sit here in my bedroom and
think I have to get to Tommy's but on this day it's like that video game
there'll be all these bad asses to overcome My Anxiety The Crazies
The People Downstairs My Grief My Guilt My Shame but I must get
to him. I wonder is there an end to this game called Life or does it go

on and on driving you crazy, is God a kindly programmer who lets you win once in a while or a greedy consultant with a marketing degree who knows just how to drive you shithouse putting in quarters all the time hoping, when you can't really ever.

The sun is coming into my bedroom like a stab. Perhaps God or whatever is like the sun, dumping goofy goodness across half the world at a time. You're not in its path, you're shit out of luck. I'm so fucking sick of thinking like this, I just want to think about normal eighteen-year-old shit like who won the game last night or who I'm gonna bring to the prom but then I can't think of that either or The Crazies will come—

Tommy—

I change: cut-off navy blue sweatpants, black Cons no socks, a Tommy H. tank top, Nike hat backward, it's black, I'll wear something black for a year in honor of Dad and Bib, I decide. No undies. But I won't think about that right now, I'll allow myself to feel this fact as I go to save The Prince but I won't think too much about it that might be disrespectful, Dad was buried today.

Dad. Ma's a mean drunk but Dad was different. Giddy, goofy after one drink,

> *Now why didn't I marry Old Mary Tunney?*
> *She's as ugly as sin—but has boo-tee-ful money!*

Morose for old Ireland after two,

> *Do you remember in Black '54,*
> *The Dead buried the dead,*
> *And still there were more . . .*

and if he wasn't home by midnight I'd go look for him up to Casey's, or The Banshee, or any other of a dozen piss-smelling dumps between home and the hospital he washed floors at, second shift. Sometimes you know I'd find him on the edge of Broadway, never the sidewalk ("I bumped into a woman with a stroller once and I'll never forgive myself,") weaving in and out of the honking cars, singing that same old, "Heart of My Heart." Other times he'd be sitting in some dark door stoop, staring out at nothing and everything with eyes like a homeless dog, finding comfort nowhere.

But his face would light up when he saw me, each time was like the first time I'd done this, Oh, Tis Timmy, Oh Look Timmy Now, Oh, Tis Glad I Am to See You Boy, My Boy, My Beautiful Beautiful Boy, like we hadn't seen each other in years, and I don't know why but we'd both cry, yeah alright sometimes I'd be high on Scooby Snacks but most times not, he'd hug me and say If I've Done Nothing Else I've Brought Someone As Beautiful As You Boy Into the World, and then he'd say what a dismal father he was, what a rotten example he'd set, he'd wanted to be an artist but got the Dengue Fever in the War and it'd given him the shakes so bad he couldn't hope to Hit a Bull's Ass With a Handful of Rice, he'd say, let alone take a brush to canvas, and that Ma loved me even though she had a Tongue Could Clip a Hedge, Remember Now Timmy She Lost Three in the Womb Before You Come To Bless Us and She Don't Dare Love You For Fear You'll Be Taken Too, and he drank, he said, because his dreams had died so Don't Ever Let Your Dreams Die Timothy Donovan, and Remember All This When I'm Gone.

Which he is now.

Bib too, buried about a hundred yards from my father, though I can never find his grave, it's Crazies Turf down there big time, that's their fucking East Coast Headquarters.

"Fly," Dad said the last time I visited him in the hospital, where once he washed floors at but then came to die in. "Get out, as far as you can go Timothy. Promise me now there's a good boy."

"Wh—where?" I'd asked, gulping so I wouldn't bawl.

"Somewhere you've never been before," he whispered, tubes everywhere. "Somewhere . . . somewhere beautiful."

I promised. Which is why my hair's a little longer now.

I begin The Game, making my way to Tommy's.

The thing about The Projects is, you can shinny down a drainpipe, hop a few fences and you're everywhere you need to be, with the lit-up-like Oz downtown towers in the backdrop. That makes me sizzle too, that view, that sizzle I told you about earlier that I'd get whenever me and Bib talked about our future, or, well, when Bib talked about it and I'd sit there and tingle staring back into his green eyes green like a perfect ballfield like my field of green the greenest field you've ever seen. I'd sit there and stare back at him and tingle. But he never knew. I guess I was always hoping The Tingles were somehow telepathic.

They're not you know.

I'm just telling you so you'll know.

I'm over three fences already. Little kids with runny noses from the sea breeze are playing ball in a dirty alley. I stop, stare, put my hands on my hips, spread my legs. Their mouths drop and their game comes to a halt bounce bounce bounce goes their ball down the alley and no one even notices it cuz I'm one of the D Street Boys and they don't know if I'm going to shake them down for cigarette and beer money or give them a beating just for shits though I never would or whatdya whatdya.

I'm on my way to Tommy's and this is another screen I have to get through first.

"Get this when you're fourteen," I say, pointing to the shamrock tattoo. "This means . . . you survive. Think of everything we been through. Starvation, war, oppression . . . we're still here." They're blinking, drinking this all in. One of them nods.

"Get this when you're sixteen," I say, showing the DSBF. "This means you stick together. This means . . . you don't let no one you love die."

I squat down. I put on my Bollé shades as my eyes are beginning to fill up. This would never do, they would dis me and everything I've just said if they saw me crying.

"What about the heart?" the tallest of them choirboy voice asks, pointing. "The heart around the DSBF?"

I pause. What about the heart.

"You get that if you're Blessed," I say. "You'll know when you're older."

I want to open my arms to them like the Statue of Jesus at the entrance to Gate of Heaven Cemetery, because some of them are already sniffing paint thinner at the age of ten. But I don't. I want to gather them into my arms. But I don't. I wanted to tell Bib that from the top of the Edison Plant you could see this island way out in the harbor, way out, you could tell it was deserted, I watched it all the time when we'd be up there drinking. I wanted to tell Bib we could go there, just me and him, we could go there and start a farm, they were talking about making a National Park out of the whole fuckin' harbor but not yet, we could go there, we could float out one night with all our stuff and start a farm.

But I never told him. That's what I want to say when I try and find his grave, I want to lift his grave up to the top of the Edison Plant and show him our island but I can't find his goddamn grave, it's the center of The Crazies Black Hole down there did I already mention that?

"Stay in school," I tell the kids. I don't gather them in, though I want to. I open one arm, but scratch my head with it instead.

Then I resume my journey to Tommy's, I need him and maybe vice versa and besides, Tommy's got Mr. Cozy and I think I might need him too.

Mr. Cozy, he's a stuffed animal, a Teddy Bear, but we were running back from the East Side one night a month ago, the cops were chasing us because we walked on the hoods of these Range Rovers, BMWs, Volvo wagons with cages in the back for trophy dogs named Josh and Sam, there's new people moving in and they're driving lots of other people out. The New People want to live in an urban neighborhood so their lives can resemble what they see in their fat smelly magazines, what they watch on TV in their Media Rooms. The cops were chasing us because **Cop Theorem Number One: When Rich People Call the Cops About Project Kids Walking on the Hoods of Their Expensive Cars, The Cops Respond.** Up this alley, over that fence—wait, there's the lights—Fuck, run!—and we melted back into the West Side like the coming of the night and we flew up this alley seven of us it was trash night and there was Mr. Cozy sitting upside down in a smelly barrel that someone threw out. I saw Tommy in front of me do a double take when we ran by, because Mr. Cozy had all the sadness of this world in his eyes.

We stopped breathless panting at the end of the alley and the glare of the streetlight behind him made Tommy's scar vanish for a minute and my breath left me more, like a punch in the belly from Hambone Kelly.

Tommy said, "I gotta go back for that bear."

"What the *fuck!*" one of the other guys said. The sirens got closer and everyone screwed over the alley wall thump thump of sneakers but Tommy just stood there didn't move so of course me and Bib stuck with him. I watched Tommy burst back down the alley just as the cops were shining their flashlights from the other end Hey You Fuckin' Kids Stop, and a flash of lightning coiled through the steamy night. A groan of thunder rumbled overhead like grown-ups fighting upstairs and you don't know why.

Tommy came back to us in three bounds we flew over the wall I could see under his arm he had that Teddy Bear we were running fast man Tommy was in front he's fastest like a greyhound with those long legs working like pistons churning and under his arm facing me I could see this liberated Teddy Bear. He had extended arms as if to hug, a little hole on his side where some of his innards had leaked out, and the words "Mr. Cozy" stenciled across his chest in floppy red felt.

We came to another alley halfway down and there was this two-story chain-link fence **Cop Theorem Number Two: Cops Will Sometimes Climb a One-Story Fence But Never a Two-Story One,** so we sprang up the fence the three of us Mr. Cozy made four and I could see our shadows on the ground below us, we looked like bugs caught in a web, then plop we're in some kind of indoor/outdoor garage neither the one nor the other with big mother concrete pillars. We stood behind one huddled close so they wouldn't see, listening, straining for the sound of fat feet flat feet running in the service of the rich because these are just the types of young urbans The Mayor wants to attract to our neighborhood and he'll be damned if any trashy kids make it uncomfortable for them by walking on the hoods of their fine automobiles.

We were a circle facing each other a triangle I could feel their breath Tommy pulled Mr. Cozy from under his arm and stuck him in the middle of us all three of us holding him up with our chests. Then cop voices harsh like dogs chasing us beams of light further down Shut Up Here They Come and I guess part of me was sticking out behind the pillar because Bib then put his hand there where no one else ever had except this drunk girl down the beach one night Nice Bum Where You From she said but Bib didn't say nothing just put his hand there and pushed in but didn't take his hand away and it's like I'm turning into liquid fire from the inside out. Our bodies were in this circle facing each other wicked close pressed together Mr. Cozy was in the middle looking scared and sad and Tommy was stroking him lightly you wouldn't think such big hands, then the flashlight beams like stabs probing for an organ like a blind surgeon or a blind priest feeling for where it hurt the most and I found I was stroking Mr. Cozy, Bib was too, you couldn't help it cuz Mr. Cozy was scared he wasn't used to this cop stuff you could tell he was trembling but I don't know if it was me or Tommy or Bib or all three of us and NOT because the cops were chasing us, that shit happened all the time, man.

Then the lights were gone.

Still we kept stroking Mr. Cozy—very quietly, you gotta be careful those cops are sneaky sometimes, our hands brushing each other's a little bit.

Stroking Mr. Cozy and now I think maybe he was like a genie's lamp in that alley just waiting to be rubbed and make Something happen cuz after all these years DSBF with a heart around it but no way to talk about it no way to think about it no way to do anything about it and now this cuz Tommy then put his long arms around me and Bib and pulled us in closer still our faces together like Origami we did once in Art Class Tommy's cheek against mine soft with tickly little bristles. Lightning flashed or maybe it was inside me. Then Bib's lips against my forehead he was shaking, a mouth I'd seen all my life tight with swears or ejecting puked-up beer or receiving Holy Communion was now soft tender electricity against my skin. And his hand was still Down There but rubbing now across back and forth and then Tommy's hand too and then both their hands went down the back of my baggy nylon gym shorts against my skin white and never before.

The rain started then Hollywood rain that was nowhere then everywhere we pulled closer still and breathing fast again now Tommy was shaking hard and his blue eyes like white in the night I watched it as it watched Bib undo his shorts and they fell with a whoosh sound to his knees and then it was like in my dreams there was a hot dog hard looking for its fellow hot dogs lurching sniffing and I heard myself gasp.

Tommy reached for it slow like he wasn't sure if it was heaven, or hell, but then his hand stopped midway. He backed up. He screamed, or maybe it was thunder. His fists clenched by his sides, his face squirming—I knew so well without seeing. Mr. Cozy fell to the concrete floor wet already. Tommy snatched him up quick like that.

"We . . . better . . . stop or . . . Mr. Cozy's gonna get us all," Tommy panted. He kind of snorted like a laugh but not funny.

"Fuck," he said.

"Whatdya whatdya," I said, attempting normal voice but no.

Bib had his head down and his face was scarlet like he was waiting to see what next. Man, the courage of him that night—Bib—

Tommy looked at us both, then flew back up the fence and was gone.

I kept watching the rain plop on the garage floor between my sneakers but eventually I had to look. See I had to.

I didn't see Tommy again till after Bib's funeral, which was three days after that night. I couldn't go to Bib's funeral, I couldn't say nothing to him after we did what we did in the garage that night after Tommy left, couldn't even look him in the eye, couldn't even walk home with him Guilt of course more Guilt now sure but lately my guilt is being joined by rage as I wonder WHO MADE THIS THING SO FUCKING BAD THAT YOU CAN'T EVEN LOOK SOMEONE IN THE EYE, CAN'T EVEN WALK SOMEONE HOME, cuz I couldn't. Couldn't even walk home with him cuz I was shaking and puking after all these years and then finally.

Just like how now, I can't gather these kids into my arms, though I want to.

Mr. Fucking Useless.

All my life I've heard from everyone teachers priests cops nuns judges parents probation officers We Must Have Laws, What Kind of Crazy World Would It Be if Everyone Just Did What They Wanted to All the Time, And You've Broken the Law and Therefore You Must Be Punished—

But I want to tell you this world is plenty fucked up for me even with all these laws and I think, I really do think it would be better the other way, if we all only did what we wanted to. But are too afraid to.

Because you know that night, after me and Bib did what we did I wanted to tell him . . . I wanted to say to him—

I wish I had said to him—

But's it too fuckin' late now.

He's dead. Bib.

Someday when I'm a man if God spares me and I make it out of here and have some money I'll go to a counselor, a good counselor who cares and isn't looking at the clock on the desk all the time and wondering *Now what fucking drug will calm this one down,* and they'll help me talk about Bib and maybe I'll get over it—

But I can't say nothing more about him right now.

I'm almost at Tommy's. I begin to slow down as I get closer. It's getting harder the closer I get. Now, what exactly was I going to say to him?

My D-Street Whistle brings him out to his back porch. It's Tommy. Jesus it's Tommy and he's very much alive. He's okay and alive and standing on his back porch. That's where they found Bib too, on his back porch.

Tommy's big hands grip the porch railing as he leans over one story above me. He's only wearing plaid boxers and his tattooed delts blue on white skin look like epaulets from a war. There's a humming inside me, like engines starting up or some fuckin' thing. My mouth's dry like the morning after the night before.

We stare at each other.

"So ahh . . . how was back to the house?" he finally asks.

"Nahhh . . . it sucked," I mumble.

We keep staring at each other.

"Sorry," he says.

I nod. Then I take a deep breath, no idea what I'm going to say—

"Tommy listen, I was ahhh . . . thinking . . . I . . . I was like wondering if maybe . . . I might borrow Mr. Cozy tonight."

Tommy freezes. Our eyes lock and I think he's holding his breath. We haven't ever talked about it ever but I think he feels like me it's now or never, the neighborhood's full up with bars where you can go and happily drown the words you can't say until you're dead and can't say them then even if you wanted to.

And I promised Dad.

"The n-nights are hardest," I say, kind of mumbly. I look up. I see Tommy gulp, the large Adam's Apple going up, then down, his smooth throat.

"I know it," he says, nodding. "I . . . .Aw fuck, Timmy. If . . . if I didn't freak out that night . . . I keep thinkin' if only I stayed the night we . . . that night." His hand makes a futile gesture, then drops slowly back to the railing again.

He looks at me. I think he's crying.

I see now that Tommy has Mr. Cozy's eyes, all that sadness. It hits me that we have more than one thing in common, more than two things in common.

We stare at each other.

"Tommy," I say.

"Yeah?" he murmurs, cocking his head toward me.

"I . . . I don't . . . I don't think I'm going to leave," I say. "I think."

I know he knows what I mean.

He's still staring at me. I see his jaw tighten. He turns away for a minute, blinks hard. He takes a deep breath, cracks his knuckles. He turns back and looks down at me again, searching for something. By now I have my arms wide open, like the Statue of Jesus.

This time for once I finally do.

I see a look on Tommy's face I've never seen in its entirety, only the beginning of it.

A sob blurts out from his mouth. He bolts from the porch. A minute or two later I hear him bounding down his back stairs. He comes through the fence door into his backyard. He stops ten feet away from me. He's put on green striped sweatpants and a white T-shirt.

We stare at each other. There are tears running down his cheeks. Holy shit. Holy Water.

"Take off your sunglasses, Timmy," he says.

Somewhere in this city, someone's raising his finger for another drink. Somewhere down the street, a very busy realtor with bright red lipstick, a little on her teeth, is rearranging her face into a smile to ask a young couple in Consuming Mode what their budget might be, deciding by their answer whether or not she could be bothered with them. Right out front there's an abandoned dog purposefully walking, intent on dog business.

But here in Tommy's backyard, I think a miracle's happening, right in between the rusted clothesline and the peeling-painted bulkhead door. There's no angel choirs or nothing, I mean you'd probably just walk by. It's a miracle of a long stare, a smile.

"C'mon," Tommy says finally.

"Where we goin'?" I walk over to him.

"You need a haircut," he says, running his hand lightly through my hair, but carefully, like my hair might burn him.

I nod my head slowly, keeping my eyes on his as his hands linger in my hair. The smile fades from his face and he gulps again.

We slide up Broadway without saying anything. We get to Dom's Barbershop. Dom's sitting inside reading the newspaper in the slanting sunlight. The place smells of geraniums and talcum powder.

"Both o' yous today?" Dom asks, rising slowly. He shakes out a nylon protective cloth with black and white daisies on it.

"Naw, just him," Tommy answers, jerking his head. I sit down on the squishy red seat and swallow hard. Dom folds a white protective collar around my neck. His fingers are cold, I notice, not like Tommy's were that night—

Tommy doesn't sit down. He folds his smooth arms across his chest. He stands right beside my chair, towering over Dom. Dom puts on little half-glasses, then pins the protective cloth tight around my neck.

"Too tight for you?" Tommy asks me. I half laugh and shake my head. Dom gives Tommy a funny look, I see this in the mirror but Tommy doesn't, he's looking down at me.

"Eh . . . how 'bout dem Red Sox?" Dom asks. I wonder why if he's a barber he doesn't trim his own nose hair.

"Yeah how 'bout 'em," Tommy says. "Regular Flattop for the young man here."

I'm looking at the pictures of pouty men on the wall and the haircuts they illustrate, The Sheraton, The Continental, The Bristol— which is way dumb, if you came in here and asked for The Bristol they'd just look at you. But to tell the truth I'm only aware of Tommy. Tommy, Tommy, and nothing but Tommy, standing so close I can feel his breath on my neck.

"Good and close now, Dom," Tommy instructs, half-pointing a finger.

"Mebbe you wanna do it yo'se'f, eh?" Dom asks, laughing.

Tommy snaps to his full height. He clenches his fists. I know this is the moment. Either we will take a lifetime of knee-jerk shit, or never take shit.

A smile breaks across Tommy's face like the sun pouring through Dom's windows.

"Yeah," he says nodding, "yeah, as a matter of fact I do. Here." He reaches into his pocket, pulls out a wad of bills and some Juicy Fruit gum. He hands Dom a twenty. "Go take a break, old man. Take your keys. We'll lock up when we're through."

"What are you crazy?" Dom asks, but he's already shoving the twenty into the pocket of his baby-blue barber's shirt. He shakes his head, shuffles over to the register, empties it, then grabs his sweater and limps out the door. He turns as he's almost through it.

"I know yo' uncle if someting's broken," he warns Tommy, waving a hairy fat finger.

"Yeah whatever," Tommy laughs.

"Crazy Irish kids," Dom mutters. The door shuts behind him with a tinkling of bells. Me and Tommy's eyes meet in the mirror. I see him swallow hard again. He walks over to the door, locks it, then turns the OPEN sign around so that it says CLOSED facing the street, the world. He lowers the big blind in the front window.

He's breathing faster when he comes back to me. I watch him in the mirror. Very gently, he loosens up my collar. "That was just buggin' me," he says, laughing, too loud. He gulps again.

He brings the buzzer to my head. He turns it on, jumps a little when it whirrs to life, then slowly brings it to my head. He presses it against scalp. A spurt of something jags through me. His breath is in my ear. He starts slow at first, then seems to get more confident. I watch his arms in the mirror, up down back forth. I notice the skin of his forearms looks like a sweater too tight to hold the muscles beneath.

"Bib," I say above the whirr. "Tommy listen, that night me and Bib—"

"Later," Tommy says, he's all business cutting my hair. He continues buzzing along, blowing the hair off every now and then with his breath, which smells like strawberry ice cream, my favorite. He puts his other hand on my shoulder, lightly at first, then harder. I don't mind. Wow, his hands are big—

When he's done he runs his hands along the back of my head where the hair's all bristly and sharp. My eyes close and a sound comes out of my mouth.

"I know," he says, laughing nervously. He tightens. "Me too . . . Baby." His last word ricochets around the barbershop like a bullet in a Saturday morning cartoon, smashing things. Our eyes lock in the mirror again.

"Ahhh," he says, looking everywhere but at me, "everybody's out at my house. For the night." His words sound like they were barbecued before they came out of his mouth.

"Ahhh . . . okay," I say. I gulp, audibly. We look at each other again via the mirror. But quick now, like birds' wings.

"Well," Tommy says after a bit, clearing his throat. He puts his hands on my shoulders. "What do you think?"

"About what?"

"The haircut, duh."

I make an appraising face in the mirror.

"Where's my hat?" I ask.

Tommy laughs, punches me in the shoulder. Really it's not that bad, maybe the best I ever had.

We lock up. We step outside into the early evening sun.

"Tommy," I say, "there's this island out in the harbor. Way out? Nobody ever goes there. You can see it from the top of the Edison Plant."

"Tim," he says. We stop. We turn and face each other. I see myself reflected in his sunglasses, and beyond me, the sky, flawless and blue, the bluest blue—

"We got everything right here," he says. "Everything."

"Tommy," I say.

He smiles and pulls out a lollipop he must've swiped from Dom's when I wasn't looking. He unwraps it and holds it like a dart beside him. But before he can do anything I snatch it quick and shove it into his shocked mouth.

"You bashtarhd!" he sputters, laughing with his mouth full, and I take off down Broadway, him chasing me close behind. I'm laughing too cuz I know I'm about to keep my promise to Dad, to go somewhere I've never been before—

Somewhere beautiful.

This Thing Called Courage

It was three in the morning when her message came in.

I was the manager on call that night, and the thing was I could've dished her call out to Sully, or Richie, any of the techs that were covering that night, that's what I was planning on doing. But then I heard the address—

What made me think I'd just be able to lie there in bed after hearing it? "The Condominiums at Taft Place," Kay from the answering service had loftily pronounced, evidently mimicking the client. "Unit B-2. The woman up there's got no heat, she says." Of course they could have called it The Taft Condos—that's what us locals did—or even The Taft—

I leapt out of bed, paced out into the kitchen as if that would help, lit up a cigarette then remembered I'd just left one burning in my bedroom—

After I slowed my breath and made my voice sound normal I called her myself. I slid back into bed, sat up, yanked the covers up to my chin—

It was the coldest night of the year, like a knife.

"Hello!" she answered on the first ring, but not with a question.

"Hi, this is Brian calling from Pinnacle Heat and Elec—"

"There's no heat in my unit!" she interrupted, and her voice was corporate crisp. "I need you to come out *immediately.*" Course I could've said to her Well, *I* Need *You* to Check the Following For *Me*—but then you're just engaging in that stupid entitlement pissing contest that passes for most human interaction nowadays—and I took my ball and went home a long time ago. Plus maybe the problem was something simple like a tripped fuse, and if I had her check a few things and we did happen to fix it over the phone, then I wouldn't be able to go out and see the place.

And all at once I needed to. It had been ten years—

"Are there any . . . ah . . . children or infants in the home?" I asked, but I was shaking. "Any aged or infirm or people with disabil—"

"Of course not!" she snapped. "What possible difference could that make?"

The Fucking Possible Difference It Makes Is That if It's Just You, I Can Warm My Ass Up in the Shower Before I Go Out in This Cold.

"It's a question," I answered, "of urgency."

"I have an important meeting in the morning, and if I don't get some heat on in this place I won't be able to sleep. How's that for urgency? Now I want someone up here in fifteen minutes or someone's going to be sorry. Is that clear?"

I took a long drag from my cigarette, blew the gray smoke up to the ceiling.

"I'll see what I can do," I said, half-stifling a feigned yawn. Then I hung up.

Great. Just my fucking luck. A Corporate Turbo Bitch.

The smoke cleared above my bed and I could see the water stain on the ceiling, the one that's shaped like Texas in a Dali kind of way. Sometimes I think that's maybe where He went, Texas, like this is some kind of sign or something. But I've been living here for seven years now and haven't done a thing about it, so I suppose it's too late. Really, it's always too late.

But He'd be waiting for me there in the basement—

I chuck the covers back, swing my thighs out, spring up to the edge of the bed, don't pull back when my outraged bare feet hit the frozen floor. I look down and see that I'm hard. I could play with myself again But What Possible Fucking Difference Could That Make? The helmet head is smiling back at me, laughing because it knows what I really need to do is pull back the tissues of my chest and play with my heart instead.

But you can't do that. Mine's dead anyway.

But I can't blame that on Him. I did it to myself.

After my shower I select my couture. Will it be the blue working-class chinos or the blue working-class chinos? I select the blue chinos. The black boots or the black boots? The black boots. The white T-shirt and socks or the white T-shirt and socks? I opt for the latter, I'm feeling sexy and, oh, I don't know, kind of dashing and frisky tonight. The one choice I don't have is the de rigueur blue chino shirt with our logo sewn onto the left breast pocket, a green mountain with a white peak and *Pinnacle Heat and Electric* in green swirly letters beneath. Above the mountain, in red writing: *Brian, Asst. Manager.*

That would be me. In case I forget my name I suppose.

I fire up the van and check the back while it's warming; Smitty had this vehicle yesterday and he's such a slob, always leaving tools everywhere and his signature Funny Doodles wrappers in the toolbox. As I'm backing out the driveway the yellowing lace curtain in the first-floor front window pulls back just a soupçon, Mr. Curtain (ironically enough) is per usual keeping a weather if somewhat jaundiced eye on my comings and goings. An insomniac, he's got the night shift while his equally inquisitive wife keeps watch by day. But really I couldn't ask for better tenants for my two-family (what a joke, family, it's just me and my two goldfish on the second floor), they're better than a fifty-thousand-dollar alarm system.

It's only a mile from my place to the Taft Condos or, a thousand pardons, The Condominiums at Taft Place. But I take a pretzel crazy way, trying to ease the boxing butterflies in my stomach. But it's no good. As I slide up the One Ways and ease through the merciless 3:30 a.m. red lights, I'm seventeen again, taking the shortcuts home from school, sweat sealing my shirt to my back and equally sticky thoughts of Him papering my mind.

The radio BEEP makes me jump and I almost drive into a police-womanesque navy Marquis, parked halfway out onto East Seventh Street because of the concrete snowbanks. The two-way radio's green light flashes and I respond like the good monkey I've been trained to be. The answering service again.

"Unit B-2 wants to know if anyone's coming and why they haven't yet," Kay from the service says.

"Uh, that's a copy, Kay. I'm en route. Over," I answer, hoping she doesn't hear the pubescent quaver in my voice.

"Roger, Brian. Sounds like one pissed-off lady," Kay says. "Lemme call her back and see if I can smooth those ruffled feathers. Over."

"You're a pal, Kay, but be careful, she's a bank vice president and they don't have feathers they have brass . . . elements. Over."

"How do you know she's a bank veepee, over?" There's a little more than idle curiosity in Kay's voice.

"Ahhhh, I just . . . somebody told me. Thanks again. Over and out."

"Hey, wait, Brian, I'm still waiting for that cup of coffee you promised me," she says. "Don't be a stranger. Base out." But I look in the rearview mirror and that's just what I see now, a very scared stranger.

The Taft School Condos can only be accessed by one street, Taft Street, and it rises arrogantly past turn-of-the-century triple-deckers and corner cig-and-lottery markets until it ends at the top of the hill, where the rose brick building sits like the Acropolis. Recessed lighting tucked into the shriveled azaleas at the base of all four sides of the Taft are neither harsh streetlight blue nor that appalling sodium vapor so prized by our master builders these days. Instead they are soft pink, and they bathe the antique rose brick in a warm love blush that belies both the building's working-class surroundings and the bitterness of the evening. But the light in the little guard shack at the entrance to the grounds is wincingly fluorescent, and it makes the man in the polyester rent-a-cop uniform sitting beneath this light look like a sallow bug. There's a lowered gate before me discouraging my further proletarian advance, written on which is **PRIVATE PROPERTY NO TRESPASSING RESIDENTS ONLY.** Of course any one of those three phrases would have sufficed, but apparently they wanted to make sure people got the point: after all, darling, we are in Southie.

It's now mandated that I keep out of a place I was once mandated to attend, the obligatory ironic architectural nod, as it were.

The guard is fast asleep. I throw the van into park and put pedal to the metal. I believe my racing motor awakens him—either that or it's a blessed coincidence. He glares at me with eyes heavy with sleep and suspicion. Even from inside my van, windows rolled up, I hear the wheezy clacking of his space heater, working beyond its capacity even if he isn't.

He says nothing. I abhor the sad demise of Common Courtesy so I glare back. At length he slides down his window and mumbles something I don't quite catch. I roll my own window down.

"Excuse me, what did you say?" I ask. "'Good evening Sir and welcome to the Taft Condos? How may I direct you this evening?' Is that what you said?"

"What unit you want?" he demands, looking like Ah yes he does remember me shooting his mother some time ago.

"The soul of balmy courtesy even in the frosty depths of winter," I smile back. "Actually I'm going to buy this whole fucking place and first thing after that is fire your rude ass. But in the meantime you can ring your match in courtesy in Unit B-2 and tell her the Boy is here."

Apparently the guard needs this job, as he doesn't come out and pound me. He picks up a phone, grumbles something, then a moment later pushes a button. The gate rises in uncertain jerks and I am admitted into the hallowed grounds of my old high school. I smile and wave like a convertible-conveyed homecoming queen as I drive in, but there's no one here.

"It's me!" I say to the imaginary crowd, students, teachers, the school board, mothers from the PTA with nostrils all aquiver in righteous indignation. "I lied," I continue. "It was me. It wasn't just Him. It was both of us. I lied."

I park where I'm not supposed to and take a petty working-class pleasure, albeit futile, in doing so. The once cracked asphalt at the side of the building is now a smooth faux-brick parking area, lavishly appointed with islands of harshly clipped yews, and rhododendrons whose shrunken leaves have closed up shop for the season, like shutters closing the eyes of cottages by the sea. This was once the faculty parking lot and was strewn with left-leaning bumper stickers holding together Volkswagen bugs and buses, old station wagons with cola cans welding mufflers together until the next paycheck came. But the area has been rechristened as well as repaved; it's the Residents' Garaging Area now, a much more appropriate moniker for the European luxury sedans and my-dick's-bigger-than-yours SUVs (none of which, I fear, shall ever be off road) all in pretty muted rows of Arctic Silvers and Metallic Frosts. It's rather inconvenient for me to be having an anxiety attack at this time as I walk to the front of the building, for I'm panting and the air I'm taking in is so cold it burns. I try not to notice the view from the front stairway as I ascend—yes, seven steps—the ocean and the harbor islands to the left, the skyline to the right. It's a view I once knew well. I open the vestibule door and buzz B-2. The inner door buzzes back instantly, as if she's been standing Doberman guard by her intercom. I wonder how she's managed to telegraph ill humor into this buzzing. I snatch at the door.

I begin to believe that I shouldn't have come after all, for the stairwell down, though carpeted now in some inoffensive color that defies identification (Wheat? Stone? Thatch?) is exactly as it was. My heart leaps to overdrive just as it used to heading down these stairs, and my testicles tingle in a kind of ball-jerk reaction. Gym class was last period, and it loomed above the horizon of the day like an iceberg one was fated to crash into again and again. And if I was often the fastest, the quickest, the strongest in gym, it was only because of the adrenaline that even now races through me like an out-of-control driverless horse at some surreal nightmare Pimlico. I wonder—if this made me excel then, will it help me now? Will I be a more effective efficient Heating Ventilation and Air Conditioning Technician because of my racing heart?

I'm sweating when she opens the door. She's wearing Armani for Crissake. She's about my age, maybe a little older, tall and big-toothed in a waspy, semi-carnivorous way. Her ice-blue eyes quickly appraise. They observe everything but see nothing. There seems something inexplicably merciless in the sharp cut of her features, the patrician sweep of her neck-length ash-blonde hair.

"I assumed you'd use the service entrance at the back of the building," she begins, and I wonder if she's purposely arranged her thin lips into a sneer, or is this an unfortunate congenital issue.

"Would you feel that the rightful order of things had beeen restored if I go out and come back that way?" I ask.

Her head snaps back a little.

"What—what kept you?" she demands.

"A contretemps with my man at the gate," I answer, trying to keep this up but her high-ceilinged unit is where our locker room was, where it all happened. "Actually that's not true. You see I breathed too heavily upon a Range Rover as I was passing through the parking lot—pardon me, the Residents' Garaging Area—and I was trying to buff out my hoi poloi breath marks. I'm sure you understand." I smile sweetly at her but really I want to weep, to scream.

Her lips fall into a frown and her thin light eyebrows swoop up like startled birds' wings.

"Wipe your feet," she orders, staring down at my boots.

"They're clean, thank you, but tell me—did you just swallow something large and unpleasant?"

"Yes," she says, "two hours worth of cold air." She shuts the door behind us.

"My!" I answer. "You should have called someone!"

"I did. You know, I was going to phone your supervisor and complain about your tardiness, but I figured I'd give you five more minutes before I got you into trouble," she says, though with less conviction.

"Ah!" I say, putting my hand over my heart. "T'would be a cold world indeed without the sweet selflessness of noblesse oblige, no?"

"Or the pleasure of customer service, given with a smile," she retorts. I can't help but laugh. She smiles and extends her hand.

"Truce?" she asks, but I want to tell her don't be nice to me, don't take away the armor of my sarcasm, it's all I've got. But of course I shake her hand. Her eyebrows lift up again when she notices my trembling hand.

"Ahhh . . . cold out," she says, but her eyes come back to mine with a bit less steel to them.

I pick up my toolbox and look away.

"It's down here," she says, turning away.

She leads me down a gallery-like hall that seems endless, as if Hitchcock did her interior and it's receding as we progress. The hall's appointed with tastefully confounding objets d'art garnered from, I presume, her hunter-gatherer business trips. The hall spills out into a vast living room—what realtors now like to call a Great Room, speaking of its size and not necessarily the things that happen there—and despite its total metamorphosis, I instantly recognize our old locker room. Sweat announces itself upon my forehead, begins trickling down my sides despite the coldness of the room and its arctic-gray color.

I shouldn't have come here.

She long-legged strides to the far end of the room and hurls open double French doors to reveal the heating unit and electrical panel. I come up behind her. She steps aside and I struggle to focus on the switches and circuit breakers.

"Do you need anything?" she asks after a minute, her hands rubbing her shoulders.

I shake my head. She stands as if unsure behind me while I mechanically begin unscrewing the bolts to the heating unit's panel. A teakettle whistles blessedly from the different-time-zone kitchen just as I feel the first dry heaves starting, the knee-jerk reaction to my anxiety attacks.

"I'll be in the kitchen if you need anything," she says quietly.

I am tempted to ask if she happens to have a spare Xanax on her, but I think better of it. "Th-thank you," I say. Then I make an absurd retching sound that pierces the high-ceilinged room. Oh shit.

"Are you . . . is everything all right?" she asks.

All I can do is nod my head. I don't hear her go, but after a minute I warily half-turn.

She's not there.

I am free to recollect.

What I mean to say is, the roofless wall of memory that I've been holding back for ten years implodes down on top of me. My hands become almost too shaky to turn the screwdriver.

It was right here, right where I am. His office was right there in the corner, the locker room right here where I'm working, our shower room up against the far wall. The wall's been cut out now and fitted with a trio of large floor-to-ceiling windows that reveal the lights of the harbor, the airport, a cruise ship nesting in its icy dock like a warm-weather bird that awakens to find it's missed its chance to migrate. Just outside the windows two shriveled rhododendron leaves flutter in the merciless polar wind; my manic eye detects something especially frantic in the left leaf's shaking. We did have windows in the locker room here, but they were casement ones, high up by the ceiling, frosted and barred, and the light that streamed through them came in steamy chunks that highlighted pink and white flesh, some smooth, some hairy. And the scent is gone now too, the odor that hung like wet sheets in unmoving air, the grasslike smell of sweat, of damply rumpled gym shorts and moist athletic supporters, of young bodies writhing and sweating, of fresh towels half wet hung up to dry on half-opened metal locker doors, of talcum powder and Old Spice swirling in the solid air like incense.

I open the electrical panel but it's really a locker door, I'm back to that day, I have no more power to resist this than I would the collapsing of the building upon my head, all four ponderous floors and ten thousand ghosts of it. I'm opening my locker door and yanking on my white briefs, white but frayed at the legs, I've grown much lately, sixteen and a half and my hair is damp lank on my forehead, my face flushed with exercise and something else, and I snatch the briefs up quick I'm only half-hard and once more I've survived gym class and the showers, once more I've exalted in gym class and the showers. Everyone else is still in the shower I hear the echoing, the laughing, the singing, the dissing, the snapping of a wet towel against wetter skin the howling, and I guess that's why he picked me, I was the first one out of the shower, he picked me, the kid who came down from the office The Beadle they used to call him, a messenger boy, a senior one year older than me and I hear him push open the squeaky locker room door and he spots me and walks over looks me up and down hands me something a piece of paper folded twice Give This To Tobin You he says, a note from the Principal's Office for Mr. Tobin.

Mr. Michael Bernard Tobin. Our gym teacher we liked Him He wasn't a hard-ass Mr. Tobin, He'd grown up here but on the West Side down by the freight yards he wasn't always trying to prove he was a hard-ass like the other gym teachers, Neanderthal Coach Kowalski, sneaky Mr. Quigley, that man in women's clothing Miss Humphries He had black hair that always looked damp but it wasn't, shiny I mean, eyes blue like the sky in winter after a storm he was quiet, like his mind was always on something else, seeing something faraway I used to wonder what, he'd been in the Service, our hometown's version of the Grand Tour, saw action in Vietnam they said, A Marine, I used to think it must be weird to have all the intense stuff happen when you're young then you spend the rest of your life thinking about it sitting around trying to digest it living in its shadow like a child star nobody calls anymore. Always dressed the same, gray T-shirt puffed out with *Taft Phys. Ed. Dept.* written across the chest, navy blue sweatpants, white socks, white sneakers, a whistle dangling from a chain around his neck.

He never raised his voice he'd just look at you. He was twenty-three.

I was a junior. It was early May.

A note. I knocked on his office door No answer but I think he's in there, I saw him go in five minutes ago when gym class ended I just happened to notice so I think he's in there, in his office which is in the front part of our locker room, but enclosed and private though. I knocked again.

No answer.

I opened the door and stepped into his office. I didn't think to put any more clothes on I guess I thought the note might be important, an emergency, somebody sick maybe couldn't wait. His office was small a desk, a chair, some black file cabinets very warm you could smell the moist heat a picture on the wall of a Marine in full dress but it's somebody else not Mr. Tobin.

I stepped in more and the door closed behind me. In the back of His office there was this closet thing but a shower stall instead, He had His own private shower why wouldn't He, He was a teacher, I'm standing in the middle of His office and I can hear the shower water running, that and my heart loud kicking like it wanted to come out and play and run around the room including the ceiling. Outside his shower closet there's a mat on the floor, a towel on the doorknob, some clothes in a pile on the floor white navy blue more white and something off-white.

The water stops.

He opens the shower door His head dripping water He looks down steps out onto the mat head jerks up when he sees me I'm staring can't help it, one time in eighth grade I ran for office Class Vice President they made you give a speech in the auditorium, but when it was my turn all I could do was stare couldn't speak no not a word I lost never done nothing since just like now because all I can do is stare into his eyes my mouth open because He is the most intense thing, the scariest thing the most beautiful thing ever of all time longish crew cut, wet white flesh, shiny hair around his nipples running across his chest gathering into a line then down his stomach, so much hair, flat muscles swollen muscles a big pink scar across his stomach but the whole time I'm looking into His eyes but peripherally I can see Everything I see It warm and rosy full from the warm shower water dripping, something familiar yet wholly different and secret and now I've seen It seen Him and I feel like crying and dancing at the same time. I didn't know people walking around all day on the street their clothes on riding the bus, taking business calls, when all along underneath some of them looked like this so unbelievable all you could do was stare your heart beating the band and I don't understand what's happening to me.

"Brian?"

He says my name picks up the towel covers His front with it, but He's still dripping there's a question in His voice but all I can do now is stare I'm shaking all over because I can't look away. And as I continue to stare I see in His eyes that He Knows. And I run out of His office, try to run out, run into the door by accident, hit my head on it I half fall back get up grab the door knob, but then I remember the note so I turn around but he's coming toward me the towel wrapped around him and he doesn't say anything but grabs me by the shoulders Electricity He spins me around, looks at my forehead but there's no blood only a bump Brian Are You Okay? but I still can't talk and He's looking in my eyes and I'm shaking I hand Him the note and leave.

And I know that He knows.

Walking home from school that day the seven of us The Gang: Sully, Richie Fitz, Eddie Fitz, Kevin, Timmy, Chris, me, we make our daily stop at McGillicuddy's Spa for cokes and whatever candy we can steal then step outside for a smoke and the establishment of our presence Hey Brian, Timmy says a few minutes later, Look Man Here Comes Brenda Casey, She's Hot For You Boy, Who, Her? I say, I jerk my head in her general direction, Yeah Man, Her Girlfriend Trudy Said You Can Meet Her Any Night Down The Beach And She'll Let You Feel Her Tits. The others hoot and holler but I puff on my smoke, pause, make a face, She's A Dog I pronounce, they think all of them I have unattainable taste, when in fact here's the truth it's them I want to feel down the beach at night and as soon as we got out of school that day my heart still racing, a welt forming on my forehead, I say I Saw Tobin Bareass, I Had This Note For Him, You Wouldn't Believe How Hairy He Is, and no one said nothing because this is what we're all becoming so it's sacred plus you just don't talk about another guy's body unless you're dissing it Fat Ass, Little Dick, Big Nose, Ugly Mug, Pigeon Toed, Zit Faced—

—but my mistake is I still can't get him out of my head what I've seen what's passed between us and later closer to home it's just me and Richie Fitz and Timmy and I say again You Wouldn't Believe How Hairy Tobin Is but Richie Fitz turns on me, screams Quit Talking About That! he's pissed off I realize I've said too much we glare at each other and I'm half-thinking of popping him one in the face but then we'd fight and it'd be all over town the next day, all over school, How'd It Start? Well See Brian Saw Tobin Naked, Right? and I couldn't have that no.

I can't sleep the next two weeks it's late May hotter every day I'm melting we still have gym three times a week and now during class I catch Mr. Tobin staring at me, he always looks away, then stares again me too, He starts fucking up, misreading the stopwatch during the fifty-yard dash, calling people the wrong names Sully mutters Hey

Bri Man, What'd You Do To Piss Tobin Off He Keeps Looking At You, see 'round here there's no reason for a man to stare at another unless he's pissed.

Who The Fuck knows? I shrug.

But then He comes to me one night. He does. Me and my family live on the first floor, the second floor's empty because the landlord won't de-lead, my bedroom's the old front porch, Dad's away with the merchant marine he comes home every six months, they stay in their bedroom Dad and Mom the whole time she comes out for air every now and again red faced laughing Shhhhh Your Father's Sleeping and she tries to cook for us but screws it up ten minutes later gives us ten bucks Kids Go Get Pizza and she's laughing as she goes back to the bedroom and nine months later we have another brother or sister. I get my own room I'm the oldest it's the old front porch and Dad's just left for six months and Mom works nights at the Necco Factory and it's hot very hot this particular night I raise the blinds to catch the sea breeze after I turn out my light and I see Him across the street leaning against the bus stop pole, Mr. Tobin His hands jammed into His pockets staring Tiger Tiger in the Night.

I'm brought to another world. I don't even think it's weird for Him to be there like in a dream when you accept anything without question it's midnight everyone's sleeping but me I open the screen door sit down on the top step I'm wearing white briefs the night's dark the City hasn't fixed the streetlight yet out front. I light up a butt.

He crosses the street. He's squinting He's not sure it's me. He comes closer.

He's wearing cutoffs and smelly sneakers with no socks and a white T-shirt whose right sleeve half-hides a Marine Corps tattoo on a swollen white bicep. His eyes look like open wounds leaking the same stuff that's in my heart but he's containing it He is after all a Marine the few the proud *Semper Fi* and all that crap He sits down beside me on the top step His bare thigh flesh grazes mine neither of us moves away we both gulp at the same time. He tells me I shouldn't smoke then a minute later asks for one we have a cigarette. I go back inside I don't say anything I hold the door open for him as we stare in gulps at each other's feet I lock the door behind us.

He finds comfort here. I don't think He understands it Himself. All over the world He's had chances, whores in Saigon, WACS at Air Force bases, any hundred girls round the way here at home who'd think themselves blessed to have Him, to give Him a houseful of red-cheeked children, kitchens happy with noise, a calendar on the fridge red-inked with upcoming Tupperware Parties and PTA. But no. No no. He has found comfort here, a remedy at last for mines decapitating his buddies beside him, children shot before His eyes I think it's as odd to Him as it would be to anyone else around here—but it's true nevertheless. He finds comfort here with a boy sixteen and a half with a body much like his own yet wholly different, as if two separate designers worked on plans from the same engineer. His calf is hairy, swollen with muscle when it's flexed in passion or standing wide-legged in the gym barking orders a whistle between His white teeth. But his calf is looser when He's lying on His stomach sleeping, one knee slightly up. The boy's calf is smooth and leanly firm. The Man's body hair is curly and black, matted in a line down the hard, scarred stomach. The boy's body hair can't be seen in most lights and when it can it's fuzzy, light, and so downy the man tries to lick it off the boy's body. The exception to this is under the boy's arms and between his legs and around each nipple where a single long, wiry hair emerges like a scout for a still-unseen army. And the man finds comfort in these as well, I can tell, and I know he doesn't know why. But that's okay.

It is what it is.

I can't really get specific about that first time every time was like the first time, a stranger in a strange land that is nevertheless Home. When summer came he had to work, He didn't make much as a gym teacher He got a job working in a moving company's warehouse on the West Side where furniture in the midst of being moved was stored like Limbo until other trucks came for it. He got me a job there too sometimes we'd really bust ass and me and him'd be moving something and our eyes would meet, sweating, panting, sweat running down our sides Wow other times it'd be slow and there were seven floors of furniture in this building, a big freight elevator too, and we'd wander among the cavernous floors making up the people's names we thought the stuff belonged to, a big wide pink crushed-velvet upholstered livingroom chair was Lady Widerear's, an indigestion-inducing severe Danish dining-room set belonged to Elke and Karl Von Sternly, and sometimes on other people's couches, sometimes on other people's beds, one time in the big freight elevator we made it stop between floors and for the rest of the day you could smell us in there but we didn't hang out much in public together, people might talk, which mostly was fine because This Thing was so intense you needed to be with this person, but also you needed to be alone so you could think about this person.

"How's it coming?"

I turn. Unit B-2 is standing before me, a cup of tea in her hands. She holds it out to me like we're filming a commercial.

"I thought you might like this."

I find myself blinking my eyes. I manage a wobbly smile, I've always been quick on my feet.

"Th-thanks."

She clears her throat. "Any luck?" she asks.

"Yes, all bad. Two burnt-out wires and a faulty coupler."

"Oo. That does sound bad," she groans.

"Well, it can make for a less than salubrious living environment. But we have the technology to fix it if that's what you're getting at. But it's . . . time intensive? Is that how you'd say it in the corporate world?"

"I'd know what you were talking about," she smiles, tossing her hair to the side of her face.

I bet you would. I gulp tea. Her eyes have become softer. I have to look away. I turn back around to my work. There's an awkward silence as I continue to strip the wires.

"Salubrious," she echoes behind me.

"Conducive to one's health," I say. "From the Latin *salub,* meaning health."

"Hmmmmph. I would have said warm," she says.

"How sad," I sigh, but she knows I'm joking, she laughs.

"Are you a writer?" she asks, sitting down on the arm of a nearby sofa.

Now I laugh. "No, I'm a Heating Ventilation and Air Conditioning Technician. Why, did you call a writer to come fix this?"

She laughs again. "No, it's your vocabulary, your quick wit. You have an amazing vocabulary for a . . . I mean . . ."

I turn my head around to face her. "For one of the Little People?" I offer.

She becomes quite ruffled, reddens.

"I'm waiting breathlessly," I chime, smiling and tilting my head.

"I'm sorry," she says. "I didn't mean it like that. I mean I didn't mean it the way it came out." She gathers up our empty tea cups, glad I think for something to do, something to take her away from me. She takes the tea things and leaves the room.

The luck of the draw had Coach Kowalski as my gym teacher when school resumed in September. Me and Mr. Tobin (I still called him that in my head, but in person I called him Mike) both thought it was better, we'd be able to concentrate maybe. It was Senior Year.

After school he'd be waiting for me downstairs in His office, He'd leave His office door unlocked for me I'd go in when the locker room was empty thinking hard about it all day. Sometimes He'd be at His desk, sometimes in the shower sometimes just sitting there his feet up on the gray desk staring at the picture of the Marine on the wall Who's He? I asked once Just Someone Who Died He said He was so kind to me, so tender, but He yelled at me once one day I told Him I could stay with Him all afternoon, all night stay at His place What About Your Homework? He asked I laughed, shrugged, made a face He got pissed, You've Got To Do Something With Your Life He said, never seen Him so serious except sometimes when I'd wake up and find Him staring at me He made me promise I'd read everything I could get my hands on, look up words I didn't know I promised just to shut Him up but I've kept my promise. Now as you can see I'm one of the best-read most highly articulate Heating Ventilation Air Conditioning Technicians around one afternoon in His office usually we waited until night, His place or mine, but this day we couldn't, a softness in His eyes, this funny smile, the smell of him lightly sweaty, his hair a little rumpled me seventeen now you know how hard that is and I drop down before Him drunk on Him high on Him my arms around the back of His thighs I ease down His clingy sweatpants His damp jockstrap He puts His hands on the back of my head groans my name like I'm hearing it for the first time and this is all happening in slow motion between us but in fast motion or regular motion His office door swings open and Coach Kowalski is there and there's no way to stop what will happen next.

They'd kill you for that where I came from or you'd kill yourself not even time to think about what to do I jumped up screamed *Fuckin' Faggot!* screamed it right in His face never saw His face like that I pushed Him away from me both hands pushed Him hard I was fully dressed His sweatpants were down at His ankles He fell backward slammed against the file cabinets I turn to Coach Kowalski, He Tried To Get Me! I say pointing at Mr. Tobin, then I bump my way past Kowalski out the office up the stairs through the doors I'm outside panting running gotta think tears streaming down my face dry heaving my first ever anxiety attack Be Gentle It's My First Time but the anxiety attack is not gentle it rips through me like a slasher and I'm home in my bed shaking under the covers dry heaving Quiet, Kids, Ma says out in the Parlor, Turn That TV Down Kevin, Brian's Got The Grippe.

There is this thing called Courage. Mr. Tobin was not in school the next day. There is this thing called Courage and it hovered above me for the next few days, hovered above me when the Principal called me into his office the next morning Kowalski was there also the head of the guidance department, some lawyer from the superintendent's office who kept picking his nose when he thought no one was looking There's to Be a Hearing on Monday, they said, Monday Morning in the Superintendent's Office Downtown, We Are Expelling Mr. Tobin You Must Come and Tell What Happened.

There is this thing called Courage and it hovered above me all that weekend like a cloud I tried to jump up and get it but it was higher than it looked.

Monday morning. The superintendent's packed office people from the PTA, the Superintendent the assistant superintendent their staff School Committee members other teachers someone from the teachers union the headmaster Coach Kowalski sneaky Mr. Quigley smug Miss Humphries a stenographer my mother sniffling anyone who could get in It's Amusing When People Get Lynched their nostrils flaring in self-righteous indignation, I imagined that some of them had done that morning at home before this meeting with their spouses or live-ins what me and Mr. Tobin had done but that was alright, and of course He was there, Mr. Tobin, all of them staring at Him like He's slime, lower than slime, won't even sit near Him in case it's catchy He's sitting there proud true wordless straight as an arrow saying nothing I can't even look at him though I want to run to him and, oddly, I think of poor starving people in Third Worlds and realize you can see just as much of Hell in the good ol' USA, the Land of The Free, even when you've fought for your country so the rich can get richer and the ranks of poor whites and poor blacks can be thinned out a bit.

Coach Kowalski reads a statement he's barely literate, he tells what he saw the audience gasps they are sickened they are outraged. For some reason my eye lights upon an especially appalled woman, a member of the school committee I think and I suspect that perhaps she is one of the people who Did That Thing this morning with her equally fat husband in fact she may still reek of it just a little here and there, but that's okay of course because after all God made Adam and Eve not Adam and Steve, or if He did make Adam and Steve they caught them and Had a Hearing, and they have all forgotten that we are made in God's image rather than the other way around.

Then they call Me.

I think I'm going to faint.

I lurch to the front of the room.

There Is This Thing Called Courage but there's only one courageous person in the room and it isn't me Is This What Happened they ask Yes I say, I do not hesitate then I go back to my seat my mother is crying beside me then they call Mr. Tobin, Is This What Happened, they ask Yes he says, He doesn't hesitate and they take turns heaping calumny on him it is after all an election year and He stands there and takes it His chest out, His back straight, His eyes distant, perhaps thinking of the Other Marine whose picture is in His office who maybe died rather than betray Him because he had this thing called courage.

They strip Him of His tenure they strip Him of His job they strip Him of his union membership there is some asshole there from the DA's office with bad breath and he asks me Are You Sure You Don't Want to Press Charges, No, I say, We Already Went Over That This Weekend When You Came to My House, and My mother says That Dirty Pervert, to Think He Can Do This to My Son and Get Away With It, and for the only time in my life I want to slap her, and I almost do but I'm shaking again, and she comes back into her living room and I'm flat on the floor I'm shaking I'm crying I can't help it because it happened right here and I loved him, loved him so much and lost him, destroyed him right in that corner over there where now hang a pair of Balinese Masks that for many cocktail parties here have been the subject of endless conversation, people are terribly interested in them and their date of origin as if any of that shit really mattered, right in that corner is where I pushed Him away, I pushed Him away but I'm the one who's been falling ever since, ten years falling and I haven't hit bottom yet or maybe at last I finally have.

"Are you all right?" she asks. Her face is alarm intensive as they may say in the corporate world.

I'm shaking so hard I can't even answer her.

Her hands twist together. She can bring home the bacon, cook it up in a pan, run a board meeting, work a roomful of anxious foreign investors, have fired upper-management types escorted from Bank Property yes all this and more, but a human being melting down before her eyes is not covered in her corporate handbook. Ordinarily she would Just Call Someone in a situation like this, but it's five in the morning and there's no one to call. Just her and me. She twists and twists her hands. They look like they might snap.

"Do you . . . should I call an ambulance?" she asks, proving me wrong. "Are you . . . are you an epileptic or something?"

I shake my head, look away utterly humiliated.

"It'll p-pass," I mumble, looking down. "I'll be all right in a minute, it's just that I . . . that I . . ." I take a deep breath and hear myself say, "It's just that I killed somebody in this room. A long long time ago."

I raise my eyes to hers.

Her eyebrows do a double swoop up. In fear? Yes I suppose, why wouldn't she be afraid. This sticks into me like a stiletto, her misunderstanding of my hyperbole or would it be ironic metaphor? I don't know how well this is known, but when you're having an anxiety attack misunderstandings that might be amusing under ordinary circumstances become five-alarm catastrophes, something to make you hysterical almost, so I squeeze my eyes shut and yell:

"Not like that not like that he, he's p-probably still alive I don't mean it like that I don't even swat mosquitoes . . . but really, I did kill him." My breath is coming in gasps and I have to stop for a moment. "Ruined his life I mean, I didn't mean to . . . but I did. Ruined his life, changed him forever, killed the best part of him, me, both of us, the whole fucking world. I killed him but he's not dead."

I open my eyes and look back at her face. She's relaxed a tiny bit, no longer shows Panic nor Alarm, only Concern at this weirdo in her condo who's Confessed Too Much, *More Information Than We Need To Know* and she takes a step back and I realize my behavior is All

Wrong, all fucked up, *Inappropriate* they would say, we've all become corporate, haven't we? We're allowed to discuss a really neat
Web site, the merits of 401K's versus 201B's sheltered rolled over de-
ferred tax antiaging supplements on demand four-wheel drive, the
plot from last night's Must See TV; but, never, It Makes Me Happy To
See You, or, Do You Think Anyone Really Loves Me, or, What The
Fuck Am I Doing With My Life, or, Oh God I'm Aching and Empty
and Don't Know Why, or, in my case, to melt down in front of someone I should be having a *professional* relationship with.

She stares at me.

Oh God. What have I said.

I picture myself getting up now, All right Get Up Now Brian, writing up the bill, handing it to her, getting the fuck out of here; but no,
instead There Is This Thing Called Despair like a cloud it hovers over
me, and, unlike Courage, it breaks like water before a birth nothing
you can do to stop what will happen next, right here in front of her I
begin dry heaving, and bellow-sobs wrack me. They're not even
attractive-sounding sobs, I self-criticize, like in a movie when You
Break Down and sniff sniff sob sob *They* come, *They* Listen, They
Take You in Their Arms and Everything gets resolved because People
Really Do Care and somehow two strangers from different walks of
life make a connection and save each other, I can see how this movie
would be scripted and pitched, she hears my story and gets misty-
eyed, I get her to open up and discover that, gee, she always wanted to
be a freelance photographer or a veterinarian and now she's going to
Go For It Girl because of something I've said, and in this movie
they've done what no one else could do, not a thousand million desperate unspoken prayers to an immovable Providence when I was a
kid, they've Hey Presto! made me straight, and now we kiss on the
couch amidst a violin fest, then comes the Shopping Montage, as
obligatory in Hollywood Romances as car chases are in Action
Thrillers, she'll try on a funny hat under the not-amused eye of a stern
clerk, later we'll have latte and I'll get a silly frothed milk moustache
over my mouth, who do *you* see playing the female lead, what about
Julia? Helena? Madonna?

But no.

This is after all not a movie this is Life, actually twice as ugly,
once, twice, three times as ugly and she sits down on a piece of sec-
tional leather furniture as vast as an airport runway that I imagine cost

more than I make in a year and I long to ask her What Do The
Banking Folk Do, What Do The Banking Folk Do but all I can do is
dry heave and sob. In an unattractive way, as I've already mentioned.

"What?" she whispers.

"I'm sorry," I say, but I'm dry heaving between the words. "It'll—
pass in a—minute. Something happened here."

"So . . . so I gather," she says. She pulls at her patrician hair.

"This w-was our locker room." I try to explain, realize I shouldn't.

She looks around her Great Room, seeing it differently I think.
One eyebrow lifts up in appraisal, like a periscope.

"They said this was the gym," she snorts, like she's been de-
frauded.

I shake my head. "The other side of this floor. Next door to you.
John Harrison's unit. That was the gym."

"How do you know that?" she asks, brightening and smiling. "Do
you know John? JB as we call him?"

"Oh, JB, is that what he's going by now? Funny, he was always
Biffy back at Choate when we were on the tiddlywinks team together."

"You're relentless," she sighs.

"Well really, what do you think? How the fuck would I know him,
the president of Tetco Enterprises? Not unless I installed his air conditioning, kindly use the service door please."

"How do you know what he does?"

"I've done research. Looked it up in the records. I know you're a
vice president at Bank Five. I'm not a stalker I've just . . . just kept an
eye on the place. From a distance, a safe distance."

"Until tonight," she says.

I nod. It becomes quiet.

"So I'm like your . . . guinea pig?" she asks, half-smiling. "You
came out here tonight just to see this place again?"

I snort a laugh. "I've used you cruelly, I admit," I say. I manage a
weak smile.

"So this was . . . ?" she asks.

"The locker room. The shower was over there. His office was over
there, right in the corner."

"Whose office?"

"His. Michael Bernard Tobin."

"And he would be . . ."

"Where did you grow up?" I ask.

"Wisconsin," she answers, making a confused face.

"Very well, that's far enough and obscure enough. He was a Native Son. Decorated M-marine Corps Vietnam Veteran. Gym teacher deluxe at Taft High School. And perverted fallen angel. Once a byword. Now a half-remembered infamy." I say this to confound this total stranger who can know nothing of what I say, but also I say it to hear the words out loud, to hear his name. I feel as if I've reached into my navel and extracted my intestines.

She stares at me.

"Yup, right over in that corner," I add sitting up, pointing. I hardly have the strength, but I do. I look at my arm, my ringless hand, I remember it was This Hand that touched Him, that did Things—this hand that now fixes rich people's electrical snafus, installs air-conditioning systems, beats off, feeds goldfish, feeds me; this dead hand that can now only point to something that happened ten years ago, like a desert signpost pointing to a vibrant city twenty miles away might as well be a million.

"You went to school here," she says.

I nod, refrain from saying You Have A Flair For The Obvious. I try to stand, realize I can't yet. I've got to get out of here—

There's a sudden noise as her heat kicks back in.

"Oh! You fixed it," she says, sitting up straighter.

"Quel surprise," I say.

She makes a face, rolls her eyes.

"Sorry," I say. "Yes, I did fix it. Right before I became almost catatonic from a less-than-lovely stroll down Memory Lane. I'm sorry. If you'll just sign for the r-repairs—"

"Tell me," she says. She leans forward, clasps her hands.

I'm waiting for her to tell me what it is she wants me to tell her: the cost perhaps, or whether this work is warrantied, or perhaps what to do if it happens again if she guesses oh so rightly that I myself will never come back here, no nay never no more.

"What?" I groan when she says nothing after a minute.

"Tell me what happened," she whispers. I look up at her. She looks smaller now sitting down, her legs pulled up underneath her. I notice dark circles beneath her eyes.

I stare at her, dully I'm sure, for after a minute I'm aware of a piece of ropy saliva stringing down my chin. I paw at it but it falls upon the Aubusson carpet, vanishing instantly.

"You gotta be kidding," I mumble.

"Please?" she says.

"Why?"

She pulls at a piece of her hair. "It's five thirty in the morning," she says. She shrugs.

"What possible difference could that make?" I murmur.

"The doctors say that I'm dying," she says.

My head snaps up like it's been yanked by a string.

She grabs at a throw pillow beside her, pulls it into her stomach with both hands. "I-I don't know anything anymore." She forces a smile. "Except that I'm always cold."

"Huh?"

I actually believe I've misheard her.

She nods. Then she laughs. Pushes her hair out of her face. She stares at me.

I stare back at her. I'm listening to the sound of the heat. I smell it as it slowly fills up her unit. I look away.

"That's . . . that's what they say," she says. "Of course I'm remaining positive, but. . . ." Her hands play with the pillow again. "Ovarian cancer."

I look back up. Our eyes lock. Her hand reaches out as if to touch something, then falls back idly on the pillow.

"I . . ."

I become truly speechless. I look down and see my fingers twirling one of my screwdrivers.

"I'm . . . sorry," I finally mumble.

"Me too," she mutters, pulling at her hair.

"No, I mean . . . I'm sorry about that yeah, but I've . . . been such a weirdo tonight, such a . . . sarcastic jerk. I . . . I might look like one and I might act like one, but I'm really not. I have two goldfish at home that'll vouch for me, I talk to them all the time, they'd tell you if they could. Brian and Mike. I might be wrong a lot but I'm really not an asshole—" I stop short as I realize I'm raving.

"Brian and Mike?"

"My goldfish. Can I smoke in here or will the Committee Against White Smoking Males make an emasculating house call?"

"Certainly not. Mike as in Michael Whatever Tobin?"

I feel myself turn crimson.

I don't say anything but I squirm. She sees my eye alighting upon my toolbox, then measuring the distance to her door—

"You . . . something happened here between you two."

"Ahhh . . . I . . ."

"You were in love with him—weren't you," she states, rather than asks.

I turn and look up at her. I can't read her eyes, but it feels like we're both in some kind of waiting room.

"Yes," I sigh, staring down at the pattern in the white rug. I don't have the energy to lie to her. She may be dying, but I'm still so mortified about this admission from her butch HVAC guy—a role I've brought to perfection after seven years playing it—that I look up and gauge her for a reaction. How's that for self-absorption?

But she just stares, a finger in her hair.

"Of course now that I've told you I'll have to kill you," I say, and we both laugh, too loudly. But there's a break in something. I think we both relax.

"That's . . . okay," she says after a minute. My knee-jerk reaction is to tell her I don't need her or anybody else's approval. But for once I hold my tongue. I find an odd comfort in her words.

"I, on the other hand, really can be a bitch," she adds, laughing. She pauses. "I had to be, they were so incredibly horrible when I first started there. At the bank. If you're nice they think you're a pushover because you're a woman and they walk all over you. If you're firm and won't take their shit you're an emasculating bitch. It'll be a nice day when people can be people, and not some label."

"Amen to that. Look, I'm really sor—"

She makes a face, waves me away, but now her hands are trembling. When she sees that I've noticed them she folds them instantly.

"Cold out tonight," I say.

She looks at me quickly. Then she smiles, and it goes into me like the rising heat.

"Yes," she says quietly. "Very cold."

There's a long pause that isn't uncomfortable. I feel my muscles relax a bit, or un-lax as I call it.

"Tell me the story," she repeats lowly. "I . . . I want to think about something else for a while."

"It seems silly now," I mutter. "Unimportant."

"No!" she cries, yells really. "No! It's . . . it's life. Life's all we have. It isn't silly." She pauses. Her mood shifts.

"Please?" she says plaintively.

I wouldn't tell the shrinks, not everything anyway, I never told anyone—

But I tell her. I tell her everything. Halfway through she suddenly laughs and cries at the same time. I stop, look up.

"Nothing," she says. "I'm sorry. I had a brother. Go on."

I finish. I tell her everything. I tell her how they spray painted FAGGOT FUCKER on Mr. Tobin's pickup truck while he was in at the hearing. I tell her how he left the next day. Gonzo. Vanished. Without a trace. Well wouldn't you? I tell her how I looked for Him for a whole year when I was twenty, then came home and tried to kill myself and had a remarkably uneventful nervous breakdown. I was in the hospital for two months. That's when they first started me being good with my dead hands. That was seven years ago. I own a house now. I'm becoming bourgeois, a harmless little consumer, more interested in my swelling home equity than who gets elected or who goes hungry. I have two goldfish who love me. I'm okay now, everything's okay. It's fucking okay.

She makes me breakfast in the techno-industrial kitchen: instant oatmeal, too-tart grapefruit juice, and honey-raisin English muffins. We sit at this artsy aluminum table with curvy legs. I stare around as the metal vastness begins to gleam in the rising daylight. When I look back at her she's watching me.

"I never consciously thought this," she says, plopping her eyes into her tea, "but if you'd asked me? I would have told you that . . . somehow all of this would have protected me." She looks around at her things. Then she looks back up at me. "You know, I don't think any of this is really . . . me. It just seems . . . so cold now. I keep thinking of my grandmother's house, and how tacky it was, and how . . . beautiful. Comfortable. *Safe.* It always smelled nice." She pauses. "Maybe I should do this whole place over," she murmurs.

"Think gingham," I reply. She laughs.

"I guess what I'm saying is . . ." she lifts her eyes to mine, "I thought this was me. It isn't."

"Y-you don't have to explain to me," I mumble back. "I should get an Oscar for the role I've been playing these last seven years."

We stare at each other.

"I . . . really don't know anything about anything," I say. I swallow.

I look away first, play with my mushy oatmeal.

"Well," she says. "You fixed my heat, Brian. That's more than I could do."

"What's . . . what's your name?" I ask.

She looks up at me and smiles.

"Joy," she says.

She signs for the repairs. We stare at each other again when I'm leaving, then laugh and embrace, awkwardly. She's staring into my eyes when we break apart as if she's searching for something. But I don't think either one of us knows what that is.

"Okay then," she says, clasping her hands together.

I follow her to the door. She turns.

"Well," she says. "Thanks."

"Thank you," I say. I pause. "Best of luck." I want to tell her about the patron saint of cancer, but she's not Catholic I don't think and she might laugh at me. Plus I can't recall his name. So instead I mumble, "I think I'll call in sick today. I feel like I could sleep for a month."

"So it's back to the goldfish?" she asks.

I nod. "And back to the bank for you?"

She nods.

"One more week," she says. "Then I'm taking some time off." She looks away. "I'd like to get back into my photog—what are you laughing at?"

"Nothing. I . . . thanks."

"You're welcome."

I walk out the door, go up the stairs two at a time like I used to when I was a kid, set free of school. The world through the glass walls and doors of the front lobby is a world of ice, but the rising sun sliding over the cement horizon turns this world into diamonds. Whether or not, it's a new day.

I stop when I reach the top stair. I turn around. She's leaning out into her hallway, watching me. She smiles, then raises her eyebrows one last time. Then she turns and shuts the door.

Jimmy Callahan, Married, Three Kids

Near the end of his sleep he dreamed.

He'd had this dream often.

Always, it was his great-grandfather at the front door of the old house on East Seventh Street—that's how they'd begin. He was a child of eight in the dreams. He'd throw open the door and find the old man waiting and glaring, as if he'd been there all night, the eyes wild and so blue they seemed frozen. A shock of still-red hair flamed around the ancient face. The old man's eyes burned into his, then he'd start talking at him, blasting away in Irish.

Dia duit! Cen ce bhfuil tu, á Sheamus?

Unintelligible words—rocky as the roaring shore the old man fished in the wild west of Ireland. Thrown at him with a terrible urgency. Little Jimmy would panic as the old man's words came at him like bullets . . . what was he saying? What? Was the house on fire? The sea, somehow at the old man's command, was the sea coming up to swallow him, as it had swallowed scores of his forebears? Who was this ancient monster? What was he saying?

This actually had happened, the seed of all this future delirium. Jimmy was eight, and splayed out belly-down on the rug in the parlor, playing with his fire engine. The front door was open to the May noon sun, flashing into the room like knives in a drawer. Then a shadow eclipsed the sun from the rug. Jimmy jumped up, expecting his friend Timmy Quinn, his father was a firefighter too. Instead the old man was at the screen door, his stooped hugeness blotting out the day. Jimmy had no idea who he was, nor even that the old man would be visiting. *We wanted it to be a surprise,* his mother explained later. It was. He'd looked up into the wild eyes, and then a stream of foreign words had been hurled at him. These, he realized now, had been spontaneous words of tumbled greeting, joy, as the old man met his namesake for the first, and, as it turned out, only time—

But Jimmy hadn't known that. A shapeless horror rising inside him like cold water, he had turned from the old man, dashed through the house, passed his mother in the kitchen, then burst out the back door.

He hadn't stopped running until he was way up by Broadway Station. They still laughed about it in his family. Jimmy didn't.

And here he was having the dream again, more than twenty years later.

He pulled at consciousness, anxious to escape the dream, wary of what the old man's words might mean this time.

He tried to stir, found he couldn't. For a jumbled second he thought he must be home with June, when he should be at the firehouse. He half-opened one eye as the old man's long-dead face flickered, then faded out like it was being pulled into deep water.

He was awake now, fully. It was still dark, he saw nothing. Not the impenetrable, ballooning black of a smoke fire, but the gray black of nothingness, forgetfulness. He found his sense of touch was heightened in the darkness. He took inventory—slowly, so as not to panic:

A long arm was thrown over his bare back;

A warm, fleshy leg was tangled up naked with his own;

His own arm lay over the back of a smooth, rigid waist, right where it began to swell into soft firm flesh.

The tumbled sheet was somewhere below his knees—but he was warm, moist with warmth.

He realized where he was.

And with whom.

He heard a sharp inrush of breath, didn't recognize it as his own for a moment. Jimmy had only heard himself do this once before: his first month on the Department when he'd found a dead infant in its smoke-curdled crib, the open eyes, blue as his own, staring up at him accusingly. *If you'd crashed through the window instead of wasting precious time axing down the door. . . . If only you'd come right in, instead of going back to the truck for the gas mask—*

The sedated part of him tried to coo himself back to sleep, to sleep, to forget . . . but he feared the old man would be lurking there in Dreamland, popping up like a fun-house ghoul. Besides—after seven years on the Department—it was impossible to regain sleep once an alarm had sounded, and now several were blaring simultaneously in his head:

An alarm that this person beside him was not his wife June;

An alarm that the musky, almost sweet odor coming from the open armpit near his face was not a feminine smell;

An alarm at the series of events that had preceded this awakening, they crashed before him one by one like huge tumbling dominoes; and—

—the loudest of all, he squeezed his eyes shut at its din—

I liked it—

It's still early, go back to sleep—

I've slept with a man and I liked it.

He lay immobile, stealing breaths carefully. He'd never slept with anyone but June. He had confessed this to no one—not even June when she used to shyly but persistently ask during the first months of their marriage.

Was it always this good? Jimmy, was it better with the others, Jimmy? How many were there before me?

A movie was playing in the dark room, he could see himself shrugging at her questions, smiling, he'd be on top of her naked when she asked. He'd been ashamed to say there had been no one else, thinking she might think him less a man if he confessed he'd gone to the altar a virgin. She stopped inquiring, finally, when she knew him better, understood—or at least grew temporarily resigned to—his silent ways. They communicated more with looks now—and of course they were busy with the kids: Jimmy Junior, tall and thin, blond and garrulous; Will, red-headed and silent like his father; little Maureen, a deaf-mute, an angelic thing who looked like no one they knew, her special-school play was tonight and he would be there to see her, June had PTA with the boys' teachers—

My God, how had this happened?

The warmth wouldn't go away.

He could inch out from the limbs covering him, the midsection pressed against his own, steal up from the bed noiselessly, he'd done it often enough when he had Early Shift and June would be sleeping beside him like a dead thing—

—in fact this was the time to get up, get out, get dressed, before what he'd done, what *they'd* done, could be recognized, talked about, *acknowledged.*

But he lingered, wide-eyed and naked in the dark.

Every event in his life had somehow led up to this utterly un-planned, unexpected occurrence—and in that occurrence, losing him-self, he had found himself: a stranger, but himself nonetheless.

It wouldn't have happened if the mayor hadn't gone to Italy. Strange. Bizarre but true. He marveled at the collision courses human lives were, grazing into something extraneous and minute and imma-terial, but in so doing, having their courses redirected, then smashing into something that smacked of destiny because of this previous meaningless grazing.

The mayor had gone to Italy for two weeks on what was routinely called a trade mission. The trade missions never happened in an elec-tion year. The deputy mayor was running the show in Hizoner's ab-sence. A nervous bureaucrat, he'd done some union busting in his earlier days, and was convinced his City Hall office would be fire-bombed or otherwise vandalized during his brief tenure as Acting Mayor. He'd ordered a fire engine to be parked in the large garage beneath City Hall, manned 'round the clock.

"Loser!" Capt. Billy had boomed, hanging up the firehouse phone. He broke into his wise-guy laugh. "What'll they think of next, hey pal?" Captain Billy had directed the question at Jimmy, who was pol-ishing the grill on Engine 7—but everyone knew it was rhetorical, ask Jimmy a question and all you got was a shrug, that smile.

"All right guys, gather round—that was some shithead from City Hall. The assistant mayor—" Captain Billy raised his nose in the air, "believes his office is *at risk*. Stupid douche bag. They're parking En-gine 3 over there for two weeks with a two-man shift 'round the clock. Guess who's been assigned the night shift?" He smiled. "Us. I need two volunteers."

Had Terry looked at Jimmy then, just for a second? Even now Jimmy wondered about this.

"I'll go," Terry said softly.

For some strange reason Jimmy could hear the blood thudding in his ears the moment after Terry volunteered.

"Count me in," Jimmy had said. This time Terry did look at him, of that Jimmy had been sure.

Maybe it wasn't all chance after all, Jimmy thought, lying in the bed.

Terry had joined their shift in Charlestown two years ago. Terry's wife had been killed one month before, hit by a delivery truck while getting out of a cab after Christmas shopping. She'd been struggling with her packages in the sleet. Laughing, someone who was there said later. Jimmy had made a contribution as nearly everyone else had; he'd remembered the incident, seen it in the papers and marveled at its almost mythicness. He'd gone to the funeral as a matter of course with everyone else. Jimmy had never met Terry before this. A month later Terry transferred over to Jimmy's firehouse when Fat Fitzy (as differentiated from just Fitzy) retired. Evidently Terry had thought a change might make it easier.

The Quiet Man, that's what the other guys on his shift called Jimmy; but Terry was quieter. They had no way of knowing if he'd always been like this.

When it was slow between calls the other guys might wash their trucks or cars, play cards, watch TV, nap. The station had one porn tape that got played once every few months. Jimmy had only seen one part of it, a chambermaid walking into a motel room and finding a man standing naked in the middle of the room with a large erection. "Looks like you've got a problem," the woman said, staring at the man's midsection.

Terry partook of none of these normal diversions. Instead he'd hang halfway out the open second-story barracks window, trying to coax a squirrel nesting in a nearby tree to eat out of his hand. He'd go into the kitchen, grab a few Ritz crackers, smear peanut butter on them, then go to the half-open window where he'd whistle softly for the squirrel. Sometimes Terry wouldn't see the squirrel all day—but still he'd look for him out the window. Jimmy watched all this carefully when he thought no one would notice. The winter came and the window got closed, but Terry still stood by it, crackers ready in the smooth white hands. He turned once unexpectedly and caught Jimmy staring at him from the small cot he was lying upon.

Jimmy colored deeply, turning as red as his hair.

"He likes this stuff," Terry said lowly, holding up a cracker. He shrugged.

Jimmy smiled.

"I don't know what else to do," Terry added, still holding Jimmy's eyes.

Jimmy nodded slowly.

Terry took a two-week vacation right before his first Christmas at Jimmy's firehouse—everyone guessed why. It was the first anniversary of his wife's death. Jimmy found himself restless, bored—he couldn't understand himself. He'd always been so comfortably predictable to himself and everyone else—high school, the service, the fire department, marriage and kids—

But in thinking of this he began to see his life as something as rigid as any caste system. June mentioned something about his mood. He began watching his behavior around the house, shocked at this. This type of filtration was utterly foreign to him and he marveled at how adept he became at it. At work, he began looking out Terry's squirrel window. He fed the animal on two occasions when Captain Billy and his caustic sense of humor were away from the station. Jimmy marveled at how close the squirrel got. He saw fear and determination mingled in the mirror-black eyes as the animal scrambled onto the sill and timidly snatched the cracker from Jimmy's fingers.

Terry came back after Little Christmas, red-eyed, looking a few pounds thinner. Jimmy found himself staring in the mirror that morning before he went in, he knew Terry would be back that day. He was thirty minutes early for work.

What's happening to me? he wondered amidst the chaos of the early morning commute.

"I think he spent his whole vacation bawling," Fitzy mumbled that evening at supper, Terry's first night back. Terry had eaten quickly, then returned to the window, even though the squirrel never came at night.

"Terrible fuckin' thing," Captain Billy slurred, his mouth spilling food.

Jimmy played with the stew in his bowl, not raising his eyes, but aware of where Terry was at any given second.

Three months later Jimmy was bounding up the stairs to their second floor barracks; Terry was running down. They both stopped, Jimmy's head snapping back a bit. Jimmy had been waiting for just such a moment, to see Terry alone. With ten men on their shift this was nearly impossible. He couldn't imagine why he'd been practicing the speech he wanted to make, why he thought about it as he jogged around Castle Island every morning.

"I, ahhh, just wanted to tell you . . . when you were on vacation I fed your squirrel a couple times," Jimmy mumbled.

"What?" Terry asked, taking a step closer, tilting his head. It seemed to Jimmy that his words had snatched Terry out of some interior world.

Terry's eyes looked into Jimmy's.

"I didn't hear you," Terry said. Jimmy became aware that Terry had his own smell, unnoticeable unless one was close. He wondered why he noticed this.

"I fed your squirrel when you were on vacation," he repeated. Jimmy gulped, he hoped Terry didn't notice.

"Vacation," Terry echoed. He scratched his thick black hair, pushed it off his forehead absently.

"Last Christmas," Jimmy said. He suddenly felt ridiculous.

"Oh. Oh! You did?"

Jimmy nodded. Their eyes locked. Jimmy got the same feeling he had when he was about to plunge into a burning building.

He didn't sleep that night.

June brought the kids into the station one day that August. The boys tried on the fire hats, sat in the driver's seat of Engine 3 making noises and punching each other. Maureen stood by her father's side, looking up at him, searching for her father's hand with her diminutive one.

"Can you watch Maureen for a minute?" June asked, pouring through her pocketbook. "I want to run across the way and get the boys haircuts." There was no reason why she couldn't take Maureen with her, but Jimmy just nodded. He had a fierce love for his daughter, a love that almost frightened him. Looking into her eyes he felt she knew all there was to know in the world, and, knowing this, said nothing. "You shouldn't favor her so," June had said—more than once. He couldn't help it. He didn't choose to help it.

June didn't like mess, Jimmy thought, didn't like the unexpected. He believed suddenly that she thought of Maureen as some might think of a ready-to-be-put-down family dog, a once-beloved pet that had grown incontinent and slightly irksome. As he watched June cross the street he felt almost as if he were watching a stranger. A chill ran through him, settling in his testicles.

He lifted up Maureen, hugged her as hard as he dared, his eyes closed. She hugged back. Somehow, lately, she represented to him all that was beautiful in life, beautiful and dangerous and wounded and invincible. He was beginning to see everything as being fragile, terminal. He didn't know what to do with these thoughts, unknown to him before. He didn't know what was happening to him, it seemed he was changing, rolling toward some cliff he couldn't avoid. He noticed people's eyes now everywhere he went, their pain, their soul. His sensitivity, his perception, seemed doubled, trebled. He'd been reading books, anything he could get his hands on. He noticed June chose the times he was reading to converse with him, keeping up an intermittent banter until Jimmy would finally put the book down. Then she'd leave the room.

He felt his eyes begin to sting as he continued to hold onto his four-year-old daughter. He opened them. He saw Terry one floor above him, at the opening of the pole ladder, watching them intently.

He held Terry's eyes as he stroked Maureen's eiderdown hair.

Terry didn't move away. He stared, his mouth set. Finally he backed off. Jimmy kept looking at the empty space Terry had occupied a moment ago. He continued to stroke Maureen's hair.

Terry took just one week off that next Christmas. June as usual had finished the holiday shopping by Labor Day, the wrapping by Halloween. Christmas Eve would be at her sister's, she announced, Christmas Day at her parents' down the street. Christmas Eve Day Jimmy was downtown at the Jewelers' Building, picking up a bracelet he'd had engraved for June. He'd almost forgotten to get her something. He ducked into St. Anthony's Shrine on Arch Street, he'd always viewed this place as a kind of oasis in the midst of downtown's turmoil of boom boxes, throngs of shoppers, and long-striding career people, their eyes glazed but wary, their teeth gritted over business deals.

He pushed through the metal and glass church doors. The sudden quiet wrapped around him like a poultice.

He dipped his right index finger into the Holy Water font, made the sign of the cross ("Don't do that!" June had cautioned the last time they went to church, "It's germy, that water!"). Then he opened the double doors that led from the foyer to the church itself.

Perhaps two dozen people were scattered about, all solitary but for a mother with two babies, and an elderly couple. He doffed his cap and sat down in the third pew. The church was dark, hushed, and almost empty, the way he liked it. Flickering candlelight glazed the walls around him. He smelled furniture polish, beeswax candles, incense lingering in the air like a prayer. He studied the crucifix above the altar, the agonized plaster face of Jesus. He saw that Jesus had Maureen's eyes.

Something stirred at the edge of his peripheral vision. Turning, he saw an old woman, her face peaceful, her eyes open and kind, shuffling out of the confessional box. Her hands were wrapped around a big black pocketbook, blue crystal Rosary beads, and several bakeshop boxes, bound, he guessed, for people other than herself. He wondered what sins these blameless women confessed.

The red light above the priest's box in the confessional gleamed steadily. On a whim Jimmy got up, walked over, swallowed hard, then pushed aside the purple velvet curtain.

Once inside the box he knelt down on the prie-dieu.

The priest slid open the screened wooden panel that separated his shrouded face from Jimmy's.

"May the peace and blessings of Almighty God, His son Jesus Christ, and the Holy Spirit be with you now and forever," the priest began.

"Bless me father for I have sinned," Jimmy answered, the words he'd been taught when he was seven.

He stalled.

"I . . . I don't know what's happening to me," he muttered.

"Yes, my son?" the priest encouraged. Jimmy heard tenderness in the old man's voice.

"I feel lost. . . . I'm . . . I'm confused." *But I've never felt more alive, more . . . vulnerable.*

"Are you married, my son?" the priest probed.

"Yes."

"Children?"

"Yes. Three."

"A good wife?"

"Ahhh . . . yes, Father."

"Feeling . . . trapped?" the priest asked.

"Yes. I guess so. Like . . . I don't know myself anymore. Like the life I'm living is . . . it's all planned. It's all been planned from the moment I was born until they bury me. Every minute. It's like I've been asleep till . . . just recently and now I see this, see everything different. My life's a big gray plan."

"Not planned by you?"

"No."

"You're feeling resentment?"

"No. Maybe. I'm feeling . . . I don't know what I'm feeling."

"What would you change if you could?"

Jimmy thought for a long time.

"I don't know. I just wish I could stop everything, like freeze the whole world for a while and just . . . think for a while. Figure things out."

"What would you think about?"

"Everything."

But mostly Terry. And why I must watch him like I do.

"What's the matter with you today?" June hissed as she helped her sister Lorraine clear away the Christmas Dinner. It was just growing dark Christmas Day.

Jimmy looked up at her.

"You've been brooding all day. Even Mom said something." She paused, hovering over him with an armful of dirty dishes. "Why don't you go out in the parlor with everybody else?"

Jimmy shook his head. He was the last one sitting at the gargantuan linen-clothed dinner table. From his in-laws' parlor came the sound of laughing, singing, children shouting—

I keep thinking about Terry, if he's all alone today. I don't want to but I can't help it.

June didn't move, Jimmy knew she wouldn't until he gave her an answer.

"There ahhhh . . . might be layoffs at work," he lied.

"Oh?" June answered, her thin eyebrows lowering. She humped the dishes onto the table and put her hands on her hips. Jimmy got the sense she was concerned not for him, but for the possible changes this event might bring to her own life, her routines: of bill paying the first Sunday night of every month in the dining room with Country Music playing, the food shopping that must be done on Saturdays even though that was the busiest day of the week—

"Dad hasn't said anything about layoffs," she intoned. Her father had retired from the department two years ago, but didn't know what to do with himself, he still walked to his old station every day, kept up with all the gossip. Jimmy'd forgotten that.

"Don't upset him," Jimmy said, turning up and around. "It's just a rumor probably. Where's . . . where's Maureen?"

"I put her in for a nap upstairs. What do you mean, layoffs? You've got seniority, right?"

"Ahhh . . . yeah. I'm just worried about some of the other guys." He played with the petrifying pie crust remnants on his dessert plate. "I think I'll go up and see Maureen."

As he left the dining room he heard his wife sigh.

He mounted the stairs of his in-laws' house, marveling at the precision of things, as if they'd measured the paintings lining the stairway hall to get them excruciatingly equidistant. He passed the second-floor bathroom. The shaggy toilet seat cover and crocheted girl covering the spare roll of toilet paper made him want to scream, he didn't know why. The too-fragrant artificial smell coming from the soap dish was, he realized, the same odor of their own bathroom at home, an odor that seemed to linger around June like a stale aura. He turned back, looked behind him, then stepped into the bathroom, shutting the door. Five small soap bars, each in the shape of an identical round seashell, nested in the soap dish. They were dirty and dusty and looked years old, but Jimmy knew they'd never been used. He emptied them into the palm of his hand, then stood over the toilet. He reached over and turned the lock on the doorknob. Then he plopped the soaps into the toilet, one by one. When the last one joined its fellows, he urinated on them. He squeezed hard, making it last longer. His heart raced. Then he flushed the toilet, watching things swirl, then vanish. He zippered and buckled and belted up, then left the bathroom, avoiding the mirror as he passed it.

Softly, he pushed open his in-laws' bedroom door. He found Maureen standing at the window, staring out. Feeling his vibrations as he crossed the creaky wooden floor, she turned, then smiled shyly when she saw it was her father. She pointed an inch-long finger out the window as if she had a secret. He bent over her, placing his hands on her small shoulders, and peered out at the gathering Yule gloom.

Outside the window, a squirrel was perched on the branch of a tree, staring back at them. Maureen looked up at her father in delight. Jimmy couldn't say whose eyes were brighter, Maureen's or the squirrel's. Jimmy made himself laugh, so his little girl wouldn't notice that he was crying.

"Running? Tonight?" June asked later, when they were back at their house, the kids put to bed. Jimmy had put on sweatpants, a nylon running jacket, and the new sneakers he'd got that morning from June. She always got them too small and he was obliged to wear them without socks. He nodded. She was at the kitchen table, a chaos of ill-fitting or unwanted sweaters and blouses and candy samplers and receipts scattered about her. She and her sisters would be downtown at the stores all the next day, returning things, haggling with sales clerks over credit amounts.

Jimmy had been slumped in the La-Z-Boy chair in the paneled Family Room, watching football for an hour. Staring around at the suddenly strange room—at the crocheted throw draped over the sofa, the artificial plant in the corner, the duck lamp on the end table— Jimmy realized there wasn't an inch of the house that June hadn't colonized.

I used to like doing this, he'd said to himself during an especially annoying, demeaning man-targeted commercial. But he was too restless now, there seemed a slow burning inside him and most things seemed absurd, pointless.

"Yeah," he said, "yeah. Just out to the Island and back."

"That's where you always go."

"I know."

"So why are you telling me?"

"You asked me if . . ." she made a face and he didn't finish.

"I might be in bed by the time you get back," she said, not looking up from the receipts. "I'm meeting Ellie and Sue early."

He hesitated at the door. *June, have you ever felt lost? Just totally lost?* They had started as friends, once, a hard to remember long ago, had shared some thoughts—he wondered if beneath all her busy-ness there was any of that care still lingering.

"Okay," he said. It was easier to just say okay.

"Can you make skim milk from the powder when you get home?" she asked.

"Ah . . . sure. Sure."

He leaned over and kissed her lightly on the top of her head. She didn't look up from the receipts. He smelled the soaps he had flushed down the toilet. A sudden anger nipped at him. He leaned back and stared at her.

"These . . . these are too small," he said.

June's head shot up.

"What? What is?"

"These. The sneakers."

"Oh." She looked back at a receipt in her fingers. "They're size ten. That's what you always take."

"Yeah." He swallowed. "Yeah, I know it, but . . . they're too small."

"How can they be too small? They're size ten and you always take size ten. Don't tell me they're too small."

"They're just . . . they're too small."

She dropped her hands to the table and glared at him over her half-glasses. "They're the same as the ones I got you last year. Same brand and everything and you never complained before. Don't tell me your feet are still growing, that's the kids' job."

"They're . . . they're too small, June."

She raised her eyes to him, searching out. How could it be that someone he had slept in the same bed with for fourteen years was someone who looked like a stranger now? A stranger whom, more disturbing thought, he didn't think he'd like to get to know?

Jimmy looked away first.

He put his hand on the door handle. She didn't notice how tightly.

"I just wanted to tell you."

"They'll stretch," she said, going back to her receipts.

It was snowing lightly when he turned the corner of East Seventh and O. Windless, timeless, otherworldly, its silent perfection made Jimmy halt. *Is the snow always this beautiful?* He stopped again at the first pay phone he passed. He pulled a slip of paper from his sweatpants pocket; he'd had it with him continually for the past two days. *T. 268-1755.* The home number. He'd gotten it from the station's rolodex.

Snowflakes, brilliant from the streetlight watching above him, fell upon the slip of paper, melting.

If the ink runs, I won't call him, I'll take it as a Sign.

His fingers were trembling. They never would at a fire. The white paper faded to gray with wetness. The numbers shone through, like sparkling rocks in a shallow sun-splashed riverbed.

He misdialed, twice.

One ring, two. He pictured the ringing happening in an empty house, echoing through empty rooms. He didn't know where in Southie Terry lived, hadn't wanted to know.

"Yeah?" he heard as he was about to hang up. His heart leapt. Terry.

The warmth held.

Jimmy thought it might be getting lighter out. He slowly lifted his left hand, marveled at it, at what it had done. He looked at his watch. It was 3:47 a.m. More than three hours till the shift change at seven. His eyes, then, were adjusting to the darkness.

He studied the face next to him, cautiously, his lids half closed. But he grew bolder as Terry's breathing remained deep and even. The black hair spilled down onto the forehead. The cheekbones were high and round—he watched how the skin was porcelain in one place, then how it merged into the one-day-beard area, seamlessly. Perfectly. The top lip was thin, the bottom fuller, and slightly open in sleep, like a child's. *How like children we are. Little children in adult bodies.* He studied the small scar on the left cheek, old and almost invisible, something from childhood probably. He marveled at how Terry's life, too, had led up to this shared moment, how every event in Terry's life had somehow led to this one here and now. The lashes on the eyelids were thick and long. Jimmy reached out a finger to them then remembered himself.

It's just the night, he thought. While it's dark, this is a different world, I'm a different kind of man. But never again. Never again. He found no comfort in this vow. He had expected some. He returned to a study of the man beside him—if this would be the only time, then he'd commit this all to memory.

Never again. He repeated the phrase in his head.

Or was it never again with anyone other than Terry?

"Ah . . . Terry?" A bus roared by and drowned out all other sound. Jimmy panicked. Who would need a bus on Christmas night at

11:00? He looked up as the bus blurred by. He plugged his other ear with his finger. The bus was empty.

"Terry? Terry?"

"Who is this?"

"It's, ah, Jimmy."

"Jimmy."

"Yeah, Jimmy Callahan from the sta—"

"I know."

"You weren't . . . sleeping?" Whatever part of the brain it was that manufactured words was closing down on Jimmy, just when he needed it.

"No. Merry . . . Christmas, Jimmy."

"Thanks. The same to—" *No! Don't!* "I just . . . wanted to see how . . . you were making out. I was just heading out for a jog and I thought—you know I just thought I'd call and . . . and . . ." *And what? What? C'mon, say something, knucklehead! Anything!*

"Where you jogging to?" Terry blessedly interceded.

"Just out to The Island." He got an idea. "It should be pretty in the snow. Quiet."

"Is it snowing out?"

"Just flurrying." *Say it, you idiot! C'mon! No, don't! Don't!*

A silence.

"Hey, Terry, would you want to meet for a dr—" But Terry began to say something at the same time.

"What?" they asked simultaneously.

Jimmy squeezed his eyes shut and blurted, "Do you wanna meet for a drink, Terry?"

Another silence.

"Okay."

They met at Brat McDermott's. Terry got there first, Jimmy was surprised at that. There were three other people at the bar, not including Carl the bartender who only worked weekends and holidays. Jimmy sometimes stopped here for a quick one on the way home from his jog when he ran at night. He didn't particularly like to drink, it was just that it kept him away from June a few minutes longer, he realized this now. Tonight's other patrons were all old men, sitting solitary, slumped over their pints, caps yanked low. They didn't bother looking up when Jimmy walked in. Thankfully, no Christmas music was playing. Terry was seated at one of the dozen red leatherette booths that lined the left side of the tavern. He was facing front. Photos of old boxers lined the walls. A smell of spilled draft beer and cigarettes licked odd areas of the room.

"I didn't think any places would be open tonight," Terry said when Jimmy sat down across from him.

"Yeah, I didn't either, I just happened to pass by it earlier," Jimmy blurted, trying not to stare. He'd never been this close to Terry, never seen him out of his uniform. He was wearing a mustard-colored work jacket with a gray hooded sweatshirt underneath.

"You got snow in your hair," Terry said, smiling and pointing. The gesture made Jimmy think, guiltily, that Terry wasn't the brightest bulb in the circuit. Jimmy didn't care.

"I do?" Jimmy said. He brushed it off, could feel himself turning crimson. "Ahh . . . what's your poison?"

Terry lifted his palms up from his lap. "Beer. A beer. Anything."

They had a beer in excruciating silence, Terry peeling the label off his bottle with his thumbnail.

Why do you stare at me sometimes? Jimmy wanted to ask. *Is it for the same reason I stare at you? Because if it is I wish you'd tell me.*

"How—how are you doing?" Jimmy finally blurted, too loudly. He gulped, audibly.

"Okay," Terry answered slowly. He looked up. Their eyes locked.

"The loneliest night of the year," Jimmy said, panicking. "That's what my father used to call it."

"Not anymore," Terry said. He put the bottle to his mouth and took a last finishing swallow, keeping his eyes on Jimmy. Jimmy looked away.

"Thanks for calling," Terry added quickly. "I been in all day."

"I . . . I've been meaning to for a while. It . . . it must be rough . . . Terry." He studied the place mat on the table before him, *Historic Sites Around Beantown*. The mat was in the shape of a bean pot.

"It . . ." Terry started. Jimmy looked up. Then Terry shrugged, shook his head, and looked down at his large red and white fingers wrapped around the empty beer bottle.

"What?" Jimmy whispered.

"It's not what you think," Terry mumbled. "It's not what anyone thinks."

"What? What isn't?"

Terry looked up. Jimmy couldn't look away. He felt everything he'd been feeling lately, all the questions, the confusion, had their resolution in Terry's eyes. How this could be, he didn't know.

You can tell me. Please, tell me—maybe if I think this hard enough you'll tell me—

"It's guilt," Terry said, looking up again. "I shouldn't have married her. I . . . I didn't—love her. I mean I did but I wasn't in . . . It just . . . I don't know, I woke up and I was married. I woke up and I was on the fire department like my old man, and married."

Jimmy's heart started racing. He thought for the first time in his life he was hearing Truth. He fought back a sob. He turned his head away and looked toward the door, as if any minute people would come in and drag them away. He turned back and found his voice for once. He leaned his head across the table until his face was inches from Terry's. Their eyes locked.

"I know!" he whispered.

Terry's blank face kept staring. Then he opened his mouth—

"Hey, Jimmy," the bartender roared. Jimmy looked up with a jump. Carl was holding the phone in his hand. One of the old men was pointing at Jimmy and grimacing. "You got a phone call. It's the Missus." Jimmy leapt up and walked over to the bar before he even thought about whether he should or not.

"Hello?"

"I figured you'd be there."

"Yeah, I just—"

"Can you leave me your Visa card? Mine's expired and they haven't sent a new one yet."

"Ahhh . . . yeah. Sure."

"Are you coming home soon?"

"Ah . . . yeah. Yeah."

"All right." She yawned. "Don't forget to make the skim milk."

When Jimmy got back to their booth, Terry was standing, zippering up his jacket.

"I gotta go anyway," he half-smiled.

Jimmy knew some people had words that could make Terry stay. He didn't know what those words were.

"Terry," was all he managed. Terry looked up, smiled again as he looked away, then brushed past him toward the door.

Jimmy grabbed his jacket and followed.

"She wants ya home, huh?" one of the old men, toothless, called after him, laughing and spinning half around on his barstool. "She knowed where to find ya though, didn't she?"

Jimmy stepped outside, pulling the door shut behind him. Terry was standing in front of him, his back to Jimmy, his hands jammed into his pants pockets. Jimmy heard Terry take a deep breath, the way Jimmy did, calming down after a fire. Jimmy took a step closer, he was right behind him now. His breath was coming faster, gray clouds of it. The miles of triple-deckers surrounding them seemed to throb in the reflection of a nearby flashing red light—lives were being manufactured even now, even Christmas Day at midnight plans were being silently laid, directives were being nonverbally communicated to children and husbands and daughters—

Jimmy watched his hand approach Terry's right shoulder, then pull back, then approach again. Finally he watched it land on its target. Terry jumped. Jimmy was shaking from the inside out. He squeezed Terry's shoulder, hard.

He heard Terry take another profound breath. Then Terry took a step forward, breaking away. He turned and began walking. He vanished around the corner.

Ten minutes later, Jimmy stood shivering across the street and down a little from his house, waiting for the blue wash of light from the TV in his and June's bedroom to flash out. After about half an hour it clicked off. He waited ten more minutes, then slipped in through the back door as quietly as he could. He was still trembling; not from the cold.

He forgot to make the skim milk, and he and June spent the next day, frozen rain outside, housebound, moody and argumentative.

Jimmy's eyes left Terry's sleeping face and moved onto the shoulders, the area between the shoulders and the neck. His eyes replayed what his fingers remembered: the smooth tautness of the skin, the rounded muscles just beneath, the way one thing so seamlessly tied into the next, but how drastic was the difference in these areas. He marveled at nakedness. Slowly, he affixed the hand that was draped over Terry's back to Terry's skin, touching. He closed his eyes. Terry half-stirred, but only to pull Jimmy in closer.

Their makeshift barracks beneath City Hall had been set up by the two-man day shift, two Hispanic guys from a firehouse in Dorchester. It was a small room adjacent to the large, diesel-smelling garaging area where Engine 3 sat idle, hostage to a bureaucrat's paranoia. In the tiny office were two chairs with a cheap metal desk in one corner, upon which rested a microwave, a week-old copy of a daily tabloid, a phone, and a two-way radio. There was a bathroom on the other side of the garage with a shower stall, a toilet, and a dirty sink with a copper-green ring around its drain. A tiny refrigerator sat on the floor of the office, with a half-empty carton of light cream, and a lemon, inside. The lemon puzzled them both. Two twin cots were placed in the middle of the room, perhaps two feet apart. The room was fetid and damp and smelled faintly of hot gasoline. The floor was dirty concrete.

"All you'll have to do is sleep," Captain Billy had said. "Fuckin' waste o' time and money. But it's a twelve-hour shift, seven to seven. Better bring a deck o' cards. Thanks for doin' this guys, I owe you one."

Their first night in the basement of City Hall was Monday.

Jimmy brought enough cold meatloaf for both of them.

"How much are you taking?" June had asked right before he left. If there wasn't enough for the kids' lunch the next day, Jimmy figured, this would change her plans, always annoying to her. He kept loading the slices into his lunchbox.

"It's a long shift," Jimmy answered, avoiding her eyes. It seemed he wanted to look into everyone's eyes now but June's. When she had asked him who the other man was on the shift, he'd told her he didn't know.

Terry had brought two peanut butter and jelly sandwiches on rubbery white bread, and a warm can of Dr. Pepper that he put in the refrigerator as soon as he got there.

It was their first time together alone since Christmas Eve, three months before.

It was so quiet in the enclosed room Jimmy could hear pulse thudding in his ears.

"At least they gave us a microwave and a fridge," Terry said.

"Yeah," Jimmy answered. His voice echoed in the small room.

They ran the compulsory check on Engine 3. It took ten minutes. Then Terry filled in the shift report. Jimmy looked at it when he was done.

7:47 p.m. and all quiet, Engine 3 checked and ready to go.

"Is that okay?" Terry asked, so close Jimmy could smell him.

"Yeah," Jimmy said. He put the logbook down quickly so Terry wouldn't see the trembling of his hand.

"What time do you want to eat?" Terry asked. His eyes seemed larger up close, like a cow's.

"How 'bout 8:30?" Jimmy answered.

"Okay."

Terry folded his arms, looked around the room. He took a step to the table and picked up the old newspaper.

"Want a hunk?" he asked, turning to Jimmy.

"Okay. Sure."

Terry pulled out a random section from the middle and handed it to Jimmy. Their eyes met again, lingered perhaps two seconds longer than they needed to. Terry sat down on the edge of the cot closest to the far wall, undid the lacings of his boots, then, carefully, pulled them off and put them side by side together on the floor. Then he lay down sideways on his cot, facing the wall, his back to Jimmy.

The cot squeaked as he shifted.

Jimmy lay down on his cot, on his back. He pulled the newspaper open above him. He had the section that contained car ads and classifieds. He didn't read, he kept the corner of his eye on Terry two feet beside him.

He could hear Terry's breathing. He noticed Terry wasn't turning the pages.

Jimmy started sweating.

"First day of spring tomorrow," Terry said after five minutes. Jimmy jumped when he spoke.

"N-nice," Jimmy said. "That'll be nice. It'll b-be nice not to have to run in the slush."

"You still running?" Terry asked, half-turning. The cot squeaked again.

"Yeah. Twice a day now." He hadn't meant to say that last part. He'd felt, after Christmas Eve, that if he didn't run he'd implode. Once before work, once after. Out to Castle Island, then turn around and all the way up to Broadway Station, to where he had run the day his great-grandfather had terrorized him at the door.

"Wow. Twice a day. Well, that's good. I mean, you look fit. I mean . . . you must be in good shape."

"I guess," Jimmy answered. He felt a smile pull across his face. "What about you? You look like . . . you look like you're in pretty good shape too."

"Ah, I throw the weights around a few times a week down at L Street," Terry shrugged. "Nothing fancy."

They went back to reading. Terry's head was propped up on his elbow, his back still to Jimmy. Jimmy couldn't help staring. He hadn't realized a man's body, too, could have curves in it, hills and valleys of muscle and tissue and terror. He began to feel nauseated.

Some time later Terry shifted, swung up to a sitting position on the bed. He stretched, then rolled off the bed and stood. He stretched again, then walked over to the edge of Jimmy's bed. He stopped. His shadow blotted out the light.

Jimmy kept his eyes riveted on an ad for a car dealership south of the city. *Zero down, zero interest, zero to pay!* He pulled the paper back slowly, until his eyes met Terry's.

"Ah . . . supper," Terry said quietly, looking down at him. "It's 8:30."

They ate at the small table. Terry had half of Jimmy's meatloaf. "This is really good," he said, five times. Each time Jimmy thanked him. Terry gave Jimmy one of his sandwiches, which Jimmy found to be just this side of inedible. Jimmy had forgotten to bring something to drink. They shared the Dr. Pepper, still warm. They passed it back and forth, keeping their eyes on each other, then looking away.

They ate the rest of the meal in silence. They finished in three minutes, Jimmy eating mechanically, quickly. He felt Terry was watching him. He couldn't look up.

Terry went back to the bed, and his paper. Jimmy checked on Engine 3 again, almost frantic. He walked back into the room, his mind made up.

"Ahhh . . . I'm ready to turn in whenever you are," he said.

Terry turned, looked up at him.

"Sure."

"I'm just gonna take a quick shower," Jimmy added. He grabbed his duffel bag and left the room again. There was no soap in the bathroom, but it didn't matter, he'd taken a shower right before he'd left home. He rinsed off his sweat, then turned the water onto cold. For the first time since he'd left the service he craved a cigarette. June had made him quit when they'd first met, she said it yellowed the curtains. Jimmy looked down at himself. He was almost painfully erect.

Looks like you've got a problem.

He opened his mouth to the cold water and gulped, but his tongue still felt parched.

The bathroom door opened. Noiselessly. Jimmy didn't hear it, but felt a sudden draft spilling like a wave over the shower stall door. Half-turning, he saw a dark blurry shape through the beveled Plexiglas stall door, motionless, filling up the doorway. His heart began racing. He turned the water to warm again, turned back, pretending he didn't see. *Open the stall door! Open the stall door, you idiot!* But the shape in the doorway reminded him too much of his dream. He felt refrigerated with fear. He turned his back to the door.

In another minute the draft ceased. He turned, slowly, rinsing his face under the water. The dark blur was gone.

He dried off quickly. The towel smelled of June, of detergent and bleach and fabric softeners and spring-fresh chemical sheets added to the dryer. He folded his navy blue uniform pants and shirt neatly, then gathered his T-shirt and boxers and white socks into a ball. He wrapped the towel around him and headed back to their room, feeling puny and ridiculous and as if he could start running and never stop.

The one overhead fluorescent light was out in their room, but light seeped in through the half-open door from the garage area. Terry was in his cot, a sheet pulled over him up to his bare shoulders. Terry, like about half the men on their shift back at the firehouse, always slept with all his clothes on. The other half slept in their underwear, including Jimmy. No one slept naked. Terry's bare shoulders, and what that might mean, leapt through Jimmy like electricity. He stood in the middle of the room, frozen. Then he walked to the other side of Terry's bed, pretending he was hunting for something. On the floor he saw what he was looking for, Terry's white briefs folded neatly on top of his boots and white socks. Another sizzle flashed through him. He could no longer pretend to himself that this . . . this *thing* with Terry was all emotional. He wondered why God had mandated that his life should unravel at the age of thirty-two. He walked to the table, closed his eyes, and removed his towel. The damp air infiltrated his midsection. He placed the towel over one of the chairs, then set his uniform across the back of the other, taking his keys, wallet, and loose change from his pants pocket as he did. Then he stood there, not knowing what to do, his back to Terry. After what seemed a very long time, he walked to the door and shut it, leaving them in darkness. A small band of light leaked under the door from the garage. He pulled back the sheet on his cot and climbed into bed.

He could hear Terry breathing again. He had never slept naked in his life before, not even with June. There could be no turning back, not now.

"Terry?" he whispered.

There was no answer.

"I don't know what's happening to me," he told the unhearing Maureen when he picked her up after school the next day. They were in his pickup. She turned and smiled at him, and reached for his hand. He started crying as he turned onto Broadway.

That evening Jimmy stopped on the way to work at a chicken place for their dinner. His eyes lingered on the tired downcast eyes of the young black woman working there. He had the urge to hold her, to stroke her hair. Suffering radiated out from him and found others in sympathy.

"Why are you wearing cologne, for Pete's sake?" June had asked when he was leaving the house.

"It's . . . wicked hot there," he said, bending over to retie his boots. "I sweat like a pig there, I don't want to smell like one too."

He didn't see her staring out the window at him as he pulled away.

Terry too had brought supper for them both, several fast food hamburgers and boxes of fries that they heated up in the microwave.

"We'll save the chicken for tomorrow night," Jimmy said, sticking it into the refrigerator.

"Okay," Terry said, half-laughing.

Terry also brought a newspaper, which they divided again. They both seemed glad of some routine to stick to.

"Hot in here," Terry said after they finished eating. He removed his uniform shirt. He wasn't wearing a T-shirt, for the first time in Jimmy's recollection. Terry placed it over his chair. He looked up and caught Jimmy staring. Terry's smooth torso was as etched with muscles and lines as the GI Joe doll Jimmy owned in his youth. He felt himself flushing, turned away. He didn't pretend to read when they lay down after supper.

When Jimmy came back from his shower, the towel wrapped around him, the light was out again, and their door half-open. He didn't notice at first that Terry's cot was empty. When he did his eyes felt like they might leap from their sockets in their haste to find him, the way they felt when he'd be in a smoke-blinded room, looking for people. He spotted him in the corner, standing with his back to Jimmy. He was naked. Jimmy's heart leapt into his throat. As Jimmy watched, Terry placed his hand over his own right shoulder. He opened it, a universal gesture.

A gasp came out of Jimmy. For once he didn't worry that he had embarrassed himself. He stepped forward, a roaring in his ears. It seemed he had never seen anything so beautiful as Terry then: as powerful an argument for the existence of a benign Creator as any Grand Canyon or the birth of his children.

He stepped closer. He reached for Terry's hand, hanging, waiting, over Terry's shoulder. Fingers touched. Terry grabbed onto Jimmy's hand. Jimmy stepped closer still, pressing his body into Terry's. A sizzle ran through his mouth. His towel fell to the floor. He thought he might not survive this. That concern was immaterial now: everything, the entire world, was sliding into Terry.

Jimmy's left hand moved across the front of Terry's body. He felt he'd been given the sense of touch for the first time. They stumbled, almost fell. Terry turned. His eyes were shining with wetness.

"I can't eat, I can't sleep," Terry began, his voice breaking.

"I know I know I know!" Jimmy repeated, almost screaming the words. They grabbed onto each other, as if for life. Terry was sobbing. They fell onto Terry's cot, which squeaked once, then oddly fell silent. It seemed to Jimmy then that there wasn't enough space in the Universe to contain the desire he felt for Terry.

Jimmy lifted his forearm to look at his watch again. It was 5:17. The day shift would be here at seven. He replaced his hand onto Terry's back. It felt like his hands started withering the moment they left Terry's body. He pulled him in, closer. Terry stirred, woke. He rolled over, facing Jimmy.

Their eyes met.

If there were a power in the universe to stop him from making love to Terry again, Jimmy thought, it was a power he didn't possess. This time they were silent, staring into the other's eyes. They continued staring when they had finished, lying side by side, face to face. Jimmy felt that if he moved one inch, he'd roll into some tar-filled abyss. On one side of him was June, the other side The Church, another side, The Department, the last side his Family. Over and above him— above them both—was the neighborhood, the community, the world, commentators in Monday Night Football booths, congressmen in the Midwest. The only safe place was tight against Terry. And that would be over in an hour.

He began sweating.

Still, he was alive. *Alive.* Finally.

The office phone rang at 6:15. Terry answered it. Jimmy got up and snapped on his clothes, as if the phone had eyes. He watched Terry's face blanch. It was Captain Billy, Jimmy could hear him over the receiver across the room.

"We gotta go!" Terry announced, slamming down the phone. They were geared up in less than a minute. Jimmy jumped in the driver's seat, fired up Engine 3. The garage roared with the echoing. Terry lifted open the large metal sliding door, then jumped in beside Jimmy.

"Whatta we got?" Jimmy panted.

"Out of control in Chinatown," Terry yelled above the sirens.

They came from the other direction, and faced the smoking tenement from the back. They drove the truck through a rotting guardrail and pulled right up to the building. They couldn't see any flame. An hysterical Asian woman was waving her arms at them as they leapt out of the truck, Terry pulling the hose with him, looking for a hydrant. She ran after Terry, screaming in a foreign tongue.

"What's she saying?" Terry roared, but Jimmy needed no translator. He grabbed the woman, spun her around.

"Where? Where?" he shouted. He shook her by the shoulders.

"Where?" He pointed, kept pointing. "Where? Where?"

The woman's black eyes were pinpoints. Then a light flared up in them. Turning, Jimmy saw a punch of fire burst from a third floor window. Glass rained down on them.

The woman began screaming again, but now she understood. She pointed to the second floor window and unleashed a torrent of words.

Jimmy was up the fire escape in three seconds, he counted *One, Two, Three.* He'd forgotten the ax. He turned his shoulder to the window and threw his whole weight against it. Most of the glass shattered, but the metal panes remained. Thick smoke curled and lifted inside the room—Jimmy could see this—then it gathered into a ball and burst out at him in a sucking vortex, roaring to life in the sudden draught. He ducked as the ocean of flame and smoke punched out over his head. More shattered glass spangled his face and helmet. He pushed at the large empty panes, the bottom ones seemed loose. He kicked at them. The grid wobbled but clung on stubbornly to the brick, like a loose tooth that will not be dislodged. Desperate, he stuck his head through a pane into the ink-black room. In the corner there was something ghost-colored. His sockets jumped at it. A young child in a long white T-shirt, he couldn't tell boy or girl, frozen in the corner, clutching a blanket. The eyes were swollen with horror, possibly catatonia.

Jimmy could see that the panes were large enough for this child to pass through.

He pushed his hands through the empty panes.

"C'mon! Come here!" he screamed. "C'mon! Come to me! C'mon! C'mere!"

The child stared back at him with unblinking eyes.

The odd feeling that Jimmy had been to this place—this exact same place, under identical conditions—began pulling at him.

"C'MON! C'MON! COME TO ME!" he screamed again, almost as much to push some sudden horror back inside himself, as to save this child. But the child only looked at him, possibly he's as afraid of me as he is of the fire, Jimmy thought, looming over him as I am, screaming unintelligible words at him—

He fell back as his nightmare became a reality. He realized he was inside his nightmare—but now he was his great-grandfather, and the child inside was him.

Something pushed him aside. In a daze he turned and saw Terry, crashing the panes with his ax. They burst asunder on his second frenzied stroke. As he watched dumbly, Terry jumped into the room, swept the child up in his arms, then handed him out to Jimmy. A lick of flame slid up Terry's arm. Jimmy stood there, looking into the child's eyes, frozen with fright.

"Take him!" Terry screamed as he pushed the child into Jimmy's arms. Terry came out immediately afterward.

"C'mon!" Terry called, pushing him down the fire escape.

They reached the bottom of the reverberating stairs. The woman seized the child from Jimmy's arms and ran into a crowd of her neighbors that had gathered 100 feet back.

"Oh God," Jimmy heard himself say. "Oh God."

"What is it?" Terry roared above the fire. Jimmy turned to him, saw only a mask.

"Jimmy, what is it?" Terry lifted his mask back to the top of his head. His eyes went back and forth.

"My dream," he said. "It was the dream!"

"C'mon!" Terry called, shaking him by the shoulders. "It's gonna go!" Terry was roaring now. "The building's gonna collapse! Run!"

Run! Run! Yes, I can run!

They ran back past the truck. Terry stopped behind the truck, searching for the radio, but Jimmy kept going. He saw the opening of an alley and headed for it, not even feeling the weight of his uniform, the clomping of his boots. Yes, this was it, this was what he needed to do. There was nothing he couldn't run from. He was through the alley in a minute and out onto Tyler Street. He turned without slowing down or looking up, he knew where he wanted to go.

But when he finally reached the Broadway Bridge, he realized too late that he had forgotten to take Maureen, and Terry, with him.

And, My God, well the whole world was on fire.

When he came back from his breakdown two months later, Jimmy discovered that Terry had left the force. No one knew where he had moved. There had been an unsigned note—*I can't do this—I can't put you through this, I'm leaving*—but Jimmy had never known of it. June opened it at home. At last she had a reason, something concrete, upon which to hang her resentment, her bullying.

Jimmy was quieter than ever now, the other guys thought; and no one ever questioned him because There But For The Grace of God.

But under June's watchful eye, it wasn't long before Jimmy was back leading the life that had been so carefully planned for him.

Sister Bennett's Crystal Ball

The Park that was our second home really couldn't be called a park at all. Parking lot was more like it—though you couldn't drive in there, except for the cops when they were hassling us. I mean there wasn't any grass at The Park, unless you counted the stiff strawy stuff that would peek up between the cracks in the asphalt every May. But even that would be gonzo by Memorial Day.

Once every couple years city workers would half fall out of a pumpkin-colored truck and take three days to plant a row of these skinny sticks out by the sidewalk, on the other side of the chain-link fence that contained our Park. But they—the trees I mean—could tell they really didn't belong there. They'd push out a few green stubs, then think better of it and be dead by June.

It wasn't big, Our Park, maybe the size of a couple of backyards. But it was ours. Sean used to say he liked to think The Park went down to the center of the earth in one direction, and up to the stars in the other. That would be Sean.

The front part of The Park had crooked swing sets, a rusted water fountain that hadn't worked in years (you'd run into it at night if you forgot it was there), and these faded painted circles on the asphalt for games no one remembered how to play. Our end was better, the back end, there was shade here from noontime on, so dark and cool you'd slosh into it like water. And these picnic tables, three of them, with faded green paint and generations of initials carved into their wooden tops. Some of these initials had dates beside them—plenty went all the way back to the Forties. Some were in pairs, and spoke of love, even spelling this out: *Tommy Loves Trudy, '42, Jack and Elaine, True Love Forever 55;* others were solitary, and testified not to love but to existence, splintered songs of oneself: *JGH '73, Dennis The Rat '84;* other messages were strictly philosophical in nature and could be used as a Rosetta Stone of shifting ideology: *We Like Ike '52; Pigs Suck '69; SORRY, I'M AN ALCOHOLIC; NEVER, 77; Drink Beers, Kill Queers,* no date given.

Probably the weirdest message was one that was hidden, carved on the underneath of the middle picnic table. Maybe whoever did it figured there was no room left on the tabletops and benches. Or—maybe—he wanted his message to be private. Whatever reason, he must've had to do it on his back, like Michelangelo. Three simple words: *I Was Sean.* No date. Carved just beneath these words was what looked like some kind of crystal ball, with rays coming out of it.

Sometimes at night up The Park if I'd be all high or just reflective maybe, I swear I'd see them all, these ghosts rising from their initials, dancing under the city stars of the sodium vapor streetlights: guys killed in wars; lovers, disenchanted now, sitting back to back, arms as crossed as their stars; these three girls my father knew who waved good-bye one night as they boarded a streetcar, never to return from the Coconut Grove Nightclub fire. "They were all dolled up," Dad used to say when he spoke about them. "All dolled up."

I told Sean about them one night, all these ghosts. He just looked at me for a minute, nodded his curly head, then asked, not with concern, only curiosity, "Do they ever talk to you, Bud?"

"No."

"What do you think they'd say, if they could talk?"

"I don't know," I said dully after a minute. Sean's questions were always predictably unexpected, but that foreknowledge never made me any better prepared for them. "What do you think they'd say?"

"They'd probably say," he answered slowly, rolling up the sleeves of his white T-shirt, they were always slipping down, "get the fuck outta here while you can."

Our Park. We'd all just graduated from high school that summer. Being the oldest group hanging at The Park now, we got the best end, the shady end with the picnic tables. If we had wanted to catch some rays we could've just moved ten yards to the sunny end of The Park; but we never did. Instead we'd slouch down to the beach three blocks away, telling the open-mouthed littler kids at the front end of The Park not to be in our section when we got back. It was just the way.

There was about twenty of us in June, but as that summer unfurled like a flower whose smell you don't know if you like yet or not, the numbers started dwindling. Eddie, Hank, and Sully went into the service on a bet, Hey What the Fuck It's Only Life After All. The twins Terry and Tommy got a job through their uncle with the Gas Company, We'll Still Hang Out but no. Three of the guys got married, mostly they had to. Animal Head Ed (Donovan, remember him?) hit a telephone pole coming back from this girl's Fourth of July party down in Quincy and died three days later. Poor unlucky bastard was only a block from his house, his mother heard the crash and called 911 not knowing it was her own son out there wrapped around the pole. His brother Denny ten months younger Irish twins pretty much stopped coming 'round after that, they'd been close and when he did he'd be all fucked up and this wild look in his eye like he'd lost something he couldn't find a word big enough for.

It's funny, it was like we'd been waiting all our lives to graduate into this shady end of the park, but then once we finally got there people start leaving and you got to start worrying about your future. The Future. It's like you're swimming along in this beautiful river having the time of your life and just when you get to the good part there's these grown-ups standing on the banks locked up in their individual cages and they keep asking, "What you gonna do now, Bud DeAngelo, what you gonna do?" and they got a cage just your size. You know it might have "Edison" written on the top of it or maybe "Fire Department," or even "College," because your family lives below the poverty line and you might be able to get a scholarship if you got halfway decent grades—which I don't—but they're all cages just the same, and all I want to do is LiveLiveLive until I DieDieDie, so I said no to Uncle Bill and his two-bit insurance business and the recruiter who came to talk to us from the Marine Corps and everybody else who had a cage just my size. And pretty soon everyone stopped asking.

Which was fine by me I had other things to do I was up The Park.

Sean most times would be waiting for me.

I'd sleep till about ten, be up The Park by eleven. Sometimes I'd be the first one up there, sometimes not, it didn't matter.

Sean had his favorite spot, one of the picnic table benches, his back slouched against the chain-link fence behind him, his legs propped up on the table, a Red Sox ball cap yanked down below his eyes. His arms folded, a King Alfred Cigarillo dangling from his full lips—that was before cigars got trendy. If you have to look in magazines to get a clue forget about it, we didn't follow trends we set them. That was one of the rules. There were others, all unwritten but you knew.

Sean wasn't tall—maybe five feet seven—but when he walked into a room, you knew it. He seemed taller, the posture of a prince without that swagger that makes some short guys cartoonish. Maybe because there wasn't as much of him to manage, he managed his movements so well. Lithe, flowing like water, most mornings he'd be waiting for me. Those gymnasts you see on TV during the Olympics had nothing on Sean. His body was all lean hard curves, the muscles inexhaustible white mounds of energy. Just so you'll get the picture.

The front side of Our Park bordered West Third Street. The two ends were flush up against triple-deckers, both vinyl sided, neither with windows facing The Park—well, why would they?—one a limey yellow whose garishness increased on cloudy days, the other a color I can only call Despair Gray.

The back section of the Park—Our section—was bordered by a two-story chain-link fence, rusted and rigid with age. Hard against this—in fact, pushing out through the fence where it could, like visiting time at Cedar Junction State Pen—was a hedge of gray-blue evergreens, their needles dense and nasty. I guess they must have been forty, fifty feet tall, and they'd grown together so tightly you'd need a tank to get through there. They didn't seem to belong here any more than the languishing city trees out by the sidewalk; but maybe they did belong to whatever lay on their other side. What that was, no one really knew. Someone said a crazy old lady lived back there; somebody else said they heard it used to be a convent that housed an order of nuns whose vow of removal from earthly things was made easier via imprisonment. My mother'd said an old lady'd lived there when she herself was a little girl in this same neighborhood—But Sure The Poor Miserable Creature Must Be Dead By Now, The Lord Ha' Mercy on Her.

Once I think I saw her. I'm not totally sure but I think I did. I saw someone anyway. What happened was, we were playing Outs—we were still little pukes, like ten or eleven—and I'd just scored from first on a triple from Sean. Panting sweaty, I burst across home and jumped into the chain-link fence to stop my momentum. It was a breezy day, gushy and spurty with wind. One of these gusts lifted some of the lower spruce boughs on the other side of the fence, I just happened to be there to see this, and a view extended into and beyond those hedgey trees. Someone was there, I saw a face, ancient, lined like a Mayan road that was busy once but deserted now. But the eyes . . . a warm brown, they zoned into mine the way eyes sometimes do. We stared at each other for a second—then the wind died and the view was blocked again. But as the branches fell back into place, she smiled at me, like she was throwing a gift to someone she'd never see again. Weird, but I saw that smile nights, when you can't sleep and your mind starts spinning.

But Sean would turn to the hedge and shake his fist at it, tiny and red when we were little, slightly hairy and larger now that we were older. See, the hedge of evergreens ate our balls. Sometimes at night I'd dream of the king's ransom of balls that I might find on the other side of this hedge; spotless balls, pimpled balls, spanking new and reeking of rubber. But even in those little kid dreams there would be something else. Further in. Calling me.

"What's up?"

It's a cloudless day, scrubbed cobalt blue and puffy white by late-July thunderstorms the night before. Sean's lips slide into a smile when he hears my voice, deep for eighteen. His baseball cap's scrunched down to his nose, which is slightly upturned, always disdaining things.

"S'up," he mumbles. His arms are folded against his chest and I think he's been half dozing in the sun. His hat's covering his eyes, so he won't see me examining his chest, the action figure pectoral lines, the little-boy nipples still hairless though he's eighteen too, the ridges and valleys of his abs rising and falling like foothills to something larger and higher down where his red nylon gym shorts sparkle in the sun. There's a funny little breeze running around, and it spurts up the back of his thighs where his baggy shorts hang half open. He stretches like a cat, shrugging his neck, arms vaulting skyward. He purrs a noise of contentment that coincides with the little breeze raising gooseflesh on my neck, bare and just showered—

—it's just that we're such good friends, that's why I look—that, plus the fact that there's only three weeks between us in age. So naturally it's just . . . normal, to want to know who's developing where. Though sometimes I wish his eyes would open at times like these so he'd know—and then maybe also I'd get to see the real Sean. Not the wise ass; not the drunken philosopher selling woe; not the nail-biting brooder . . . not the invincible overachiever, terrifying in his self-confidence—

"Toss me a cigarillo, will ya Bud?" he murmurs. No one else's here yet so I comply instantly, knowing they're in the pocket of his white T-shirt, which lies like a piece of him on the asphalt. I snatch at it and pull it as close to my nose as I dare, pretending I can't find the goods at first. Fragrance—light, sweet, just-mowed grass from a far-off field—rises shyly through the air. Now I smell him now I don't now I do again. Yup, it's Sean all right. I pull out one of the tan cigarillos, close the box and the low-cut lady on the front is supposed to look sexy but to me she just looks silly playing on this small harp or some fucking thing.

I exile her back to Sean's pocket, drop his T-shirt to the ground, doff my own. I watch it fall on top of his. I always think I can hear a sound when my T-shirt hits his. Soft, yielding. An odd thought—but then I've got the Odd Ways, Grandma Higgins used to say so before she died, she'd come visit Sundays.

"Look at himself now with the odd ways all over him," she'd say in her lovely lilting brogue (that's what Dad called it anyways but what the hell's a lilt?), we'd be sitting in the parlor after Mass and roast beef dinner me busting anxious to get out, Walkman covering my ears but way down low so I could hear them.

"Stop it Ma, he'll hear you!" Mom'd half laugh. "And he doesn't neither."

"Sure'n he does, t'won't do a bit o' good sayin' he don't. Look at him now, the big brown eyes and never knowin' what they're thinkin'— and his nose always shoved into a book. I never knowed nothin' good to come from that—lookit what it did to the English. Ach, t'is what comes of ye marryin' an eye-talian for sure, ye get a gypsy mutt like him."

"Frank's only half Italian, Ma. Besides, you like Frank, you told me so."

"Well your hubby Frank's a pleasurable man and no mistake, always singin' and laughin'—but so was the Village Idiot back home and I didn't go and marry the man now did I? And that name, God help us—Bud! Where in the world did ye get that one? Is it even Christian, I'm wonderin'?"

"Ma! It's . . . we like it. It's a nice friendly American name and we like it."

"Never mind friendly. Sounds like a dog's name God Help Us."

"Here," I say, standing over Sean, I'm rolling the thickness of the cigarillo between my thumb and index finger. He *is* half sleeping, I can tell. He keeps his hairless arms folded across his chest. His shining lips part slightly. I hold the cigarillo like a dart. I stick it in. Nice and slow. My hand brushes against his square chin. His lips close on the cigarillo like the completion of something.

"Thanks, Bud," he mumbles. The cigarillo lurches up and down with his words. He gropes into his ratty sneaker and extracts a red Bic lighter. He's the only one I know who always gets it on the first try, even in a gale. He puffs in deeply, then exhales with an Ahhhh.

I plop down beside Sean, throw my legs up on the picnic table beside his. We're still for a minute. Then I say, "Gimme one."

My eyes are closed in the sea-washed sun. I feel him sit up. I can tell he's looking around to see if anyone's here. They're not, just little pukes at the front end of the Park, two mothers with strollers bellyaching together near the entrance. A second later a cigarillo is poking electrically at my lips. I open up. He sticks it in. He lights me up. He sits down beside me again. We puff in silence for a minute.

We say nothing. The sun pours down, honey from a bottomless jar, a benediction. The fat seconds plop by, each one a universe to be savored, made more pleasurable by the knowledge that there are more many more where they came from. And here they are now.

We say nothing, but there's a stream between us, unseen, full of color. I notice our breathing has fallen into unison. He's a mirror of my own contentment. No job, no future prospects, no amount of money or 401Ks or profit-sharing plans can compare with this. I think of the sitcoms I see on TV, every blessed one full up with young urban somethings, constantly opening up restaurants or working for advertising agencies, interacting wittily, beautifully in their clothes and haircuts—nothing. Nothing compared to this. A person and they say he is wise, a success, works himself to death from twenty to sixty-five so he can do this when he retires, sit in the sun somewhere; but we're doing it now. And we're eighteen. And we know it, know how to use it.

We say nothing.

God's in His Heaven all's right with the world. It can be so nice between us when he's like this.

But see there's this other Sean—

"Guess what I got?" he murmurs, his voice a buzzing tongue of delight in my ear.

"VD?" I answer. He jabs me in the ribs, keeps his elbow there.

"How should I know?" I say.

He leans over away from me, reaches down. I hear the crinkling of a brown paper bag, the thin crisp ones from Five and Tens, pregnant with delight, so I know he's been to Woolworth's earlier this morning up on Broadway.

"Now keep your eyes closed," he instructs.

"Okay," I say, opening them.

"I mean it, shit-for-brains."

"All right all right."

He puts something in my lap. One. Two. Three. I smell India rubber. I open my eyes and see them nesting in the V of my lap, spang new pimple balls. This means there will be Stickball this afternoon. I can't overexaggerate the delight this creates.

"Nice," I say, closing my eyes again. I leave the balls there. I put my hands behind my head. I smell a sweetness from under my arms, wonder if Sean smells it too.

"Where'd you get the dough?" I ask.

"Aunt Tilly was over last night," he says.

"Nice," I repeat. Aunt Tilly was always good for a twenty.

"It was fifty this time," Sean says, reading my mind as he usually seems to. "For graduation."

"God love her," I say.

Sean murmurs, "I figger meatball subs for lunch . . . haircuts this afternoon . . . then a couple of sixes tonight." He's talking like he's a king granting favors. He is.

"Nice," I say again.

It's just the way it is with us, we hook each other up. When things are okay between us.

"When I run this City, Bud . . ." he begins. He says it all the time. Going to Law School after college, going into politics, going to be mayor someday . . . there's a long pause. I feel him tighten beside me. Sean's great-grandfather almost won a mayoral election seventy years ago. His grandfather was a state senator but got indicted. Sean's family has always believed he'll succeed where these others failed.

"Yeah, what then?" I finally ask between puffs.

He blows a few expanding blue rings out into space, dreams he's launching.

"I'll take care of you, Bud," he says. "That's what."

I don't say anything. I don't ever say anything anymore when he talks about this.

"Mean game of Stickball this afternoon when the others get up here," he continues.

"Mmmmmmph," I answer.

"And I'm going to kick your ass today," he mumbles drowsily.

"You're going to lick my what today?" I ask.

"In your dreams," Sean says.

I say nothing.

Unfortunately, he's right.

Stickball is murder in the July afternoons, whoever's pitching is in the sun and the batter's in the shade and you get to whip the ball all your might when you're pitching, and when you're the batter, trying to pick the ball up in your sightline as it travels from sun to shade is a bitch. We play for sweaty hours once Matty and Timmy and Paul come up. Matty and Timmy are brothers and look like twins but one an economy version of the other. They got a sparkle in their blue eyes as if they knew things you didn't but no. Paul is a big quiet redhead nicknamed Herman as in Munster. He's got a sister Liz even bigger than him that Sean calls Lizilla, he's quick like that. Timmy and Paul and Matty basically do what me and Sean always want to do, but we don't look down on them for that. They're kind of like an arm, or a leg, it'll do what you command without complaint, and you look at it once in a while and you're glad, grateful you got it.

Eventually the last ball goes slam awry into the hedge behind us and the game comes to an end. Sean tells Matty, Timmy, and Paul that me and him got something to do, and the two of us take off, tucking our dangling shirts into our waistbands behind us. The sea breeze is puffing up West Third Street and it cools the sweat running down liquid lines on our chests. Sean's nipples respond to the breeze. I look away as he turns to see what I'm looking at.

We stop at Ma McGillicuddy's Spa and Sean springs for meatball subs, the foot-longers. We wolf them down at the beach, straddling the seawall like it's a horse between our legs, facing each other. One of the red drippy meatballs slips out of the open-mouth sub roll as Sean tries to stuff it into his mouth, and it rolls down his bare chest, leaving a track of red as it goes. I can't help but stare as he wets a finger and swabs away at his smooth skin, cleaning up the mess. He looks up at me. Our eyes meet for a second before I look away. Sean's are so blue they seem like peepholes to the sky behind him.

After a while we're stuffed, our small bellies distended like puppies after a feeding. We throw little pieces of the soft leftover sub rolls to the screeching gulls, they're always ravenous. We're both that Irish that we can't abide the sight of hungry things. Then we go get haircuts. Sean treats from the Aunt Tilly windfall.

"This is for both of us," Sean lavishly tells Dom the Barber when we're almost done, saying it loud enough so that even Dom's chairbound Old Man coterie can hear him. I look down and see my black hair on the floor, mingling with Sean's brown locks. I let my eyes go soft out of focus, and the hair mingles, becomes one.

We part at the corner of O and Broadway, we're each rubbing the nub on the back of our just-buzzed heads.

We stare at each other for a minute.

"What time tonight?" I ask.

"Figger about eight. I'll bring some beers."

"Cool. Later."

"Yeah."

We stare at each other a little longer than we need to before Sean turns away and struts off. I watch him till he vanishes around a corner.

"Sean," I whisper to the empty air that just contained him.

There are some things, memories or maybe vibrant imaginings, which become such strong metaphors they overshadow the object itself they refer to. Like I can't hear the word Christmas without thinking of the bike I got when Dad's number came out Christmas Eve. When I hear the word summer now I go zip back to that night, the first stars out when the sky to the west was still cornflower blue, the lights of the office towers downtown twinkling back like they were exchanging messages, the brilliant vermilion that freaked the sky some minutes later, the drunk breeze staggering up from the South and smelling of some fruitier land far away from here, the near full moon stretching up from the ocean like it was just full last week but needed to come back again on such a night as this. And Sean's face in this light—ruddy, dusky, flushed and quick, ready for anything.

The night grew warmer, stickier, as the five of us polished our beers off up at The Park.

Kids from the Projects 'round the way were stealing yuppie cars that night, and the screeching cop cars, the sirens, and the car alarms started pissing us off around ten.

"Let's get the fuck outta here," Sean said, disgusted, flipping a spent cigarillo to the ground. "Let's go swimmin'."

We hopped a few fences on the way down to the beach, practicing random acts of clothesline snatching as we went, for the necessary towels. The Boulevard along the ocean was alive with the roar of open-windowed cars joyriding on such an electric night, warm tropical air blowing into these windows, festive music from the radio and shrieks of delight blowing out. We played Dodge-Em as we crossed The Boulevard, tipping our ball caps to those we knew that stopped for us, giving the finger to those who honked that we didn't know. A few people were on the beach, but we headed way down to the area just behind the old pumping station, which was always pretty deserted. We always went there when we swam, at my insistence.

"Tell me again why you hate the big beach," Sean muttered, the other three guys lagging behind us.

"You know," I say.

"I know Bud but I like that story," he says. The tender tone of his voice changes my mind.

"Awright. I guess I was about four—"

"You said last time you were five," Sean interrupts, like he's been swindled.

"Do you want to hear the fuckin' story or not?"

"Yeah, but the last time—"

"Well maybe I was five. I was four or five." I pause. "We were down at the beach, me and Ma and Dad. I was like digging in the sand, making stuff—"

"What were you makin'?" Sean asks.

"Castles and moats," I say immediately. Sean nods.

"Yeah," he says.

"And then I found this thing. It was green and wicked shiny, about the size of a small button—like a button for a doll's dress maybe. But not in the shape of a button, like kinda square."

"Yeah."

"And I thought it was treasure. Some kind of gem or something. Like you know how it is when you're a little kid? Anything can happen? The world's full of . . . possibilities, you know? Magic? Like you could find a treasure on a beach in Southie even?"

"Yeah." He licks his lips.

"So I showed it to my parents. I couldn't even answer when my mother asked me What's This? I was that geeked-out. She gave me a piece of tissue to wrap it in, and I put it under my pillow that night when we got home, I figgered I'd bring it to the jeweler's the next day and collect my ransom."

There's a pause. We can hear the ocean sighing as it dreams the night away, we're that close.

"So what happened?" Sean asks.

"You know what happened," I say.

"I know Bud but tell me."

"My Dad came into my room later that night. He was in one of his moods. He took my jewel and flushed it down the toilet. He said it was just a piece of glass, just a lousy piece of somebody's busted beer bottle. He said I might as well find out then."

"Find out what?"

"That . . . you know. That shit like that can't happen. There's no such thing as Magic, I guess. Life's a shit sandwich and then you die."

Sean's quiet for a minute.

He turns and looks at me. I see moons in his eyes.

"He mighta been wrong," he says. "Bud."

We strip down to our briefs wordlessly when we reach the back of the pumping station, like we're taking part in some ritual. I turn my back on the others but it's no good, the moon throws their purple shadows against the back of the old brick building and it's worse than seeing the real thing, everything's blown up and huge and bigger than life. I turn and dash into the water, I'm always the first one in. The moon on the flat ocean seems a golden path you could walk all the way back to Ireland. I wonder what the rules are there? I dive into the ocean's fire. The others I hear behind me doing the same.

Sometimes we'd swim out to the old Navy pier, as we do this night. It's no surprise when Sean turns it into a race, beating me to the old wooden platform by half a length. The other three I hear way behind, galumping in the water like walruses. Sean draws his arms out of the water and lifts himself onto the platform by hands pressed flat against the wet wood. I can only watch as his body materializes before me, his ivory skin alchemizing into wet moon drench, his white briefs turning pink as they cling to his backside, revealing not enough, and yet too much, of the mounds of flesh beneath. As he gains the platform he throws one knee upon it. The moon finds the open area between his legs, showing me a plum-shaped package that seems to contain all the beauty, and wickedness, of Life.

"We're not going all the way out there," we hear behind us. Turning, I see the heads of Timmy, Matty, and Paul bobbing in the water like beachballs some fifty yards away.

"We'll see you up The Park in about an hour then," Sean yells back, cupping his hands. "And don't drink all the beers!"

Sean stands up on the dock, rising above and before me. He turns and and faces me, putting his hands on his hips, his breath bellowing through his body like a pump. Every inch of him is outlined in the moonlight, like he's tonight's featured event, Live from Planet Earth.

He looks down at me still in the water.

"You might be smarter than me, Bud," he pants quietly, "with all that book reading you do. Maybe. The jury's still out on that one. But I'll always be better than you at everything."

Sometimes I can't tell when Sean's kidding. He squats down and extends his hand to me. I reach up and take it, then yank him back into the water, hearing, "You bas—!" before he goes under again. He comes up spluttering and laughing to find me halfway onto the dock, my legs still in the water. He grabs at them, loses them in their slipperiness, then lunges again from the water, hitting my back. As his hands slide off me again they catch at the waistband of my briefs. With me wiggling to gain the platform, and him yanking from behind, I feel them jerk down to the back of my knees.

"You—bas-tard!" I pant, for my breath has left me. He gives one more almighty tug as he falls back into the water, my now-torn briefs in his hands. I crawl onto the platform on my belly sucking wind, my mind spiraling away.

I hear him come up on the platform behind me. Water from his body drips onto mine. Our panting joins, becomes uniform.

"You gonna—buy me a—new pair—of underwear?" I gasp. It's all I can think of to say.

He doesn't answer.

"Huh?" I repeat, too loudly.

"I'll give you one o' mine," he says, but his voice is quavery, like it's become part of the lapping water around us. I don't dare turn and look at him standing right behind me. I come to a profound but frantic understanding of the meaning of the old cliché feeling naked.

"It looks like you got a white bathing suit on," Sean says lowly after a minute, like he's accusing me of something almost. Then I feel his foot, his wet toes, lightly graze my butt. Just once. This time I can't answer him, not even a wiseass knee-jerk snap. My mouth opens, but nothing comes out. I realize I'm shaking, not cold though.

After an hour-long minute he plops down right beside me, also on his belly, his triceps all slickety and wet sliding across mine.

"Them others are pussies," I finally manage, snatching at words like sand running through my hands. I turn to face him. His head facing mine is mere inches away, propped up on one dripping elbow. His usually curly hair is smeared onto his forehead. There's a fire in his eyes which may be the moon. Or the beer. Or neither.

"Are you afraid of me, Bud?" he whispers.

We hold eyes for a moment. When I look away that's his answer. I laugh, turn back around, but I still can't say anything.

But if I could I would say, "Afraid? Of you? I'm not afraid of anything. Except for maybe being afraid this dock might fall to pieces beneath the hardness of me when you're beside me like this. Or, possibly, of the way I dream about you every night. Of the way, maybe, that I'd sacrifice my whole life, any future plans, for the epiphany of maneuvering a cigarillo between your lips. Or possibly just a little bit afraid of Uncle Pat, who's been trying to get me to join the Knights of Columbus now that I'm a man of eighteen—you know Uncle Pat, he's the one who's on that committee to keep the fags from marching in our St. Patrick's Day Parade. Or maybe a little bit afraid of what's going to happen between me and my father, who says all the time when he's not putting me down how nice it is that his only kid turned out to be a boy, that way the family name can continue—as if the fucking world would roll over and die if there were a few less DeAngelos around. Other than that, nothing scares me. Except maybe my high school cumulative D average, since it was all I could do to show up every day, my mind boiling over with thoughts that I've been cursed with This Thing, a sleeping beauty sting while I lay dozing in my infant crib and, more, that I'm the only one in the world that's like this and Normal, wants to play sports and not become an interior decorator and dress up in women's clothing like those freaks they show on the TV every June when they have their own Parade. Not to be compared with (my D average, I mean) Sean's 4.0. Perfect. With a scholarship to college in September. Though sometimes I think he won't go, even though he says he will. He's gonna go to Law School after that he says, gonna run the City someday. Other than that I'm not afraid of anything. Except for maybe one thing, the only thing, okay the biggest thing, the chance, the very good chance, the strong possibility, the inevitability, of you, Sean, not being like this, of me not having the one thing the only thing I ever really thought was worth anything in this lousy fucked-up world."

You, Sean.

Maybe the truth at this point would have defused what happened later.

But instead I just laugh and turn my head away, because speeches like that never get made in this life.

Sean is still for a bit. I'm biting my lip to see what next.

After a while he says, "Who's the pussy?" then gets up and leaps back into the water.

"C'mon," he snarls from the water, "let's go back and get all fucked up on beers." I don't like the sound of his voice. I shudder, it's the voice of the Other Sean, That One, the one with the chip on his shoulder the size of Toledo.

I can't move for a minute. But I know he's watching me, waiting. I jump up quick and dive in, keeping my eyes open. Seeing Sean's moon-whitened briefs and scissoring legs beneath the water for a second. Then I burst out, gasping for air. I start swimming, Sean behind me.

"Bud," I hear him, I am swimming fast like I'm Tarzan and the crocodiles right on my ass, "do you have a boner?" but I decide quick to pretend not to hear, not certain if I've heard derision, or hope, in Sean's voice. We swim in silence for a bit until something white flies above me and lands plop ten yards in front of me. It floats weirdly in the water for a minute like it's laughing, then sinks out of sight. Sean's underwear. He is naked now too. For a second my eyes stop seeing. I can feel them narrow as this realization hits me. Me. And Sean. Naked. Together. In the water. And the shore just ahead. My dick is so hard it hurts.

"There's the fuckin' pair of undies I owe you," he says behind me.

I keep swimming. I stop when I'm standing waist-deep in the water close to the shore five minutes later, clueless. Stuck. Cemented there hard for all time.

Sean is there beside me in a minute, his waves lapping against my back growing stronger and then he's there next to me up to his waist. We're both panting, face forward, like we're about to begin a race, some kind of competition or sneak quiz I haven't studied for. I won't look at him.

Our jagged breath falls into unison again.

"Let's go, Bud," he says, jerking his head forward. He pushes me, forward a little but I resist. His hand on my back is like the third rail.

"In a minute," I say. I try to think of a dead litter of cats I found once in the alley behind my home, old lady vibrant violet lipstick on crushed-out cigarette butts, any gross image that will deflate my tell-tale tumescence. But it's no good, he's next to me and naked and there's nothing in the world more important or vivid—

"Now," he says. He pushes me forward again. I start walking straight ahead, my back to him, maybe I'll be okay after all. I see my clothes in a heap just ahead like a life preserver, the safety of my towel, somebody else's that's mine now with a sun-faded Darth Vader on it.

"Stop!" I hear behind me. My mind's so fucked up it's ready for any suggestion, and it latches onto this one like a pit bull's jaws. I instantly comply. I freeze. Once more I'm shaking, but again not from the cold, it's hot like the tropics. A breeze blows where it never has before.

"Just stop right there," Sean says. "Bud. Butt. Fuckin' white-ass."

I can see my shadow right before me, I realize the moon is spotlighting me from behind why is it so fucking bright it's not supposed to be here in the city where are the fucking clouds when you want them oh shit oh God oh hope oh everything and nothing.

"Turn around, Bud."

I notice a change in Sean's voice that only I would, like Nice Sean's trying to hold back Mad Sean, Wild Sean—

There's this bridge over Fort Point Channel, they've torn it down but in younger days we were twelve, thirteen we'd dive off it to prove something and in the second that you'd leap you couldn't believe you were doing it—

I start to turn. I don't know anything. The balloon of what's happening now has swelled too large for my brain to contain, so it leaves me, floating away slowly.

I don't know anything except that Sean is behind me. I turn around and face him.

He hasn't moved. There are only two things in the world, yeah there are three: the water; the moon; and Sean. They swirl and meld together, becoming One like the Trinity, the water spurting moonlight, the moon having fallen in the water, Sean brooding, as black and unreadable as the ocean five hundred miles out. The moon spins through his hair, streams between his fingers that are placed on his sides, right at the level of his waist.

But—

There's one other thing, not me, I've floated away, this other thing that, to an alien maybe, might be responding to the moon, pulsing to life, lifting, rising like a tide. Or maybe it's a marker, some piece of primitive pagan wood whose long shadow up the calendar of my sunburned belly foretells Something, an equinox, a solstice, a plague, a thousand-year era of peace and harmony, or, maybe, the end of everything, a disaster of Biblical proportions.

Or maybe just something ridiculous to laugh at.

If only I could read his eyes, read his body—I wonder if I'll spend my whole life reacting, reacting, waiting for somebody else to do something and basing my actions on that—

Fuck it.

I turn around.

"Here I am," I say. Everything I thought to hide forever is revealed now. "Here I am."

Sean says nothing. The moon stings my salty eyes, blinds me, floods over the front of my body like spilled milk.

"You—you wanted me to—turn." I can hardly talk for panting. "Well . . ." I throw out my arms, then drop them to my sides. I think about how I might have to leave town tomorrow morning, first thing.

Sean remains silent.

"S-say something, you bastard," I whisper through chattering teeth.

Sean says nothing. The sea is silent too, straining to hear. The not-too-distant Boulevard is ghost town empty. The whole world's empty, everyone's gone to the moon that's why it's so bright—

"Say something," I repeat.

Nothing.

"If you don't say something," I say, "I'm leaving, I'll fuckin' lea—"

"Don't," he whispers. But nothing more. A second eternity passes.

Finally he lifts a hand from the water, points at me, like a sea god rising from the water, pronouncing my doom.

"*Ecce Homo,*" he says.

"Huh?"

"*Ecce Homo.*"

It comes back to me I remember now, from Religion class. Pilate's words to the bloodthirsty crowd as he displayed the whipped and thorny-crowned Jesus. *Behold the Man.* But maybe in this case Sean means *Behold the Homo.* In typical double-entendre Sean fashion, his utterance is open to debate, I see opposing teams of hoary-bearded scholars arguing in my head, arms flailing, fingers gesturing—

Then he says, "Oh, Bud," like he's in anguish. For himself? Or for me? Or for what was our friendship, now revealed, at least on my part, as it's ripped up by its root, to be an oak, and not just a radish; a wild and steamy jungle instead of a *Have A Nice Day* smiley-face daisy—

He starts sloshing forward, slowly. The moon turns liquid as it radiates around Sean, like he's made of gold and he's melting into the water.

I start shaking—

It's not just that he knows now; not just that he knows it's *him* now—

It's that he's coming for me.

I close my eyes like I'm about to be in a car wreck.

He wades through the water full of some purpose that I feel rather than see. I open my eyes. The moon behind him outlines his body like neon. He's up to his thighs but he's in shadow the moon behind. I squint, but only hear, don't see. His sloshing, sloshing. Then laughter, a voice, harsh crow's cackling. Sean's head goes up like an animal's sniffing danger. He melts back quick into the water. My head yanks left and I see them, two figures along the beach, stumbling, touching, staggering, laughing, shrieking—

They freeze, seeing me. I turn and grab for my shorts, wrest them on over my impertinent hardness—

"Who's that?" a voice drippy with boozy testosterone booms from thirty yards away.

I pull the towel up from the sand, start drying off my legs, my chest. Sean's bobbing in the water up to his neck, saying nothing.

"Who's that?" the voice repeats, almost wet with ominousness.

"Who's *that?*" Sean asks back from the water, the standard neighborhood response. At least they know now it's some of their own. They press on toward us. I recognize Dougie O'Brien, a hulking refrigerator of a man two years older than us, a ne'er-do-well neighborhood Macawber who's waiting to be picked for the fire or police department. The girl I recognize, she's from 'round the way; we went to school together but I can't think of her name.

"S'up Dougie," I mutter, still reeling.

"Hey," Dougie says. He turns and peers into the water as the blonde girl bounces off his chest again and again. The stale smell of booze rises up from them like vapor from a landfill.

"Hey, my man Sean!" Dougie bellows when he recognizes Sean. "Watta yese doin'?" and his speech is a throwback to an earlier era—Pleistocene maybe.

"Wassup Dougie!" Sean half laughs, like he's delighted to see this interrupting loser and his bimbo girlfriend at a crisis point in his life. Only I hear the phoniness in Sean's voice, the nervous cliff off of which his words tumble. I remember the girl now, some tough-girl-name Donna Dora Dara she'd be waiting after school with high hair and white lipstick and her tough-girl cohorts waiting to beat the shit out of other girls who pissed her off or had the balls to date someone she liked, I remember now a note one time from one of her girlfriends saying this same girl liked me but of course I couldn't be bothered and now she's smiling at me but I see malice in her italic-drunk eyes Hell Hath No Fury and I get a tingle in my nuts I smell Trouble.

"Hi, Bud!" she bursts to me, sicky-sweet. Then she looks between Sean and me. This girl set a new standard for dubious achievement in the SATs but she has animal instincts when it comes to sniffing out people and their motives and she leans forward puts her hands on her chubby bare knees and says, "Ain't cha coming outta the water, Seannie?"

Sean doesn't move.

The girl starts giggling, then she whispers something into Dougie's ear. I hear the f word, not that one the other one. Dougie's face scrunches up.

"Nah, I don't think so, Doreen," he slurs. "Seannie's good people."

Doreen, that's her name.

"Why should I come out?" Sean calls from the water. "Why don't you come in, Doreen?" I cringe to hear the tease in Sean's voice, it's as fake as his greeting was a minute ago, more than cringe, I die to hear this, the saddest song in the universe, the groveling of my prince so that he'll fit in with these creeps—or am I all wrong? Sean knows about me now but I still don't know about him, no one's ever taught me what to look for how to tell Son Can I Have a Word with You, You're Getting to That Age Now Son Where You Might Want to Start Dating and Getting Serious with Another Young Man, But of Course You've Got to Know How to Tell the Normal People Like Your Mother and Me from the Freaks Like You, So This Is What You Want to Look for yeah right, so I have no clue if he's Dear God Please like me or just baiting me to eject me from his life forever tell everybody have me run out of town on a rail—

Doreen looks quite pleased with herself, her groundhog cheeks are chuck full of smiling delight. I feel an especial rage puffing up inside me, choking, something I've never felt before and I wonder if this heirloom anger derives from some Irish brawler who swung for his temper, or perhaps from my father's people, Sicilians, I've seen the old pictures dark-eyed monosyllabics dressed in black that you wouldn't want to fuck with—

"You boys was frolickin' in the water bare-ass, weren't cha?" she says. She repeats the word. "Fro-lick-in'." She says it like it's sticky pink candy in her mouth. She's still got the same complacent smile on her face and she looks back and forth from me to Sean. Dougie's mouth is open like a flytrap and his dark eyes move back and forth mechanically, digesting this.

"You ain't On the Hog, are you, Seannie?" Dougie asks, a local term for an alternative lifestyle, its etymology from such phrases as On the Dole, On the Bottle, On Drugs, and the like.

"They never date girls, neither one of 'em," Doreen eagerly stage whispers.

Dougie's head tilts to think about this, my guess is it's impossible for his brain to process information without a sympathetic physical demonstration.

"That's true, ain't it?" he asks, more to himself. There's an awful quiet and I think the sky's about to fall in.

"We hate fuckin' faggots more'n we hate niggers," Doreen says. Then she titters and covers her mouth with one hand, like she really didn't mean to say this. Dougie clenches his fists like a Rock 'Em Sock 'Em robot come to life.

Sean's head twists to the side like he's been hit. The moon catches his face, slashes at it, and for the first time I see the real Sean: open-mouthed like a child, utterly at a loss, the eyes agape, full of terror. My breath evaporates. A wellspring of tenderness, protectiveness, love, endless, unstoppable, geysers up inside me.

"Wait'll the gang finds out!" Doreen gushes, faux seriously, and I decide instantly that these will be the last words her sewer mouth backs up into this world. A stiletto-brandishing Daddy ancestor combines with a red-faced chortling murderously raging bogtrotter from Ma's forebears and the three of us decide to go for Dougie first, to tackle him quickly into the water then hold his block head beneath the waves till he drowns. Then Doreen we can take care of slowly, torturously slowly—all for my Seannie, the Real Seannie, the one I've always loved, always knew was there like a blind bee guided by fragrance alone—

I take a step toward Dougie—

"C'mon, let's get outta here," Doreen says, trying to sound bored. Dougie glares between Sean and me for a minute, sees something in my eyes perhaps, then heads off up the beach, shaking his head. He puts his arm around Doreen.

They say something but I can't hear what. And they leave as they came, trailing crow laughter.

It's very quiet when they're gone, like they've taken all the sound in the world with them. I haven't moved. My heart's racing, my chin prickly like before you puke. I turn to the water. Sean's head is still there, bobbing. Then suddenly he starts slamming the water with his fists, punching up and down like a madman, spinning round. A sound comes out of him, a wail that could be all the anguish the world's ever known, the groan of tree crashing to earth, the shriek of a refugee mother trying to shake her dead baby back to life, the unbearable weight of stone grinding against the open pink flesh of the earth—I can't bear to hear this—

"Wh-what's the matter with you!" I scream. "Stop! STOP IT!"

"Fuck!" he screams. "FFFFUUUCCCKKKK! Why didn't you . . . why didn't you fight for me? I couldn't do nuthin' in the water! Why didn't you fuckin' fight for me?" I realize we will not be picking this up where we left it.

"They're . . . they're not worth it," I say, stumbling over the words. "I'm a lover, not a fighter."

"You mean you're a pussy, you're a faggot pussy!" he chortles. He comes out of the water, trembling—he is beautiful, beyond my greatest imaginings, beyond what I've even dreamt, but his words slash.

"Don't fuckin' look at me, Faggot!" he cries. "Turn around! Turn the fuck around!"

"Fuck you," I mumble, stung by his words. I look down at my bare sandy feet, fishbelly white in the moonlight. All at once there's nothing in this world worth anything, every jewel's a broken beer bottle.

Sean doesn't even dry off. He yanks his T-shirt and shorts on, stomps into his sneakers. He storms off, me right behind. He stops at the sidewalk at the edge of The Boulevard, even though there's no cars at this late hour. He puts his hand up to his forehead.

"Aw fuck," he moans. He sounds like he's on the verge of crying. I put a tentative hand on the back of his shoulder. I would do anything for him at this moment. He flings it off like it burns.

"Get the fuck outta here!" he screams.

We walk back to The Park wordlessly, me reeling, yet still keeping an eye on the torturous beauty of his sockless legs, the curve that slides down to his sneakers and ends as a dagger to my heart. Danny and Timmy and Matt are sitting on the picnic table in the corner, quietly discussing the pennant race or some other absurd nothing, drinking methodically, the beers underneath the table like treasure they're guarding.

Sean says nothing but grabs the case from beneath the table, slides it out. He chugs one fast; then another. He hurls the empty cans against the chain-link fence when he's through. Beautifully, I can't help noticing, a perfect marriage of intent and bodily effort.

"How was the swim?" Matty asks knowingly, looking at me with a question in his eyes. I shake my head, look down, drink my beer.

"It sucked," Sean snarls, like he's ready to fight over this appraisal. "Everything fucking sucks. Next stupid fuckin' question." He chugs another. He turns around and stumbles into the corner, grabs onto the chain-link fence with one hand, undoes his pants with the other, starts peeing. His stream creates a river between his legs, one side of it washes up against the edge of his left sneaker but he doesn't care. When he turns around there's a devil light in his eyes.

"I know!" he says. "I wanna see what's on the other side of these fuckin' trees! Wanna get some o' my fuckin' balls back!"

Paul says, "You can't get through—"

"C'mon!" Sean screams, and the veins stand out on his neck like ripcords. "C'mon!"

The other three look at me. If nothing more than to protect him from going alone and hurting himself, I decide we should go. I nod. Sean's at the top of the two-story fence already, scaling it like a monkey despite his growing inebriation.

Going up for the rest of us is easy, but coming down on the other side is another thing, the trees fighting kicking scratching all the way—but we make it, Sean taking off into the trees as soon as we join him on the ground.

Now the Wild Sean reigns supreme. His madness, his rage, goes before me, rising from him like a hot stove, and he tears through the evergreen boughs as if he were the one bristling with needles and not they, as if he were making them bleed in a thousand different places, instead of the other way around.

There is a new smell here, new to me anyway—if I'd grown up anywhere else, ever been anywhere else I would've recognized it as the smell of woods, of Nature. But it is new to me this night, as is the benign give of the soft pine-needled earth beneath my sneakers. Sean pushes on though, as if his intent were not to find balls at all, but to go on, as if something is waiting for him, for all of us, beyond these trees.

And it is.

The moonlight squeezes through the trees in smaller and smaller chunks as we press on, my mind numb from what has just happened down the beach, the first thing, then the other, as well as the chilling realization of what I am capable of doing.

The woods go on. Who would've thought there were so many trees in the world, let alone Southie? I hate people who don't live in the city suddenly, hate the refuges they have. I wonder if maybe me and Sean—but this isn't a movie, this is Life.

We come to a wall, two stories high and cracked here and there, mossy green with lichens and ferns the size of my thumbs—

But we were weaned on climbing walls, and we ten-finger over it with barely a struggle. We land with a plop on the other side. And then it is like we aren't in South Boston anymore.

Even Sean for a minute is lifted out of his rage.

"What the . . ." I heard him murmur in front of me.

We are on this lawn, or really a sweep of grass, as close cut and flawless as a golf course green. This statue of a lady is right beside us, in fact we'd just missed her coming down. Moonlight is the only adornment she wears, and one of her hands is cupped to her ear as if she has heard us, and will report this intrusion now to Headquarters.

On either side of the statue this row of high, perfectly square bushes marches on down, with an eight-foot wide strip of the lawn running down the middle. Between the bushes and the lawn are flowers, more than I've ever seen, it is like Flower Heaven, and this the place where every blossom that has ever unfurled, and every bud that has withered before its time, has come to swell and bloom forever into its own invincible dream of itself.

We wander down this green alley. It intersects with another, going left and right, the crossroads marked by a trellised arch running riot with roses, and the air is almost wet with their scent. They touch my still-damp hair as I walked underneath, forty different shades of moon-drenched and shadow-sprinkled pink against my black hair. I take the right alley, no particular reason, caught up in this dream where you wander aimlessly, but with an intent that you understand only later, at the end. The swath of grass continues, moving through even wider drifts of flowers, their faces raised to the moon as if this light were as beneficial to them as sunshine. I can almost see the faces on each one, like this is a little kid's drawing come to life.

I know nothing of flowers, less than nothing; but I can see how different each clump is, the many varieties here. Because here are bell towers of things, ringing toward the back of the borders; open-mouthed trumpets, fluorescent in the moonlight, their eager throats sticky with pollen; radio-tower stems, rigid in their architecture, crowned with flat umbrae of varying color; gushy, billowy things, half-drunk on their own honey fragrance and flopping into their neighbors; neat mounds of buttony things at the edges of the borders, enabling the excess of their neighbors into something resembling Order—and all, every one, pouring out scents like confessions to the moon. Eventually this path begins to curve, and meets the main axis again, but further along, further in, closer to some center that each path seems to be leading us on to.

As my eyes adjust—but the garden is all glimmery with the moon, I guess I am making a kind of emotional adjustment—I start noticing small plaques here and there throughout the garden: some are in foreign languages beyond my comprehension, but others I can read: *Be Love,* says the first; *Flowers Are the Thoughts of the Earth,* says the second; *I Shall Live Alone in the Bee-Loud Glade,* says a third, right next to this roundy-pyramid shaped thing attached halfway up a tree that I guess is a beehive—imagine! Bees in Southie! Where did they first come from, I wonder? Over how many train yards, over how many rat-and-roach-infested cold water flats and housing projects did they fly before landing here? And how did they know they would find what they did here? What is this thing called Hope, and why has it, so far, failed to land on me?

I keep going. The path curves again. Now I can see a clearing at the end of this flower alley, an old stone archway through which I will have to pass and beyond this an opening, a center, the end of all the paths. As I pass through the last archway, as smothered with roses as the others, I notice another one-foot-square brass plaque. This one says, *Embrace Hope All Ye Who Enter Here.*

I pass through the archway, and stop.

I have come to the center of this place, where all the paths and avenues meet like a collision between Fragrance and Awe.

I find myself standing at the edge of a perfect circle, ringed with flower and shrub beds. The end of each path that spills into this circle—there are twelve in all, including this one I've just passed through—is marked by a stone archway, each one more smothered in roses than the other. An open, perfect lawn marks the center ring, in the middle of which is another circle, which seems the heart of this universe. In this center is a round pool, about ten feet across, edged with what looks like wicked old stone, scarred and crusty with lichen, like it came from an old church or castle on a cliff by the sea. The surface of the pool's water is black and totally still—I wouldn't know it is water at all if I couldn't see the moon in there, which is now being escorted by mother-of-pearl Man-o-War clouds. These, too, are etched in the pool, so accurately I think another world might be down there, better than this one like all dream worlds are.

But there's more. Rising from the center of the pool a slab of stone, taller than my own six feet, rough hewn, solemn, somewhat ominous, tapering to a smaller, jagged point. At the top of the stone slab rests a crystal ball—one of those garden globes. It's a shining, translucent emerald green, but much larger than usual, almost surreal in its size.

I dump myself upon the pool's rock wall edge, the coolness of the stone a gasping relief against my flanks, sticky with the monster humidity. I become aware of the crickets now—in Southie!—chanting like the deep-voiced older altar boys during High Funerals or Solemn Masses at Gate of Heaven Church.

I slip into the water.

I feel with my toes for bottom, and hit it about three feet down. I slide into the water's coolness, and start wading toward the ball. I have the urge to remove my shorts. As I get closer I see that the crystal ball's surface is a mosaic of hundreds of small pieces of glass, each one reflecting the moon's brilliance, as well as its own, and its neighbors', the cumulative effect being it glows from within.

As if by Magic.

Reaching the stone that cradles the ball, I see these weird characters carved into its surface—not letters or designs but something of both. I run my hands across the slab's rough surface, wondering what strange stories this ancient thing could tell, thinking that probably the oddest tale of all would be the one explaining its presence here. And then the ball itself—shimmering on top, radiant—my hands approach it but not to touch, only to caress from a distance, to marvel—

"Right here, Bud!"

The hiss of Sean's voice—turning, rushing back to other reality highspeed through a tunnel. I see him on the other side of the pool, one foot saucily up on the rock wall edge, his arms open as if to catch something, a nasty grin garishing up his face—

"The ball!" he cries, seeing my stupor. "Right here!"

Matty and Timmy and Paul are dawdling idly behind him, hands jammed in their shorts pockets.

I remember Brown Eyes, their softness, her smile, and what that softness had done, creating this world here. But there were other reasons—

"Naw, don't," I say. "We might . . . ahhh . . . break it."

"Who gives a fuck?" Sean chortles, his brows lowering till they look purple. "She's got all our balls so fuck her I'm gonna take one o' hers." His rage is sobering him up by the second. I see his fists clench by his sides.

It is a bad time for some angel of goodness to perch on my right shoulder. Then I think, it's me that's being good, for the real Sean, the one who's being smothered now by Mad Sean.

I shake my head.

"No," I say. "Sorry dude."

I pull my hands away from the ball, radiant. The most beautiful thing I've ever seen, besides this garden. And Sean. And Sean wants to kill it, destroy it. I position myself in front of the stone. I fold my arms across my chest. My hands I notice are shaking. But this of course is about more than just the ball.

One of Sean's thin dark eyebrows goes up. His chin lowers. Our eyes lock. His never leave mine as he pulls his sneakers off one at a time, lofts them carelessly over his shoulder.

He slides into the water.

"I said gimme it, Bud," he says. A puff of big wind gushes through the garden. The moon flickers between the thickening clouds.

"No."

"Faggot," he says.

"Fuck you," I say, though I still love him. But his words no longer sting. I had seen the real Sean. He can call me every name in the book now—it won't change who he really is. Like a Prophet who has seen his God, I fear nothing.

I stride to meet him in the water. If we fight, we won't fight anywhere near the crystal ball.

"You gonna give it to me?" he says.

"No."

He comes at me, lunging instantly. I knew he would but still his quickness catches me off guard, and we go bowling over into the water. My open mouth gasping is quick full and I come up sputtering and choking. We're at the wall at the edge of the pond, wet hands locked on the other's slippery shoulders, fighting for balance. I let up pressure then redouble it, and we both go sailing over the wall onto the ground below, grunting, half-swearing, panting. We wrestle and push and roll a bit, and then I find we've reached the end of one of the flower beds, in fact we're rolling in it. I try to pull us out and roll back onto the lawn, but Sean's anger is making him too strong.

The others stand by uselessly. It never has been entirely resolved just who is the leader of our little gang, and now the issue will be settled, at least one aspect of it anyway.

"You faggot," he mutters again between gasps, his mouth dirty and grass-stained.

"You're the faggot and you know it," I answer. And then I laugh—for suddenly the truth of this comes to me like a loved lost dog trotting home at last. Joy leaps up inside me. Now all I have to do is defeat Mad Sean, Frightened Sean, and Real Sean, My Sean, the one I will succor forever, the wide-eyed open-mouthed clueless thing of tenderness and love, will come to the fore—

His punch catches me unawares, so savage and strong it is, right to the face. Before this we had wrestled, grappled, took the measure of the other's grip and intention, wanting, I think, just to have contact, a better kind than this but this would have to do until we found a way to have that better one; but now Sean sees me as That Thing, the Monster within. Plus possibly I've also turned into Dougie and Doreen.

His third smack to my face snaps something inside me, the Irish Brawler and stiletto-wielding Sicilian spring to life as if this were the tag-team signal they'd been juicy salivating for, and now We Fight. We Fight among thorny roses that crash beneath our weight then bleed too much fragrance as we roll over crushing them. We Fight among innocent-looking, almost shy mounds of flowers tucked into secret corners, ripping them up with our exerting feet, I almost think I can hear their screams or maybe Brown Eyes is screaming from afar or maybe me, We Fight in an area I haven't seen yet, a patio full of pots of lemon and orange trees I think brought out to take the summer sun just for a while because winter is deadly here but we are deadlier, tipping over and shattering the terra-cotta, the individual specimens vomiting out of the pots to wilt under the vanishing moon as the wind gusts increase and far away the rumble of thunder as if something were Displeased. The other three Timmy Matty Paul bolt at the sound of the crashing pots.

And then my rage is gone, as quickly as it came. At least I haven't kicked him. He gets on top of me effortlessly, without my anger I am like a ragdoll. The sky behind Sean's red swollen face, bloodied here and there with the marks from my hands . . . my own hands have done this . . . oh God . . . the sky grows ominous and lightning sizzles, I can feel it wiggling inside me. His knees on top of my thighs, his hands pinning down my wrists both panting breathless bloody tears in both our eyes why, he sees the lightning in my eyes and turns his head to the sky. He keeps his hands and knees where they are but his grip loosens.

We both understand the fight is over. He turns back and looks into my eyes, I can't see his too well.

We say nothing, we're panting trying to catch breath. Something leaps between us. We stare at each other, panting in unison. My face feels like Sean's looks, thick and mangled. I'm sore all over and never felt more alive. He's over me panting holding me.

He turns and looks at the sky again. I can tell he's rearranging his squirming face.

He turns back to me, after scanning the now terrorized garden and making sure we're alone.

"The m-moon . . ." he finally begins. Then he sniffs. I feel something, a raindrop but it hasn't started raining yet. He's shaking on top of me the way you do right before you cry.

He takes a deep jagged breath.

"The moon's gone behind the clouds to cry," he says. He shakes his head. I'm one big sore but there's Something Coming that cancels out everything else.

He's looking sideways at the Big Sky.

"Bud," he says, whispering. He turns back to me, lowers his face until it's inches away from mine. "Did you ever," he whispers, "did you ever feel like . . . it was raining all over the world?"

All I can do is stare at him. His eye is like a hand now, caressing.

"Oh man," he sighs, still looking at me, eating me with his eyes.

"Sean," I whisper, like it's the only sound in the universe.

"Jesus Christ, what have I done?" he says, gulping, his voice rising. He lets go my right wrist and brings a tentative finger toward my swollen-shut left eye, the welt that's forming on my right cheek. Sean has touched me one million times over the years, the bum slaps in Little League, ten thousand high fives during Outs games, wrestling and pushing and shoving and back slapping and horseplaying and even some dozen arms around the shoulder—for a second—when the shit hit the fan as it does on a regular basis in Southie. But now, for the first time, he will touch me in that Other Way—

His finger lowers, approaching my mouth. I can't help gasping and closing my eyes. His touch is so soft that I think I'm imagining it at first. His index finger lands on my lower lip, traces its outline. I moan and open my eyes.

"My God . . . what the . . . what have I done to you, Bud?" he whispers, his voice breaking. His jaw tightens and he swallows hard, but his eyes grow larger and swell into my own. Finally a sob breaks through him. "I love you, Bud," he weeps. "I've always loved you."

I hear myself say, "I . . . I *am* you, Sean." I don't know where these words come from.

Sean—

Something jolts through him like electricity. His head jerks back a little.

"It's true," he says.

He lowers his face to mine and kisses me on my swollen lips, tenderly, as if mine were rose petals that must be put back together carefully, excruciatingly—

He's weeping silently and his salty tears fall through my lips like so many cigarillos. I drink them in, anxious for any part of him, to take any part of him into me. His hands are everywhere as if he'd devour me through the sense of touch alone. My arms wrap around him, pulling in closer. He leans all of himself on top of me.

The rain begins. We roll over, and over, until it's hard to tell if the storm is above us or below us or inside us.

"Oh, Bud," he says, again and again. I begin to believe that the garden, the whole world, is healing itself around us. The softness of his skin, the realization that my hands are free to roam the length and breadth of him is too much. By an accident of alphabetization, we sat beside each other in kindergarten, and we haven't tired of each other's company yet. And now it has come to this.

After a long time we're lying quiet holding each other and he says, "They'll all know tomorrow . . . what are we gonna do?"

He sits up and stares at me. The rain washes over his face, slicking his black hair onto his forehead, but his cobalt eyes burn. He looks a little different after what we've done. I become afraid of the power of my love for him, if such a short word can contain the ocean of everything I feel.

"Ahh . . ."

"What are we gonna do," he says, not asking. He stares at me. His lips set together in determination. A chill goes through me, settling in my testicles.

"No," I say.

"It's us or them," he says. "It's a . . . matter of survival. Like if someone came into your house and . . . and tried to kill you. You can kiss everything good-bye if everybody finds out."

"No," I repeat.

"For me," he says. He stands up, pulls me up by my hands. He sticks his hand out, palm up, then grabs me where no one has before tonight. He keeps his hand there, stares at me until I look in his eyes.

"For us," he says. He stoops behind him, picks a flower, brings it to his lips, kisses it, hands it to me.

"We can leave town," I say, "we can leave tonight. You're the only thing keeping me here anyway and—"

"And do what?" Sean chortles. "Have spittin' contests all day? Smoke cigarillos till we're fuckin' eighty? Bud, I got plans! I wanna *be* something!"

I'm ashamed I don't admit all I ever wanted to be was his.

"People like us . . . we get killed every day," he says, like he's already a lawyer and making arguments. "Sometimes slow day by day, sometimes fast." He pauses and grabs my forearm. "Bud, look what they did to that fuckin' kid in Colorado, that guy in the Navy . . . all those others!" I'm surprised Sean knows about Stuff Like That. "What about all the people who've killed themselves! The fuckin' kids who get the shit beat out of them . . . fuck, Bud! Let's fight back for once!" He pauses again. He grabs me by my shoulders and brings his face right into mine.

"You know where your Dad keeps his gun," he murmurs.

Hand in hand we walk back to the center of the garden, the world. The damage we've done is appalling and no it hasn't healed itself.

We come to the pool, with the crystal ball rising from the black water. There's no light in the sky but still the glass ball glows, though less strongly. Sean stiffens beside me, lets go my hand. I follow his eyes to see what he sees. There's a woman standing beside the pool— so still she could be the stone monolith.

We face each other for a bit. She smiles weakly. It's Brown Eyes. She's dressed simply, in black blouse and loose-fitting pants belted with rope. A heavy cross dangles from a chain around her neck, so large it almost looks surreal. She has an ageless face the color of milk but I guess she's at least eighty. Instinctively I draw myself into Sean's side. He tries to nudge me away but I won't let him.

"Hello," she says, tentatively. "I'm Sister Bennett."

I guessed she was a nun from her un-bouffanted hair, the size of the cross that dangles from her neck, big enough so people wouldn't sit next to you on the bus.

"Hi," we both say at once.

"Quite a night," she says, making the understatement of the year.

"I'm sorry," I say. My head drops beneath her gaze.

"Sorry," Sean mumbles.

"I've been watching you," she says. "I think I understand." She smiles again, tentatively.

Sean turns scarlet beside me even in the night, puts a little distance between us.

"We'll fix everything," I say.

"Everything," Sean echoes.

"Don't be afraid," she says. "Come closer."

We take a few steps forward. Her eyes are like a doe's, liquidy, full of wonder. They go back and forth from me to Sean like we might be plants from her garden she's never seen before.

"What ahhh . . . is this place?" Sean asks, looking down, scuffing his feet.

"A place to heal," she says. "We . . . we're a missionary order. South America. We come back here when we're old or sick. Or injured."

"Injured," Sean echoes.

She nods.

"We get shot at and beaten from time to time," she says.

Sean makes a sound of disbelief.

"We . . . have the radical idea that the poor are people too," she explains, smiling.

There's a silence. I find myself wishing she'd acknowledge the dead body lying at our feet: the sundered garden, the crushed bushes, the shattered pots, the uprooted plants—

"Are you the head . . . nun?" Sean asks.

She smiles.

"No. We don't really . . . we're kind of a democracy. I'm retired now and it's my job to keep this place up."

My wonder increases. It would take truckloads of City workers to do the work that's been done here.

Her eyes fix upon mine. I can't look away. Something passes between us. She takes hold of her cross, fingers it like a familiar lover.

"I . . . I've been thinking of hiring someone, I could use some help here," she continues. With her healer's intuition, I think I've become an object of interest to her. I believe she wants to try and rescue me. I come to think I might want to be rescued, a necessary part of the equation that's usually ignored.

"I've been thinking about that a lot lately," she continues. "The weeds have always been fast, but now they're faster than me, for I've become so slow."

Sean won't look up at her, I know there's only one thing on his mind now and it isn't This.

"I . . . won't be here forever," Sister Bennett goes on. "And we'll need someone to take over when I'm gone. We really can't spare anyone from the field, there's so few of us now and so much to be done."

She lowers her head and stares intently at us.

Sean finally looks up.

"I'm going to college in September," he says flatly, like he's full and she's offering food. "Ahhh, then law school after that."

"Good for you," Sister Bennett says. "We can use some good lawyers."

Sean grimaces, looks down at his feet.

She returns her gaze to me. I examine her face for sarcasm but see none. I see that she belongs to that special category of nuns, the There's No Such Thing As a Bad Boy school.

"And what are your plans?" she asks me.

"I . . ." Her question catches me unawares. But it's her eyes on mine that make an answer useless, when there isn't any answer.

"The pay's good," she continues, "and the work's steady. There's a huge library inside the house. And from the chapel tower you can see . . . everywhere."

I say nothing. Perhaps it's my paranoia, but I suspect she's trying to pull me from the upcoming wreckage of the unwinnable war between My Heart and My Head.

The moon comes out again, igniting the wet crystal ball.

"I'd . . . I'd like to come back tomorrow and start cleaning up," I stall. "That's the least I can do."

She smiles, shakes her head dismissively, but she's compelled to look around. Her face falls.

"My only concern is . . ." She begins. She gets a little shaky. She turns behind her and looks for something, maybe a chair, that she doesn't see. She takes a deep breath and steadies herself. "My only concern is you've—uhm . . . the butterfly garden is destro—is gone now, and they'll come tomorrow and find nothing to eat. Milkweed and Joe-Pye Weed. I . . ." and then she brings her hands to her face. She starts weeping, and the sound is more painful than Sean's punches.

My heart breaks.

"I'm sorry," she apologizes, for nothing.

Sean turns to me, sensing my discomfiture. We exchange a long, long look.

"I know, Bud," he whispers. "This is . . . this is awful and we'll fix it up . . . but we gotta get going. You know what you gotta do. You know Bud. Before it's too late. For me. Please? Please?"

I see my two and only two possible futures, clearly. I'm almost calm as I examine both scenarios. Working here with Sister Bennett. Living a life alone here, but growing, always growing like the flowers. Educating myself in her library. If I can find anything I care to study. There must be something, other than Sean. Climbing the tower, watching, waiting for Sean to come to his senses—when he's eighty or something—

The other option is equally vivid. I'll leave now, get my Dad's gun, find Doreen and Dougie for him, for Sean, do what he wants me to do. I'll admit it all later, say it was all my own doing. Sean'll say he was in bed sleeping this night, and I'll vouch for that I will.

I'll get life, with parole possible in fifteen to twenty. That's a given. We grow up around here knowing the system the way suburban kids can rattle off the names of colleges they'd like to go to.

I'll do the time.

He'll pick me up on the day I get out, I know it. He'll probably have a Mercedes by then, a BMW, somehow he'll have gotten the City to pay for it. That Sean—my Sean—what an operator.

He'll maybe be married by then—

—that would be hard. But he's got his career to think about, his image. He'll make me understand.

I'll hop in his car. We'll look at each other. We won't say anything at first. He's expecting me to look nasty after fifteen years Inside, but he'll be surprised, I've been working out every day, become a Buddhist or something. He's got a bit of a paunch from all those political dinners, but he's still playing hockey. He'll be fit enough. And the eyes will still be cobalt, unexpectedly softer when he smiles.

We'll drive down to Castle Island in the dark, pull the car over. He'll lean back in his seat, put his hands behind his head, close his eyes just to have me near him again. We'll both be Old. Thirty-three.

Eventually he'll turn to me, study my face for a bit . . . I know this now.

"Toss me a cigarillo, will ya, Bud?" he'll say. "They're in the glove compartment."

The Rain

"Chk-chk-chk-chk-chkchkchkchkchk!" the squirrel jabbers, on a tree branch right above my little home on the hill here. Kev, I really think it's the same squirrel you used to throw peanuts to off your paint-peeling back porch, when your mother wasn't looking. (She said squirrels were nothing but rats with tails—Sacrilege! Get into the dead man's garage and do some soul-searching, woman!) I look up at him, take off my baseball cap, try to figure out what he's saying to me. I know he's trying to say *something,* Kev. I reach into my hooded sweatshirt's pocket, take an acorn out and—

Wait.

All that comes later.

Let's talk about the rain first.

Oh, yes. The rain.

Swish of wind wet with rain and here it is again I'm safe. The rain, the rain.

Blessed be the rain.

It tiptoes over Fort Point Channel—remember Kev how we used to diggity dive there sweaty neck summer nights before they bashed the bridge down? The rain must drink up some of this water as it crosses over, for it gathers shapeless strength, then sweeply sweeps down Summer Street. There's this one moment when the beginning of Summer Street is shiny half-seen with rain, and three blocks down I'm here is dry yet, I'm peering at the corner, watching, waiting, its coming is inevitable—I love that moment. A puff of wind—ahh, then all's well. I stick my hands out into it—the rain, the rain. The rainly rain.

Everybody wants to hear about the other thing, Kev, and what happened—but The Rain came after, and it washes things away. I'd rather talk about The Rain.

The rain's not a car, not a person: when it comes to the corner of L and West Broadway, it doesn't have to decide whether to turn right, or left, or keep going ahead past the barrooms and triple-deckers down to the beach. It does all these things at once, then goes starry straight up too, and sideways. Because it can. The rain, the rain, the rain.

Oh the rain.

You can tell when it's comely coming. I can anyway. Sure, part of that's practice, but I got me a good spot too, right up here on the hill where the easty east wind meets the westy west. See it's the wind tells you first—meaning the trees, which are the million little mouths of the wind. Then of course there's the smell. You know what I mean. Even here in the city.

Other smells ooze in with the rain, like the scent of someone you love right before they get here. If the streets have been frizzy-hair frying in the sun all day, the rain goes splat! onto them and you get that smell—like boiling water on asphalt; only much much better because it means The Rain—sometimes a little vapor. You ever lived in the city you know just what I'm talking about. If rain keeps raining, it washes that first scent away, comes in with its own smell in a billion little bouquets. Rainly rain smell, which of course washes things away including thoughts and stops me from wondering whose idea it was that night.

Not that it matters now.

There's different kinds of rain. Most people don't know this. Not around here anywayslywise. Like Billy Hogan? Works over at Fenway Park? You remember, Kev. I saw him late this afternoon. Rain was just unloosening. He crossed the street to the other side when he saw me coming. They all think I'm kickity crazy, Kev. I crossed over too. Directly. Not like the squirrels, who cross only halfway, then stop.

"The rainly rain, Bill!" I announced, smiling, standing in front of him, pointing up.

"*Fuckin'* rain," he says, look-to-everywhere but my eyes. I like to STARE now Kev, see everything. Just in case you're higgledy-hiding in some corner of my vision. I guess it spooks people, this staring. Boo!

"Fuckin' game got rained out," Billy blurts on. "I lost a hunnert bucks." He thinks I hate the rain. Man, life's tough enough without being stupid, huh?

"Yo, *Bill!*" I cried, clapping him on the back. I'm that pleased to think the rain might last through the nightly night, they don't call off ball games unless it's supposed to keep on, and only on. (Those are the best nights, Kev.)

"And just what kind of rainly rain was she over at Fenway?" I asked Bill.

He looked at me for a spazy second.

"The oozling, puddling, gurgly gurgling kind?" I quizzed, helping him out. "Or sudden and hard like? Coming at you sideways? Or puffity puff puff puffy in gale winds, like buckets tossed at you? Hah!"

"Ahhhhh," he stalled, like he was at the doctor's. He took a step backward—

Our eyes met just for a second, Kev, mine and Billy's—and I could see that Billy was afraid. Afraid of me, Kev. I sighed. You know there's nothing inside me but tenderness. But how to show it in a world like this, Kev. That would be the question. How to show it, in a world like this. I could say, "Billy, I'm not crazy, just tender." But what then? Billy's not interested in my tenderness, Kev. He's only interested in my absence.

So I said, "Forget about it, Billity Boy. Go on and get outta here." That's what I told him. Really, why punish him further for his ignorance, right? Ignorance is its own punishment. You don't *see* things, don't *know* things—like a dog being color blind. Aquamarine and vermilion are shining there—but they might as well not be. Like the difference between Cleansers, and Cleaners. Just as an example.

Billy left and I turned around and faced the westerly west. A row of tripilty-deckers marches up both sides of Broadway, canopied by the sentry trees. They're not moving, none of them, not the houses, not the trees but above them over me this flying carpet of pregnant clouds scudding sweeping toward me, coming to me.

Bringing rain. Blessed rain.

I throw my arms up, raise my face to the sky—

"The rain!" I cry, I gasp. *"The raaaaaaiiiiiiiiinnnnnn!"* I spin around—

I guess I should tell you why I like the rainly rain. Ah, I will. Soon.

I tell you about Billy Hogan because he is The Average Normal Person. He'll get a pull over here, ATM, credit cards it's in here somewhere, buy a house do you like this one honey, a big-ass SUV look at me next to you now, get married SHIT!, have a kid or two was I this bad when I was his age. He'll die, and think all that stuff was his idea.

But really? If he lived five thousand years ago? He'd screamly raid a neighboring village, have a manhood initiation look at this thing growing now, throw stones at his enemies FUG!, find a little cave for himself and his mate someday. Then die, and think all that stuff was his idea. Just the average person, doing what they're told. But me?

Well I'll tell you, I'm getting to be a rain expert. *By choice.* This is what I'd say . . . but nobody asks. Were I to fill out an application, it's what I'd tell them. *Occupation: Rain Expert,* I'd write. And not like a scientist—c'mon. Some tie-dyed T-shirted bushy-haired nerd'll tell you .7 of an inch of precipitation fell last night when the (shivery) cold front moved in or whatever, and some of them get all giggledy geeked out on the *science* of it, you can see their eyes wild, hands sweeping over maps, getting a biggity boner over millibars and so many inches of pressure and all that shit. C'mon—you don't know fucking Jack Sprat about it if that's how you look at it. But I'll tell you—I'll tell you all about the rain. How it looks. *Infinite.* How it feels. *Like liggity life.* How it smells. *Like liggity life.* How it tastes. *Like liggity life.* How it sounds. *Blue and gray and green.* What it washes away. *Everything.*

I'll tell you everything, really, including why I like the rain. But I won't be able to tell you one thing, why people run in from it. Talk about crazy.

But first let's do some quick statistics. So I'm standing on the side of biggity Broadway spinning around and calling out The Rain, after I dismiss Billy Hogan. Let's say there's a hundred people within listening earshot, most of them locked in their boxity houses. Let's say half of them—which makes fifty—can hear me—the others are watching tickity TV way up loud, or going to the bathroom, or maybe listening to some radio talk show and you know how liggity loud those are, all those fucking loud people complaining about the city giving out too many piggity parking tickets or whatever—and let's say half of *them* are nosey enough to come to their windows and see what's up. (Huh like they'd know. What's up is *the rain!*) And so half of them, twenty-five of them, come to the window and they see this kid, this nineteen-year-old kid, spinning around in the rain. There's older gravelly voiced ladies in housecoats and scuff slippers pushing up from their couches on the arms of which are their Kent Golden 100s in maroon velveteen cigarette cases with a slot on the side for a lighter, shuffling to the window—there's young mothers, they never sit still, most of them come running to look out the window, they're used to miggity manic running, they can't stop running and when they feel bad about this they think of themselves as being in an ad playing the role of Today's Busy Woman Who Can Do It All—there's kids, watching TV, getting instructions on what products they need to pressure Today's Busy Woman their mother into buying, or maybe they're playing on the computer trying to download dirty pictures— they lean to the window, just stare out—

Now most of these people, they just sigh—"Joey McInnis," they mutter, shaking their heads. "God help us." The young mothers if they're Southie don't really care either. But if they're not Southie they become Concerned and they call the cops. Or if they're viggity vinegar grouchy old men they call the cops. Let's say three of them do this. They call the *cops* at this kid twirling in the rain! What a world. But why am I surprised? The Indians did Rain Dances, and look what happened to them.

"Yeah lookit, there's some kid out here, screamin' in the rain." They point in the direction of the street, even though they're talking on the phone Your Voice Being Recorded For Your Protection. Even if only three percent call the cops that's three people calling the cops. Sometimes the cops come. Most times it's Sergeant Upton, and somebody else riding with him, it varies. A woman cop, a black cop. He doesn't have the same regular partner like on TV.

"Wassup, Joey?" Sergeant Upton always begins, smiling, sliding out of his cruiser. Whoever's with him gets out and just stares. Not Sergeant Upton though, he's got this big Dog Day smiley face, you almost need your shades to look at him. Like he just happened to be driving around and saw me and got nothing better to do than pass time of day.

It's not that I don't like him. He's Southie, and he's a pretty nice guy, for a cop. It's just that big smiley Dog Day face—I'm Concerned it might dry up the rain, chase it away.

Somebody must have called cuz he came today, sliding out of his cruiser again. Another cop was with him, he just got out and stared.

"Wassup, Joey?" Sergeant Upton asked. He was wearing his orange rain slicker.

"The rain," I said, but carefully. "Now don't be chasing it away with that face of yours."

He looked at the other cop for a second, then back at me. "No, no, I wouldn't do that," he said. The other cop looked shocked for some reason—as if he didn't know. C'mon—gimme a billity break!

"So. What you up to, Joey? Jus' hangin'?"

"Yup."

"Not causing no trouble?"

"Nope."

"So ahhhh, tell me, Joey—where you livin' at these days?"

"The Island of Unopened Packages, Sarge," I answer.

He started laughing. "No really," he said.

You tell people the truth, Kev, and they don't want to hear it.

"C'mon Sarge, what are you, Sherlock Holmes wit all these questions?"

"Well I just . . . I mean you're out here in the rain . . ." he said.

Jeesh, it's like it's a crime, digging the rain. Wassup with that? There's people been in their houses for days on end, but that's okay, you don't see the cops hassling them, dragging their parched asses out into the rain.

"I'm fine," I said.

"I'm just worried about you, that's all, how you makin' out, where you livin'."

"I'm makin' out fine. I'm livin' at home, where you think."

He puts one leg up on the side of the blue and white cruiser, leans his arms onto his knee. This is his Buddy pose. The other cop, this guy, folds his arms across his chest. This is the Non-Buddy pose.

"Well ah, your mother says she ain't seen you in a month," he says, quietly, like he doesn't *really* mean to contradict me.

"She ain't seen me in a month Sarge cuz she changed the fuckin' locks on the doors."

"She said you were gettin' outta hand, Joey."

"Not me. I was makin' her new boyfriend nervous, that's all—and she must get laid, Sarge, at all costs. But that ain't my home anywayslywise. Not anymore."

"Yeah, Joey, but you ain't been at Sherman Street neither. I was over there the other day and Mr. Franklin said he hadn't seen you in a coupl'a weeks."

"They're all fuckin' nuts over there," I say. "That's like a druggie rehab place. I never had no problem with that shit."

"So where you livin' then?" For a minute Sergeant Upton's Dog Day face gets partly cloudy. I get the feeling this is its natural state, don't ask me why.

"Here and there . . . wit friends," I answered. Well it's true, Kev—*you* know that. Course I can't tell him exactly where—people are so touchy about some things.

Sergeant Upton looks me up and down. Not like you used to, Kev.

"You eatin' at all?" he goes on. "Looks like you're wearing away to nothing, Joey."

Eatin'! Like I got the time for that shit, man!

"Look Sarge, I'm fine. It's rainin'. *Rainin'*. And I was spinnin' in the rain. Big diggity deal. I gotta get goin' now. You should too. There's a bank bein' robbed somewheres, and some old lady's gettin' the shit beat out o' her even as we speak." Remember we used to say that to the cops all the time, Kev, when they'd be hasslin' us or askin' too many stupid questions because we were just . . . *breathing,* for Christ's sakes. Hanging here and there.

"Joey," he says, his eyebrows lowered, his gray eyes sad—which is weird, it's raining. "I'm . . . sorry about what happened. Everybody is. But . . . you gotta . . . you gotta move on, you know?" He makes this churning motion with both his forearms, like he's runnin' in place.

"That's what I'm doin'," I answer, doing the same thing with my arms, but pulling away, backing up, melting into the rain. I dodge up a few alleys, cut through the school playground . . . just in case he follows me, Kev. I can't have that. I wanna go home now.

It's just getting dark when I get home, up here on the hill, where the easty east wind meets the westy west. The wrought iron gates are locked up for the night but I'm over them like in a dream, Kev. Nice view of the city as the sky melts into the dark ground like a painting left out in the rain—everything blurs, day drips into night. I breathe deeply. Rain, Kev—nothing but rainly rain. Like liggity life. I unfold my washer machine box, which I've stashed under some leaves, then crawl inside, bringing the leaves with me. I lie flat on my belly, staring out at the rain.

The rain. Listen to it.

My head is full of thoughts tonight. Thoughts of you, Kev. My head full of you. Am I doing this? Or you? Or is it the rain, parachuting thoughts of you down to me, soaking my hood, wetting my hair, leaking into my brain? I guess it doesn't matter.

These thoughts:

Tonight, it's the times you used to do handstands—no reason—and your T-shirt would fall down loose over your head. It'd cover your face yeah but more important I could see your chest and stomach, the top band of your white underwear blue stripe against the just-starting tangly auburn hairs running south from your belly button. Or north, since you were upside down. Kev, do you remember Sister Claire from Eighth Grade? She had a nervous breakdown and I guess the archdiocese or whatever had shut down the nun hospital, so she went to this other hospital and when she came back a few months later she was wearing sandals and was like into incense and weird religions? 'Member when we'd have Morning Prayers after that, she'd always look at the crucifix on the wall above the blackboard and say, "Forgive us for worshipping you in these symbols, when you are everywhere?" She said it was some kind of Zen thing, or from India or someplace.

I never knew what she meant, Kev—until I saw your underwear like that, and those tiny reddish-brown hairs on your stomach . . . you were everywhere, Kev, and you were everything, but I worshipped you in those kinda small, dumb symbols—

This never happened, Kev, but I imagine you handstanding in the rain, how those hairs, your hairless white pecs, your red nipples, might look wet. Shiny wet with blessed rain. That thought makes me quiet. I have to lie down on my belly and think when I think like that Kev. There's other thoughts a million others that'll do that too, make me lie quiet and stare so hard I can see them, almost see you.

What hood? I'll explain. It's part of the uniform. You can't be Southie without the uniform. (I'm not talking to you now, Kev, but the people out there. They have to know all this.)

The uniform: this time of year (it varies with the seasons naturally). Fall. Hooded sweatshirt. Black or navy blue. Sometimes red but no more. Got no love for red no more. Hood up. Picture the five of us, slinging badass down the nickity nightly streets dressed this way. Our streetlight shadows looked so cool—remember, Kev? You commented on that once. (But now there's only one, I sling alone—kind of.) (Sometimes we'd let our dicks hang out as we walked at night, just on a dare. 'Member? I do.) It gets colder, you throw a flannel shirt on top, hood still up. Hood always up. Except when you go in a house, or chiggity church. That would be rude.

Momma Nature's uniform now: Fall nights. Leaves rattling across my footsteps like black cats. Quick cloud-scudded Moons in alleys. Then they're gone. Trees, gnarly, reaching out to grab you. Just one more thing that can get you 'round here if you don't watch yourself. Even if you do watch yourself. Like when we climbed the—

So why do I like the rain. Okay. **Reason Number 4322: Each little drop bringing thoughts.** This can be good and bad. But they keep you occupied, these thoughts, no? Each little drop has a thought in it, you can see them, like each drop is a clear wet glassy balloon floating down with a little thought-picture inside it. I lie on my belly up here at my home on the hill where the easty east meets the westy west and raise my head, peering straight out at these rain-thoughts: here's a thought there's a thought everywhere a thought thought. Keeping me from thinking about the way it looked when you were falling from the—

Reason Number 514: It's clean, the rain. It's cleansing. It washes things away. Dirt. Blood. I asked Ma about a month ago, right before she changed the locks: "What's the difference? That place around the corner where you brought the tablecloth when everyone was supposed to come for Christmas Dinner but nobody showed so you got drunk and cried and smashed dishes the rest of the day? Old Colony Cleansers? Then there's that other place farther up Broadway, West Side Cleaners. I been wondering, Ma—cleaners, cleansers. What's the difference?"

She just looked at me, got on the phone, closed the kitchen door started crying to Ruthie up the street I Can't Take No More, He's Goddamn Crazy. But now I know, see. Cleansers use rainwater. But for some reason it's this big secret, I went into Old Colony Cleansers the other day to talk to the guy, and he denied using rainwater. But I know. The rain is cleansing. Of course they use rainwater.

"Don't worry," I smiled, walking out of his place. "I won't tell anyone."

The squirrels are asleep now, Kev. It's dark out here at my home on the hill. At least they're pretending to be asleep. I think they're like me, lying quiet on their bellies in leaf nests. Peering out at the rain. Quiet. Thinking. Maybe trying to forget. There must be some squirrel thoughts they wish to have washed away. The time one of them got run down by a car; the time one of their babies fell from the nest—

Tonight, I'm thinking maybe it was Peter who came up with the idea; each night I have different theories, Kev. Not that it matters—it doesn't. Not now. But I just get to wondering. I'm not placing no blame, Kev, and it's not like we hadn't talked about it before. . . . I just get to thinking If Peter Never Said That, That Night, you'd be here with me now. Or would you? Or are you anyway?

Can you help me out with this, Kev? I'd like to know whose idea it was—not that it matters now. We were down at the beach, remember? Probably the ten thousandth time we were down there—drinking, goofing—but different this night: the twins Peter and Paul were leaving the next day for the Marines. Little Will was starting electrical school the next week. After that, there'd just be me and you. You remember. It was our last night together, so we were hanging and drinking.

It was our last night together. September 3.

We were looking back—at least you guys were. I was pretending to. I was looking forward, Kev—you know that now if you didn't know it then. For the first time in my life I was looking toward the future—could *see* it almost. "When the others are gone," you said—remember, Kev? I do. It wasn't raining. I really didn't know about the rain then. It was raining moonlight—it rose like a spotlight from the end of the ocean, piggity pink—never seen a moon like that before, Kev. It pumped up over the ocean like a gas station sign the color of love, swollen and pinky-orange. The sand was water-bottle warm from the day's heat, we were sitting on it, our backs leaned up against the sea wall, facing the ocean. I could just make out some of the harbor islands, loosening up the sea for the shock of the continent ahead. (The harbor islands. Remember when we were twelve, Kev, and me and you were down at the beach on our bikes one night, and we gave those islands names? Our own names? *Crayola Island* you called one of them, Kev, you always wanted Crayola crayons when you were a kid and you never got them. Remember? "And not the little box neither," you said then, Kev. "The big one with sixty-four, and the built-in sharpener." I called one of them Mystery Island. Which was lame. I guess I'm just a lame kind of guy, Kev. Then you named the third one *The Island of Unopened Packages.* I loved that, Kev. *The Island of Unopened Packages.*) Back to September 3 now, Kev. The gang's last night together. Sitting on the sand drinking. Just a few months ago, Kev, if you can believe it.

You had your knees up like you always did. You were wearing your baggy Notre Dame nylon basketball shorts. They were shiny in the moonrain. So were those little golden hairs on your bare legs. I knew each one, Kev—like stars in a constellation that only I could see. While you were laughing at something Little Will said, you unconsciously kicked your Nikes off, Kev. They smelled a little. Like grass. You wiggled your toes in the sand. Just then my own feet shivered.

I just keep wondering—again, I'm not looking to lay no blame—I just keep wondering whose idea it was. It might have been Paul's. "No one's ever done it before," I do remember him saying that. His brother Peter agreed *something* crazy was called for—The Gang's last night together. Somebody said what if we steal Old Lady Gallagher's car and drive it into the ocean—remember that old Rambler she had, like forty years old? With like twenty miles on it? She used to call the cops on us for just leaning against it when we were kids. Remember when we were kids, Kev? We got matching crew cuts for First Holy Communion when we were seven—so many thoughts, Kev. They parachute in with the rain, every drop a thought. The rain washes thoughts away, Kev, but it also brings thoughts in—weird, huh? In, now out—like breath, Kev. Like the ocean. Like anything living—I bet you Sister Claire could explain it all. But they shut down our old nun school last year. There weren't enough nuns anymore. The ex-nuns are all at the gym now, Kev, losing those flabby triceps. Getting fit. Drinking Crystal Lite. Or something.

The car idea kind of didn't go anywhere—we hadn't been much into running lately, Kev, I think that's how we knew we were becoming men—no more running, and of course stealing Old Lady Gallagher's car that night would have meant running. Kickity kids stuff, Kev.

And then somebody mentioned doing the other thing. Climbing to the top of the Edison Smokestack.

Little Will didn't want to, which I thought was weird, he was the smallest and almost always trying to keep up with the rest of us. Not that he *said* anything. C'mon—you know him, Kev, he'd die before he'd say anything. But he got real quiet, started drinking faster. And you remember what a mournful drunk Little Will was. The twins though—they were psyched, all muscle and bone and blood—Kev, there's a thing in life that's tender and healing, and it finds delight in all things that grow. (Here's a for instance—when the oak leaves push out in May, and they're the softest green you've ever seen, the squirrels have a ceremony—they told me so—and delight and wonder and gratitude shine in their mirror eyes.) But Kev there's something else that snarls and eats and tears and rips—and whatever that something is, it flowed through the twins like . . . blood. Sniffing this kind of thing out, they lived for it really. The way I live for the rain now. The rain versus this other thing—it's the eternal struggle. I should know, Kev, I'm right in the middle of it.

We decided we needed spray paint—not that people wouldn't't've believed us, that wasn't it—the thing was, you take the trouble to do something like this, you got to leave your mark. For the whole world to see. "JUST US," that was what we wrote all the time growing up when the five of us did something. We'd spray paint JUST US.

"We'll meet you over there," I told the other three, me and you, Kev, were going to your father's garage to nab some spray paint. He'd died three years before and your mother hadn't had the heart to clean it out, your Da's garage. Neatest garage in Southie, all kinds of tools and gadgets and wood and shit—like a suburban garage, a Mr. Dennis the Menace garage, all those tools and very little to do with them. Your father. Remember when he died? He'd never said an out-of-place word in his life—then the week before he died he spewed nothing but nonsense. Must have been the medication.

I went with you the last time you saw him alive, the day before he died. Remember? Three years ago. You said I was your brother when the big fat black nurse said Family Only. I felt good about that, Kev, although I felt a little guilty feeling good when your father was dying. Man, what a sight he was. All those tubes sticking up his nose and in his arms, and his eyes big and buggy, like he was a specimen the hospital had captured and they'd pinned him under bright fluorescent lights for the curious to gawk at.

I wanted to hold your hand then, Kev, entering this Cold Zone. I could tell you were close to crying. I guess you know that now, that I wanted to hold your hand.

"Hey Dad," you said in a little voice. He was staring at the ceiling. "How you feelin'?" He just looked at you. He glared at me for a second and I got the creeps. Then he looked back at you. Everything was quiet for a while.

But then, "Not so good!" he chortled all of a sudden, in a voice way too loud for his own. We both jumped. Remember?

But the weirdness was just beginning.

"That's right, not so good. Not like Higgledy-Piggledy over there," your Da went on, tossing his head to the empty chair in the corner. (I didn't like that chair, Kev—it was just simulated wood and red fake leather upholstery, it looked innocent enough, but it had a bad feeling about it—not the kind of chair you'd pick out for your home. Institutional Furniture. Why do they make that stuff, Kev? Is it so inappropriately good feelings will be banished from certain places? Hospitals? Offices?)

"Who, Dad?" you asked. You couldn't believe it. I could though.

"Higgledy-Piggledy!" he repeated, annoyed at us, nodding again to the empty chair. "Comes in to visit now and then. Looks like the piggity picture of health, doesn't he? That billity bastard!" Then he started laughing. Not his normal laugh at all. Vinnie Price material.

You went into the bathroom then, Kev—when you came out a few minutes later, your nose was red. I knew you'd been crying—I'm sorry. The man who knew everything, who never made a mistake, who yelled at you when you fucked up stupid useless Handyman Junior projects he'd give you, who always told you what to do—was totally wigging out. It must have been a big-ass shock.

"Higgledy-Piggledy's mickity mad now cuz I didn't introduce you," your Da said when you came out of the bathroom.

"M-mickity?" you said.

"Yes, mickity. Of course mickity. So let's observe the piggity proprieties. Higgledy-Piggledy, this is my son Kevin, and his friggity friend Joey. Boys, say higgity hello to Higgledy-Piggledy."

You just stared, Kev, your beautiful mouth open like a kid.

"Wassup," I said with a nod to the institutional chair, just to appease the silence.

We left right after that. I saw your finger when you pushed the elevator button, trembling—I wanted to hold you then.

But I didn't do anything. When we stepped out of the smelly elevator into the lobby you stopped, like you didn't know what to do anymore without your Da telling you. You turned at me. "What should we do?" you asked, hoarse, biting a nail—your green eyes then,

Kev—ablaze. So lost. I had to look away for a minute to keep from holding you forever.

But I pulled myself together.

"I'll tell you what we should do," I said. "I say we get the figgity fuck out of this higgity hospital."

Your mouth fell open. Your sandy eyebrows jolted up. I kind of shrugged my shoulders. I mean, what else was there to do, Kev?

We headed for the door. Then you started laughing, Kev. Quiet first, but then so loud hospital people in half-glasses poring over Accounts Payable computers at the front desk looked over stern at us. I started laughing too, and for ten minutes waiting for the stupid bus that's all we did, laugh. Holding our stomachs. And that's when we started with the nonsense in our speech, Kev, the liggity language, a tongue all our own. A survival thing. It spread to the others too, Kev, the twins and Little Will, but only when they were drunk or high. Tell you the truth I think it bugged them that we had this thing that was between just me and you. (The squirrels do it too, Kev, but I think they've always done it. Maybe it's this ancient thing, and your Da just like tiggity tapped into it before he diggity died.)

Kev, you never cried for the Da again. But you know really, why should you have? You were just another piece of wood to be shaped and cut by him, chucked onto the scrap heap when you didn't turn out quite the way he'd planned. But the piece that was rejected, Kev . . . what's that old saying? I forget it now, but I know what they meant. Really, I do.

Really.

"Orange or black?" you asked me in a crew-cut whisper when we got to your Da's garage that night. September 3. Two months ago— hard to believe, Kev. Of course he had spray paint, several cans of it. Three years dead and your Da still had everything you were looking for in that garage. Talk about fucking efficient.

"I dunno—what color is the tower?" I asked you—see, your question kind of yanked me: I was a jillion miles away, Kev, behind you looking at you right in front of me, thiggity thinking.

"I think like . . . like brick. Like the color of bricks," you answered, your rich voice so soft it was like those milkweed seeds that are unlucky enough to blow into Southie from somewhere out in the country. You were holding a spray-paint can in each hand. Like you were weighing them. You paused—I heard it in your voice. You were definitely . . . stalling. Waiting. For what, Kev?

My heart started beating funny. I noticed how quiet it was in your Da's garage (it could never be yours, Kev, that garage), how dark too. But still I could see the color of your hair, Kev. That beautiful thick red hair, cut in a flattop. Sticking out the opening in the back of your navy blue Red Sox baseball cap. Not angry brilliant red, like Margery McKillop's (remember her, everyone used to tease, "Hey Margie, what color's your bush?") or ugly matted frizzy red, with Carl Sagan-like numbers of freckles, and skin the color of flour to match, like my poor cousin Joe Barry. Yours was like . . . Golden Red—the color of many of the sunsets up here at my home on the hill, the only good thing about the non-rainly nights. Kevin Red, they should call it, a color all its own, and sell it in tubes to artists agreeing to paint only the beautiful, the sublime.

I'll tell you what I was thinking, Kev, what I was thinking when you asked me what color spray paint we should take with us. I was thinking of some words. I don't know where I'd read them—somewhere a few months before that night, maybe in a magazine at Dom's Barbershop or something. *Do's and Don'ts for a Man* was the name of the article, some stupid article about the things you could and could not do as a man. *You can stand up to pee. You can carry everything you need in a wallet.* Other stupid stuff. But one part of that smarmy article really jumped out at me, Kev. *There are three places you can't touch on your buddy's body: his privates, his face, and his hands.*

Kev, I don't know why—but it all changed for me then, with that article. The things I'd never been able to admit, the half dreams of you and me I'd wake from, shake off as just dreams—they took on a shape after I read those words, Kev.

They took on a name: Shame.

But Desire too. Starting at my toes and burning up until sometimes I couldn't see for wanting you, Kev. A combination of Shame and Desire, some bastard child of these two, like they'd met at a dance and went out and fucked in an alley shitfaced and had this bastard child. Nothing in common and a lousy miggity maddening match to begin with, but now there's this kid that half the human race is descended from.

Or ten percent anyway, Kev. Ten percent. So they say.

It started with your hands, with wanting to touch your hands—I allowed myself that much at night in bed in my dark room, neighbors fighting next door: *Why can't I touch his hands?* I'd ask myself, the ceiling, the world, God. *Why not? What's the big deal about his hands?* At first I'd been confused—a man touches another man's hands in a handshake, right?—and I hadn't known exactly what they'd meant, Kev—

—until that moment in the garage when you paused, your back to me, each of your hands holding a can of spray paint.

"Then . . . then we better go with the black," you said then Kev, and you put the orange spray paint back on the shelf, neat like your father would, label facing forward. Then you put your empty hand down on the worktable beside you. You rested it flat, palm down.

I knew then, Kev. I knew in an instant what they'd been talking about in that article. I watched that resting hand, Kev—the smooth skin of it. The little red hairs on your wrist. The supple fingers, the gaping thumb, the bitten-down fingernails, two of them dirty—and I knew. This hand of yours, this right hand, owned you, Kev. It knew you, did things for you, *was you*. It crossed the boundaries between you and the rest of the world, effortlessly—it could give me a sweaty high five during a game of Outs one minute, ruffle the greasy grateful fur of a stray dog on Broadway the next, then an hour later in your home . . . in your room, Kev—

Private and off-limits, Kev, but in that instant in the garage I saw all those things that hand did and probably did.

It would smooth out the downy stray hairs of your flattop, after you'd slide your white T-shirt off. It undid the top button of your cut-offs. Oh Kev—

—it glided beneath the waistband of your underwear. Soft on softer. It carefully wiped the crumbs from your red lips, after you ate. It cleaned you. It shook you, after you peed. It wrote down doubtful answers to confounding essay questions during Fifth Period English Class—

—and at night, Kev, under your covers—

—(even now I feel the fire of this thought Kev, and I have to pray it doesn't burn away tonight's rain). Like I was saying, under your covers—

Oh Kev—

. . . it was no stranger, this hand under your covers. It sailed up and down your body, the charted waters that we all knew and saw every day yeah—but the unknown places too. The deep places, Kev. The secret places. The caves wrapped in constant night, the bottomless lagoons. The ends of the world, Kev, where the ignorant mariner proves Columbus wrong, and falls off.

I saw all this as I watched your hand in your Da's garage Kev.

I decided I wanted to be part of all that.

So I reached out, Kev.

If there was a power Big Enough in this universe to stop me, Kev, they haven't thought of it yet. We hadn't turned the garage light on for fear your mother might discover us in our piffity pilfering, and we were standing there, a bit of the streetlight smearing through the diggity dirty windows. And I reached out. I watched my hand (with secrets of its own) travel through the space between us.

I extended my fingertips. I lowered them, softly as a lunar landing, onto your hand.

I did what I was forbidden to do, Kev.

I touched your hand, as carefully and tenderly as if it was your heart, beating.

Blessed be the beer that gave me the balls to do this. (I wonder if they make beer from rainwater?)

For a minute I was figgity falling, Kev, and the only thing keeping me standing in this dizzy world was being locked onto your hand like that. Cemented by the gentlest of touches. And as the garage spun around, I thought—*No wonder they've forbidden this. What wars would be fought, what business deals sealed, what dirty plots hatched, what bogus trials prosecuted, if all the world were to touch the hand of one they were forbidden to?*

You froze then, Kev. Of course. And started trembling, like electricity was jiggling through you. There in that dark Da crippity crypt of a garage, you know we could hear the cars roaring by drunk on the late summer night, but still it was quiet. Too quiet almost. I could hear your breathing. Could you hear mine? You were trembling, Kev, for only the second time in your life that I knew of—this moment right now, and the other time when your dying Da had wigged out in the hospital three years before. And you never had trembled before, Kev, when we took on the D Street Gang when we were sixteen, and five of them got us in that corner with baseball bats—remember? Or when we cleaned out that West Side barroom, after that stain Dougie O'Brien called your sister a whore? You were steady as a rock then, Kev. Or how about when the cops kicked and handcuffed us, Kev, for breaking into the liggity liquor store Christmas Eve when we were fifteen—you were defiantly self-composed then, Kev—

But now you were trembling.

Funny, Kev, how the gentlest of touches could do what baseball bats and ferocious stomps couldn't, make you shake in your size 11 Nikes like that. I know, Kev. I was shaking too.

You didn't move your hand away.

Time heated up, melted, stretched out. It seemed like a very long time, standing in that garage, touching your hand. I could smell old oil, tools, wood—and you, Kev. That little smell all your own. Kind of a combination between . . . oranges and grass. And something else. We stood there like this for a very long time, Kev. And the world started to turn into color. You didn't move your hand away, didn't turn to punch me.

Then you started turning. Very slowly, Kev. Turning around toward me. That moment of moments, Kev. It was like we'd been two rivers all our lives, running beside each other, in our own separate channel like, and now—now . . . what would happen? What would I see in your green eyes, Kev? The thing I was looking for, hoping for, scared shit of? Or condemnation? Accusation? Horror? I think I would have died on the spot, Kev, if I saw any of them bad things.

I panicked, Kev. I had to protect myself, see? I'd come this far, this far after so long, touched your hand, brought things to this point—but I couldn't go any farther. The fiery engine that was driving me on sputtered, ran out of gas. You turned, Kev. And I pulled my hand back and looked down at the oil-stained floor. As if the floor contained everything I was looking for, hoping for praying for, and not your South Sea-green eyes.

I couldn't look at you.

I could hear the blood thudding in my ears, Kev. Then I spoke.

"The others," I mumbled, keeping my eyes riveted on the unseen floor. "The others'll . . . they'll be waitin'." Like I gave a shit about the others right then. Like I could remember the names of those lifelong companions just then. Like I really wanted to climb the fucking Edison Plant smokestack and spray paint JUST US on its top.

"The . . . others," you echoed, and your voice was husky. Kev—I'll never hear your voice again—sometimes it just hits me—let me try this again—

"The others," you said, and your voice . . . your rich voice . . .

Excuse me.

I have to stop now and lie down for a minute and think of something else. **Reason Number 217: The Rain Makes You Believe You Can Start All Over Again.** Even when you know you can't. This period of lovely denial has a variable duration. Sometimes only a minute—sometimes more. But I'll take that minute.

Let me just take a breather for a minute, breathing in this lovely rain. **Reason Number 416: No One Can Tell You're Crying When It's Raining.**

Kev—

I hear a noise in the tree limb just above me. I look up—here comes one of the squirrels, Kev.

They don't come out too much at night.

He moves nimbly but slowly to the end of the limb right over my head. He stands up. He pauses. He folds his little hands across his white belly, leans his head down toward me. His black eyes shine in the rainly night, with tenderness. He looks like the kind of kindly house-calling Doctor they don't make anymore.

"A tough night?" he asks.

My throat is sore from the balloon of a sob that's stuck there, trying to get out. So all I can do is nod. He nods back—slowly, knowingly.

I take a deep breath. "Which is weird," I finally gasp, "because it's a rainy night, and I love the rainy nights."

"A *rainly* rainy night," he corrects. I smile a little. He's right of course. "But really, Joey," he says, "don't wonder at this irony. Every thing in this world, contains its opposite within itself."

I think about this for a moment.

"You sound like Sister Claire," I tell him, raising up on my elbows, sticking my head out of my washer machine box a little.

"My father used to sit outside her clackity classroom window," he answers. "She was wise. She knew stuff—for a person, I mean. Here," he says, reaching behind his back. "You should eat." He drops me down a chestnut. It's about the only thing I can eat now, Kev. It makes me feel a little better. So. Where was I? Ahhhh, your Da's garage—now I remember. As if I could forget—

"The others," you said. You were echoing my words. But I could hear confusion in them, Kev, like you couldn't understand why I was pulling back now. But now you know—right, Kev? Then you cleared your throat and said, "When the others are gone," but at the same time I said, "They'll be waiting for us." I gulped. Did you hear my gulp, Kev? I hadn't heard exactly what you'd said. I kept my eye on this oil stain on the concrete garage floor that looked just like Ohio but upside down. Just to steady myself, I was falling, now that I wasn't holding onto your hand anymore.

"Yeah. Yeah they will," you said, answering what I had just said.

I turned around and headed out of your Da's garage, Kev—empty handed but full of everything. Hope. Shame. Hope. Self-anger. And a punchy siggity sizzle from the holding of your hand, like I'd been whacked on the head with a two-by-four.

We took the ziggity zigzag shortcuts, to meet the others. By the time we got to East Seventh Street I was able to think again. By the time we reached East Broadway I started realizing you hadn't pulled your hand away, when I touched it. When we got to the corner of L and East Broadway, it dawned on me what you'd said. I replayed the words, in rhythm to the scuffling of our sneakers as we approached Power House Street. *When the others are gone. When the others are gone. When the others are gone—*

I guess it was about one in the morning then, and we were sliding down L Street toward the three-block long Edison Plant. We weren't really looking at it I wasn't anyway but I could kind of *feel* it looming above us in the nightly night, its hugeness blotting out the few Southie stars. I could hear its hum, and smell the tang of the sea (the ocean's right on the other side of the Edison Plant cuz I guess they bring coal in big boats to keep it running) but every step I took, Kev, brought me closer to the meaning of how you hadn't pulled away, and your words—When The Others Are Gone. My breath started coming faster, my fists clenched themselves involuntarily—when you become a man you don't want to run as much, kickity kids stuff—

I stopped.

Just dead stopped. You walked a foot ahead momentum then stopped too. You turned, I saw your baseball cap turning around to face me. I didn't look away this time. You looked at me. Our eyes locked. Your head lowered a little. I could just see your eyes peering out from under your cap's brim, they looked like this deer's eyes I'd seen once on Cable three in the morning couldn't sleep, some vulgar hunting show and they'd shot this deer through its heart and its eyes were liquidy and wondering why as it fell to the ground.

A late-night cab rumbled by us bouncing over potholes but we didn't care. Trash blew by in the puffy late summer stale-city-smell-ing air, but ditto. Nothing else in the world. "What?" anyone else would've asked me in a murmur but you didn't have to. Too old to want to run away anymore but not old enough to know what to say, or know how to take away the hands over my mouth, suffocating hands of everyone we'd ever known and everything we'd been taught for-ever all our lives by thought, word, and deed, including, how weird, the billboard right above you then across the street on top of the diner, an ad for soap, Lifebuoy it said in big letters above a man and woman hand in hand walking the beach, but not L Street Beach.

But your eyes tender cut through these gripping hands like a laser. Kev, if your eyes right then had been fierce, hard, they would've failed in this but they were gentle so gentle they tore the suffocating hands to ribbons. So I could say something. So I did. I didn't stutter when I said it, didn't pause or stare at the ground or scuff one no-sock sneaker against the other like a tard.

"You know when I touched you, I meant it," I said, "Kev."

A plane roared overhead just then so low I could see out of the cor-ner of my eye the little passenger windows full up with littler identi-cal miggity mannequin-looking people, these Other People who lead Other Lives of trip taking and major purchases and pension plans thrown like mattresses against the buckling doors of this world's Chaos pounding to get in. But our lives, really, aren't that different, us and them, we share the common American cup of problem solving: *they* are trying to find an architect who will expand their living space while preserving the Integrity of the Light that comes into their home, while *I*—at this point in my life, Kev—am trying to solve the problem of how to keep my hands clean, blood free, in between rainstorms. Not all that different really. Nor are the squirrels' lives all that differ-ent from ours—it's all about conundrums, Kev.

"What *your* problem is," one of the squirrels said to me just the other night, "meaning humans' problem—is that you people just don't know how to love. It's so simple. But you're always concerned with all this other useless crap—and you only go halfway with love, if you go at all." He shook his head. "We go all the way with love," he said. "*Our* problem is we only go halfway when we're crossing the street. Some kind of survival thing from ages ago I think, when we'd wiggity warily cross a meadow, stopping to look around every now and again." He sighed, shook his head. "We still haven't solved this problem yet."

"Jeez, that's easy!" I laughed. "Just go all the way to the other side, quick!"

"*You* go all the way with love quick," he said, hurt. "That's easy too."

Kev, some things are just meant to be. Or not. Which is it? How long did we stare at each other then, scared shit but unashamed, letting it all show in our eyes? Could've stayed that way forever, Kev. Maybe we did. Ten seconds? Ten minutes? Then Little Will's voice: "Yo! Yo! Up here! Yo!" Remember how deep his voice was, Kev, how very deep for such a little guy. His black hair was already receding at nineteen and his white full face shone like a little moon from the Edison Plant one story up half a block down as he called to us. They were waiting for us one floor up. We both jumped a mile, Kev, me and you like we'd been caught doing something which of course we were, expressing love in a No-Love Zone. We started heading toward him and the twins behind him immediately—but as we did you bumped into me on purpose, leaned your solid slightly sweaty body into mine. You looked up quick with that I-got-something-to-say-look.

"We got all the time in the world, Joey," you murmured.

Hmmm.

"What are you guys doing?" one of the twins hissed, appearing behind Little Will. "C'mon!" he waved. They were about thirty yards away one floor up. My head still spinning, I plodded along, you beside me, Kev. I never knew words could make you drunk. I half stumbled into you as we reached the building, then we cut up an alley running alongside. The moon was right above us, like a spotlight. We shimmied up a drainpipe, you first, Kev. Your lean calves, swollen with muscle, were lightly dusted with those little blond hairs of yours, things too beautiful to be dragged along for the ride through the mean streets of Southie. Sorry, Kev, but like I said I worshipped you through those small symbols. They were practically in my face, Kev, as you went up before me and I reached up my hands, Kev, and placed them there, then up behind the back of your baggy Notre Dame shorts, Kev, and felt the softest substance I've ever hoped to touch, Kev, which caused a volcano inside me and this softness surprised me as you were all muscle and bone and blood everywhere else, but not like the twins were. The others couldn't see us of course climbing up they could just see your head as you stopped froze and I liked the idea of other people almost being able to see what I felt for you, Kev, but not quite and I liked your discomfort like a joke wanted to see how you'd explain it, I felt more comfortable being the usual Wise Guy while at the same time doing what I never dreamed I'd have the balls—or the chance—to do—

You turned back down to me, Kev, your face like the sun before this all my life living in night and I understood every commercial then I'd ever seen, I was welcomed into the two-by-two ark of American Couples Culture and hadn't been thrown out quite yet because no one knew who I felt this Love for. "C'mon," one of the twins half-yawned, wondering what the delay was, you started laughing, Kev, and I wouldn't take my hands away, Kev, I was rubbing them where I wasn't supposed to not your hands or your face or your genitals but somewhere just as good soft yet firm and nothing else between them. You reached the roof of the little guardshack that brought you up to one floor up, Kev, you were still laughing and Peter said, "Is Joey playing games down there?" and then his brother Paul said, "No funny stuff now," not quite in the Marines yet but already on the look-out for the enemies of this Great Country, things that would undermine if not the Constitution, then Our Wonderful Way of Life. When I only wanted to love you, Kev. That's all.

I pulled my hands back, you moved on and I jumped onto the shingled guardshack roof and then walked over to everybody else and had never been so happy, Kev.

"What took yous?" Paul griped while Peter stared and Little Will swilled the remnants of his beer with joyless eagerness.

"Chill," you said, Kev.

There's this area where the first floor roof takes the corner which we did and then there's the ladder attached to the side of the building going up the side of the rest of the building to the top floor which is like the thirteenth no windows just light green steel all the way up and then the smokestack starts from the top way up there. Way up. One of the twins—I wasn't paying attention so I couldn't say just which one—was wearing socks so you gave him the spray paint and he shoved it into his left sock and we started up the metal ladder the twins were wrestling each other as each tried to go up the ladder first and then finally Peter whacked Paul in the back wicked hard and Peter flew up quick with Paul in flushed pursuit. Then you. Why, Kev? I was trying to hang back so I'd be the last and you the second-to-last so I could touch you there again, Kev, touch you other places but it didn't quite work out that way because Little Will whose round Irish face was full of woe I could see by the sodium light, seemed to suddenly make up his mind to do this and just *flew* up the rungs right after you. I had lit up a butt which I thought we'd share so I just finished it myself enjoying it watching how the smoke in the dead calm night went straight up like a sacrifice, not thinking there are times when God or whoever wants more than lousy smoke as a sacrifice, not realizing that perhaps Heaven is now a smoke-free environment not thinking this because see I was enjoying the possibilities that the future now held, the possibility of looking in your eyes while rubbing your ass and saying Forgive Me, Kev, for Worshipping You in This When You Are Everything to Me.

When the others were gone.

I launched my cig butt off the side of the building with my figgity flicking fingers. Then I walked over to the ladder and put my hand on one of the metal rungs, it was green too. I stopped for a second, surprised at how cold this half-rusty rung was. There is a thing that delights in that which grows, Kev, we talked about that already and this other thing that delights in snarling violence and blood yeah we talked about that too already as it flowed through the twins—but also there's this third thing, a cousin I think to the second thing that pumped through the twins, it's a thing that's changeless and old and unmerciful, a thing that remains cold and dark and jealous even in the summer, and I felt it then when I first touched that rung, it was cold and a shudder went through me, not so much at its coldness, but at this thing's hatred of the warmth, this thing's refusal to ever be warmed. Even in the summer. Then I started climbing.

Fast. Third floor fourth floor fifth floor lotions potions and notions and what the fuck were we doing this for anyway when you and me had a life to live now. As I climbed I looked up to see how far you other guys had gone, and first thing I see, there was the round rump of Little Will working up the ladder like melon pistons. He was further up from me than I figured he'd be, about thirty yards maybe. Then I got this stray thought from nowhere *I wonder if Little Will's ass is as smooth as Kev's.*

Sorry, Kev.

I didn't invite this thought, or want it even, and Kev listen I sure didn't worship Little Will the way I did you—the thought just came on its own, like you're standing somewhere all alone and then all of a sudden there's a bird flapping in your face in panic and confusion. *I must be wicked queer,* I thought next, then quick I was eight years old and watching TV with Dad right before he left for good and the news was on and they were showing a parade and the paraders looked nickity normal to me but slouchy slovenly Dad in his La-Z-Boy said, "They oughtta put all them queers on an island and drop the A-Bomb on 'em." And I didn't know who queers were then, but I remember thinking at the time they must be pretty bad for Dad to say that, he didn't even say that about black people and Dad didn't like black people at all. But Kev, even that tender childhood recollection went down in the face of your smile, the power of your words *When the Others Are Gone.* And as for wondering what Little Will's butt felt like, I figured just because you *thought* something that doesn't mean you'd actually do it. Cuz I wouldn't, Kev. Honest. Not with anyone but you. So I kept climbing, and looked at the only other part of Little Will I could see, his white legs and arms, flailing along up the ladder. He was moving all mechanical-like, I could tell he was wicked freaked, which is not a good thing when you're drunk and seven stories up, which he was, and every now and then he had to stop, I guess to wait for you guys ahead of him to keep climbing. I started going faster to catch up. A puff of blowsy wind came up and molested me through my baggy shorts on its way to somewhere else, and I thought how it must have stopped and run through me like that because it wasn't expecting me or anyone here up so high, then I thought of a poem we had to memorize in third grade about stopping by these woods at night or something and I made up my own version—just weird things you do Kev—that went like this:

This gust of wind must think it queer /
to find people this high with no elevator near.

Then I changed that or my conscience did to:

This gust of wind must know I'm queer /
cuz I keep thinking about Kev's rear

and I thought about what would've happened if I had recited that to the class back in third grade. Just weird things you thiggity think of, Kev. Then I made up a full, fantasy version of that poem, which I called "Stopping by Kev's Garage on a Snowy Night for a Blowjob." But that's private and I won't reproduce it here. (Kev, forgive me for worshipping you in these symbols, etc.) But I will say I got a woody while composing that poem, and it snagged on one of the rungs as I climbed up until it went away when I looked down at its weirdness and saw beyond it the roof, the first floor seven stories below, and this puking feeling spurted through me, so quick I looked straight ahead and kept climbing.

Then another gush of wind and another, dead calm in between, and looking up again I could see the back of Little Will's T-shirt puffing out in the wind like sails on boys/buoys out in the harbor walking on the water like Jesus and I knew then that the higher up we went, the windier it was getting. Not a nice wind from a nice family but an angry hot wind, the smell of it tainted and fallen like what vents out of subway grates.

I kept climbing. Then some brightness kind of lazily called to me from the left (I guess I was about eight or nine stories up by then, Kev, you guys must have been ten or eleven), these lights out of the corner of my eye and I just half-turned half-wondering Huh What's That and the lights were Summer Street, West Broadway, the whole sodium-spangled West Side *below* me, row after row of streets laid out *below* me, the streets we knew by heart by gum by sneaker, our streets, but not where they were supposed to be, not among me or beside me or around me but *below me,* where they'd never been before and it was like the view was sucking me Kev out of the corner of my eye I could see the ocean behind me yanking me like a tide, and all of a sudden this *whooooosh* running through me and quick I was sliding off the ladder into the dance of the slippery falling world and I pulled myself fast back into the ladder, too fast and I banged my head on one of the rungs BONG! it went and I closed my eyes against the whacky diggity dizziness. I felt some warmth leaking down my face and when you grow up where we did you know right away it's blood, again. I didn't really think I had a fear of heights but then again Kev I'd never been more than ten feet above Southie sea level in my life.

"I ain't afraid of heights, I ain't afraid of heights," I kept repeating like a mantra to an unconvinced god with gleeful punishment on his mind, but still I couldn't move and the blood was leaking down my face and into my mouth now. We all of us walk around all day squirrels too with this vast amount of blood in us without realizing how easily it can be spilled. I rolled it out of my mouth with my eyes closed still, then took a few deep breaths, I had those little pickely prickly things you get in your chin before you puke and my legs felt like they were somebody else's that I was just dragging along for the night. I opened one eye. Then the other. I looked at the rung right in front of me. It had some blood on it (not bad or scary blood, it was only *my* blood) but the important thing was the rung was not moving which was crucial cuz everything else was, or had been. (I'd really prefer to talk about the rain.) After a few minutes my forehead blood lava flow slowed to a trickle. I oozed out the last mouthful of it, carefully, closing my eyes as I positioned my head downward and rolled out its thought-provoking taste.

Then—slowly though—I lifted my head up. Then I looked up.

I couldn't see Little Will anymore. I couldn't see anyone.

I was alone.

Kev, did you know that people have cement inside them? Most people don't know this—it's like blood in that respect: Always there. We lug gallons of it around with us, blanch at the sight of somebody else's—yet how often do we realize One False Move, And My Blood Will Spill Out? Just like the cement. It's always there I guess, for I could feel it then, solidifying at the edges of my fingers and toes, then flowing inward, upward through me. Filling me up. Turning me into concrete. I tried to move my hands up to the next rung, but like I say by then they'd turned to cement. Half-heartedly I watched them remain bolted onto the rung in front of me—not the bloody rung but one five rungs below.

"M-move!" I commanded my hands, saying it out loud. "Fuckin' *move*!" The wind gushed and made a wind sound, but nothing else. I concentrated, *willed* my hands to move.

"Sorry," they answered, "we can't. We're cement now."

Sweat announced itself in tiny bubbles all over me. Not the kind Don Ho sang about that my mother liked. Unless maybe I'm mistaken. The moon dodged behind a cloud, like a woman turning away from the bloody finale of a violent movie her boyfriend has taken her to.

At that second, Kev, This New Thing sliced into me, a jagged knife of This New Thing (that nameless thing that makes people scream in mental wards), and it combined with This Other Thing that you get sometimes when you're crossing a high bridge on foot: the crazy desire to hurl yourself over the very edge that you instinctively pull back from. The first thing punched into me like a wave, Kev. At the same time the Second Thing grabbed at me from below like a vicious sucking undertow—the ol' one-two, Kev. I jammed my eyes closed again.

"Just go down, just go back down," some Selfish Gene spoke up then.

"The others—" Peer Pressure said, "the others will think you're a pus—"

"Fuck the others," the selfish gene interrupted. "Just go back down. *Now. Right now.*"

"We're going back down," I said out loud to my hands, like I was trying to fast-talk someone right next to me out of shooting me. There was this awful pause like in a dream before the bomb you're reaching for explodes—

"Not so fast!" my hands snarled. "It doesn't matter what you say—we're cement now!"

I knew I was a goner then, Kev, that it was as impossible for me to scuttle down from the ladder as it would be for me to climb up. The wind blew again, cold against my sweat. My teeth chattered together, twice. Then they turned to cement too.

For a few minutes nothing happened—it's wicked quiet way up in high places—and I was beginning to think my brain had turned to cement as well. But then something said it would be easier to just let go now, rather than wait until I plunged off from sheer exhaustion some higgity hell hours—or days—from now. Just let go. How so easy this would be. Cement, stubborn before, seemed to be okay with this last suggestion. I opened one eye. I watched the small finger on my liggity left hand spring free. I turned my eye to my right hand to watch it do the same. My right hand, Kev. A little black hair on the fingers, a few black hairs on the fist. The hand that had touched your hand. You remember, Kev.

Then I remembered too.

This hand touched Kevin O'Shea where it was forbidden to. This hand was not flung away when it did that. This hand has saved your life.

Kev, all of a sudden in those thoughts, cement melted. It was like I'd been penniless pleading at the door with an evicting landlord, and all at once Hey Wait A Minute remembered I'd won the lottery the night before and you laugh in his face and tell him to go fuck himself. This hand, this right hand of mine, I could see now, was a strong hand: strong enough to overcome whiskey-breath Father McCarthy red-face chortling (when he had his annual "Boy Talk" with us in Eighth Grade), "*That* perversion (you know the one, Kev) is the worst in the book!" strong enough to overcome my father's A-Bomb Gay-Bomb plans, strong enough not to despair over the fate of Francis "Faggot" McMurdy, who earned his nickname when he had the misfortune of popping a boner in the showers after baseball freshman year, and lived with that nickname until one rainy March midnight two years later he walked, just walked, into the ocean, and never came back, strong enough to dismiss every remark and nonremark, every billboard, every ad in the paper, every song on the radio, every TV sitcom, every yoked boy-girl couple joined at the hip or the hand or the mouth or the grinding groin parading unending before us. Strong enough to dismiss what the twins always said our constant companions along with Little Will all our lives, the twins had called Francis that name loudest and oftenest before he checked out even though they used to beat each other off, Kev, remember we caught them at it once and they said, "It's just cuz we're twins and there's no broads around to do it"? And remember how they howled, Kev, the twins and really nearly everybody else, the year that gay Irish group marched in the St. Patrick's Day Parade, how they howled when those poor brave bastards walked through the gauntlet that was the parade that year? 'Member how our eyes met, Kev, yours and mine, just for a second as they walked by? 'Member my own overly rouged mother, Kev, across the street from us shitfaced, a Virginia Slim thrust out from her lips like a rhino horn, as her and her boyfriend-du-jour (Denny, I think, 'member him, the plumber with the huge beer belly) held up the sign she'd made that morning GOD HATES FAGS. "What are you doing, Ma?" I asked her that morning when I awoke to the smell of cig smoke and magic markers. "It's just for laughs," she said. "Let 'em march in their own fuckin' parade."

In touching you Kev, *my* hand had been strong enough to overcome all those things—and more Kev. And as this occurred to me, I wasn't surprised anymore at all that *your* hand (not having pulled away from mine) had injected something into mine that was strong enough to melt cement like it was a bad dream WHEW! that you wake from and smile that it was just a dream.

I snatched my right hand away from the shocked rung like it was a feather, looked at it, turned it around, brought it to my crusty-blood lips and kissed it, Kev. As I did this I smelled you on my hand, Kev, and I kissed it again, placed this smell of yours on my T-shirt heart. Then I felt carefully at my forehead, at the bump that was already sprouting there.

Then I began climbing again, Kev, no problem at all like I was a careless precocious suburban kid going up the top of bunk beds, carelessly, happily and you waiting for me. Cuz you were, Kev. You were waiting up there at the bottom of the smokestack a couple of floors above me, you and the twins and Little Will but mostly you, Kev, and our future When The Others Are Gone. The light green steel-runged ladder curved out Kev at about the thirteenth floor, then went flat as it reached the roof of the power plant. Toward the middle of the roof there was a cage of two-story chain-link fencing, in the middle of which was another cage of one-story fencing with barbed wire at the top. In the middle of this area was this concrete and brick house like, out of the center of which rose the smokestack, like a big cannon pointing to the stars in a war against heaven.

I couldn't see the top of it it was so high.

But you know how high it was, Kev. God knows you do—

"What took you so long?" one of the twins boomed, he was twenty feet away sitting down with his back leaned up against the first fencing, smoking a butt his legs wide open his brother beside him same position like I was seeing double from my headwhack. Little Will was pacing back and forth spitting and smoking a butt too but like those expectant fathers you see in black and white movies. You were close to the far edge of the roof, Kev, looking at the unbelievable vickity view of the world including the ocean by moonlight leaking through late-summer clouds. But you turned when you heard Peter or Paul ask where I'd been. I watched your face, Kev, flushed under your baseball cap get whiter when you saw me, saw the dried blood of my face, you kickity came right over and it was all worth it, Kev, worth anything to see the look on your face, the way your voice sounded when you said,

"What happened, Joey?"

So very tender. Right here in Southie.

"I just bumped my head," I shrugged, like ahh it was nothing. You touched my face then, Kev (that was forbidden too in that stupid article), your index finger softly touching the bump, the cut as if to heal. There was a window underneath your armpit, Kev, and I happened then to looked through this and saw knee-jerk disapproval squirming across the face of Paul.

"Hey, Kev, you wanna kiss it and make it better?" he half-laughed.

You turned and (I iggity imagine) glared at him.

"Maybe I do," you said then carelessly, Kev, and you turned back to me and liggity leaned in and kissed my forehead.

"You okay?" you whispered, and my soul sprung a boner, Kev. That's the only dumb way I can say how I felt then.

One of the twins laughed then in an ugly way and you didn't even bother to look at him when you languidly snarled, "Fuck you, Paulie, go beat off your biggity brother," which of course shut them both up.

"They have only forgotten their Godlike perfection," Little Will joked, imitating the postbreakdown Sister Claire, who proselytized that there was no such thing as a bad person in this world, everyone was perfect and if anyone did anything hurtful or hateful they had merely forgotten their own God-made perfection and the merciful Christ Within. Of course we peppered her with absurd situations, urban myth-like atrocities of things we claimed to have heard about or read in the paper, What About if a Man Kills His Mother by Putting Out Cigars in Her Eyes, or What About That Guy in California Who Hijacked a Busload of Nuns and Force-Fed Them LSD Then Raped Them and Then Drove the Bus Over the Golden Gate Bridge, but to everything we threw at her she just smiled and replied, "They have only forgotten their Godlike perfection." So we all kind of chuckled at Little Will's joke and the fidgety discomfort it caused the twins.

A minute later me and you, Kev, walked over to join the others. The moonlight brushed the side of your bare legs and I saw the starry little golden hairs again. Little Will produced a peace pipe joint which we all smoked, eventually standing in a mannish spread-leg circle as we passed it one to the other, and soon the contrite-via-narcotics Paul leaned over to me as it was approaching roach time and asked, "You 'kay, Joey? That looks pretty fuckin' nasty, bud," and so peggity peace was restored in our time.

But all the same, Kev, I couldn't help half-looking at that soaring smokestack, how its top mingled with the little stars then vanished in the night sky, wondering over and over why anything would want to be so tall, so stupidly tall, so . . . *institutional*.

I guess it was around two in the morning when we landed with a plop onto the tar-paper-and-gravel surface of the space behind the two fences where the concrete house that held the bottom of the smokestack began. (The cops would ask me the time later and I told them, "Two," Kev, but it could have been two thirty or one thirty or three or one thirty seven but what difference any of that could make I don't know.) I guess the smokestack was probably about twenty feet in diameter at its bottom here, with a ladder going up the side, and it was skinny this ladder, like the one going up the side of the building we'd just climbed. This ladder was black though. Black against the dirty red bricks. There was kind of a weird humming noise coming from inside the smokestack. Little Will even in the semi-dark was snow-white against the red. But like I say, Kev, he'd die before he'd ever say anything. And I'm not kidding. The twins went first again, Kev. Little Will this time was reluctant and wouldn't go after the twins but I wanted him to so you and me could bring up the rear as it were and be together more or less. "Go ahead," I told him, jerking my head toward the ladder. Why did I do that, Kev? Why didn't I just say Little Will I Know You Don't Want To Go So Forget About It And Just Wait Here For Us, but something tells me he would have gone anyway, Kev, what is it about this place (where the highest thing you can aspire to is to be known as a Nut) that everything you think say and do must be wrung through the filter of What Will Everyone Say? I guess maybe it's because all most of us have here is our reputations, Kev. Or at least that's what we think. I was beginning to think differently ever since I had put my hands on your smooth butt, Kev. (Forgive me for worshipping you in these things. . . .)

So Little Will was stuck at the bottom of the ladder while the twins scrambled upward and soon were lost to view Kev the moon was behind the smokestack now and anyways these clouds that had been waiting in some dark alley of the sky came out of nowhere and jumped the moon and when they got through with her she was a bloody smear against the sky and not much else. "They're going too fast," Little Will said, looking up, his blue County Kilkenny (where the Lakes are) eyes growing wide in fear.

"C'mon, Willy-Boy," you said then, Kev, grabbing onto the ladder, "I'll go next and you can stay close to me," which of course was you all over, Kev. I opened my mouth to say something but then Little Will turned around and kind of mumbly said to me, "You'll be right behind me, right Joey?" and Kev, what could I say to that.

So deep biggity breath up we went.

First thing I noticed, these rungs were even colder than the ones we'd left behind on the side of the building, which reminded me of That's The Wicked Witch of the East, She's Even Worse Than Her Sister. Also there seemed something garishly ominous in the red light bulbs that ran up the side of the smokestack next to the ladder, each one imprisoned in its own little cage they kept flashing off and on which I guess they always did but being so close at hand they seemed to be screeching out a warning that we couldn't hear because we'd gone deaf. But I kept reminding myself Kev of your hand, my hand, the power inside those hands and When the Others Are Gone and I just kept climbing Maybe This Won't Be So Bad After All. And so we went up. And up. And up. I tried *not* to remind myself that the smokestack was twice as tall as the building upon which it sat. But as we got higher the smokestack started thinning out, and soon Kev the lighted-up edges of the Universe far below and beyond began appearing on either side of me. So I kept my eyes riveted to the rungs right in front of me. I was doing okay until a huge 747 roared by in its approach to nearby Logan Airport, and it was *below* us, Kev. Did you see that? Did you get as freaked out by that as I did? No miggity mannequin thoughts now, Kev—no theories about conundrum solving or anything else like that. Just one thought. *Fuck.* Which, despite its baseness, is closely related to the next thought I had:

God—

God, help me—

Look at the ladder! Keep your eyes on the ladder! the selfish gene said then, or maybe it was God, far away in Heaven watching us on His very wide-screen TV. Any suggestion at a time like this is of course a, well, godsend so I snatched at it. I looked at the ladder.

This ladder against the sooty brick was attached with metal bolts one on each side every four rungs, I noticed, but I also thought I noticed, Kev, that they were rusty and some of them looked like they weren't holding too well anymore. I can remember thinking how horrible it was that a ladder even went up the smokestack anyway, I mean why would they do that? Maybe to repair bricks that had fallen out once in a while? But whatever the reason had been, Kev, we soon learned no one had climbed up here in quite some time—if ever—cuz next I heard (and you and Little Will must have heard it too), "Fuck!" a story or two above us where the twins were, the unmistakable but indistinguishable growl of one of the twins. And then immediately following that, these weird coo-coo-coo, coo-coo-coo noises. The twins had come across a pigeon's nest built into the ladder and as we climbed higher we stopped and you yelled down, "There's pigeons up here!" and I looked up and saw Little Will's rump again and part of you and then above that there were three pigeons flapping around. Next I saw this stuff coming down, flying by me in the wind which had started up again, clumps of straw and some other unidentifiable stuff and rather than just bypass it the twins were pulling the nest apart and throwing it off into Space. Which of course was the twins.

We started climbing again after a minute and pretty soon we slowed down again and then we came to the nest, or what was left of the nest, and then I heard Little Will scream out. I looked up and one of the birds probably scared and homeless now had flown too close to Little Will's comfort and I looked up and saw it flapping between his face and the ladder and then I saw his left Nike slip off the rung and his body came down about one foot before he caught himself and he screamed a second time UHHHHHHH! I think you didn't hear him in the wind, Kev, cuz I couldn't see anyone beyond Little Will but he was blocking my view in that direction so I can't be sure about that. For a second I had doubled my clench onto the rungs as some part of me I guess was expecting Little Will to keep coming straight down knock me off maybe, but he caught himself in time. It felt like there was a hammer inside my chest banging to get out like an avenging ghost hammer from your father's dead garage How Dare You Steal Spray Paint—so I can only imagine what Little Will was feeling, who was never meant to climb ladders 500 feet above L Street but instead to drive on L Street as he came home from, or went to, Electrical Jobs until he died. How stupid, some people might be saying now, this is why most of these kids never get anywhere and you feel complacent, we get what we deserve for doing brainless things like climbing the Edison Plant's smokestack you think, and then you pick up a book about some bored patricians scaling Mt. Everest because it's there and you think How Noble, How Very Courageous and Admirable and you wish your daughter Brittany or your son Joshua would do such a thing to bring honor, distinction to you at your next suburban coffee klatch. Or whatever.

I reached up and took hold of Little Will's ankle putting my other hand through the rung up to my elbow just to be sure. "You okay, Will?" I asked, but my words were grabbed by the wind and hurled downward, as if the spirit of this place would fling anything of ours it could down to the ground. So I roared the words upward. His ankle felt like petrified wood and I knew then that he was a believer in the Cement Theory I had first come upon on the first ladder an hour ago. He didn't answer me. He didn't move. Neither did I. *We'll never get down,* I remember thinking then, Kev. And then after that: *There's only one way we'll get back down.*

Idle thoughts will go on, Kev—I don't know why—but it's like a car roaring in fifth gear 2,000 miles an hour smoke bursting out the engine and it just happens to slip into neutral—for a second, just a second, and I found myself thinking of these steel rungs in front of me, the steel rung my left hand was frozen on to. I thought of the factory where these had been manufactured—somewhere in the Midwest, I thought. I wondered whether this rung had been painted black at the foundry, or had that happened later? I thought about the people who might work at that factory—I saw them taking lunch, or talking to each other, looking up with welding guns in their hands and goggles across their eyes—I wondered what they might have done if some angel had whispered into their ears, "Make this rung extra strong, for by-and-by a young man will be clinging to it for his very life." Would they then look up at the large clock on the wall, speculate how much time—if any—they could devote to this? To making this rung a little sounder? But even idle thoughts all lead back to the same thing, Kev, for then I had a picture of the large clock on the factory wall (institutional of course) its hands spinning too fast out of control and I thought Why Am I Thinking This? And then I realized I was seeing Time Fly, just like we'd soon be flying off into space—all roads lead to Rome, Kev—who used to say that? One of our teachers . . . never knew what she meant till this moment. Amazing, the amount of enlightenment up on that smokestack. But Kev—Kev—you were waiting for me for the rest of our lives. Again that realization jolted through me—nothing else mattered. I felt myself again.

I squeezed Little Will's ankle, screeched his name again. His face was buried into the rungs. He was shaking. This high up I noticed now the smokestack was resembling more and more a needle, tapering to a thinner and thinner end. There might have been two feet of smokestack now on either side of the ladder. Who's fucking idea was this anyway? My heart was saying You and Kev Forever, but to be honest, Kev, my brain was freaking out, my body. If only I couldn't see the curvature of the earth to my right as the ocean slid out to Forever, or the twinkling skyscrapers half a mile away beside us, and behind them nothing . . . nothing. Just screaming, empty space too high up. Then I heard somebody yelling something from above. Not Little Will—he was right on top of me—but one of you guys way further up.

"What'd they say?" I shouted to Little Will. "What did they say?" I began shaking him by the ankle. He half turned a flour-white face down to me. I hardly recognized him, Kev, for the fear. Then I guess he must have seen beyond me below me to the world waiting down there some thousands of miles away. He whipped his face back and buried it into the rungs again. He started shaking harder. "WHAT DID THEY SAY!" I screamed, really shaking him hard this time. He yanked his foot real hard then Kev, trying to get loose of my grip I'd much rather talk about the rainly rain, see, even then the clouds were building, puffing up like balloons I bet, moving in, the moon, the stars, didn't want to see what happened next cuz I wasn't expecting Little Will to yank that hard and he took my right hand with him Kev and I started losing my balance, all my weight on the right side there started veering off to the right and my hand slipped off Little Will's ankle and for a second it was just punching through the air hanging on to nothing so I threw it upward, Kev, I mean anybody in that situation would've done the same don't you think and I hit a rung with it and grabbed on to it with all my might cuz all my weight was on that side now Kev see, and I don't know I guess the bolts holding the ladder against the brick were old and rusty or something Kev cuz one of them popped out then Kev BOOOUSSSHHH! it sounded like, then another over my head BOOOUSSSHHH! then one up by Little Will, then they started popping out like dominoes Kev going up it was the weirdest thing, not below, not where I was but over my head Kev running up the ladder and the ladder started slowly coming backward and, "FUCK! FUUUUCCCCKKKKK!" Little Will screamed as he clung onto the ladder but the ladder had nothing to cling to anymore Kev cuz all the bolts were flying out now above me BOOUSSHHH! BOOUSSHH! one caught me right over my left eye Kev that's what the little scar is from, when I banged my head earlier there's no scar there now Kev but that flying bolt left a scar.

"C'MON! C'MON!" I screamed then to Little Will and, Kev, I started flying down the ladder no more cement taking two and then three rungs at a time then for some reason it sounded like machine gun fire all those bolts snapping off going all the way upward Kev where you guys were did you hear it I keep wondering, did you know what was coming Kev BOUSH BOUSH BOUSH and I saw Little Will's little white sock with the little Champion logo on it start to move backward above my head and it kept going and I couldn't figure out why until I realized his foot was going with the sock and his leg with his foot and his body with his leg and the screams with everything and the ladder snapped Kev about ten feet above me and if Little Will had only moved down with me Kev he would've been okay but how can you ever know these things Kev maybe he couldn't move anyway and the little Champion logo on his sock went flying by me with the same screams I hear when it isn't raining because the rain washes things away Kev and then the rest of the ladder I think it snapped some more cuz a big piece of it flew by the other side of me not where Little Will's part of the ladder had gone and a shape went screaming by me Kev then another, and then oh God another with more ladder and rungs clinking off the brick smokestack and dust and powder and ladder and bolts and screams.

And then it was very quiet.

Even the wind.

I looked down, Kev. I kept blinking I'm not sure why and I looked down.

A truck was moving along Summer Street. I bet the driver was listening to country music though I don't know why but I heard nothing so far up.

And then nothing else mattered so I climbed down.

I was halfway down the smokestack when the rain started Kev. Quietly, like it didn't want to cause any offense. The rainly rain. Soft at first like a whisper in a dream, then steadier. Straight down. No more wind. It began washing things away, cleansing things. It washed away the piss soaking through my pants, Kev, I'm not sure at what point that happened but I hadn't even realized it at first.

I got to the bottom of the smokestack. Little Will was on the roof of the power plant, right beside where the smokestack began thirteen stories up. His arms and legs were funny like a crab's, Kev, or like he was trying out for the circus we snuck into in Fifth Grade (remember?) and he'd been frozen in this funny mime pose. A pool of inky blood was spreading out from his head as I walked over to him. The rain made little droplets into it—like it was just another puddle on Broadway you'd drive through. I believe this is when I began to appreciate the rainly rain.

Little Will's eyes were open. His face was still very white.

"Little Will," I said.

There was this weird buzzing in my ears, Kev. I squatted down beside him. I took him softly by the arm, shook him. There was a bone sticking out of his arm, Kev, right near his shamrock tattoo. "Little Will, you gotta start electrical school next week," I said. He didn't answer. I shook him again. "Little Will, c'mon, the others are waiting."

The thing was, Kev—you were waiting.

He didn't get up so I closed his eyes, Kev. He had those beautiful blue eyes—remember? They open up again at night sometimes up here at my little home on the hill. They don't say anything they just look at me, Kev. "I have to go cuz Kev's waiting," I told him. Then I climbed down the second ladder. Thirteen floors I went. I reached the roof of the guard shack, hopped onto it, then shimmied down the drainpipe. I was in an alley by the side of the power plant. Then I walked out front.

There was a big piece of twisted ladder in the middle of L Street, Kev, when I got back down. It looked bigger and wider down here than it had when we were climbing it. There was another ladder section, smaller, that looked like it had smashed into the roof and the windshield of this old Chevy parked a little further down the street. Then I noticed there was a car in the middle of the road, its engine running and its lights on. There was a gray-haired chubby guy in this car, he'd stopped in the middle of the street with his car running, leaning out his window, looking up, squinting into the rain. He must have been driving by when the ladder and . . . and the other stuff started falling.

"Hey what the hell's going on here?" he said to me, like he'd been swindled or something.

I walked over to his car.

"Little Will," I said, pointing up, I had to yell the words, Kev, even though this guy was wicked close to me, because the buzzing clacking noise was louder and louder. "He needs a diggity doctor," I said.

The guy looked at me, then he rolled up his window and locked his door Kev, I didn't know why.

"Well, I told you!" I yelled at him as he took off. I banged my fists on his trunk, Kev. "I have to find Kev now, but don't blame me, I *told* you Little Will needs a doctor—asshole!" He disappeared down L Street.

What a world, Kev.

I walked over to the big piece of the ladder in the middle of the street. It was nice and clean, the rain was washing it. I walked down to the other section, the one that had crashed into the parked car. That was getting clean too. I walked further down L Street, past the end of the power plant, almost to the bridge, looking. Then I turned around and headed back. I heard the first sirens then, Kev. When I got back to the power plant, I hopped the fence, then walked up the other side of the building, right by the water where they dock the boats that bring the coal that runs the plant. There were a few young sumacs growing out of the cracked asphalt, their leaves limp and discouraged looking. I didn't go much farther before I found the twins. They were sprawled funny like Little Will, and half-in and half-out of an icky-brown security light shadow. They were resting quietly. For once. Peter had his hand reached out in the direction of Paul, three feet away. I got down on my knees into the gathering blood that was getting less bloody and more rainly rainish, and rolled Peter over, twice, until he was right on top of Paul. This wasn't as easy as it sounds, Kev, because one of Peter's legs was missing, and something from his insides spilled out as I rolled him. The buzzing inside my head turned into a clacking, Kev. I could hardly hear the sirens, the ambulances and fire trucks, and they were just pulling up to the front of the building then, I could see their lights flashing everywhere, barely hear their crackling two-way radios blasting tinny.

"You guys need a doctor too," I told the twins, weaving their smashed fingers together. "There," I said, finishing. I held my hands out into the rain, letting it wash away the blood. It was really starting to come down now, Kev. I paused. "Hey, ahhh, you guys—where's—where's my Kev, do you know?" See, I figgered it was time we told them, Kev. Told them about us. That's why I said *my* Kev. The twins didn't say anything, I guess this was a big-ass shock to them. Too bad though, I wasn't through yet.

"It's true," I went on. (I could hear more and more sirens but I didn't care.) I squatted down. "See, I love Kev. I've loved him all my life, you guys. And I always will. Not like brothers. I mean like *in love*. Like you guys love your girlfriends. Only better cuz I'm not gonna talk dirty about his body when we do things, the way you guys do. And we will do things. Everything." I waited for a response, Kev, but nothing—the ol' Silent Treatment. Well, whatever, Kev. You can't change the world overnight. Too bad if they didn't like it. But really, I wasn't surprised. "And you guys were wrong to scream at those queers that day o' the parade," I added. I paused. It hadn't been that hard to tell them after all, Kev. "But listen you guys—I'll still get you a doctor though," I said, standing up. "You're still my best figgity friends." I paused again. "Faggoty friends," I said, laughing and walking away. I headed further down the side of the building. I had to find you. There were some more limpy sumacs, a chain-link fence, and then another dock, this one old and like they didn't use it anymore.

You were on that dock, Kev. A few feet from the water.

"Kev," I said, trotting over. You were facedown—but not in a funny position like the others. Your arms and legs were spread out, but not in a weird, buggy way. Your T-shirt was gone though, except for just the collar, you know that band right around the neck. Weird, huh? I kneeled down beside you. The rain, Kev—it had washed most of your blood away. There was just a little here and there, Kev, which the rain hadn't gotten to yet.

I touched your hand again, Kev. Once again, you didn't pull away. I started crying, Kev. I guess I was just so overcome, that all the years I'd been dreaming of tiggity touching you, and now I finally was and you weren't pulling away. "Kev," I whispered into your ear, which had a little blood trickling out of it but not that much. I nuzzled into your ear, Kev, slid in beside you, threw my arm over your back. Your skin, Kev—so soft, and shiny with the wet. But it felt a little chilly, probably from the rainly rain. "Here," I said, pulling off my own shirt. I put it over your back. There was some blood on my shirt, Kev, I hope you didn't mind. Hopefully, I was keeping you warm. Our first night sleeping together. I licked the blood as it came out of your ear. "You better see the doctor too," I whispered, "but not just yet. I been waiting for so long, Kev." The clacking inside my head was very loud now, Kev. I didn't really care though; I only mention it cuz that's probably why I didn't hear the firemen, clomping over the dock with their boots, some EMT guys too, until they were right on top of me. "We got two more!" one of them shouted, scaring me.

"Shhhhh!" I snarled, turning and lifting my head, "he's trying to sleep!" I think I scared the shit out of the guy, cuz he just stopped dead and his eyes got all buggy.

"We got a live one!" one of the others beside him yelled, and then more people came running clomp clomp onto the dock with their big-ass clodhopper boots. They were all wearing big boots except for this one EMT woman, she had the siggity sense to wear sneakers.

"You're gonna be all right, you're gonna be all right," a third said to me, pulling at me trying to get me away from you, Kev, trying to get me to lie down. Some others started grabbing at you, Kev, flipping you over, touching you everywhere with their latex gloves like you had the cooties or something, putting their head up to your chest in the rainly rain. "GET THE FUCK OUTTA HERE! GET THE FUCK AWAY FROM HIM!" I screamed. Two of them tried to pin me down but I kicked one of them right in the face, BOOM! dove into the two EMTs who were all over you like a cheap suit. "LEAVE HIM THE FUCK ALONE! HE'S MINE! MINE!" but then four of them got me, Kev, they held me down and one of them big face right over my face yelled GIVE 'EM THE GODDAMN SHOT! WILL YOU GIVE HIM THE GODDAMN SHOT? And they stuck a needle in me, Kev, and somebody else said The Other One's Gone and then everything started getting funky, Kev, and the clackity clack inside my head got louder and then they let go of me and one of them took a scissors and started cutting off my gym shorts and underwear No I said, crying but they kept doing it I don't think they could hear me No I said again but they kept cutting and then everyone could see my bush brown against my white thighs and belly Kev, my pecker all small and shrunken up No I said in my head and then they brought down a black bag Kev with zippers and started putting you in it No I said Bring Him to the

Doctors but they put you in it No I said and then they pulled up the zippers Kev No I said and they wheeled you away, Kev, and the rain washed your blood away and that's the last thing I remember.

There's some blurs next: a hospital blur and a guy was yelling at a nurse cuz she said she couldn't find where my blood was coming from, some police What Happened Up There, Get Him Out of the Bag I said, then another fight then another needle and a big blur and a long several-week hospital blur with a guy who looked like Lenin with a little ugly scraggly beard and no kindness at all in his eyes I'd see him every day I think it was the nuthouse, Kev, and all I kept asking him all I wanted to know over and over Did My Kev Get Back from the Doctors Yet, What About the Others Little Will and the Twins, Are They Back from the Doctors Yet, and he kept saying Your Friends Are All Dead. And he finally made me cry and I think that's what he was after all along.

Bastard.

Then there's this dreamy time I only half recall and they gave me shots every day and pills and some of the stuff that I remember—I'm not really sure it happened, like when Ma somehow found out about me and you, Kev, and she paraded right outside my bars-across window back and forth with a butt in her mouth carrying a sign that read GOD HATES JOEY. And when I started crying she looked up at me and said I was supposed to laugh, it was just for laughs. Then she went into the bushes where her boyfriend was waiting and he fucked her.

Finally—this part is real—a woman saw me instead of Dr. Lenin with some kindness in her eyes and I told her everything, Kev, that I just told you and she said she could get me into the halfway house because I told her I didn't like to hear the screaming at night, it sounded like people falling off a tower, and why couldn't I wash my hands more often or at least be let out into the rainly rain.

And then they sent me back to Southie, to the halfway house.

So I was there for a while and they said I was getting better and then Ma got all freaked out when I went home for my third visit and merely asked her what the difference was between Cleaners and Cleansers. Plus she said I made her new boyfriend nervous and we can't have that, Kev. So she changed the locks and when they let me, more and more, out of the halfway house (which was really for people who had trouble with drugs, Kev, that one over on F Street) I didn't tell them that I wasn't going home. That's when I first started coming up here, Kev, to my little home on the hill. I found an empty washer machine box, Kev, and I stashed it under some leaves right by this stone that had your name on it while you were at the doctors.

It was one of the squirrels finally broke the news to me, Kev.

I think it was the same one you used to feed off your back porch.

"*Chk-chk-chk-chkchkchkchkchk!*" he jabbered at me, from a tree branch right above my little home on the hill. It was my first night here. I took off my baseball cap, scratched my head, tried to figure out what he was saying. It was obvious he was trying to say *something*, Kev. He kept staring at me with those mirror black eyes, his head cocked to the side.

"Can you say it in English?" I finally asked him.

"You were a friend of his?" he asked me, jerking his head at the stupid stone right next to me with your name on it, Kev.

"More than a friend," I answered. "Much more. I told the twins, so I guess I can tell you. He's the one I'll spend the rest of my life with. But what's up with this past tense? He's just at the doctor's."

The squirrel looked down at me, pursed his little squirrel lips. He sighed. "We loved him too," he said. "He was a noble one. He used to feed us. He'd always slow down driving his car down Broadway if one of us was crossing the street—you know we have a problem with that." He paused. "He's . . . he's gone to Heaven."

"I don't believe you," I said.

"He's gone to heaven," he repeated, tears filling up his squirrel eyes. They have gray tears Kev, like the rain—did you know that?

I looked at the stone right in front of me. It had your name on it. Some dates too.

Heaven—

I guess I really knew it all along, Kev—just so hard to believe.

I stretched out onto your grave, grabbed up the loose soil, the little baby grass trying to grow there that I didn't want to grow there. Something cracked in my throat. I started sobbing, Kev. I sobbed until I thought I'd die. The squirrels came down then, Kev. One by one. Unlike Dr. Lenin, who just stared at me, they came down. Slowly at first, tentatively, but soon they gathered all around me, snuggled in against me. They joined me in my weeping. They make this very sad sound when they're crying, like a cross between a whistle and a moan.

"Come back tomorrow night," the first one said after a long while. "We're having a service for him."

"Of course," I said. "I'll be back every night. This is my home now."

It was quite a funeral, Kev, the squirrels' memorial service. It started at midnight, that next night. We met at your grave. There were so many squirrels, Kev—they passed through the trees like the wind. They formed into units at the gate of the cemetery, and slowly marched out, me bringing up the rear. There were 40,000 of them marching up Broadway. Two hundred rows of solemn squirrels twenty abreast. Divided into various divisions, stepping in time to a dirge that only me and them could hear: "Requiem for a Fallen Squirrel," they told me later. With its own ritual march. Left front paw forward, slowly, then down to the ground head to the right, march; then right paw forward, slowly, then down to the ground head to the left, march; this was the opening contingent of the squirrel delegation, the Silent Mournful Marchers. These were followed by the Standard Bearers. Each one of these was two-fisted carrying a figgity flag-leaf: not a golden leaf, Kev, no not a red one neither, but black, black from decay and mildew, black from sorrow and agony, gathered in distant, brooding woods of ill humor by silent women squirrels who knew the meaning of sorrow, grief. Of what might have been. Of what should have been.

Next came the Soldier Squirrels, with their plaid forest green Tam-O'-Shanters and shields of acorn tops, slowly blowing "Amazing Grace" on pinecone bagpipes—it would've been enough to break my heart, Kev, if it wasn't already busted. On the sidewalks other squirrels gathered, some of them holding little tree-bark signs that read GOD LOVES KEVIN LOVING JOE. When we passed St. Francis de Sales Church, I heard the singing going on in there, 1,000 men and women squirrels up in the old balcony, singing a Mass for you, Kev. It was Eastern Orthodox Rite, but I knew you wouldn't mind, the rain touches us all. It was quite a tribute to you, Kev. For my sake they sang it in English, so I could understand.

And so on, Kev. Like I say. It was quite a tribute to you. Until the cops busted it up.

Whatever happened to respect for the dead, Kev? All of a sudden I was trooping solemnly down the middle of Broadway behind the squirrels, and the police came—the squirrels screwing of course up drainpipes, down gutters, to any tree within a mile. I suppose, Kev, if you had been some politician, some overswelled ego of a thing that coerced business deals and took smelly PAC money and railroaded various projects onto an already overburdened world, then the police would have been ordered to come and serve as the honor guard, rather than to break it all up.

"What's up, Joey?" Sergeant Upton asked, pulling up beside me, but I was too broke up to answer.

"Do you need a ride somewheres?" he asked, slowing his vehicle down to the same mournful pace I was walking at. I shook my head. Eventually he took the hint and left, Kev, but it was too late, the squirrels had already screwed. A prophet is never recognized in his own town, Kev—you know that now. And I don't want you to take this the wrong way, Kev, when I tell you that to the world, you meant very little. But to me, Kev, to me—

The rain's stopped now, Kev.

I got so wrapped up remembering all this and telling it to you, that I kind of didn't notice. It was supposed to be an all-night rainly rain. That's why they cancelled tonight's game at Fenway. Maybe this is just a break in the action. Regardless though the air smells clean, Kev, fresh and cleansed. My hands are clean. For now. As long as I don't think about whose idea it was that night.

I look up. My squirrel friend is back again, the one you used to feed. But there's a sense of urgency in his eyes.

"Hurry," he says.

"What?" I answer, sticking my head out a little from my washer machine box.

"They're coming for you," he answers, scampering down the tree. "They found out you've been living here!"

He's right, Kev. My head tenses and lifts a bit, smells the air like an animal sniffing danger. I see three cop cars, their lights off, prowling quiet sneaky like cats into the cemetery.

"Shit!" I snarl. "It'll be back to the nuthouse for sure!"

"Never mind that," the squirrel says. "Drink this." He holds out to me a half-chestnut shell, filled with this thick green liquid.

"What is it?" I ask.

"No time!" he says. "Quick! Hurry! Drink!" I hear car doors slam, harsh voices. Flashlights slice through the curtainy night air. "Come on!" he squeals. "Drink!"

I chug it down, Kev. Immediately there's this burning, then a thickness, an unbelievable thickness, on my tongue. This travels down my throat and then quick I'm jumping or spinning or falling or something, and Kev—Kev! Holy Shit! My hands, Kev! My feet! *My paws! My tail!*

"You'll be siggity safe now!" the squirrel says. "Safe from all their liggity lunacy. Follow me!" We fly up a tree trunk, Kev, scamper out on a branch, leap to another tree—but for some reason the cops' flashlights are on me as if they know it's still me, even though I've been turned into a squirrel. We get to the edge of the cemetery. I pause.

"C'mon!" the squirrel cries, but quick I get a better idea, Kev: I love the squirrels, I trust them, they know things, but I think *in this one matter* they might be misinformed, Kev—it's just a hunch but I've got to check it out, got to get to your house and see if you're not waiting there for me on your back porch with a bag of nuts. To feed me, Kev. I have this funny feeling you are.

I scamper down a tree, fly over the gates, dash up the sidewalk—

"Come back! Come back!" they all yell, squirrels, cops, but there's no stopping me now, Kev—

I come up to Broadway. I dart across the sidewalk, leap into the gutter—

I dash into the street—

I stop halfway. Just freeze.

Something makes me. I'm confused all of a sudden, or certain that I need to look around some before crossing the other half of the street. There's traffic everywhere, cars roaring—I look to the left and see the Broadway Bus barreling down, its lights blinding me and I can't seem to move, Kev. But then—wait, Kev . . . more important . . . much more important . . . I think . . . maybe . . . yes! *Yes!*

There's a smell, Kev, *that smell,* that wiggity wonderful siggity smell, my nose lifts up just to breathe it, to feel it, and then a noise above the traffic, a sigh through the trees, a gush from Heaven above. And I turn my head away from the bothersome bus lights, Kev, the blaring of its horn, and here it is again, sweeping down Broadway, dancing up and down, cleansing the entire world—

The Rain, Kev! The rainly rain! Ahhhhh!

I close my eyes, spin around, lift my furry tail, sing out, *"Chk chk chk chkchkchkchkchk!"*

Which, loosely translated, means just this, Kev:

The rain, the rain, the rain—

Oh, the rain.

Peter Pillsbury's Pride Parade

They found out when he was seventeen, and threw him out of the house. He spent three nights on the street, each evening venturing closer to Downtown. He became aware that something was going on on a certain block, cars would slow and young men very much like himself, their hands jammed into their pockets, would approach these cars.

On his fourth night out, hungry, shivering, an older man picked him up and brought him to a home Peter O'Sullivan had never seen the likes of before. He didn't realize at first that the man's kindness was based upon Peter's youth and looks, the baseball-trained body. Peter was overwhelmed by the man's kindness—though he never told him so—and had no problem repaying the man in ways the man liked.

During his fourth month of living with the man, Peter overheard him on the phone in the next room. Peter had been napping.

"Oh, just a little Mick nothing from Southie," the man was saying lowly to a friend. "Well darling, you haven't met him for the simple reason that he's too embarrassing to take anywhere. My God, his English is so bad I can hardly understand it myself. *But*... a hotter little nothing you never saw before."

Peter sat up in the bed. The clock said it was 11:12 p.m. The man was laughing now, that snickery laugh. Peter had been devastated but not shocked at his family's abandonment. He hadn't expected the man's generosity in a world that thus far had shown him only isolation and judgment, and the man's kindness had revolutionized the way Peter looked at things, at life—

He realized now how wrong he had been.

He felt something inside him close down.

He saw now that he was no more known, no more important to the man than the Aubusson carpet that lay beyond this bed, the armoire that had been custom made in Provence the summer before that house guests stole into the bedroom to stare at and touch with ringed fingers.

Peter got out of the bed, dressed, and slipped out the back door.

No one will ever laugh at me again, he said.

Ten Years Later

At the edge of the continent was the city. At the edge of the city was the ocean, and the sun lifted itself from this ocean and stabbed light into the city. It was a June morning. The sky gleamed cobalt. The world seemed flawless, which was only right, it was Gay Pride Day.

In one section of the city, wisecracking civil servants ran yellow crowd control tape along the edges of sidewalks. Street vendors hawking everything from rainbow condoms to hot dogs secured strategic corners. Police began arriving, establishing either a comic or resigned blue presence.

More passersby than usual were about for an early Saturday morning. Some idled about gawking. Others moved quickly in and out of the morning shadows. One of these latter, his step full of purpose, emerged from an ancient brick building still sleeping in darkness. Once a piano factory, then, for decades, a squalid rooming house, the building now housed a predominantly male gym with a two-month waiting list if you didn't know someone. Peter Pillsbury crossed the street and stepped into the sunlight, revealing a black nylon running suit with white stripes down the sides, and dark hair that became no lighter in the sun. He smiled back at a threesome sipping latte at a neighborhood café, one of whom had knocked at the window and waved to him, hoping for an audience. But Peter had no time on this day of days for idle chatter; besides, conversation was an investment for Peter, and he always chose his investments carefully.

The tolling of the old church bells fell upon him five minutes later as he inserted three different keys into three different locks at the front door of his building. At first he took this tolling, somber as it may have been, as a good omen—until the tenth gong fell upon his ears with a distinctly sour note. Ten? Ten o'clock? He lifted his wrist as he passed into his building's hallway, but was greeted only by tanned flesh straddling a fish-belly-white ribbon. He remembered that his designer watch was ensconced in the designer canvas gym bag slung just so over his shoulder. Turning, he caught a glimpse of the church tower as his front door closed behind him. He shook his fist at it in panic and anger—but not without a slight pleasure at the pumped state of his bare forearm, a pleasure that mingled with but did not overcome his sudden franticness. Ten o'clock! The old church tower must be wrong—yet he'd never known it to be in the five years he'd been living across from it. He was glad now in his anger—as if the church tower clock was the master of time and not simply its messenger—that the church had been defrocked, desanctified, and compartmentalized four years ago into thirty fashionable condominiums; but he would have been glad anyway. He remembered five years ago, his first year in this condo, when the church was still serving its original purpose, and he would see decrepit persons tottering to and from the building of a Sunday morning. Hardly people that added anything to their up-and-coming neighborhood. An old building was something else—that could be rehabbed—but Peter had little use for old people. And now, designer fabrics, techno-industrial furnishings, and scintillating conversations had replaced the hushed mutterings of bead-telling fools and their cane-wielding, echoing footsteps. Peter had been to every party that mattered in the church condos since its gala opening three years ago, and couldn't imagine life without the California-cool café on the ground floor, with its retro barbershop chairs and gothic, kiddie-pornish watrons.

But ten o'clock—shit! That left him one hour—one!—to ready himself for the Pride Parade!

He flew up the hall stairs two at a time, feeling the pleasant pump in his just-worked hamstrings. He could almost see, in fact could see in his mind's eye, the smooth, muscle-swollen calves as well. But in that same perfectly arranged chamber he could also see the stubbling hair on those calves and hamstrings that would have to be shaved. Oh it couldn't be ten!

Two more keys fumbled into two more locks and Peter Pillsbury burst into the clean, exact space he called home. The metal postmodern clock was staring him in the face—

Ten o'clock.

He felt the color rise into his already flushed cheeks. For an instant he was swept with the panic of the fire-stricken, who have only seconds to prioritize which objects will be grabbed in the mad dash for safety.

"*Damn* those New Yorkers!" Peter said aloud. He dumped the canvas gym bag onto the Italian white leather sofa. The two out-of-towners at Peter's gym this morning had been two of the hottest guys

Peter had seen in ages, so of course he had to talk to them, be seen
talking to them, to consume them as it were. They had shuttled in last
night for Pride today. Like Peter, they'd been getting one last workout
in before the high-noon kickoff. But now he could see that he'd lav-
ished too much time on them—after all they'd only be spectators,
faces in the crowd while he, Peter, would be on a float; and not just
any float, *the* Float.

Damn them, and damn the church tower!

But—

—at least he had determined by his conversation with them that
they weren't *quite* as hot, *quite* as handsome, as he himself was. To
calm himself before plunging into the chaos that must now inevitably
follow, he closed his eyes and saw their flaws again. Both tall, both
built, one a brunette, the other a blond, with all the right words spilling through bleached flawless smiles—nevertheless, nevertheless, all
this could *not* hide the crow's-feet of one and the weak chin of the
other. True, they were just barely visible, these flaws, and Peter had to
search somewhat to find them; but they were flaws nonetheless. The
thought of them now spread joyously through Peter like, well, crow's-
feet; for other than the occasional blemish, Peter *knew* he himself was
flawless, as did many others using the same criteria. He smiled. It was
always L.A. this and South Beach that, but it had been Peter's delight
to show these Big Applers that Boston wasn't the dreary little back-
water it was sometimes dissed as, and it's A-List could compare with
any city's. And Peter was about as high on his gay city's A-list as one
could get. If he were now running late because he had proved this
point—well, maybe it was worth it after all.

He opened his eyes and saw his face reflected back to him in one of
the eleven mirrors that were strategically scattered about his condo—
and he liked what he saw. Yes, he was hotter than they were, and yes it
had been worth it, well worth it, worth more in fact.

He recalled with a smirk what Brad Kent, a definite wannabe, had
said behind Peter's back two years ago, that you couldn't stand anywhere within Peter's 2,000-square foot condo and be out of view of a
mirror.

"Well," Peter remembered quipping at the time, "if the same can't
be said about Brad's place, maybe there's a very good reason for
that." That retort had henceforth become known as The Comment,
and it had cast Brad from the approaching glow of A-List Perhapness

back to some lesser, darker place from whence he'd crawled. Not that Brad was ugly . . . actually he was quite handsome—as long as the light was right. But only one year older than Peter, Brad looked ten. He was aging like a cheese, Peter thought. It didn't occur to Peter that he should feel anything other than delight at this. And what trip down memory lane would be complete without a revisiting of *the night,* the night of his housewarming that people were still talking about three years later. All of gay Boston was there, as well as just the right amount of hotties from L.A., New York, and South Beach. The hottest DJ du jour had been hired—Peter couldn't remember his name now—and then *he* had shown up, the man who had taken Peter off the streets years earlier. Of course two of Peter's friends were working the front door, making sure that the unattractive, unknown, and unimportant didn't get in, and Peter had given a slight shaking of his head when the man showed up, friends in tow.

"But I know Peter!" the man had blustered, his fat face reddening and a snarl puckering his face.

"Sorry," Peter's friend had said, smiling blandly as others younger and more attractive streamed in. "We only have room for so many, you know."

There *was* a God, for someone had at that moment asked, "Who's *that?*" and Peter, answering loud enough for the departing man to hear, said, "Oh, just a fat old nothing I used to know."

But enough—now to action! Peter flew into his bedroom and stripped off the designer running suit and black jock strap beneath. Ahhh, he thought, flexing in the mahogany cheval mirror, this morning's two-hour workout had been just the ticket, gilding the lily of his musculature with a fresh pump.

He thought again of the ad he'd seen a year ago in some fat smelly 'zine at the gym, the ad that had summed up life just as Peter saw it. The ad was too successful, at least for Peter, in that he'd forgotten the product it was shilling—but there had been an exquisite, blue-black-and-white butterfly, wings spread in full glory, antennae richly crenellated, sitting on a twig beside a tiny, rather ugly common moth, the color of crinkled parchment. The copy read: "Either You Have It. Or You Don't."

Precisely.

It had been an epiphanic moment for Peter. Irreligious not so much from a dogmatic point of view but more as a matter of scheduling, in his better moments Peter would feel a warm gratitude pulse through him toward whatever deities had deemed him one of those who had it.

He examined himself minutely, front . . . back . . . sides. He'd been highly disturbed to read on the Internet some months ago that the human body contained in excess of 420 muscles; previous to this it had been enough to work his chest, shoulders, and arms one day, his back, legs, and abs the next, with cardio every day of the week. But since that revelation he had been troubled by a recurring nightmare, in which all 420 muscles had to be worked out separately, exhaustively, and he would awaken from such nocturnal terrors drenched, feeling some oppressive, overwhelming weight upon him, crushing out whatever joy might still exist within him. Peter would employ at times like these the same game he used to put himself to sleep when a hectic schedule, or a bit too much of the drug du jour, would render him sleepless. This game involved ranking the myriad people he knew, based on a number of criteria: obvious things of course like appearance, musculature, leanness, fat/muscle ratio, the straightness and whiteness of teeth, eye color, fashion sense, bone structure, hair, skin, and nails; but also other equally vital considerations such as address, wealth, occupation, intelligence, and social circle. There were perhaps fifty people he would rate in this way, and numbers two through fifty would often exchange places from time to time as if there were a mad, exhausting dance going on inside Peter's head; but numbers one, and fifty, were invariably the same: Peter himself in the former; and someone Peter referred to as Fatty, always, in the latter position.

But sometimes even this calming practice would produce a nightmare of its own, in which everything went topsy-turvy and those on the bottom of the list swung up to occupy the top positions, and vice versa. In these dreams he himself would be standing in front of a mirror, exhaustively aware of a thousand-item regimen he would have to get through to make himself presentable, but no matter what he did there was still someone inherently, profoundly ugly staring back at him from the mirror. These were the worst dreams of all, repudiating as they did everything Peter believed in, and at such times he would call out, sometimes in his dream but other times audibly (myriad bed partners had confirmed this), "Help! Help me! Please, *please* help me!"

But on such a day as this Peter Pillsbury—he'd changed his name some years ago to something less ethnic—did not belong to the dreaming class of men.

Some minutes later he reluctantly dragged himself out of a mirror reverie in which there were two Peter Pillsburys—as if the munificence of nature could be imposed upon—and stepped into the multi-directional shower, carrying with him a not small plastic bag of sundries.

The chest was the first to be shaved. This was easy, and Peter marveled at how rounded and defined the pectorals were, like fine hills in a Hopper painting—then, oh so carefully, the legs: a nick here would be most inconvenient on this day of days. Fifteen minutes later—done! And not a scratch! Next it was time for, in this exact order, the exfoliating mask, the deep cleanser, the pore filler, the clarifyer, the moisturizer, and the sunscreen.

Now it was the hair's turn. Giogio's cut two days ago had been his best yet—it ought to have been for $125.00—but talk about money well spent! High and tight on the sides, razor trimmed in the back, the soft dark locks on top spilling with seeming abandon onto the unlined forehead, a perfect foil for the killer sea-green eyes. The hot oil treatment came first, then a thorough rinse before the highlighting chamomile shampoo, which was followed as inevitably as night follows day by the Super Conditioning After Rinse with Ginseng and Evening Primrose Oil.

He was toweling off and about to pluck an errant eyebrow from the bridge of his nose when the buzzer rang.

Peter watched himself make a purposely bemused face in the mirror, thought for a moment what an incredible actor he would have made, then wondered who . . .? Everyone he knew was doing, at this precise moment, exactly what he was, getting ready for the big event.

"I won't answer it," he mumbled.

The buzzer persisted. Louder, longer.

He pulled on his white terry designer robe and padded out to the hall. He watched himself push the intercom button with a freshly manicured nail.

"Yes," he said rather than asked.

"Hey Peter? It's . . . it's just me, Ken. Ken from downstairs."

Oh God, of all people—Fatty!

"Yes?" Peter didn't bother hiding the annoyance in his voice. He supposed it was a free country, but why the condo association had ever let anyone so fat, so sloppy, so . . . unattractive! buy into this building was beyond him—and especially directly downstairs!

"I . . . I heard you upstairs so I figured you'd be home, I'll be right up."

Before Peter could tell him I'm busy, don't bother, he could hear his neighbor's vast avoirdupois plodding up the stairs. Peter stomped to the door and flung it open, catching the surprised Ken in the act of picking his nose. The perpetually pimpled red face blushed even deeper.

"Oh, hi . . . sorry," Ken stammered. He grasped the railing and tried to catch his breath.

"I'm kind of busy," Peter snapped, already closing the door on this visual pollution.

"Oh wait, I just . . . just wanted to show you, I . . . I took your advice and bought something dark to . . . to hide my . . . weight."

"Advice?" Peter echoed, more to himself. His annoyance grew as Ken undertook an awkward pirouette, bumping into the just-polished banister. He grasped onto it to catch his balance—Peter hoped Fatty's plump fingers weren't sticky with chocolate, Peter would no doubt be bringing someone home later and people noticed such things, Peter always did.

"You . . . you mentioned once that I might not look so . . . big if I wore darker clothes," Ken explained lowly. He made eye contact at last. His eyes grew radiant. Peter couldn't see this, he was thinking Ken looked like a burnt, overstuffed sausage in the ill-fitting, already sweaty black shirt and blacker chinos.

"I . . . I just bought them this morning," Ken fumbled on. "I read about that, uh, Pride Parade going on today, I saw it in the paper last night and I thought, you know, I thought maybe I'd go."

Last night? My God, Peter thought, some people really were pathetic! He himself had been preparing for this weekend for almost a year now!

"Ah, yeah, great, great Ken," and Peter began closing the door. But Ken lurched forward, alarm in his face.

"Wait, I was wondering maybe . . . maybe I could walk up with you. I mean to the parade I mean." Ken gulped audibly. There, he'd said it. It wasn't as flowery as he'd seen it in his head last night practicing the words over and over, but he'd gotten them out, that was the main thing. Ken wasn't kidding himself that this would be any kind of date—surely his upstairs neighbor could have just about any man he wanted—it was just a friend thing, someone to go to Pride with, surely no one would exclude him on this day when the community celebrated its solidarity, its survival—

Peter's face registered shock. Where did these people get the nerve to think someone like he, Peter Pillsbury, would be interested in even casually conversing with someone like Ken, let alone be caught dead walking the streets with him? And on Pride Day!

"I—I need to be there early. 11:00 a.m.," he said, beginning to shut the door again.

"I can go early, I'm already ready!" Ken exclaimed. But he said the words to Peter's closed door.

Ken thought at first that Peter would return, that he'd gone only for a moment, maybe to get something. But a full minute went by. Then two. Nothing.

"What an asshole," Ken mumbled. As he turned to descend the stairs he heard the phone ring inside Peter's apartment. Ken heard the familiar, worshipful tread of Peter's bare feet as they flew out of the bathroom.

"Hello?" Ken heard, muffled, but still he heard, and as always the sound of that voice thrilled him. No, he shouldn't listen, that wouldn't be right—but he loved that voice, and heard it so infrequently; besides, what else did he have to do today, now that he wouldn't be going to the parade? For he couldn't go alone: he'd reached some critical mass where he just could not do one more thing utterly by himself; and try as he had, Ken had met few gay people in the city other than Peter since moving here a year ago. It wasn't for a lack of trying, he'd done the clubs and restaurants and bars, even walked the streets . . . but he felt more and more invisible, people's eyes would kind of glaze over and shift away as he approached, as if he were a leper almost.

"Oh God, I'm incredibly late already, I got talking to these two really really hot guys from New York at the gym this morning who were cruising me big time," Ken heard. He forgot who he was, and a vision was his for a moment: of attractiveness, of making new best friends wherever he went, of numbers exchanged and received, of laughs and thrills and parties and a phone that never stopped ringing.

It was a vision that couldn't have been more unlike his own life.

Ken could not know this, but for that moment his face softened, his eyes growing tender and evocative as they always might have been had his life been something different than what it was. A stranger seeing this face might have pronounced it almost angelic in its wistfulness.

"And then as if I wasn't already late enough," Ken heard next through the door, and that world that had been his for a moment was snatched back to Peter Pillsbury, "who rings my buzzer but Fatty from downstairs! Can you believe it?"

Ken visibly jolted just outside the door. *Fatty* . . . but there was more.

". . . Oh gross, like a burnt overstuffed sausage!" (Peter liked this phrase, and thought it clever.) "Oh who knows, he must have been hallucinating or something, he thought he looked thinner, he kept insisting I'd advised him to go out and get dark clothes . . . I know I know, as if I could care less about anything he said or did or thought. But wait—that's not the half of it! He asked me if we could go to Pride together! Hello? I mean, what are these people thinking? Like I'd be caught dead. And he was picking his nose too if you can believe it. What a loser. My God, fat, ugly—he probably has a little dick too. Talk about a faggot triple disaster. Cologne? No definitely don't wear any till tonight . . . I haven't decided yet . . . You did? Oh God, where'd you see that tired old thing?"

The voice blurred into babble as Ken, more quietly than he had ascended, moved back down the stairs. He gripped the railing tightly, looking neither left nor right. For the second time in five minutes things seemed misty; but this time there was nothing of fantasy about Ken's vision.

A faggot triple disaster. That's what they called him: a faggot triple disaster.

They were right of course, Ken saw this now. Better he had joined a gym than volunteered at the local hospice. Better he had invested his money in a dermatologist's care than spend it on the flower garden he'd made down the street in the abandoned lot. Better he had learned cutting, witty put-downs so he'd be popular albeit in a vicious, freakish way, rather than spend all that time dreaming—dreaming!—of friends that never did materialize.

He saw this all clearly now.

He quietly closed his apartment door behind him. He found the chocolate bars he'd been denying himself all morning on top of the refrigerator. Slightly mushy from the day's warmth, he carried them into his bedroom and sat upon the unmade bed. His eyes were still vacant. He pushed the bars abstractedly into his mouth.

He realized he, in his search for community having moved here, had never felt more profoundly alone. Not even back in tenth grade, when the whole school had somehow found out about him, and the beatings and harassment were doubled as he was found to be no longer just fat, but a fat faggot.

His eyes cleared, thanks to the sound of the very hottest and latest dance CD thumping from Peter's stereo just above. He looked across his bed and found Ferdie, his fattest and favorite Teddy Bear. He clutched Ferdie to his chest with one hand, then with the other retrieved the plastic shopping bag his new, darker clothing had been carried home in so hopefully earlier this morning. He slid it over his head, then pulled the strings so tightly they cut into his soft neck flesh. Then he pulled Ferdie into himself with both hands, staring into the stuffed bear's dark glass eyes, bottomless with understanding.

When he fell forward to the ground three minutes later, his face blue and a broken blood vessel in his now inactive brain, his neighbor above heard nothing. The thud had occurred in perfect synchronicity to a bass thump on this latest and hottest CD, falling like a hammer at the exact instant. In the bedroom directly above, where the music originated, Peter Pillsbury practiced a few dance moves in his full-length mirror, something new he had seen only a week ago down at South Beach. In the corner of his room a shaft of sunlight had gathered, and in the mirror's reflection it seemed to be growing. Annoyed at this distraction, which was taking him away from matters of consequence, Peter spun round to find a pillar of light—brighter than just the sun—assembling in the back corner of his bedroom. The light seemed to be fluid, it moved like water but in the midst of this growing mass were individual specks of even brighter light, so bright Peter felt himself squinting. And then a figure took shape within this light, a figure of a woman dressed in blue and white, her face timeless, full of light yet full of woe.

Peter unconsciously backed up. The cheval mirror crashed to the ground behind him. He fell backwards, landing on the floor. The woman seemed to tower above him. Peter tried to scream but found his tongue cloven to the roof of his mouth. He could feel his heart laboring as if under a tremendous strain. He frantically tried to recall if he'd taken any X yet, they were planning to for Pride—

The woman opened her arms to Peter. A flood of ferocious light came at him like a train, he was struck by it.

"We have heard your calls for Help," Peter heard inside his mind. "Therefore . . . a Gift we bring you."

The last thing Peter remembered was the feeling of passing out, of drowning in this sea of light . . .

He awoke, sore and totally unconnected; as if from birth. Then in panic he thought of the time. It was 10:45. He was due at Robert's condo across the street *now*. All Pride participants had to be at the kickoff point by 11:00 a.m.

Then he saw the mirror, its curved legs unnaturally askew, its shards sprinkling the Aubusson carpet. His mouth fell open and he almost wrenched his neck turning his head to the corner of his bedroom where only moments before . . . what? A quiet shaft of sunlight was there, as it always was this time of day.

"What a dream," he said aloud, standing up. He quickly cleaned up the mess; it would never do to bring someone home with his condo in this state. He stood before the bathroom mirror for one last look. He zoned in immediately on his eyes. Something in his very foundations seemed shaken. His eyes looked different—larger, deeper—he remembered something vaguely, then literally shook the feeling off.

When he emerged from his shadowed apartment building moments later, Peter felt a chill immediately. He considered for just one second changing into something more substantial than the tight black short shorts and white mesh tank top he had selected months ago for this day of days, complemented by the slouching snow-white socks and gleaming black construction boots, unsullied by anything even remotely approaching work.

Peter had desired to be particularly quiet coming down the stairs, lest Fatty hear him and once more make nauseating suggestions. But unfortunately Peter seemed suddenly full of a clumsy something, and he'd bumped into his brass coat rack right at the top of the landing. It clattered down the stairway with enough noise to, well, wake the dead; but at any rate it did not bring Fatty out into the hall.

Peter crossed the street and ascended the steps of his friend Robert's condominium, the ancient church. Peter buzzed Robert's number, then stepped back to check his look in the polished glass of the ponderous double-doors. He saw nothing to dismay him. But when the doors swung open moments later, expelling Peter's friend Robert Burrows, a chill breeze blew out like a breath from the old building, a breath that seemed to go right for Peter. It tossled Peter's hair quite out of place despite the layers of spritz he'd applied only moments ago.

"Hi," Robert smiled.

"Shit!" Peter hissed, and Robert visibly cowered, as if he thought the expletive was directed at him, for some fashion faux pas he had committed in his dress.

"What?" Robert gasped, frozen. Peter didn't answer, he was busy arranging his hair in the glass. But somehow he couldn't make it right, damnit—and it'd been perfect, as it usually was, only moments ago—

"I need your bathroom," Peter announced. "Wait here and gimme your keys." Robert complied instantly, extracting a rainbow key ring from his own slouching snow-white socks.

Peter pushed through the doors and passed into the building's lobby, the only part of the interior that retained the look and feel of the church's original purpose.

"It's like a tomb in here," Peter commented aloud. He had said the words lowly, or so he thought, but they seemed to echo loudly throughout the stone chamber.

Robert's bathroom was a disgrace, but it had a mirror, and hairspray, so it served Peter's purpose. In five minutes Peter was back outside. He and Robert wordlessly began the four-block trek to the parade's kickoff point. But every reflective storefront they passed showed Peter a deteriorating mess where once the winsome locks had been; then Peter caught Robert stealing a glance at his hair for the third time.

"Nice ears!" Peter exploded. Robert was an almost hypnotically beautiful man facially—he wouldn't have been Peter's friend if he wasn't—but the classically chiseled face was somewhat lampooned by the jug ears that vented out almost perpendicularly. It was Robert's only visible flaw. Intensely self-conscious about those ears, he colored immediately at Peter's retort—especially in the ears.

The day, despite the sun, seemed to be growing decidedly chillier.

Peter remained silent as a stone as he strove to unravel the Gordian Knot that was now vexing his brain: why was his hair continuing to blow in this fucking East wind, when he had lacquered it—twice!—almost to the point of petrification?

He held his head stiffly to one side, so that the wind would blow with, rather than against, his hair; but just at that moment the wind shifted, and the locks became all awry again. He turned his head to the other side; the wind paused, then shifted back again.

Two or three people in the crowd of passersby were people Peter should have stopped and talked to, their stars were rising in their rehabbing neighborhood; but in his angry discomfiture he had barely nodded at them, plodding by with the silent Robert at his side. In fact he'd heard one of these say to his companion, "What's *her* problem?" right after they'd passed by.

By the time Peter and Robert reached the Parade's kickoff point, a chaotic scene of costume, cacophony, and caricature, Peter was livid.

Everyone else selected by Peter to be on their float—there would be twelve of them in all, including Peter and Robert—was already milling about. A simple flatbed truck, draped in black cloth, with two immense stereo speakers attached to the back, had been fitted with a dozen circular platforms of varying height, one for each participant. While the other floats in the parade represented fraternal organizations, charities, or specific clubs, Peter's float represented, as the silver and black banners attached to their truck proclaimed, "The Pride of Our Neighborhood."

Peter was slightly mollified to see that his fellow float participants had followed orders as to their dress: black boots, white slouch socks, black short shorts, and mesh tank tops of varying color so that the conglomerate effect would suggest a rainbow. But everyone knew the tank tops would be coming off, sooner rather than later, to unveil the results of vast amounts of gym time invested, and fat eschewed. Already four of the brethren were shirtless.

A small crowd of camp followers had already gathered at the rear of the float. Peter hoped their numbers would swell into the hundreds as the fast-approaching kickoff time drew near.

Peter yelled to the float's driver—he had come as part of the package deal with the truck—to turn on the stereo system. The driver had been given several tapes the night before, tapes that Peter had personally commissioned from a disc jockey he knew: nothing but the latest and hottest music, and the more Euro and obscure the remixes, the better. The music kicked in with a heart-pounding bass intro. An electric jolt raced through the crowd. People began streaming to their float. Peter and his cohorts mounted their assigned platforms—Peter's was slightly higher than the others, and dead center—and began moving to the music. Tank tops flew off.

Peter heard the shrill microphoned intonations of some charity queen kicking off the parade a block away, and then a deafening siren went off. Thousands of pink and white balloons let loose, and the opal sky became lost in them for a moment. A mighty roar went up from the crowd. The truck's engine growled to life. The float began lurching forward—it was about the seventh or eighth item in the parade— and Peter turned, in time with the music, to scan the back of the float.

As he had hoped, dozens of men were now trailing the float, arms waving in time to the music—or perhaps in adulation—eyes filled with a greasy swipe of lust, adoration, and envy, just what Peter had wanted. He undertook a trickier dance in response to this attention, the one he had just seen on the dance floors of South Beach. He closed his eyes, and let this vox populi wash over him like a love blush. Individually each member of the crowd was, most of them, clueless, a flabby herd lacking in a sense of what was really . . . *important* in life. But collectively they were a different thing, when one couldn't see each oily pore, the very cut of the sweaty shorts; collectively he loved them, loved the fact that they were looking at him and not just wanting him, but wanting to . . . *be* him.

Just then the woman of light came back to him, an intrusion he didn't want, or appreciate.

"Therefore . . . a gift we bring you," he heard again.

Then an earthly voice cut into this reverie.

"You've changed your hair!"

Turning—not that he had to to identify the speaker—he saw the slightest of smiles on the fleshy lips of the dancer just to his right, Jeffrey Trowbridge. The second member of the unofficial triumvirate that commanded their neighborhood's society (Peter himself, and Scott Breton, another dancer on the float, being numbers One and Three respectively), Jeffrey looked as shiningly flawless as Peter had an hour ago.

In fact he looked better than Peter had seen him look before, ever. *Bitch.* A tang of intense dislike jabbed through Peter.

"What horrible timing for a bad hair day!" Jeffrey gushed, full of mock sympathy. Hearing no retort, he smelled blood and continued.

"Do you need a ball cap? I can get you one." Among their set, ball caps were the last refuge of the folliclely challenged; tactful veils for haircuts gone gravely awry; or the trappings of the Bridge and Tunnel Set—suburbanites who knew no better.

"No thanks!" Peter smirked, putting on his wrap-around shades, trying to look cool somehow, anyhow. "Oh Jeffrey!" he continued, "I saw Thomas this morning at the gym with this gorgeous, gorgeous guy. I thought you'd want to know." Thomas was the unpredictable artist type who had unceremoniously dumped Jeffrey a week ago, a humiliating first that Jeffrey had vehemently denied. But people were talking—and Peter always listened when they did.

Jeffrey snapped back around, his face flaming.

This business finished, Peter turned back to matters at hand. The crowd was swelling. The float turned a corner crowd-stretched to overflowing. A roar like a tidal wave went up from the masses. The dancers increased their ferocity, each one trying to determine how many of the adoring throng were looking precisely at him alone. Many at the corner abandoned their coveted front-row stations and fell into the mad swollen troop behind the float. Something close to what Peter thought would be the short-term reward for all this tugged at him; but then an especially blowsy gust found his hair, and wreaked additional havoc upon it.

He would've screamed if he weren't in public.

He turned to see if any of the other dancers were suffering the same ill effects. Immediately his eye went to adjacent Jeffrey, in particular to a quite large, angry red blemish on Jeffrey's otherwise porcelain skin, right in the midst of his right calf—no, actually it was more like a boil, half-dollar size at least. Having been so preoccupied at the parade's outset with his own hair issues, Peter had failed to take a closer, critical look at his fellow dancers beyond their outfits. It was for just these things that Peter had prepared two or three alternate dancers, should there be some kind of last-minute unpleasantness like this. Damn! He wished he'd seen this before, Jeffrey never would have been allowed on the float!

"Don't look now, Jeff," Peter shouted, using the shorter form of his friend's name, which Jeffrey loathed, "but you're sprouting a third eye on your right calf!"

Jeffrey stopped dancing midbeat, as if Peter had said a poisonous serpent was crawling up his leg. Jeffrey turned—and Peter gasped: at least a dozen of these appalling eruptions were sprouting up all over Jeffrey's arms and chest, like a chain of suddenly active volcanoes.

Jeffrey's instant cessation of movement drew a few looks from the crowd. Some of them visibly started.

"Put your shirt back on! Put it on!" Peter hissed, not in sympathy but in the embarrassment of association. Jeffrey grabbed his red mesh tank top from his waistband where it had been waving with his every movement and swiftly put it on. But it did nothing to hide the boils on his arms.

The wind blew again.

Peter screamed out loud—this was becoming a disaster! He jumped off his pedestal. Leaning over the edge of the truck, he grabbed the first hat he saw that wasn't too offensive, a plain black cap, and pulled it on tightly, saying nothing to the man he had liberated it from, a sense of entitlement similar to an eminent domain land seizure dismissing any second thoughts.

He turned back to Jeffrey.

"You've got to get off!" Peter screamed, almost gagging at the sight of the boils, which seemed to be developing pea-green pus heads even as he watched. They were on Jeffrey's face as well now.

"Don't look at me like that!" Jeffrey screamed back, almost writhing. "Plus you've got them too—asshole!"

Peter looked down. A roaring that was not the crowd flooded his ears. He saw a dozen similar marks coursing across his own chest, along his arms, up and down the just-shaved legs. With hands almost frozen into inaction he donned his own tank top. A horrible thought occurring to him, he ran his hands lightly across his heretofore-flawless face—he felt at least five or six of the boils on his cheeks alone.

"Oh, they've gone psychedelic, with polka-dots!" a huge drag queen in the crowd screamed, pointing an endless dinner-gloved arm at Peter Pillsbury, whose dance had become an almost catatonic shuffle, and not at all what the boys in South Beach were doing. Thus he was not surprised when, turning around, he saw similar pox on each of the other dancers, who were just now beginning to notice. Their dance became a grotesque tottering, oddly in perfect time to the music that was now pouring through the speakers like rotten rank water—music that Peter had never heard before—

Perhaps it was due to his state of mind that Peter didn't notice exactly when the music had changed—but changed it had, how he did not know, and instead of the latest and hottest dance mixes the huge speakers were now moaning forth almost a funeral dirge, some fantastically horrible wail—he was about to pound on the Plexiglas window directly behind their driver when an instant and fierce itch exploded halfway up the inside of his right nostril.

If there were a power on this earth to resist such an itch, it was not within Peter Pillsbury. In desperation he drove his newly manicured right index finger as far into the offending orifice as it would go. Everything in his mind, everything he was, rebelled at his actions, and he ordered his finger to stop, especially as they were fast approaching the most fashionable, truly exclusive, section of their gay neighborhood. But in answer his left index finger now joined in the hunt, for a sympathetic itching had just now erupted in his left nostril. He could see peripherally that the other dancers were similarly engaged; but what tore at his attention now, above and beyond this uncanny itch, was a growing distrust in his own eyes—for surely Jeffrey—surely David and Michael and Brad—surely all of them!—were in better shape than this! He *knew* they were! But what then were these suddenly slouching bellies, these triceps gone loose and flabby, the saggy breasts that had been firm mounds of muscle only minutes ago? A horrible thought occurring to him, Peter drove his eyes downward, and for the first time in his life could not see below his waist, which had become a doughy mass of jellied flesh!

Whether it was the morbid, discordant cry pouring from the stereo speakers, or the sight of themselves, Peter could not determine; but an open-mouthed silence now gripped the crowd as the float passed by, a silence that was horrificly surreal because of the very number of the thousands gathered to watch. Peter would have thought himself gone deaf had it not been for the music. He tried to scream—but nothing would come from his throat but animal-like guttural groans of satisfaction as he continued to scratch away at his enflamed nostrils. A sudden gust of wind tore at his hat, blowing it back into the crowd from whence it had come.

He found that he couldn't move, except for his fully engaged fingers.

He had to get off.

Fat, riddled with scarlike boils, both hands engaged in picking his nose—he had to get home, had to get out of view, had to flee this nightmare in which people—thousands of them!—were staring at him, Peter Pillsbury, not with swift approving appraisal, not with rapt admiration nor even envy—but with deep, essential disgust, utter revulsion.

"It's me, it's Jeffrey!" Peter heard beside him, Jeffrey screaming to someone in the crowd. "Remember you told me I had the hottest ass in the world? Remember?" and to Peter's horror he watched Jeffrey rip his hands from his nose and wriggle his impossibly tight shorts down to his knees. Peter gagged as he saw a vast quivering mass of cellulite exposed to the crowd. Some in the crowd looked away, others groaned. Peter drove his own hands backward and felt with unbelieving fingers a similar jiggly hugeness where only moments ago his own sculpted buttocks had been.

Peter dove off the float, landing on three spectators, knocking them down. He picked himself up. An older queen next to Peter stared, struck a pose, then sniveled, "You're drunk, honey."

"Fuck you," he said, or thought he said, but the voice he heard coming from his mouth was not his own rich bass, but a high prissy lisp instead.

Peter took off in a panic. He was breathless in less than a block. Away from his float the parade seemed to be going along as normal, a feisty crowd and thumping dance music obliterating the nightmare silence he had just escaped. But something was wrong, something he couldn't quite put his finger on, there was this eerie quality to things, people's faces were a blur and they were—yes! Laughing! They were laughing at him, Peter Pillsbury!

He pushed his way down a side street, away from the crowd. Words that had never before been directed at him came hurtling his way like stones.

"Hey, beautify America! Put some clothes on!" he heard from one group hastily making their way up to the parade.

"It's Mirth and Girth . . . and I do mean Girth!" someone else catcalled from a balcony gathering, and titters of laughter rained down—home. He must get home—but amidst his desperation a seed of anger was taking root—

He found moving along the street incredibly difficult, he guessed he now weighed 250 pounds, and somehow most of this was fat. He would awaken at home; perhaps some jealous queen had slipped something into his latte this morning—home!

He had to stop halfway up his stairs to snatch at breath. He was shaking with rage. Fumbling in his slouch socks for his keys, he wondered whose elephant legs these were, drooping with fat—

For the first time in as long as he could remember, there were no flashes announcing messages on his answering machine. But he didn't care. The mirror, the full-length mirror in his bathroom—

He flicked the switch on out in the hall. The air was still moist from his shower, which seemed a lifetime ago. The mirror inside the bathroom, he knew, would not lie. He had to stop again outside the door, but this time his breathlessness was due to anxiety. What would he see? Who was he now? An absurd high sob exploded from his throat.

He stepped inside. He closed his eyes and felt his way to the middle of the room. The scent of Evening Primrose Oil still lingered in the air.

He became aware of some vague, vast regret, a prodigal wasting of time and energy and life—

He found he was sweating. Feeling his way with his plump hands, he placed himself before the mirror.

He opened his eyes.

Staring back at him was the face of himself, but 250 pounds worth, riddled with boils—

He pressed his eyes tightly shut. He opened them again.

No change. Peter winked, raised his fleshy hands to his face, pulled at the heavy chins—no change. He could have been his downstairs' neighbor Ken, Peter thought; but it was Peter's face now, uniquely his own.

He dropped to the bathroom floor upon all fours, nauseated. His rage blew up inside him, something foul and all-encompassing.

His raised his head. His eyes narrowed and he actually growled as he remembered the strange dream, the woman—

He got up and marched into the bedroom, the light of battle in his eyes. He kicked the pieces of the busted cheval mirror out of his way without a thought. He planted himself in front of the corner where the light had first gathered, his chest heaving with rage—

"Wh-what have you done to me!" he screamed, almost alarmed at the power of the voice coming out of his mouth. "Who are you? What did you do?"

Out of the corner of his eye he saw something. Turning, he saw himself in a wall mirror. He closed his eyes. Then he roared, like there was something inside him writhing in its death agony.

He fell to the floor upon all fours again, trying to control his breathing.

His eyes remained closed.
He remained there for some time.

He became aware that something inexplicable, otherworldly even, had happened to him, something that could never be explained in this world; yet somehow this all had some kind of strange inevitability about it, some logic, even if he couldn't penetrate it. Oddly, he felt this face, this body, belonged to him in a way that his previous features had not. How this could be he did not know; but nevertheless he knew this to be true.
He remained on the floor.

The sun slanted into the silent apartment. It shifted slowly as shafts of light moved from room to room, illuminating various objects in the apartment, objects which Peter now felt a strange and vast disassociation from.
Then the light began to fade.
"Therefore . . . a gift we bring you."
He recalled the words from his dream, if dream it was. He closed his eyes and shook his head.
Finally he got up, with an effort. He fumbled into the living room, toward the large bay window, one panel of which was open. Choppy sounds of celebration filtered in from several blocks away, then were gone. The horizon was a clear rose color. He kept his eyes upon it, but he was seeing something else.
He sat down again upon the floor, his head full of thoughts.

When Jesus Came to Town

I wicked wish you could read this in my beautiful penmanship—the letters swirling like angels, written on the crisp paper Grandma Flynn gave me. She got it at a stationery store. It's rustley, and the color of the inside of an apple. See, then even when I wrote about the bad things that happened, you wouldn't mind as much.

Okay. I guess I should start now. I guess it all started when Sister Marie came to our school.

Sister Marie wasn't like the other nuns at Gate of Heaven School. Even in my dreams she was different—you couldn't even dream her into normal. Sometimes at night—earlier, before she came to our school—I'd dream of nuns—just nuns—standing in a slanting line, sideways—you couldn't see their faces. Motionless. Quiet as snow-flakes. Even after she came here, I never dreamed of Sister Marie in that line. But if I did, she would have been standing on her head, or singing, or maybe just looking at you. With those big eyes the color of crows. That could see Heaven, and Earth.

Even before everything happened, I could see she was different. She talked different. Ma said, "She's got an accent, that's all." Ma would explain things in one sentence like that. If you didn't get it, that was too bad. You never got any more.

"But what's an accent?" I asked. But no more. So everyone who talked funny had an accent. Tommy Regan sat behind me. He stuttered. "He has an accent," I whispered to my best friend Brenda Mc-Carthy at recess one day, when Tommy lurched past us, his little red fists jammed in his pockets. He'd lean against the school wall by himself every day. "He's so cute," I sighed.

"I know it," Brenda said. Then she laughed. "I wonder what he sounds like when he comes? 'Oh, G-G-GOD! I'm c-c-c-c-commmmmmmminnnnnnnnnnn'!'"

Brenda's a year older than me, she's thirteen, because she got kept back when she was seven, and she's got more experience with boys than I do, and loves to talk about them.

"Stop it, Brenda!" I said, trying not to laugh, "he'll hear you!"

So Sister Marie had an accent. She said she grew up on a very poor farm in this place called the Middle East, where almost everyone spoke a different language. She came from a family of farmers and shepherds, she said. But she'd been all over the world, and could speak tons of different languages. After she told us all that, I dreamed of all these rows of Middle Eastern people rising up from the ground like corn plants, their heads bowed, their hands folded in prayer, and when the sun came up they all started speaking in foreign languages, like birds singing in the morning.

"They all speak crazy languages over there," Ma said when I asked her about it.

"Why?" I asked. But she just kept ironing. Pounding into the clothes.

During Music, Sister Marie taught us French songs. She said French was one of her favorite languages. We couldn't understand a word of it, but it sounded nice I guess. The next time that I dreamt of where she grew up in the Middle East, the people sang in the morning instead of just talking. But afterward they asked each other, "But what does it mean?" in English. And nobody knew. But they all agreed it sounded pretty.

Sister Marie looked different too. She was smaller than the other nuns, and her skin was almost the color of the bag I would bring my lunch to school in every day. One bag a week. "Fold it and bring it home neat, they cost money," Ma said, and when I'd forget, I couldn't watch TV that afternoon. So on those days I'd go up to my blue bedroom and wait for Jimmy with my door open a specky so I'd hear him coming home, my older brother. Because once in a while he likes me to hang with him while he lies on his bed. Sometimes, he cries. But don't tell anyone because I'm not supposed to tell. It's because of What Happened. But he hardly ever comes home before suppertime anymore. I love Jimmy.

I don't know what color Sister Marie's hair was because like the rest of the nuns she had her nun thing on that covered her head all up except her face. Nancy Riordan said they were all bald, that's how God let you know you had a Calling to be a nun, He struck you bald and then you knew. But Ma said, "They're not bald." I was going to stand up on the toilet seat and lean over so I could check the top of my head in the mirror that night after I brushed my teeth to see if I had a Calling and was going bald. But after Ma said that, I didn't bother— sometimes you'd slip on the toilet seat's shaggy pink cover. All right all right, I'm kinda short for twelve. So sue me.

"How do you know they're not bald?" I asked Ma. But no more.

Sister Marie's eyebrows were dark and they flew up like blinds sometimes, especially when you told her something strange (like, some kids in our grade huffed, and then someone told her that meant sniffing paint or glue or aerosol), her eyebrows would leap up and she'd say, "Eez dis truuuue?" She said the first week of school that each one of us had a Guardian Angel that watched over us. There was a great big poster of one of them scotch taped to the blackboard. He was helping two nerdy-looking kids on bikes not get hit by a car. After school the second week of class, when it was still September Hot and our classroom still smelled like sharpened pencils and paper nobody wrote on yet, I asked Sister Marie when everybody left, "So. Was ahhh . . . Johnny's Guardian Angel sleeping when he got hit by the train, or what?"

Her head snapped back a little.

"Who ez Johnny, den?" she asked, standing up quickly from behind her desk.

"My brother that . . . ahhh . . . went to Heaven this summer. Two days after the Fourth of July."

Up close I noticed Sister Marie's eyes were the color of the crows that sat on the telephone wires outside our class sometimes, and they got bigger now. She came around to me, her starched white habit rustling, like the paper inside a Christmas present box.

"Ez dis true?" she asked, but sadder, and her eyebrows didn't swoop this time.

"Uh-hmmm," I said. "Yup."

"You are . . . Christine, no? Christine Flynn?"

"Yes, Sister."

"The one wit the beautiful handwriting, no?"

"Yes, thank you. So, was he sleeping?" I pointed to the poster of the Guardian Angel.

"I tink God wanted him, your broder," Sister Marie said after a minute. "What do you tink?"

"I don't know, that's why I'm asking you," I said. I had to look away her eyes were so . . . I don't know, deep-like, penetrating. I could feel myself turning wicked red.

Sister Marie said, "But you must tink something."

"Grandma Flynn said God had a job for him in Heaven," I said, staring at my shoes. Grandma Flynn is way cool and nice, she's Dad's mother who moved in for a little while when Ma was in the hospital after Johnny died.

"Yes, perhaps," Sister Marie said.

"That makes sense," I said, "because Dad said you have to be sixteen to get a job." I was cracking a joke but Sister Marie didn't smile.

"And how old was he, Johnny?"

"Sixteen. Just."

"And you, Christine—you are twelve, or tirteen?"

"Twelve. I'll be thirteen in May."

"Uhm," she said. She thought for a moment.

"All of dis—it ez . . . a Mystery," she pronounced. "We cannot know ev'ryting, ma chere. There is an ant goes crawling down the sidewalk, and he cannot know about . . . China, for example. Or Math. That does not mean these tings do not exist. Hmmm? So it ez for us on dis eart. We cannot know some tings. Like det. Especially, sudden—and so young. So tragic. I am so sorry. You must be devastated, still."

I looked down at my shoes again, at the wavy gloss of the green linoleum floor.

"Tell me Christine Flynn, who ez at home?"

"Just Ma."

"Where is your father, den?"

"Working at the gas station. He fixes cars."

"Ahh, no—who else ez in your fam-i-ly? Who lives wit you at home?"

"Ma and Dad and Jimmy."

"Jimmy ez your broder? Another broder?"

"Yeah. He's eighteen. But nobody talks at supper anymore. Do you want to see Johnny's grave? It's right next door. I won't charge you a buck like I did the little kids this summer."

Sometimes I like to see it, just to make sure he's really not coming back.

"Well! That is very kind of you. Of course. Shall we . . . shall we pick some flowers for the grave? I know where some are growing."

"I guess. So why is the Guardian Angel wearing a dress if he's a man?"

Sister Marie smiled. "It is what an artist tinks a Guardian Angel wears. But you know that."

"One time we were taking the subway to the dentist's and a man got on wearing a dress who smelled like likker. Ma said he was a fruit. What's a fruit? You can only ask Ma one question."

Sister Marie's eyebrows lowered.

"A fruit?" she repeated. "I cannot be sure what she meant by deez." She paused, and her eyes looked into mine. "But—leesten," she said, "I do know God made us all deeferent. But we are all God's Childrens. His beloveds one and all. When we see clearly, we see little of the physical, and more of the Spirit. Please to remember dis, eh?"

"Yeah. Sure thing, Sister."

We left school together that day, me and Sister Marie. We walked through the nuns' special entrance to the school, which was a hall that was a tunnel almost. It was quiet, and smelled like pine cleaner, and sun hitting geraniums. The sun came slanty through the hall's glowing frosted windows. It felt almost like angels might be around every corner. The hall-tunnel connected Gate of Heaven School to the Convent of Our Lady of Hope, where all the nuns lived. My penny loafers made echo sounds, but Sister Marie's were black and quiet.

"Do you have this tunnel so the nuns won't run away?" I asked.

Sister Marie laughed, high and clear like the bells at Consecration during Mass. If you're not Catholic, that means when bread turns into Jesus' body. "We don't want to run away. Dis ez the life we have chosen."

I said, "But you never get to go out."

"Of course we can, if we wish," Sister Marie said. "But . . . it ez . . . see, we are *in* dis world, but not *of* dis world. Understand?"

"Not really."

We went through another door and were outside, in the convent's backyard. There was a brown fence all around so you couldn't see in from the outside. The grass was wicked green. There was a great big clothesline with white clothes blowing on it, like happy sails on the boats out in Pleasure Bay. Sister Marie's white habit blew in the puffy wind too and for a minute she looked like the clothes on the line. Around the corner of the building there were flowers sticking out of the ground, mostly pink, white, red, and purple. But there was one tall spiky one, it was yellow, over by the edge.

"Dis ez my little garden," Sister Marie said. She stood back and folded her hands and smiled.

"W-what's it for?" I asked. I'd never seen so many flowers all at once, except at the funny smelling funeral parlor where everyone came to stare at the closed box Johnny was in when he was dead.

"How do you mean?" Sister Marie asked back. Her eyebrows didn't leap, they bunched together.

"Well . . . what's it for, exactly?" I asked. I hated not knowing things, that's why I ask so many questions.

Her eyebrows leaped now.

"A garden? You do not know a garden?"

I shrugged. "Not really. I've heard of them, never seen one this big really."

"Hmm. Well. *Dis* ez a garden. A . . . home for flowers. Dis is where they grow. You plant a seed, they grow, no? A place you can come and maybe make it look like Heaven. When I come here dis summer, it ez the first ting I do, even before the soup kitchen." She looked around. Then she leaned closer and murmured, "I don't tink the others understand. But I must have a garden," she said. "Do you like? These are all roses, my favorite. Smell."

I breathed deeply. Spice and fruit and perfume all in one.

"It's okay I guess, except it reminds me of when Johnny died."

"How ez dis?"

"Everyone came to see him at the wake. They put him in a box and there were flowers everywhere."

(I hate wakes. They're boring and there's billions of people, and they'll always be some wicked wicked old lady with eyes that look spider-huge behind her glasses and she'll clutch my hand like a lobster and say something like, "I'm your Great Aunt Nora's sister-in-law's cousin." Me and my brother Jimmy always seem to end up outside for air, and one time outside during this wicked boring one, we changed the name of the funeral parlor and gave it a new name based on what everyone would always say at wakes, the same boring things over and over, and we called it, instead of the Daniel F. Cassidy Funeral Parlor, the Daniel F. Cassidy Step-into-the-Parlor-and-Have-a-Highball, the-Good-Lord-Have-Mercy-on-Her, She-Looks-Good-Doesn't-She-They-Did-A-Nice-Job She's-Out-of-Her-Suffering-Now

Funeral Parlor. And we imagined them putting that sign up out front with all those words on it, and we couldn't stop laughing, and just then some old lady shuffled out of the wake we were at with an even older man by her side and she gave us a wicked dirty look, then walked down the stairs, and finally she turned around and said, "You kids shouldn't laugh at wakes, you bold things! Someone will be laughing at yours someday, you kids!" and that was even funnier.)

"Ahh," Sister Marie said, "Flowers remind you of wakes. I see. Well, maybe a trick you can try. When you tink sad of when your broder die, instead you can tink of a garden. The other way around. No?"

The tall yellow flower near the edge of the garden didn't look anything like the flowers they had at Cassidy's Funeral Parlor. It was tall and spiky and its flowers looked like thimbles. They were the color of pale lemons. Its leaves were grayish green and fuzzy. When I looked closer I could see that the fuzziness came from little silvery hairs on the leaves. They were big and floppy, these leaves, like baby elephant ears.

"I like that one," I said, pointing.

"Eh! The Mullein! You cut me to the quick!" Sister Marie laughed. "You pick out the only one I did not plant!"

"Then how did it get here?"

"It ez what gardeners call 'A Volunteer.' It just showed up."

"But . . . how?" I was thinking that maybe it just walked over from some other garden, maybe a garden that was all yellow flowers, and this way it would get noticed. But then I thought no, flowers can't walk.

"Perhaps a bird dropped the seed," Sister Marie explained, and her hands made like a flying bird. She was kind of goofy like that but you didn't really mind. "Or perhaps it was the wind blew the seed from somewhere." She paused. "Or maybe," she said, lowering her voice, "one day the eart thought, 'Mullein!' and so it grew."

"What do you mean, Sister?"

"Perhaps flowers are de toughts of the eart. Perhaps there are such tings as magic, and joy. What is that old line from the poem? 'The eart is so full of many tings/we all should be as happy as kings.' Is dat it?"

"I don't know," I said. But I thought about it silently. Maybe for somebody else—not for me.

Not after what I've done.

"Pick some flowers, Christine, and we go make a visit to your broder's grave."

"How do I know which ones to pick?" I asked.

"Perhaps you say in your mind, you ask the flowers, Who Would Like to Come Make My Broder's Grave Pretty? Den see if you tink some of them want to do dis ting."

I told you she was kinda weird. But I didn't mind.

Walking over to the grave later, we cut through the church, lit a candle for Johnny, then out a side door and the cemetery's right there. Makes it easier for the pallbearers I guess. Tons of graves. The trees are old and twisty and they meet overhead and at night they look like ghosts might hang out in them. "And you say nobody talks now at supper?" Sister Marie suddenly asked. "Why ez dis?"

One of the good things about being Catholic is you can talk to priests and nuns about almost anything. And even if they yell at you or give you lousy advice—usually they don't—you can get stuff off your chest and not go mental.

"My mother thinks it's Jimmy's fault that Johnny died, that's why," I said. Sister Marie stopped. We were at someone's grave with an angel crying on the headstone. Sister Marie rapidly brushed the leaves off the angel, but I could tell she was thinking.

Then all at once, "But how ez dis? He was hit with a train, no?" Her eyebrows went up again.

I nodded. "He followed my other brother Jimmy," I said. "Jimmy was ahhhh . . . taking a walk up by the tracks, and Johnny followed him. Then the train came."

"Den how ez dis Jimmy's fault?" Sister Marie asked.

"I don't know." I paused. "But . . . Jimmy thinks it's his fault too." I paused again. I opened my mouth, then shut it. There are some things you can't tell anyone, even a priest or nun. Like how it was really *my* fault.

A few minutes later we went up a path on our way to Johnny's grave and two men in green pants and shirts were lying on their backs on the ground, smoking butts and laughing. A yellow lawn mower was idle near them. They jumped up when they saw us. They tipped their baseball caps to Sister Marie.

"Ahh, we were just taking a little break there, Sister," one of them said.

Sister Marie laughed. "As you were," she said. She laughed again. "Dis ez not the army, and I am nobody's boss. It ez a day to take one's leisure, eh?" And we kept walking until we got to Johnny's grave. We said the Rosary there, if you're not Catholic that's tons of prayers to the Blessed Mother. Sister Marie did the first part of each prayer, and I did the second. After a while she said, "Do you want to hear the prayers in French? They are beautiful."

I thought for a minute.

"Will they still count, Sister?"

When we were walking back from Johnny's grave Sister Marie said, "What ez it you would you like to do wit your life, Christine?"

I answered right away. "I'm going to write letters. I'll have me a beautiful office and a beautiful dress. And I'll sit in my beautiful office all day and write letters for people that come to me, and the people who get the letters will be happy even if the letters say something nasty or sad, because they'll be written in beautiful penmanship. And everyone will give me lots of money for my beautiful letters."

"Ahhh! Dis sounds wonderful! You do have very beautiful writing, as I have said."

I stopped walking for a second. "You're the first person who's ever said something good about my plan," I said. "Most people tell me everything's computers now and no one's gonna write in the future. But don't you think some things should be written in person like?"

"There is nothing to compare wit the personal touch," she said, and she smiled like the sun in a little kid's drawing.

Later when we got back to the school Sister Marie took me by both hands and looked me in the eyes like she had something very important to say. I wanted to pull away because no one touches me anymore, but I didn't want to embarrass her.

She looked right through me with those crow's eyes.

She said, "Tell your broder Jimmy to come and see me."

"Where were you?" Ma asked when I got home. She was at the kitchen table, stirring her tea.

"I was with Sister Marie after school."

"Didn't I tell you to come right home when school lets out?"

"I know but I was with Sister Marie. She said—"

"I don't care if you were with the Blessed Mother. You come home from school right away, see? Every single day." She paused, and stared into her tea. She used to look over her teacup and talk to you but now she stares into it, always, like something more than tea might be swishing around inside her cup. And when she does look at you it's like she doesn't really see you. Her eyes look like they're always looking for something she can't find.

I brace myself for What's Coming Next. I never have to wait long.

Ma's red nose sniffles. Then she moans, "That's how it was that day . . . I was waiting for Johnny and . . . and he never came home!" She starts crying. Again. I used to stare but now I look away. It's not doing anyone any good. Especially Jimmy. Me, I can take care of myself.

"And h-he'll never come home again!" she wails.

No shit, I think.

Every talk with Ma now always ends up like this, no matter how it starts. It's like walking home from school. You can cut through the church parking lot and squeeze through the thorny bushes with the little orange berries on them that the birds won't eat. Or you can take the normal way by the streets. Or you can go around the long way by Teresa McNally's house, and her weird mother might give you red jellybeans sometimes and ask you to pray for her. But you always end up at home, no matter how you do it.

"Set the table and peel the potatoes," Ma says as I'm leaving the kitchen. "And make sure you wash your hands first."

"This organic lady on TV the other night said it's better not to peel the potatoes," I say. "The skin has good things—"

"Don't you try and weasel out of your chores because of what some freak said!" Ma snarls. "You just peel them! And set the table too."

"I gotta put my stuff away first," I say. I really want to go upstairs just in case Jimmy's home yet. But I check his room and he isn't. I change my clothes, then sit down on my bed. I take a deep breath, then get up and head back downstairs.

There's a window over the kitchen sink. I peel the potatoes and I look out and see a brown bird sitting on the chain-link fence at the end of our tiny backyard. I can't hear it, but I can tell it's singing. Its head is raised up and tilted and its throat is vibrating like. This reminds me of the first song Sister Marie taught us in French. I start singing:

"Frear a jock-a, frear a jock-a, Door may voo, door may voo," I think it was about football players. Johnny was a Jock, before he died.

"Hush that racket!" Ma says right behind me.

"Sister Marie taught us—"

"Singing's for happy houses!" she screams. "This house isn't happy anymore!"

I keep peeling, getting madder and madder. Then I turn and say, "It might be happier if you stopped the goddamn funeral you've been having since . . . since the summer!"

I don't say this for me, I can take care of myself. I say it for Jimmy.

Ma's blue eyes get huge. Before I can make a move she picks up her tea mug and whips it at me. Lucky for me, her tea's not scalding, like before. The cup hits me in the elbow and it hurts, but I won't cry. I try to make it out of the kitchen quick but Ma's smart, she heads for where the kitchen goes out into the hall, instead of for me, so she cuts off my escape. There's a light in her eyes as she starts coming closer.

"How dare you!" she hisses, hunching over and sticking out her scrunched up hands, like they're claws. "How dare you!" Tears are running fast down her face. She gets me in the corner. I turn my back and cover my face so she won't bruise me there. I don't want anyone to know. Yet. There will be a time for others knowing. Later, after I help Jimmy. I could hit her back but I just can't. For some reason I think of when Ma would dance around the kitchen with Johnny when the radio played her favorite song "That's The Light When The Nights Went Out in Georgia." I hate that song. It sucks and it's way dumb.

Ma comes into me. She beats me hard. I can't help crying, but I do it so she won't hear me, my mouth's open but I'm quiet. "Why wasn't it you, you little bitch!" she screams. "Why wasn't it *you!*"

* * *

"She wants to see you," I whispered into Jimmy's ear that night after supper when nobody talked again. He was lying on his bed, his face to the wall. But I could tell he wasn't sleeping. He always stays in his room now, after supper. I was wearing a sweater so he wouldn't see the new bruises on my arm.

"Who?" he asked. His voice was all muffley and soggy, like a week of rain.

"Sister Marie. She's my teacher." I waited for him to say something but he didn't.

"She's nice," I added.

"Why?" Jimmy asked.

"I don't know," I answered. I did know, but I also knew if I told Jimmy why he wouldn't go. He doesn't like to talk about It, talk to anybody about It, not even to me, and I was there. "Maybe she's got some questions about tires."

"Yeah right," Jimmy said. Jimmy has a job at a tire place over on Old Colony Road, putting new tires on people's cars. Dad got him the job. Jimmy hates it. A friend of Dad's owns the place, Mr. Brennan. Jimmy says he's an asshole. Jimmy was going to go to Art School even though Ma and Dad didn't want him to, but now he says he's changed his mind. He doesn't even draw anymore. Which is too bad, he's really awesome at Art.

"She's a nun, she probably doesn't even have a car," he said. He lifted his head up and turned toward me. He'd been crying again. Jimmy has eyes the same color blue as Ma's but they're not crazy or still and mean like Ma's. And Dad's curly black hair. My hair's straight and light brown. Ma says it's mousy but Grandma Flynn says it's like silk. Grandma Flynn is so cool.

"Well?" I asked after a minute. My fingers were double-crossed behind my back. I would've said a prayer but God's too mad at me. "What should I tell her?"

"Each of us—we are like the onion," Sister Marie was explaining. It was first period, Religion Class. Not usually my favorite class, no offense, God. That would be Penmanship. Every year I win the Penmanship Award for our class. Just like Jimmy used to win the Art Award every year when he was here at Gate of Heaven School. But Mom and Dad always got more excited when Johnny got his baseball or football or hockey trophies. This makes me think of the time I had meningitis. I was asleep for two days in my room. Finally Grandma Flynn was over and had me rushed to the hospital. I almost died. Jimmy said Grandma Flynn blasted Ma, and Ma blasted her back saying, "Well I didn't know! I'm not a Goddamn Doctor, you know!"

About a year after that, Johnny got really sick. He had a high fever. He was talking crazy, saying that Jesus was coming to town. Ma burst into my room when I was on the phone with Brenda without even knocking. She looked like the Holy Ghost on acid or something, all freaked out.

"Hang that up!" she said, grabbing the portable from my hands and shutting it off. "Pray! C'mon! *Pray!*" She pushed me down on the floor and shoved blue crystal Rosary Beads into my hands.

"Wh . . . what are you doing?" I asked, annoyed and pissed.

"Pray!" she said.

"For . . . for what?" I asked.

"For your brother!" she hissed, taking me by the shoulders and shaking. "He's got a fever of 104! The doctor's on his way, but you pray, missy, do you hear me? *Pray!*" Ma ran out of my room and went downstairs to wait for the doctor.

"Dear God," I said, getting back up and reaching for the phone so I could call Brenda back. "Let Johnny get better."

Johnny did get better, but two things stayed with him. His fever was so high he lost most of his hearing in one ear, which really bothered him because he said he wouldn't be able to be a Marine when he turned eighteen; and the other thing was he still thought a little that Jesus was going to come to town someday. He asked me about it once, that's how I know, it was like the only polite conversation we had in five years. He kinda got nastier every year—finally the people at school said he had to go see a shrink, he was always getting in trouble and fights and stuff. Ma brought him to three different psychiatrists before she found one that didn't say Johnny was just a troublemaking punk. They found out that Johnny had ADD and DDT and all this other stuff, and they gave him pills which he didn't take all the time because he wouldn't be able to drink beer with them, and whenever he lost his temper or started breaking things we all had to "support him," Ma said, if we knew what was good for us.

"Yes, each of us . . . we are like ze onion," Sister Marie repeated.

Sister Marie pulled an onion, a small yellow one, out of her nun pockets, which you could never see. They were kind of hidden in the folds of her white habit. If you're not a Catholic, that's a nun dress. Some of the kids laughed. Just because this was weird.

"Ef you peel the first layer," she went on, doing this, "what do you get? Anoder layer. Ef you peel that layer, you find . . . wait a minute . . . look here, anoder layer. See? So it is with us. Dere ez someone we are that we show to the world. Riding the bus, let's say. Dis ez our first layer, no? There is another layer beneat dis one, which maybe our classmates see—they know a little more about us den strangers on a bus. Beneat dat layer, dere ez anoder one. See? Like the onion. Maybe our close friends see dis layer. Den dere is anoder layer—our family maybe see dis one. And so on. And if you go to the very middle . . . dis is who we are. Our . . . essence. Our soul. Maybe only we know dis layer. What we really tink. Who we really are. Et ez this inner essence that is so beautiful. God loves dis inner essence. It ez where we are all different. But all de same. We are perfect love, in dis essence, dis middle. Know dis about yourselves. Don't ever tink you are not precious, or worthy of love. We find God in dis middle. We find ourselves. Picture a beautiful light inside you—"

"Good morn-ing, Fa-ther."

Everybody stood up all at once as Father McCarthy opened the classroom door and walked in. Sister Marie's head jerked back a little as she watched us do this, then it swept to the left. Her eyebrows bunched together and she stopped talking. As Pastor of Gate of Heaven Church, Father McCarthy would sometimes make surprise visits to the classrooms. Especially the classrooms of new teachers like Sister Marie.

"Hello, children," Father McCarthy smiled. He called us children even though we were in the seventh grade. "You can sit down now." Father McCarthy always smiled. I don't think I'd ever seen him without a smile. Except for maybe when he was giving the Homily during Sunday Mass. Two of his teeth—the ones on either side of his two front top ones—were kind of pointy. That's probably why he looked meaner when he smiled than lots of other people when they frowned. Like a wolf in an olden-days cartoon. He was skinny and had white hair and always seemed tanned. And his eyes kept moving around all the time, going from side to side.

"And what are we doing this morning?" he asked, smiling even bigger. Debbie Pickett raised her hand. One good thing about sitting in the back is you see everything—who's got the hots for who, untucked shirts, notes being passed, who's trying to cheat, who picks their nose and wipes it under the desk, stuff like that. And Sister Marie staring at Father McCarthy in front of her like she didn't like this and was annoyed.

"Yes!" Father McCarthy smiled, rubbing his hands together and nodding his head at Debbie. That meant he couldn't remember her name. There's over 1,200 families in Gate of Heaven Parish, so he couldn't remember everyone's name. Especially the families from the Projects, it seemed, probably because most of them had big big families and couldn't give much in the weekly collection.

Debbie Pickett stood up immediately, as we all did when we were called on. Even if you didn't know the answer you had to stand up.

"Sister-Marie-was-saying-how-we-were-like-onions," she said rapidly. Then she sat back down.

"Ahhhh!" Father McCarthy said, very very slowly, like either us or him was an idiot. He kept smiling but his white eyebrows bunched together. "Onions!"

Some of my classmates nodded.

"Uhhmmm . . . how, exactly?" he asked, folding his arms across his chest and sitting down on the edge of Sister Marie's desk, blocking her from our view. A few kids raised their hands, but instead Father McCarthy pointed to Danny O'Brien. "Mr. O'Brien!" he said. Danny's father owns O'Brien Ford, and they all sit in the front row at Sunday Mass. Mrs. O'Brien has a fur coat, and attitude.

"Ahhh . . . she said we all got these layers, like," Danny said. "And ahhhh, the bottomest layer is perfect, like."

"Ohhhhhh!" Father McCarthy said, slow like we were all retarded. He put one of his hands up to his chin. His lips stuck out as he thought about this.

"I can't *exactly* agree with that," he said after a minute, when it was so quiet I could hear the ticking of the clock and some other class outside at recess. "You see, boys and girls, inside there is . . . *sin*. Black sin."

All of a sudden I felt the blackness come back. There had been this blackness inside me, eating me away little by little ever since—

"Wouldn't you agree, Sister Marie," Father McCarthy said. He didn't turn around to look at her. His smile got wider.

"Well—everyone has made mistakes," she answered after a minute. "Even nuns and priests."

Then for once Father McCarthy didn't smile.

I had to duck down I was laughing so hard. I felt the blackness stop eating me for a minute.

* * *

Jimmy went to see Sister Marie. He got a note. I brought it home from school. I wrote it during Penmanship. I signed it "Sister Marie." This was a little lie but one of my outer layers did it, not my inner layer. My inner layer just wanted to help Jimmy and I knew he wouldn't go see her unless I sent a note or something. And after all— she did say she wanted to see him. The note said, "Dear Jimmy, Please come and see me. I would like to speak to you about some- thing important. Sister Marie." I did it three times before I finally had her writing right. During lunch I asked Sister Marie if she might have some nice paper that I could write a nice note on instead of my messy spiral notebook with the ripped edges.

"Such beautiful penmanship as yours calls for equally beautiful paper!" she said, opening her desk drawers, one then the other. I had figured she'd say something just like that. I smiled. After a minute of rummaging she gave me a pad of nice thick whitish-yellow paper that had *Sisters of St. Joseph* written on the top in black letters. It was very real looking. I put the last version of my note on this paper.

I left it on Jimmy's bed when I got home from school that afternoon.

"I have seen your broder," Sister Marie said to me a week later, af- ter class. I held my breath—but she didn't say anything about a note, so I guess neither one of them had mentioned it. "He's a very nice per- son," Sister Marie said. Her eyes looked sad, like a doll's alone in a toy store.

"Can you help him?" I blurted. It was what I was thinking, but I'm not sure I wanted to say it.

She looked at me quick.

"How much do you know?" she asked.

"About what?" I asked back.

"I tink so," she said.

"Oh, I just remembered—she's gonna get fired," Brenda McCar- thy whispered to me as we walked up to the front of the church on our way out. It was a few weeks later and not hot anymore. You needed a sweater now walking to school in the morning and the blue skies were bluer and colder in the morning. I didn't get any new school clothes this year which really pissed me off. (Ma said she didn't have the heart because it reminded her of when she'd go new-school-clothes-shopping with Johnny. Loser. Grandma Flynn gave me a hundred bucks a few weeks later to get some. But I put the money aside instead.)

The next day was a Holy Day and our whole school had just attended Mass after classes.

"Who?" I said. We walked by the statue of the Blessed Mother near the side entrance of the church and her eyes always seemed to follow me as I passed. "Who's gonna get fired?"

"Sister Marie," Brenda said, blowing a pink gum bubble like what she just said didn't really matter too much.

I stopped. Her words felt like a punch in the stomach.

"Shit, she can't!" I said, and my voice echoed a little. Sister Mary John, an eighth grade mean nun, turned around and looked very cross in our direction. Brenda looked away and we walked faster until we were outside. Brenda blew another bubble.

"Wait till we get to the store," Brenda said. There were some things we didn't talk about on school and church property, mostly sex stuff.

"My aunt told me," Brenda said as we went down the stairs that led from the church parking lot out to Broadway. Brenda's Aunt Teresa was the cook at the Gate of Heaven Rectory. If you're not Catholic, a rectory's this place where priests live, like a convent except it's priests instead of nuns. "She heard the priests talking at suppertime. They don't think she can hear but she does. I heard her telling my mother last night. They don't think I can hear them from upstairs but I do."

"Why?"

"Because they think I'm too far away to hear."

"No, duh! Why do they want to can Sister Marie?"

"In . . . insubordination." Brenda said the word importantly, like she knew what it meant, but I knew she didn't.

"What's that mean?" I asked, but I was thinking of something else. I could figure out what it meant. "But . . . how can they fire a nun?"

"They send them to another school, far away somewhere. In the ghetto or something, or some shithole overseas. They reassign them. Ohmigod, do you wanna see the note Pinky McGurl sent me?"

"Not right now," I said after a minute. Later when we were outside the store, I asked her, "do you remember that story Sister Marie told us a while ago? About Our Lady of Fatima? The girl who got special messages from Our Lady?"

"Yeah, so what?" Brenda asked. She was pissed because I didn't look at her note from Pinky. Also she was trying to get the braids out of her hair. You had to wear your hair in braids to school if you had long hair, so Brenda always undid them on the way home. She has such beautiful hair, thick and black, not like mine.

"Do you think," I said. I stopped for a minute. "Do you think that could happen nowadays?"

Brenda said, "Beats me. Maybe they'd do it on computers. That way more people would know."

After supper that night I was doing homework in my room when a familiar smell seeped in under my door. I know my mouth fell open. I raised my head from the paper, sniffing just to be sure. A second later I was in Jimmy's room.

"You're painting again!" I whispered, afraid that if I talked too loud the spell would break. He was sitting backward on his chair the way he used to with a large canvas propped up on his desk. He'd put his lamp on the bed so the light would shine on what he was painting. It was all black, his painting, with these white things floating around like ghosts, and splotches of red. It was scary looking. But he was painting again!

"Sister Marie says you have to paint the feelings out," he mumbled after a minute, not even looking at me.

"What is it?" I asked. "What are you painting?" I had to sit down, my breath was coming funny—Jimmy was painting again! I knew Sister Marie could help him!

"I don't know yet," he said after a minute.

Then a chill came over me, like when some loser runs their long fingernails down a blackboard just to be funny. I remembered what Brenda had said about Sister Marie getting fired.

I watched Jimmy paint for ten minutes, in silence that wrapped us like blankets. Warm, scratchy blankets, the kind Ma used to cover me with and kiss me when I'd be half-asleep before Johnny died. That kind. I was letting the image of Jimmy painting go into me like water. But still I was thinking of Sister Marie getting fired.

"Don't bite your lip, Sweetheart," Jimmy said, half turning. I smiled. I didn't even know I was doing it. I got up to leave, to think in my own room. There had to be a way.

"Thanks," Jimmy said when I was leaving his green bedroom, adjusting the baseball lamp he got when he was twelve that he painted over, until the baseball looked like an owl's head.

"For what?"

"Sister Marie," he said. "I ahhh . . . see her twice a week now,"

"Isn't she awesome?" I whispered.

"Yeah," Jimmy said. His eyes strayed away from mine and went back to his painting.

Sunday mornings are not like other mornings. We learned four years ago in third grade about B.C. and A.D. B.C. was Before Christ. A.D. was after, though I forget what the A and the D stand for. Something that's not English I think. They said everything changed after Jesus was born, that's why they had to change the years and call them A.D. or B.C. It's the same in our house now. Everything changed after Johnny died. I made up new initials. B.J.D. and A.J.D. If I knew another language maybe I'd make one of them in a different language to make it more official sounding. But I don't. Before Johnny Died and After Johnny Died. Sundays have always been different, both B.J.D. and A.J.D.

B.J.D. they were like Grandma Flynn's tablecloth that she keeps up in her attic. Her attic smells like dust and books and velvet. There's lots of trunks up there. They're all black except for one that's white. She keeps the key to the white trunk on a chain around her neck. The skin around her neck is saggy like a chicken's. It's interesting, you never see that kind of stuff on TV.

"Look Christine," she said once, we were up in the attic looking for her Christmas lights. She was babysitting us. Ma and Dad had gone on a boat because they had been married fifteen years, exactly. It was raining out and I wanted snow. Johnny was playing in Grandma Flynn's basement three floors below us with her old-fashioned ironing thing that had a pedal and a big round thing like the dry cleaners. Jimmy was in the parlor, reading. I was nine. It was three and a half years ago.

"Look," Grandma Flynn said. She slipped the chain off her neck. She slowly bent down on her knees, then blew dust off the top of the white trunk. The dust went into the gray light that was coming through the window in a slant and started dancing like fairies.

"So that's where the key to that trunk is!" I said. Grandma Flynn turned her blue eyes to me. They're soft and watery, not like Jimmy's, which are faraway, then steady when he looks at you. Not like Ma's, which are mean, and cold—like a blue marble you dropped in very cold water. A.J.D., I mean. I don't remember Ma's eyes B.J.D. They were just there, just eyes.

"You've tried to open this before?" she asked. I nodded my head.

"Curiosity is a good thing," she said. She patted me. "It means you're smart."

"What's curiosity?" I asked. I knew, but I wanted to enjoy being able to ask as many questions as I wanted, you can do that with Grandma Flynn. She chuckled.

"Wanting to know things." I love Grandma Flynn.

"Look here, Christine," she said. She unlocked the dark gray lock. It made a solid CLINK sound, like the old silver dollars Dad collects on his bureau when they splash together. She undid the lock, then lifted the trunk top. I helped her do that part.

The underneath of the trunk lid had pink cushion stuff in it. A smell lifted out of the trunk like the incense at Mass. It reminded me of old dresses, carefully folded.

I breathed deeply.

"That's Lavender," Grandma Flynn said. There was tissue on the top of the trunk. She pulled this out. It was white, and also smelled pretty. Then there was more tissue. And more. She turned around and looked for a place to put it. "Put this on that chair over there, sweetheart," she asked me. I did. When I came back she was lifting something out of the trunk with her forearms. She wouldn't touch it with her hands, like it was Holy. I didn't come any closer.

"What is it?" I whispered.

"Irish Linen," she said. "My mother made this." It was a tablecloth, she said, and twelve matching napkins. They were all white.

"Look closer," she said. I came closer. In the dazzling white there was more white, just barely showing castles and shamrocks and designs. "The finest embroidery. She made it for my wedding day. All done by hand," Grandma Flynn said. Then she paused. A tear fell on the cloth. She didn't wipe it up.

"All done with love," she added. She put the linen back. It rustled.

Sundays B.J.D. were like Grandma Flynn's linen. You would take them out carefully, like they were Holy. They smelled pretty. They were full of rustling sounds, as Ma put on her best dress, and I put on my silk. You could smell Dad's hair tonic. Ma would make pancakes "from Scratch," Dad would always say. I never got to find out what that meant. I asked Ma the other day but she wouldn't answer me, she

just stared into her tea. (I could see her red nose and her angry eyes reflected wavery in the tea, so I knew not to ask again.) After breakfast
on Sundays B.J.D., Dad and the boys would put their shirts and ties on.
Me and Mom had to be careful not to spill the maple syrup on our
dresses. But the boys and Dad couldn't be trusted not to be slobs.
They got to eat in their T-shirts. I think it would have been easier if I
were a boy. They painted my room blue before I was born, expecting
a boy. "I felt the same way carrying you that I did Johnny and Jimmy,"
Ma used to say all the time. "That's why I thought you'd be a boy." I
always waited for her to say, "But I'm glad you weren't, I'm glad
you're you." She never did though. And my room never got painted,
it's still blue. As soon as I get a job when I'm sixteen, I'm going to
buy paint. Yellow paint.

After breakfast on Sundays B.J.D., Mom would rush to wash the
dishes, and the boys and Dad would run upstairs to put on their shirts
and ties. In the summer the birds would call through the screened
open windows—I don't remember them doing that any other day of
the week. I used to think they were saints that got tired of Heaven and
would fly down to earth for the day. Just because it was Sunday.
There's not that many birds around here usually, see. The smell of
Mrs. Morrison's roast beef cooking in her oven next door would drift
in too, just little bits of odor like it was shy. She always ate her big
supper at noon. "Roast beef every Sunday at noon," Mom would say,
shaking her head, "come Helen Highwater." I guess that was a rela-
tive of Mrs. Morrison's or something that might or might not visit.
Mom would rush to wash the dishes but sooner or later someone
would call her to go upstairs and find something. A tie. A shirt. Cuff
links. She said nothing when Dad did it, her face would be blank.
She'd get mad when Jimmy did it and always asked him to look
harder, don't be so absent-minded, she didn't have time. When
Johnny did it she'd laugh, say, "Oh, that one," and go running up the
stairs, "he's all boy." She always said that about Johnny. She never
said that about Jimmy.

Then we'd all walk to Mass together. Dad would hold my hand,
when I was younger. The sun shone down different, maybe because it
reflected on my yellow silk dress and shone everywhere. Dad wore
After You Shave, and he smelled different than when he came home
every night from the garage stinking like hot gasoline. Johnny knew
everyone, from his playing football and baseball and hockey and the

Boys Club and the Touchdown Club, and so Ma knew them too because she'd go to his games and fund-raisers and make phone calls when they needed money for equipment or trips. We'd all have to stop while Johnny and Ma and These People talked. It was always stupid stuff they talked about, boring, what someone wore to the Awards Banquet, next year's prospects. "Tiny talk," Jimmy called it. "Tiny people tiny talking," he said, and I thought that was so silly that I laughed in church after he said it until Ma gave me a knuckle to the head. The foolish teenage girls we'd see on the way to Mass would tease Johnny and he'd tease them back and Mom would smile. The girls would stare at Jimmy, but they'd never say anything. Jimmy always walked behind, his hands in his pockets, looking at things. Everything, but mostly down on the ground.

"C'mon!" Ma would growl at him, half turning around. We'd sit in different places every Sunday, it would depend. Mostly we'd be a little late and have to stand. Mom hated to stand. She'd wait until some man would turn and see her, and offer her his seat. If no one turned around she'd cough until someone did. She'd smile and shake her head, mouthing, "No! No!" when someone offered her their seat, but she'd always take it, and if no one offered her a seat she'd complain about it all the way home, saying chivalry was dead whatever that means and also saying she shouldn't stand with her very close veins.

"You shouldn't talk then on the way to Mass, and then we wouldn't have to be late and stand," I said once. She lunged at me but then people were around she remembered, so she stopped, but she got me later that night when Dad went out bowling with his friends from the gas station. B.J.D. she'd just spank, but A.J.D. she punches. Hard as hell.

A.J.D., Sundays are still different, but different the way death is different from life. It's so quiet you want to scream. Mom tried making pancakes once but had to stop halfway through she was bawling so much. Jimmy doesn't go to church with us anymore, so it's just me and Ma and Dad, and Johnny's not with us of course and when people see us coming they seem to always look away quick so there's no one to stop and talk to and we're never late.

It was a Sunday, the first Sunday in November, when I made the announcement. I had to, because Brenda's aunt had told her mother that they were going to fire Sister Marie that week. I slept a little the night before. I woke up at 4:17 or :18. It was still dark and the big dresser looked like a monster until right before six, when it started getting lighter. I studied some holy pictures I had under my mattress of the different children Our Lady had appeared to over the years. They all looked pale, and kind of Goth, and like they might be in pain. *Remember this,* I told myself. Dad got up at 6:47 and peed with the bathroom door open, then he went back to bed. I could hear muffled talking in their bedroom, then nothing else. At 7:30 I got up and made my bed then said prayers for the first time in a long time.

"God," I said, "help me do it today."

Then I went down to the living room and turned on TV. One of my old favorite cartoons was on which I watched, but it seemed boring and not enjoyable anymore. There were lots of holy shows on but I wasn't sure if they were Catholic or not and if I was supposed to watch them. Plus they were boring too. I had cereal at 8:30, Frosted Stars. There was frozen orange juice in its container that Ma had left out on the counter to defrost. Some of the thick yellow juicy stuff was leaking out of the bottom of the can. But I didn't feel like making it. At 9:00 the Showcase of Homes show came on, which I love. The nice lady would drive around to new neighborhoods and go visit new houses for sale. I liked to pretend she was my real mother and one day she'd drive up to our house right in the middle of her show and say to everyone out there in TV land, "Before we look at the exciting new development at Canton Woods, let's pick up my real daughter at the house she's been living at for a while." And then we'd drive around to see new houses, me and her, and if we saw one we really liked, we'd send the cameras home and just live there. And Dad and Jimmy could come live with us too. At 9:22, Dad got up.

"Hey Sport," he said to me. He rubbed my head, then went out into the kitchen and had cereal. Then he went out jogging. Dad used to smile a lot and watch sports on TV and say nothing B.J.D. Now he just says nothing.

At 9:44 Jimmy got up, took a shower, then went back into his room. The smell of oil paints tiptoed downstairs from his bedroom. I smiled, even though I was nervous. At 10:17, Mom got up, and I hated her footsteps. She came down the living room stairs, then looked out the curtains sneaky-like, which is the first thing she does every day.

"Is your father back yet?" she asked.

"No," I said.

She shuffled out to the kitchen, then came back in.

"Why didn't you make the orange juice?" she said.

"I don't know," I said, not looking away from the TV. "I . . . forgot."

She walked over to me and slapped me in the face.

"That's so you don't forget again," she said. Then she walked back out into the kitchen.

"Isn't this fabulous?" the lady on the TV said, looking at a huge bedroom closet in a new house.

When Dad held the church door open for me and Ma an hour later, I scooted in first, then walked all the way down to the empty-ish pew second closest to the altar, listening to my patent leather shoes. Ma hated to sit up front because she said everyone looked at her, but I think she didn't like to because then she couldn't look at everyone else. But I found seats in the second pew, and so Ma and Dad were forced to come and sit with me. Dad didn't care—he didn't care about anything really, it was like someone gave him a Numb Pill A.J.D. But Mom glared and pinched me after she sat down next to me.

"You know I hate sitting this close!" she hissed.

"Really?" I said back, lifting my eyebrows. Then I made the Sign of the Cross and knelt down. The church was full of sound and light and smell. People murmuring, whispering, talking low, the organist Mrs. Cassidy warming up (Jimmy whispered to me one time B.J.D., "Christine, what if Mrs. Cassidy all of a sudden started playing scary *Phantom of the Opera* Organ Music, and she locked herself up in the loft and no one could make her stop," and I got the giggles thinking about this), the sound of crisp Missal pages being turned, the smells— of beeswax candles that somehow never got drippy like mine did in Girl Scouts when we made them two years ago, of furniture polish, and people's wool coats, this was like the first cold Sunday of the year.

The O'Briens (O'Brien Ford, remember?) were in the front row like they always were except for summers when they went to the Cape and probably sat in the front row of some church down there. Mr. O'Brien has a big nose that always looks bigger because he lifts his head high like he's the priest instead of the priest and Mrs. O'Brien had a gross fur coat on that two hundred animals must have died for so people would look at her fat furry ass. Mr. Dooley was the Lector that day. If you're not Catholic, that means like the announcer.

He stands at a pulpit thing that they call the Lectern. He had glasses and a black suit that didn't fit good and a white shirt and a white tie. Someone in the back of the church kept coughing. Mr. Dooley kept pushing his glasses up against the top of his nose even though they weren't slipping, and peering to the back of the church. That's where the priest who was going to say today's Mass was gathering with the altar servers (young kids), and the Eucharistic Ministers. If you're not Catholic, those are the people who help the priest give out Communion at Communion Time.

Finally Mr. Dooley said into the microphone, "Good morning." But he said it too close to the microphone and it came out all loud and deep, like in a horror movie but instead of Good Evening like they say in horror movies it was Good Morning. Nobody said Good Morning back, I'd never noticed before if they did or they didn't. My breath was coming funny. Then Mr. Dooley said, "Today's Entrance Hymn is Number 432, 'A City Upon A Hill'." Everybody stood up. The lady in front of me was jumbo and blocked my view. She was a wearing a tan coat made out of some shiny material. I slid over closer to Ma even though I didn't want to, so I could see. Mrs. Cassidy started playing on her organ and the altar servers and the Eucharistic Ministers and the priest started walking slow down the aisle. The priest today was Father Bryne. He's one of the two regular priests that help the pastor, Father McCarthy, who's like the boss of the parish. Father Bryne is younger than Father McCarthy, maybe thirty. Grandma Flynn says he has beautiful hands. To me they just look normal and very white, like Wonder Bread. They were very smooth though. Not like Dad's, which are big and red and rough looking, and always gasoline-ish, no matter how hard he scrubs them with Lava. Father Bryne was holding a big book over his head as he walked past. His vestments were bright green today. He was the last one in line. First came the altar servers (two boys and a girl—Timmy O'Toole, Jack Cotter, and Maria Sullivan who I can't stand), then the Eucharistic Ministers, then Father Bryne. Only about half the people were singing. Father Bryne was singing loud. It sounded like he was in pain, he didn't have a good voice. Then they all got to the altar and climbed up the steps. Father Bryne kissed the altar, and everybody genuflected. Then they started the Mass.

Maybe it was because I was very very very nervous, but I could hear things better, and smell things better. Somebody still kept coughing in the back. I could hear a baby's breathing. I could smell Dad's spicy After You Shave, Mom's perfume, which smelled like roses after they've been in a vase for a week and time to throw them out, the candles, which smelled high and light and sweet. It got warmer in the church as the Mass went on and I could smell people. I could see things better too, how Mrs. Donaghue one row beside us blew her nose in a tissue that she got from up her dress sleeve, how her sister Mrs. Barton stared at her afterward like she'd done something wrong. I saw how Mrs. Kenny, one of the Eucharistic Ministers, had a little bit of lipstick on one of her teeth, you could only see this when she opened her mouth to make a response to the priest's prayers. Things started to slow down. Jesus on the cross, hanging way behind and above the altar, had his head hanging down sad like he was thinking about Johnny and how it looked when the train hit him. I tried to see if I could see a guardian angel behind Him, or anybody else in the church, but I couldn't. I wanted to look over to the right side of the front of the church where the Shrine to Our Lady was, but one of the big pale yellow pillars was in the way. I wanted to see if the statue of the Blessed Mother, the one where her eyes followed you, was looking angry over at me. I guess it was just as good that I couldn't see it. I started getting a little scared but then I thought of Jimmy, and Sister Marie. I was doing this for Jimmy, but also I was doing it for Sister Marie, I liked her and she did good things. She had started a soup kitchen when she first came to our parish. Lots of people said we didn't need one and that Southie Took Care of Its Own, and Father McCarthy tried to stop her but then the first week they ran out of like a million gallons of soup and tons of bread and they did a story in the paper and the mayor came down to get his picture taken so there wasn't any way anyone could shut it down without looking like a loser.

"Who does she think she is, coming in here and doing that?" Ma had said about the soup kitchen.

I don't remember too much about the opening prayer that morning. Or the Kyrie. Or the first reading, or the second reading . . . none of the official stuff. I remember the little things, like I mentioned, and a little buzzing in my ears like I hadn't eaten in a while, but I had. Then Father Bryne got up from his chair and walked to the altar.

Everybody stood up when he did. The fat lady in front of me took off her coat, and slung it over the pew behind her. She stared at me when our eyes met, as if to say Don't You Touch This Expensive Coat, Girly. As if, Mrs. Jumbo.

"A reading from the Holy Gospel, according to Luke," Father Bryne said.

"Glory to You, oh Lord," was the response, like a rumble of far-away thunder running through the church. Out of the corner of my eye I saw Mom and it looked like she was giving dirty looks to Jesus hanging way behind and above the altar. She thinks He should have stopped the train from hitting Johnny, but if He didn't stop His own death, then why would He stop anybody else's? I think He died so we wouldn't fear death anymore. That's what Sister Marie says anyway.

Father Bryne read the gospel story for that day. It was about they all went to a wedding and they ran out of booze and Jesus turned some water into wine and everyone said it was the best wine they ever had.

Then everyone sat down.

Father Bryne took the microphone from the Lectern where Mr. Dooley made his announcements from (he was sitting down in a chair on the side now, Mr. Dooley, with everyone else, we were all sitting now) and then Father Bryne took a few steps down from the altar and began the Homily. If you're not Catholic that's when the priest gives a lecture about something. I noticed I was beginning to sweat. I held up the glass face of my watch so I could see my own reflection, I wanted to see if I looked pale and in pain, the way the children had that the Blessed Mother appeared to. I couldn't tell too good. Father Bryne kept talking. He was saying how miracles could still happen today. Then finally he finished. He went back up to the altar and everyone stood up again and said the Profession of Faith. It was 12:32. There was a bunch more prayers and then everybody said the Our Father and then it was just about time. Time for Communion. That was the time when I had decided I would do it. Somebody said once that Protestants go to Communion row by row, but we don't do it that way because then everybody could tell who went to Communion and who didn't, because you weren't supposed to go to Communion unless you were in a State of Grace, so I guess Protestants gossip more about each other, talking about who's in a State of Grace and who isn't. What happens here is just this, the priest gives out these golden chalices that reflect light all over the place full of Communion to the Eucharistic Ministers, then he keeps one for himself, and they spread

out at the bottom of the altar, the priest right in front of the altar, a
Eucharistic Minister on either side of him, and then two Eucharistic
Ministers on the other two sides of the altar. Then everybody that
wants to goes to Communion and the organist Mrs. Cassidy plays
something that's supposed to make you concentrate on what you've
just done, because people come back from Communion and kneel
and sometimes put their faces into their hands so they can Reflect. Ma
did not go to Communion. I felt bad for her for a minute because I
knew she wasn't going because she felt she hated God and wasn't
good enough to go because of her anger, like I said she was bull with
God for not stopping the train that hit Johnny and he burst into blood,
but then I remembered how she hits me now when Dad isn't around
and I didn't feel bad for her anymore and I hoped God was mad with
her too. Dad went though, and I went behind him. Dad went right up
to the front of the altar. I didn't. I had it all planned in my head. He
was in front of me and he kept going straight. I took a right up the
main front side aisle, and headed over to the right aisle. There were
two lines of people there waiting for Communion and I got in the lon-
gest one. I peeked up at the statue of the Blessed Mother and she was
watching me, but she didn't seem especially mad or cross. You
couldn't figure out what she was thinking. I had thought earlier how I
might faint at this moment, so close to doing what I had to do for
Jimmy and Sister Marie. But it wasn't that way at all. Now that I was
really going to do it I felt strong and I knew I had to do it. I was doing
it for Jimmy and his blue eyes and curly hair and kind ways and Art
talent, I was doing it for Sister Marie and her kind ways and her
crow's eyes. And no one could stop me now. Ma was far away and
Dad never knew what was going on anyway. I didn't even look when
Teresa McKillop stuck her tongue out at me when she passed me as
she came back from getting Communion. I was the last one to get
Communion in this line. After I got it I stood to the side and blessed
myself and held my head down to stall a little more, because sometimes people did that. Then I looked out of the corner of my eye and
saw that I was the last one in the whole church that had received Holy
Communion. That was good, this was what I had planned which is
why I didn't get too much sleep the night before, I was planning everything in my head. But I wasn't tired. I was wearing my yellow
dress even though it's getting a little small for me. Then I started
walking back to where we were sitting. Father Bryne and the Eucharistic

Ministers were putting the Communion back in the Tabernacle, which is like a little house they keep the leftover Communion in, way over to the left of the altar. As I walked by the altar with my hands folded, I took a right instead of a left and went up to the Lectern. Mr. Dooley was there, but he had his head turned and was waiting nervously for Father Bryne to come back. I reached up and took the microphone from the lectern. Then I turned around. The whole church could see me and I knew by now that everyone was staring at me open-mouthed like when someone runs onto the field bareass during a professional baseball game. I didn't raise my head or look at anyone, I knew that would ruin my concentration. I know how to concentrate from Penmanship, making each letter just so is perfect for developing Concentration. Then I walked the few steps to the center aisle, right at the foot of the altar. I held the microphone up to my mouth.

"I have an announcement to make," I said.

Unlike Mr. Dooley, who did this every single week but could never seem to get it right, I had beginner's luck or maybe God was watching out for me, for my voice came out perfect, loud but not too loud, and very clear. I kept my eyes on the choir loft way at the other end of the church that seemed twenty miles away. I didn't look at anybody's face, but out of the corner of my eye I could see every single person sitting in the church staring at me. I could hear Mr. Dooley say something about Miss, Miss, What Are You Doing, but I paid him no mind, I didn't even turn in his direction. It was November 3. I knew I only had a minute.

"The Blessed Mother appeared to me," I said into the microphone. I paused. "She gave me two very special messages to tell everybody."

Finally, even the sound of that one person coughing went away. The only thing I could hear was my heartbeat in my ears and a dog barking outside the church. It was so quiet, like the time at the crowded noisy Mall when someone shot somebody else and for a second after the shot, it was the quietest I ever heard in my life. Until now.

"The first message is that she is pleased with the Soup Kitchen and the job Sister Marie has done. The second message is—"

I don't understand how it could have been so quiet, and I didn't hear Father McCarthy coming. He wasn't even saying this Mass. I guess he must have been waiting in the Sacristy, which is this little room off the side of the altar where the priests put on their vestments.

All of a sudden he was there, and he had his two hands on the microphone. I grabbed on tighter.

"Gimme that!" he said, but the microphone was right under his mouth and his words came out very loud all over the church. I tried to grab the microphone back but his red hands were like claws on it. Mr. Dooley was on the other side of me now, pushing his glasses very fast up his nose and hovering like he didn't know what to do, a wild look in his eyes and some drool on his lips.

All of a sudden, "Let her talk!" somebody yelled from the back of the church. But Father McCarthy didn't pay it any mind, and he finally got the microphone from me. I decided I'd have to say it without the microphone. I ran up to the top of the altar. Father McCarthy came after me. I ran to the other side of the altar. But Father Bryne grabbed me from behind. I saw Dad stand up.

"Get her out of here!" Father McCarthy said to Mr. Dooley and Father Bryne, and this time he covered up the microphone. They started pulling me toward the Sacristy. Then I got a better idea.

"It's a very important message!" I yelled, as loud as I could, "She wanted me to tell you! She appeared to me!" Everybody out in the crowd started talking at once. A few more people yelled, "Let her talk!" They pulled me into the room. Dad was there, looking like he'd just woke up from a seven-year dream and he didn't know what to do. I guess he'd run up after me, when they were pulling me into the Sacristy.

"Is this your daughter?" Father McCarthy asked, who for once wasn't smiling and his face had turned red.

Dad just nodded, his mouth open.

Father McCarthy spun me around by my shoulders and shook me.

"Why did you tell that lie?" he asked. The veins on his neck were sticking out.

"Owww!" I said, because his hands were on a bruise I had from the week before where Ma had punched me.

"Leave her alone!" Dad said. I couldn't believe it. Dad put his arm around my shoulder and pulled me toward him. I hugged him hard and started crying, not because of what I'd just done but because I didn't know Dad liked me. Father McCarthy was breathing hard and nobody said anything for a minute. Then Dad turned us around and we walked out of the little room. All the talking stopped as soon as everybody in the church saw us reappear. We went across the front of the church, then around the altar and to the front of the main aisle. Ma wasn't there where we had been sitting, I noticed. Dad's grip on my hand tightened. Everyone was staring at me. I thought of Sister Marie, I don't know why. We started walking down the main aisle. I don't think anyone knew what to think or do. Everyone was staring at me. There was something very scary about so many people being so quiet. No coughing, nothing. We were about halfway up the aisle and I started crying again because I thought my plan had failed because of stupid Father McCarthy. Then Mrs. McAllister, who owns a bake shop on West Broadway—she's big and tall and always has a mean look on her red face, and she snatches money when you hand it to her and holds it up to the light—pushed to the end of the aisle she was sitting in. She was wearing a purple coat and had lots of makeup on her face. I thought maybe she was trying to get out of the church, away from all this nonsense that had made her late for something. But instead she pointed at me and said, "Look!" really loud. Dad stopped instinctively. She pushed her way closer to the edge of the aisle, still pointing. By now I could tell she was pointing at my arm, part of my dress sleeve had gotten torn during the Sacristy scuffle, and she was pointing at a spot right below my left elbow.

"It's the Sign of the Cross!" Mrs. McAllister said.

There was a rushy noise like everybody in the church lost their breath at once. I looked down. Mrs. McAllister was pointing to another bruise I'd got from Ma the week before when she'd gripped her thumb and fingers really hard on my arm. It was kind of in the shape of a cross, I noticed then for the first time.

Mrs. McAllister reached the end of her aisle. She had a look on her face that I don't think anyone in Southie had ever seen on her before. I know I never had. Her face was lit up, and her eyes were huge.

"It's a miracle!" she said. She started crying. "A miracle!"

Then she reached out her hand, slowly, the way Grandma Flynn touched her Irish linen. And she touched me.

She was shaking.

Everything changed after that.

All of a sudden everyone started pouring out of their seats like someone had said there was fire, run for your lives. But they all came to me. People started trying to touch me, my hair, my head, my dress, my arms, my back. All these hands, old hands, red hands, smooth hands, hands like parchment clutching light blue crystal Rosary beads.

"What was Our Lady's other message?" Mrs. O'Toole, who's about ninety, said to me right in front of me, all of a sudden her face was in mine and she's about as tall as me because she's all hunched over. "Yeah, what did she say?" forty other people said all at the same time, and the hands kept coming toward me. Somebody fell that was trying to get to me. I had to get out of there, I had to get home. Plus I didn't want anyone getting hurt, it was like when the boys at school called out "Pig Pile!" and everyone jumped on top of everybody else at recess. And someone always got hurt.

"She said," I said, and everything stopped and got quiet again. I looked around. I made my way slowly to the back of the church. Everybody followed silently. No one touched me anymore. Dad was able to catch up to me again.

I turned around and faced the crowd. There were hundreds of people there, all crowding the main aisle, or wedged into the ends of pews. The priests and Eucharistic Ministers were all up at the front of church, their arms folded, listening.

"She said," I said as loud as I could, "that her son Jesus would be coming to town."

There was a funny noise then that I'd never heard before, it was like the breath went out of everyone at once.

"He's going to come here," I said.

Somebody laughed, but at the same time Mrs. Gallagher fainted.

"When?" someone called out from the back of the crowd, and then everybody started asking When? When? It was the like the crowd was made up of tons of people, but only one mind, like an octopus with a million arms.

"December 1," I said. The gasping sound again.

Then I turned around and went home with Dad.

He didn't say anything all the way home. Everybody stared. No one said hi.

When we got home I went right to my room and shut the door. Jimmy was out somewhere. Mom and Dad were talking downstairs at the kitchen table, but I couldn't hear what they were saying. The phone started ringing.

"She's not home," I heard Ma say. As soon as she hung it up it rang again. And again. And again.

"That was someone from the newspaper," I heard her say to Dad at one point. I laid down on my bed and tried to take a nap. About an hour later I heard something outside my house and looked out my bedroom window to see what it was. There were people outside, so I ducked back quick before they could see me. Then very slowly I pulled back the navy blue curtain with the little ships and lighthouses on it, and peeked out the little opening I had made. One floor below out on the sidewalk, there were some of the people from Mass—three old ladies, one couple with two little kids, and Mr. O'Shea, the church's janitor. As I watched the three old ladies knelt down on the sidewalk and took out their Rosaries. They started to pray. It was cold out, and the wind blew their hair and turned their noses red raw. I watched for a while. More people came. By the time I left the window there were about twenty people out there.

Then Ma came into my room.

"What are you doing?" she said. I couldn't tell what kind of mood she was in, so I didn't say anything. She sat down on the edge of my bed. Her tongue was running up and down the inside of her cheek and she was staring hard at me.

"Do you know how embarrassed I was in church?" She kept eyeing me carefully, it reminded me of a cat I'd seen watching a mouse hole on one of my cartoon shows earlier that morning.

"You don't believe me?" I asked her.

"Like the Blessed Mother would appear to you!" she scoffed.

"It says in the Bible," I said, "that a prophet is never recognized in their own town. I didn't expect you to believe me." I paused. Ma's eyes got large with rage, but she didn't move from the edge of my bed. "I don't know if Dad told you," I continued, quick before she could strike, "but when we were leaving the church, Mrs. McAllister saw this on my arm and said it was The Sign of the Cross. And then everybody believed me." I rolled up my sleeve and showed her the bruise. By now I had changed my clothes and was wearing a New England Patriots sweatshirt that Jimmy got for Christmas a few years ago and never wore and he gave it to me. I looked Ma right in the eye, then I said, "Why don't we go outside and tell all those people how this really got here?"

Ma's black eyebrows bunched together. Her face didn't move but her eyes shifted to the window, where you could just barely hear some people. Then she leaped up and went over to it. Her mouth fell open, I don't think she knew people were out there. She turned around and looked at me. I could see rage in her eyes—but fear, too. Then they must have called out to her or something, because she turned and looked back out, then started smiling, crooked like, like she was trying to remember how. Then she waved to the people. Then she pulled the curtains tight and stepped back from the window and looked at me.

"It's payback time," I said.

"You wouldn't dare tell strangers what goes on in this house—"

"Oh you don't think so?" I asked. "If you ever touch me again, I will. And if you don't start treating Jimmy nicer, I will." Ma's head snapped back a little. "So help me," I said.

When I went to school the next morning there were about twenty people outside. Most of the kids at school made fun of me. Sister Marie asked me to stay afterward. She was quiet and serious.

"Tell me what happened," she said. I told her. She looked at me very serious. I could tell she wanted to ask me if this was all true, but she didn't. I wanted to tell her I was doing this for her, and for Jimmy, but I didn't. I felt like crying.

"Do you . . . are you sure of all this, Christine?" she said.

I had to look away and trot out of the classroom.

By Thursday there were 100 people outside my house. More and more every day after that. They'd be there at night too. Singing, praying. The cameras and TV came. I got sick of talking to them after a while. But they gave me money when I did.

The oddest things happened. It got bigger than me, the whole thing, and started changing people. Even if I huffed—sniffed glue, which I don't and never will—but even if I did, I couldn't have imagined the things that happened, and they say you imagine the craziest things when you huff. Things like: Sister Marie Soup Kitchens began popping up all over the country—in Milwaukee, New Orleans, Los Angeles (some famous people got involved with that one, but only for a week until they got their picture in the papers), two in New York.

One even in Paris, France, where they said Sister Marie's family originally must have come from.

Like: Mrs. McAllister (the bake shop lady) started giving away things in her store for free, every Sunday. If you were poor and couldn't afford anything, you could have it for free. Like: a lot of the barrooms in town had to start serving food so they could stay in business, I guess a lot of people quit drinking. Like: the advertising people took down all the cig and booze and violent movie billboards in town. It said in the papers that they did this because we weren't "a good market for their clients" anymore, whatever that meant. Like: people started being nice to each other. It got to the point where you'd see the cops sitting in their cars or leaning up against them, nothing to do and the whole day to do it. People were talking more to their neighbors, planting gardens in the front of their houses even though it was November, walking the streets again at night. Like: the local Red Cross put out their monthly desperate appeal for blood—and for the first time in their history, they had to turn people away the next day so many showed up.

Like: they put my picture, with Sister Marie's picture and Father McCarthy's picture in the background, on the cover of this big magazine. After that Father McCarthy became my new best friend, and started hanging out with me all the time. I was on the cover of a few other magazines too. One of them was funny, it had a picture of me on the cover with my arms folded and the headline under my picture said, "Christine Flynn: Who Is She? What Does She Want?" They gave me more and more money for interviews. There was even a story on the front page of one of those cheesy newspapers they have at the checkouts at Flannagan's. It had a way-ugly picture of me from two years ago and then this big row of pictures of some of the boys in our school and the headline said "Christine's Secret Teen Lovers!" Which was a huge lie, they had Chris Whitney's picture there and everyone knows I can't stand him. I gave a lot of the money from the newspapers and magazines to Sister Marie for her soup kitchen, but most of it I put in a special bank account in Jimmy's name without him knowing it.

Like: Sean McBride whistled at me one day when I was sneaking home from school with a hat pulled low over my head, then he ran across the street to talk to me. He's from the Projects and a drug dealer and everyone says he's his own best customer. He's a big tough twenty-year-older that bit somebody's ear off one time when they owed him money. He always carried a gun down the back of his pants, I saw it once when he was playing basketball without his shirt when he jumped up. I started running but he caught up to me. He was out of breath.

"Hey," he said. I was so scared all I could do was pull my books tighter into my chest. I couldn't say a word. "I'm clean," he said. I wasn't sure what he was talking about but Brenda told me later that meant he was off drugs.

"It's killing me, but I been clean for a week now," he went on. He smiled at me. His two front teeth were chipped. But it was still a very pretty smile. "I didn't know nothing good could happen around here."

I smiled back.

"I just wanted to tell you," he said. Then he reached his hand out and touched me. Then he smiled again, shrugged, and walked away. When I told Brenda about it the next day, she told me he was volunteering now at the Soup Kitchen, which they had to move to the high school auditorium because so many people went there at night. They came in buses all the way from Quebec and Maine and New York, just to see it and help out. All the nuns were working there too now.

Sean McBride said it was nearly killing him to be clean. Actually, it did kill him. A week after I saw him, one of the other drug dealers in another project across town found out he wasn't carrying a gun anymore and shot him as he left his house. I tried to go to his funeral, because there was something about what had happened that made me cry and cry and I didn't even know him. But as soon as I left the house they started following me, people from the newspapers and TV stations, so I just ran through to the backyards to Grandma Flynn's. But I saw Sean's mother in church a few days later. I thought she'd be mad at me. But she took my hands and kissed them instead.

"Thank you," she said, with big gray tears in her eyes. "His days were numbered anyway, the rate he was going," she sniffed. "Now . . . he died with the Lord."

I never meant for that to happen.

It seemed most of the people you wouldn't think were holy started changing, being nice and turning their lives around, while the people who were holy started getting nervous and almost mad at me.

"What did you have to go and start all this trouble for?" Mrs. Cleary said, she was the head of the Ladies Sodality that put flowers around the church every day.

I should tell you about the announcements. Every Sunday night I'd go to the church and say what the Blessed Mother had said to me that week in her messages. Father McCarthy would stand on one side of me smiling while I said this. But I also insisted Sister Marie stand on the other side of me. She didn't smile, she didn't say anything. She looked very uncomfortable. It got to the point where people never left the church anymore, they wanted to be there when I made the announcements Sunday nights.

The first week I was nervous and just said, "The Blessed Mother is pleased that so many people are turning back to their faith now," and then I sat down and wouldn't say anymore. But throughout the next week I thought a lot about it, because so many people were listening, and so the second week I said, "It's important to go to church and pray and all that stuff, but The Blessed Mother and God really want people to change from the inside out. Be kind to one another. Love one another. Do something good each day that you wouldn't ordinarily do. Cook a meal for the homeless person down the street. Pay a compliment to everyone you meet, for three straight days. Call someone you had a fight with and haven't spoken to in a while and forget about your pride. Be love." I meant the last part to come out "Be loving," but I was nervous.

"Is that what she said?" a reporter asked. "Be love?"

"Yes," I said. And that kind of became like the slogan of the whole thing.

The third week I said, "The Blessed Mother says people on this earth worry about two things too much. They worry about dying and they worry about money. People spend their whole lives worrying about these things. The Blessed Mother says, Don't Be Afraid. Just love yourself and love one another. Enjoy life. Be good to yourselves and be good to each other. And then there will be nothing you can't accomplish, and no wonderful paradise that the world can't be turned into. And be nice to animals and every creature, God made them all."

Things really changed after that one.

But all the time, the days were going fast and lots of crazy things happened, but the big thing was that December 1 was coming quicker and quicker. Everyone kept asking me where Jesus was going to appear. A lot of people thought the world was going to end that day and they quit their jobs and started freaking out. Not just in Southie but all over the world. I kept saying that the Blessed Mother hadn't said anything about the world ending, so people shouldn't worry about that. I said I didn't know where Jesus was going to be. We all moved to Grandma Flynn's because we couldn't leave or go into our house, there were so many people shoving and pushing and screaming when we did. But they found out about that too. It was agreed that I'd live in the rectory with Father McCarthy, which I didn't like, but I had my own room and cable TV and telephone and could eat anything I wanted, I just had to tell the cook. There were police guarding the rectory twenty-four hours a day because some kooks made death threats and when I'd go to the church and school every day they came with me to keep people away. Finally Father McCarthy said it was best if I stopped going to school because it was causing too much disruption for everybody else.

I kept giving the money and checks and stuff to Grandma Flynn, who'd come and visit me every day at the Rectory and she'd put it all in Jimmy's bank account. Jimmy would come and visit too but it was always hard, he didn't believe me and kept asking me what I was doing this for and we finally agreed that we wouldn't talk about it anymore. He said the tire place was doing twice the business it ever had now that everyone knew Christine Flynn's brother worked there, and Mr. Brennan his boss was being nicer to him and had doubled his salary. But he still hated the job and seemed very depressed.

"You should think about going to Art School. About leaving and going to New York or someplace and going to Art School," I said.

I was glad when December 1 finally got closer. I wanted everything to be over with now. I wanted to go back home and see Dad and Jimmy all the time again. Jimmy wouldn't be home much longer, I'd taken most of the money I got from the interviews and enrolled him in Art School. Sister Marie helped me write the recommendations. Ma I didn't miss much. But I just wanted to be normal again, and not have everyone see me and recognize me and touch me and chase me.

The traffic started the week before. You couldn't really get in or out of the city. Lots of businesses in Downtown Boston had to close because people couldn't get to work.

It was about midnight the night before when there was knock on my door. I was watching *Saturday Night Live.*

"Who is it?"

"Father McCarthy. May I come in, Christine?"

I rolled my eyes and wondered what that pain-in-the-ass wanted.
"I'm busy," I said.
"Just for a minute?"
I made a noise and slumped off the bed, snapping off the TV as I passed it. I whipped open the door to show my disapproval, and there was Father McCarthy with a tiny old lady, all hunched in the back. When the light from my room flooded onto her face, she smiled, raised her face, and clutched her shaking hands together.
"I'm sorry to bother you so late, Christine," Father McCarthy said, and for once he didn't sound so smarmy. "This is . . . my mother. I just picked her up at the airport."
"Hi," I said. "I suppose you want to touch me." I was tired and a little cranky.
The woman nodded, her eyes growing big like a child's. I dropped the attitude and invited them in. Mrs. McCarthy could hardly speak, with ecstasy.
"Did I tell you," Father McCarthy said, taking his mother's hand, "that this poor girl lost her brother last summer? He was hit by a train." The woman's face saddened with genuine sympathy.
Her voice went shaky and weak when she said, "Oh my dear! But . . . but isn't it nice that Our Lady appeared to you, after the horrible tragedy you've been through?" She paused, shook her blue-hair head. "That must be devastating, my dear, to lose a brother when you're young like that. I'm sure you were very close."
That was really the final straw. I almost guffawed.
"Well," I said. I stood up. "I'll see you all tomorrow."
I showed them out.

You're probably wondering why her words almost made me laugh. All right. I guess it's time.
I should tell you what happened last summer. What really happened. Okay.
It was two days after the Fourth of July. Last summer. So hot you could smell it. Sizzling and quiet. The sea breeze hadn't kicked in yet, usually that happened around three or four in the afternoon.
Jimmy was working at the tire place then, but only part time for the summer. He was going to go to Art School in New York City in Sep-

tember. He was waiting to hear about some scholarships and loans and financial aid. Ma and Dad wouldn't pay for such, "foolishness." It wasn't so much Dad—he went along with anything Ma said.

I was on the phone to Brenda. Ma was down street, food shopping. Johnny was out playing ball or working out or hanging down at the beach whatever.

Jimmy came in a little after noon, I heard the screen door slam. He came up the stairs two at a time. He stuck his hand through the crack in my door and waved it funny, like he always did, just his hand. I started laughing.

"What?" Brenda said over the phone.

"It's just Jimmy," I said. I heard him go into his bedroom and kick off his big clunky work boots. There were rushy sounds wherever Jimmy went back then, it was like he couldn't wait to do the next thing. Except when he was painting. Then he'd be still. Quiet and still, but all this energy around him in the air. Like the ocean the night before a storm.

"He's been wicked happy lately," I said to myself, while Brenda went on and on and on about what she did with this boy she met down at the beach the night before, a friend of her cousin's. A minute later Jimmy knocked on my door lightly. He popped his head in, grinning with sweaty grease all over his face and his white teeth shining.

"Are you going to be long, Chris?" he asked.

"I'm getting off now," I said, though I hadn't been planning on it. I heard Brenda wail, "Hey, I'm not through!" But the thing was, Jimmy always asked so nicely. When Johnny wanted the phone he'd just pick up the extension and start dialing, and when his stupid call wouldn't go through he'd seem truly bewildered, until he realized I was on the other end.

"You hoggin' the phone *again,* loser?" he'd snarl. "Hang up, I gotta make a call," and he wouldn't hang up until I did, making obnoxious fart sounds and stuff all the while. Jerk.

"I'll call you back," I said to Brenda. Then I handed Jimmy the portable. "How was work?" I asked. I was lying on my bed.

"Nasty!" Jimmy said, making a silly face. I laughed. "Thanks, Angel Girl. I'll take it in the other room." He hustled back into his bedroom and shut the door.

"He's *happy!*" I repeated, this time out loud in a whisper. Not that he was unhappy before . . . it was just he was always so quiet, so . . . *intense.*

I wasn't really spying, but I heard Jimmy say, "Is Denny there? Yeah, Denny O'Keefe." It's just I have wicked good hearing. Grandma Flynn's getting deaf and sometimes I watch *Oprah* with her and I have to repeat things for her, except for the kind of kinky things, which I don't repeat, that would embarrass her. "God Bless your hearing, My Dear!" she'll always say to me.

But Denny O'Keefe? I wondered what Jimmy was doing with him. He worked at the same gas station Dad did. He was old, like twenty-two or something, and all the girls would get their gas there just to look at him. He was a Dream and a Half.

A second later I could hear Jimmy laughing, and then him imitating someone. More laughing. He came out of his bedroom with the phone pressed against his right ear and just a towel wrapped around him. He scooted into the bathroom, laughing still. He turned the shower water on.

"No! No way!" he laughed again, like the other person on the line was trying to make him do something silly. "Okay, loser!" Jimmy finally said—laughing still—and then I heard what sounded like a slap. Then more laughing.

"*What* is going on with him?" I asked myself.

Then right before he hung up and got into the shower, I heard him say, "Okay. Twenty minutes. Our place." He said the last words like he was Humphrey Bogart. I looked up from my bed and caught a glance of my own puzzled face in the mirror.

He came out of the bathroom ten minutes later in a whisk of steam and the towel pressed around him. A minute later he flew out of his bedroom wearing a white T-shirt and cutoff sweatpants. There was a hint of cologne in the air.

"Where—" I began.

"I be going out, Angel Girl! Be back later!" he rattled, bounding down the stairs three at a time, like a herd of panicked animals.

Now, you have to understand, this was the summer of Nancy Drew. Grandma Flynn had given me two Nancy Drew books the Christmas before (plus fifty bucks) and they sat under my bed collecting dust until one time in March when I had a cold and was so bored I thought

I'd scream. So I read one. Then I read the other. Then I couldn't get enough of them. I had seventeen of them by then.

But even if it wasn't The Summer of Nancy Drew (who Brenda said was, "nerdy and a closet lesbo"), I don't think I could have resisted following Jimmy. I went into his room, snagged a baseball cap, then went back into my room and put on my shades. While I was there I happened to see Jimmy out my bedroom window, hopping our fence in the back yard.

"A-ha!" I thought, "he's going up the tracks!" That was the only time when we'd use the backyard cut-through, to get to the tracks.

As I flew down the stairs, my hands against the walls so I wouldn't fall (they were sticky with the heat, the way some walls get in a heat wave), I heard the screen door slam again. I thought Jimmy had come back for something.

But when I got into the kitchen, I stopped short. It was Johnny. His shaved head was poked into the refrigerator, which was always his first stop when he came in.

He turned around when he heard me.

"Where you goin'?" he asked. He was all red-faced and sweaty and icky with his shirt off and his baseball glove on his head like a hat.

"None of your beeswax," I said.

"Make me something to eat," he said, grabbing the gallon of milk and starting to chug it from the bottle.

"Yeah, when pigs fly," I said.

"Ugly bitch," he said, in between slugs.

"Up yours," I said, "and don't do that, the rest of us don't want your bad breath germs!"

He lunged at me like he was going to punch me, then pulled back.

"If you don't make me something, I'll tell Ma you swore," he threatened. "And she'll keep you in for a fuckin' year and a week."

"Oh yeah?" I said. "If you do that, I'll tell all your loser friends you thought Jesus was gonna come to town. For *years* you thought that." This was the only thing I had over Johnny.

"Ugly bitch, ugly bitch, ugly bitch," he said.

I stood in the doorway with one hand on the hot back door screen. "You're such a loser," I said.

"And you're an ugly little bitch," Johnny said. He chugged the milk again. "Speakin' of losers, where's Jimmy? He's only working half a day today. He was supposed to put all the trash out when he got home." Ma and Dad had had their big Fourth of July cookout two days before, and there were like forty bags of trash to go out. He sniffed suddenly.

"What's that cologne smell? Did that loser take my cologne?"

"I don't smell anything except your stinky pits," I lied.

"Don't tell me the world's oldest virgin had a date. Where'd he go?"

"I don't know."

"Well, he's gonna catch full shit when he gets home for not putting out the trash."

"Who died and left you boss?" I said. "You do it for a change, good-for-nothing."

"What are you, on crack?" he said. "I been playing ball all day, I'm too tired." He wiped his milk moustache away from his mouth with his sweaty forearm. "Besides, Ma told him to do it."

"You know," I said, really getting mad, "you think you're so much better than Jimmy, and Ma's stupid enough to believe it. Well you know what? You're nothing, *nothing* compared to him! He's . . . he's got talent and he's a nice person and you . . . you just got your obnoxious self!" Then I ran out the door before he could get me.

"Ugly Bitch!" I heard him yell after me. I ran across the backyard and was over the fence in a heartbeat, sweating already. I turned around to make sure Johnny wasn't chasing after me, and I saw his face watching me out the kitchen screen window. Before I could look away he gave me the finger and mouthed, *"Ug-ly Bitch!"* one last time. For once my timing was perfect, I heard Ma's car pulling into the driveway. I turned away and scooted into the O'Brien's backyard, saying, "I'm not going to cry, I'm not going to let him make me cry," over and over, so when I felt water running down my face I pretended it was sweat. I stopped and peeked at my reflection in the O'Brien's dark garage window. Grandma Flynn said all the time I was pretty, but still whenever Johnny said that . . . I believed him. And I cried.

Enough about that.

Okay, this is how you get to the tracks. You cut through our backyard, which goes into the O'Brien's backyard. Mr. O'Brien (not the O'Brien Ford ones) died about a hundred years ago. Mrs. O'Brien is like a million years old. She watches TV in the dark all day, so loud we can hear it in our house, summers. She only goes out on Sundays, to Mass, and she leaves about two hours before because she walks so slow. She hates it when we cut through her backyard, but by the time she comes out to yell it's like two days later. Then you walk up the side of their house, then you cross the street and cut through the Dwyers' backyard, but the Dwyers don't live there anymore, other people do that are never home. In the Dwyers' backyard there's a chain-link fence and you hop over that and go through some sumac bushes and then there's the tracks.

The tracks are really straight there and you can see for a long way off in both directions before they curve into the distance. I couldn't have been more than a minute behind Jimmy when I got to them. Someone was walking way ahead of me, right before a curve in the tracks. I squinted. The air was shimmery from the heat and I couldn't really tell at first. But then I saw that it wasn't Jimmy, this person was wearing long pants, like navy blue chinos. I could see it was a man. His shirt was off and hanging over his right shoulder. I walked very fast, then stopped and squinted again. I saw a red rag waving out of the back of this person's pants, back and forth as he walked.

"It's Denny O'Keefe!" I said out loud, and I got a little ping in my stomach. He could've been in the movies I bet, but instead he was a mechanic like Dad at the gas station.

Then he vanished around the curve in the distance.

Up the tracks I went, faster. Even though the trains come through here three or four times a day, tall weeds and grasses grow in between the tar-smelling railroad ties. I would have thought the trains would've cut them down, but I guess they bend when the trains come, then bounce back. I could feel the heat rising up from the shiny metal rails. I wanted to balance myself on them and pretend I was at the Olympics trying to win a gymnastics medal for the United States, but I didn't have time for that. Plus I'd forgotten to change my shoes and I was only wearing my yellow flip-flops, and they would have been too hot on the rail. They were slowing me down enough as it was, and I was trying to hurry. I stopped walking in between the ties and went over to the gravel outside the tracks. After a while it was so hot I thought my flip-flops were going to melt, so I went back to walking tie to tie. Every now and then you could see the back of a small factory or printing company, or the back of somebody's triple-decker, but mostly along the tracks you'd almost think you were out in the suburbs because bushes and trees choked out the view from both sides. I think that's probably why Jimmy always liked coming up here to read and sketch, even when he was a kid. But what was Denny O'Keefe doing up here, and why was Jimmy going to meet him? It was an Exciting Mystery and so far that summer it had been pretty dullsville. Except I got my first period, which I had been waiting for ever since Brenda got hers six months earlier. *You bleed,* she told me in school the day after it happened to her. But that's another story.

I came up to the curve. The sun was starting to burn my neck, I was glad I'd worn one of Jimmy's ball caps, but wished now for something around my neck. I have fair skin. There was some old-fashioned thing right beside me that I think they used to switch tracks in the olden days. It was all rusty and there was an old birds' nest on it. But I didn't have time to look. I saw a real butterfly for the first time in my life but I couldn't follow it, I was on a Case. The view up the tracks opened up again as I walked a little further.

I couldn't see anyone.

And you could see for about a mile ahead there.

I stopped. To the left about fifty yards ahead, right after this old bridge, another set of tracks went off to the side just for a bit and ran beside an old wrecky building there. Sitting on those side tracks were three old brown train cars. Two of them had no writing on them (unless you counted the silvery graffiti spray painted on them), and the third had its roof gone and said Southern Serves the South. Nancy Drew always said, when you eliminate every other possibility, the one that remains is the solution. I was standing still, thinking, trying not to get too excited thinking about how I could write this whole story in my beautiful handwriting and call it, "What Happened Up the Tracks."

It dawned on me that there were only two possible answers to this riddle: Denny, and Jimmy, had left the tracks and gone somewhere else, which meant I wouldn't find them because there were too many possibilities; or they were behind, or in, those abandoned train cars off to the side. The only thing to do was to go over there and investigate. The thing was though I had to cross over the bridge that the tracks were on just ahead if I wanted to get to the train cars fifty yards away. And I hated going over the bridge because you could look down in between the ties and see the street thirty feet below you. It gave me the creeps. I came up to the edge of it and stopped.

"Nancy would go," I said out loud. I took a deep breath and began moving my feet from tie to tie. The thing is, you have to look down to make sure your feet go from tie to tie, but when you look down at the ties you can see the street way below you. My shirt was sticking to me by now I was sweating so hard.

I came to the other side. "Thank you God," I said to myself. I could talk to God then, that was the last day. The train cars were only about thirty yards ahead now. I got off the tracks and went over to the side where it was all gravelly. There was a lot of junk around, pieces of barbed wire fencing, trash, broken bricks, and cinderblocks.

I got closer. The abandoned train cars were only twenty feet away. Then ten. I heard something in front of me, like the wind coming, then it turned into a rumble. A train appeared and before you could hardly do anything it came whizzing by. It was loud, so I ran fast the rest of the distance between me and the abandoned train cars, knowing no one would hear me with all the train noise. As the train passed by I could feel it rumbling inside me. Then quick it was gone.

Everything was quiet again, except for the humming of a heat bug. Then I heard a noise, like a laugh almost. It was coming from behind the abandoned train cars. My ears went up. I got a shiver down my sweaty neck. *"Yes!"* I said. To myself.

I crept closer. I heard another noise, then another. Definitely human voices. I took off my flip-flops.

I reached the first car. I waited. Nothing. Then I squatted down to look underneath. I couldn't see anything on the other side, except for weeds, and an empty busted beer bottle. I moved up a little more, very slowly, very quietly. I counted seventeen seconds between every step I took, just to make sure they didn't hear me. One Mississippi, two Mississippi, all the way up to seventeen, that's my lucky number. I put my flip-flops down so I could use both hands for balance against the hot wood and metal of the first train car. I crept along. I stopped when I came up near the space between the first car and the second one. I was behind the big train wheels, rusty and brown. I waited. I felt something on my leg. I looked down and a huge Daddy Longlegs was crawling up it. I almost screamed but didn't, Nancy wouldn't've screamed. I brushed it off, but carefully so I wouldn't kill it.

I waited for a long time, but I couldn't hear anything. I realized I had to go to the bathroom, number one. That would have to wait. My nose started itching. I tried to think of something else. I was about to move up a little further when I heard something right on the other side of me, right on the other side of the train car. I heard it very clearly. It was just the width of the train car away from me, maybe five or six feet.

"Ohhhhhh."

A low sound, like a moan. It was Jimmy's voice. Definitely.

"You like that?" somebody else said, lowly. It must have been Denny O'Keefe, though I hadn't heard him talk enough to remember his voice. I got a funny feeling in my stomach. My eyebrows bunched together all by themselves.

"Yeah," Jimmy answered, almost whispering. "Yeah Denny."

I felt like I was near something very different and strange from everything I'd ever seen or thought about before. But I didn't know how this could be. It was just my brother, and another guy. I didn't know what to think, then thought maybe they were looking at some of Jimmy's sketches or something. I wondered again how they'd gotten to be such good friends, Jimmy'd never mentioned it. Maybe Denny liked to draw too and they came up here to draw together.

There were more noises. But no words. Just more groans, and sighs, like. And sounds of things moving and rustling kind of. Half of me began to wish that I was home again, and had never come here, I didn't know why. The other half wanted to see. I knew if I just stuck my head out from behind this wheel I was hiding behind, I'd be able to see.

One Christmas when I was seven Johnny kept saying there was no Santa Claus, and I cried and cried and cried and wouldn't believe him. But just to be sure, I hung my stocking that year on my left bedpost. My bedroom door was to the right of me and the left bedpost was in the corner against the wall. That way Santa—or whoever filled my stocking—would have to lean over me to do it. I kept myself awake, and at 2:37 someone turned the handle of my bedroom door and came in. I squeezed my eyes shut. They leaned over my bed. I could feel their warm breath on my face. I thought, All I Have to Do Now Is Open My Eyes, and I'll Know.

But I was too afraid to.

But I promised myself that if I ever got in a situation like that again . . . I'd look. For sure. And find things out.

I scrunched over a bit, and turned so that I was facing them. Slowly, slowly, holding my breath. I began inching my head past the big rusty train wheel. My eyes were open wider than they ever had been, I think. I didn't know why.

And then I moved my head noiselessly past the wheel.

First one eye. Then the other.

I saw everything.

The first thing I saw was Jimmy's sneakers, quivering slightly, white with blue and yellow stripes. But his navy blue cutoff sweatpants were yanked down on the top of them. His legs were far apart. The old wreaky building that was right on the other side of the train cars had this platform that they must have used in the old days to unload stuff from the railroad, and Jimmy was lying on the platform on his back, his legs spread apart and dangling over the edge. His T-shirt was on the ground, in a pile mixed up with Denny's navy blue gas station shirt. And Denny was standing with his back to me, at the edge of the platform in between Jimmy's legs and bent over him. Denny's pants were down to his ankles. I could see his bum, all muscled and hairy and white. His hands were moving all over Jimmy's chest. His head was bobbing up and down near Jimmy's stomach somewhere.

This funny feeling came at me like I was going to hyperventilate, or maybe start laughing. I felt like I was watching something secret and private, forbidden, holy almost. Like the time when I was ten and saw a mother squirrel out in our backyard with babies squirming out of her, and she looked at me with big eyes like she didn't want me to watch but couldn't do anything to stop me.

I couldn't look away, couldn't move. Then Denny climbed on top of Jimmy, and Jimmy lifted himself up a bit until he was sitting, and they started kissing. Hard like they do in movies, like they were in pain, and noises. Then I saw both their Boy Things, they were red and sticking straight up and big. And then Denny put his hands on both sides of Jimmy's face and looked at him. Jimmy looked into Denny's eyes. I lost my breath. I'd never seen that look on Jimmy's face before. On anyone's face, except maybe some of the holy statues in church. But it was what I always wanted for Jimmy, to be happy, beyond happy.

I guess I made a sound when I saw that look on Jimmy's face. Both their heads whipped around. They looked around wild for a second. Then they saw me. They froze. They could see me right there, half-under the train car on the other side. But still I couldn't move or say anything. It seemed like a very long second that all three of us just stared with loud beating hearts.

Jimmy's eyes got bug huge. His mouth fell open. His lips moved, but no sound came out. They were wet and shiny.

"Fuck!" Denny cried, like he was seeing a monster. He closed his eyes, then made a weird sound and roared the word again. *"Fuck!"* He yanked up his pants and grabbed his shirt. The heat bug sizzled again like nothing had happened. Before Denny had his pants even hooked up all the way, he took off. He stumbled down the tracks about ten feet, then practically dove into some bushes on the side, and vanished. It was like I was watching a movie, but in real life.

When I looked back at Jimmy, he was trying to pull his cutoffs up. But they were all sweaty and rolled and bunched up like, and they were stuck around his knees. I don't think I've ever seen anyone look scareder in my life.

"It's . . . it's . . . it's okay, it's okay J-Jimmy," I heard myself stuttering. Then something grabbed hold onto my wrist from behind like a vice.

"Okay? Okay? What the *fuck* are you talking about?"

I whipped around. It was Johnny right there. His eyes were wild, almost white, and his face as red as Jimmy's.

I guess he'd followed me.

"Your brother's a fuckin' *faggot!* And you think that's fuckin' *okay? Are you fuckin' nuts?*"

Johnny pushed me hard against the train car. The back of my head whacked against it. But I couldn't even make a sound, couldn't even cry out. Everything was happening too fast. Johnny brushed past me, toward Jimmy.

"I'm gonna be fuckin' *SICK!*" Johnny screamed, roared really loud, his face all red like it might explode. His hands swelled into clenched fists. Jimmy kept yanking his cutoffs up. He finally got them to cover his Thing, but still his face hadn't changed, not a muscle like he was in shock.

"So! You're a fuckin' queer, huh? I should'a known it! I should'a fuckin' known it! A piece o' shit *fag!* Wait'll Ma finds out! And Dad! They'll throw your faggot ass out o' the house so fuckin' fast—"

He stopped. I could see his eyes squint. I felt a thing of sweat drip off my nose.

"Who was that who ran off into the bushes?" Johnny said. He took a step closer to Jimmy. "Who was it? Who's your little faggot fuck buddy? Huh? WHO WAS IT?"

Jimmy still couldn't seem to move, or say anything. He was just watching Johnny with eyes that looked dead. Johnny turned around one way, then the other, making these noises like a dog, breathing heavy. Then he saw something and dashed about ten feet into the bushes. A second later he came out with a big pipe, thick like a baseball bat except rusty and metal and longer. I felt like I was watching a dream, the worst dream, slow and unstoppable.

Johnny raised the pipe over his head. He advanced toward Jimmy, who still hadn't moved from the platform.

"You fuckin' *tell me who that was!*" he screamed. Jimmy just looked up.

"Fuck you," Jimmy murmured. But he didn't move.

Johnny wound up and swung, with a roar. The pipe whistled WHOOSH as it went through the air. I felt like I might throw up. *"Noooooo!"* I heard, then realized it was me, screaming. Jimmy scooted to the side but not quick enough. Part of the pipe slammed into the platform wall and cracked the cement, but the rest of it crashed onto Jimmy's bare leg. Jimmy screamed out in agony. He reached for the pipe with one hand but Johnny was quicker and yanked it back.

Johnny raised the pipe again, getting ready to wind up for a second time. Jimmy was wedged against the platform door, there was nowhere for him to go. "Oh God," I heard him moan. I screamed again, and that seemed to wake me up.

"It was Denny O'Keefe! It was Denny O'Keefe!" I cried, freaking out, coming closer, not to be a squealer but because I thought maybe Johnny would stop now. The pipe froze in the air.

"Huh?" Johnny panted, not even turning around, like he'd forgotten I was there.

"It was! It was Denny O'Keefe!" I repeated, my voice breaking.

"Jesus Christ," Johnny snorted, resting the pipe onto his shoulder, but still clenching it hard with both red hands. "The fuckin' grease monkey? Works with Dad? He's a faggot too? Je-sus Christ. Wait'll I tell Dad. He won't have that fuckin' job long."

"NOOOO!" Jimmy screamed all of a sudden, I don't think I'd ever heard anyone scream so loud. He jumped up. His face was all twisted. "He'll kill himself if anyone finds out! He will! He will!"

"So?" Johnny said, smiling. "One less fag. You should kill yourself too."

Jimmy sprang from the platform, and crashed on top of Johnny. They both fell to the ground. They rolled around a bit. I felt tears streaming down my face. I noticed two of my fingers were in my mouth. Johnny got loose and stood up. Jimmy tried to, but he couldn't. I saw his leg above the knee where Johnny had whacked it, it was all bloody and pulpy. Both of them were gasping for air. Johnny had a look on his face like he was almost enjoying this. He raised the pipe again high in the air. Jimmy put his hands over his head.

"No!" I screamed. "No!" I ran over to Johnny and grabbed him by the back of his white T-shirt, but I tripped as I did it and fell. His T-shirt ripped a little as I lost my grip. I grabbed onto the back of his leg and dug my fingernails into his flesh.

"Get the *fuck* outta here, you little bitch!" he screamed, half turning. He kicked at me, but I fell back and he missed. I felt a whoosh of air go by me as his foot swept past my face. I jumped up quick and backed off.

"You'll kill himmmm!" I screamed, losing it for a minute.

He turned away from me like I wasn't even there. He raised the pipe again. There was a broken cinder block on the ground. It was right there, like on purpose. There were some others scattered here and there but this one was right here beside me. I picked it up.

"Johnny!" I said. The pipe came back, he was winding up, he wasn't paying me any mind and was making animal sounds.

"Look!" I shouted as loud as I could. "Jesus! It's Jesus! Jesus came to town!"

"Huh?" Johnny panted, half turning toward me.

"Here!" I said, and I was crying. I crashed the cinder block into his face with all my might, both hands.

There was this crunching noise—

—I don't like to remember that part. That's when the blackness started inside me.

Johnny fell. He didn't make any sound at all. He just crumbled and fell. He lay motionless for a minute, then one of his legs kicked out.

Then he was still again.

Then it was very very quiet. Even the heat bug stopped.

I was shaking. I felt wet all over from my sweat, like I'd just climbed out of the ocean. I couldn't stop shaking. I heard a weird wheezing noise and couldn't figure it out, then I realized it was my breath. Jimmy still had his head covered with his hands, but he was staring at Johnny lying there.

"Oh God," he said, all wavery, like his voice was coming through water. He half got up and staggered over near Johnny.

Johnny's sneakers were brand new, they were always brand new, Ma was always buying him sneakers but not me or Jimmy. "He's an athlete, he needs them," Ma would say. "You two don't do anything." But now Johnny's sneakers, at the ends of his feet spread apart, one of them had splotches of blood on it.

I turned afraid and threw up.

"Oh God!" Jimmy repeated. I turned back around. He was leaning on one leg. He ran his hands through his hair. There was white dust like chalk on Johnny's face from the cinder block. Part of his forehead, and his left eye, were crushed in. Blood seeped out, like a leak from under a door during a flood. I watched Johnny's T-shirt to see if he was breathing. It didn't move.

"Johnny!" Jimmy wailed. He had all his weight on one leg. He reached down his hand like he was going to touch Johnny, but then his hand stopped halfway. Jimmy started sobbing. Our eyes met.

"I had to!" I said. I was shaking and couldn't stop. "I had to, he was going to kill you!" I burst into Jimmy and we held tight tight tight onto each other.

"I'm sorry!" Jimmy wailed, "I'm sorry, I'm so sorry—"

He turned away from me.

"It . . . it wasn't your f-fault," I said. "He was gonna kill you! Is . . . is your leg . . ." I continued, but I could hardly talk.

"Nothing's broken," he said. Then he raised his head. His eyes moved back and forth.

"I gotta think," he said. "Oh Jesus help me think."

I was crying and I didn't even know it. Then Jimmy said, "I don't want you getting into trouble. Don't . . . wait a minute . . . Jesus Christ . . . don't say you were anywhere near here today. Do you hear me? You were nowhere near here today."

It was a relief for someone else to have an idea, to take charge.

"All r-right," I said.

"C'mon," he said, but he didn't move, he was still standing over Johnny.

"What?" I said.

"We have to get him on the tracks."

I couldn't say anything. I just stared at Jimmy. Finally he looked up at me.

"We have to," he said. "It has to look like he was hit . . . b-by the train. Come on."

I walked over, keeping my eyes on Jimmy. Then I looked down. Johnny—my brother Johnny—

We both grabbed a hand. I didn't know if I could. The one I grabbed was still warm, hot even, still sweaty. It felt almost like Johnny's hand grabbed back. Tears started pouring down my face so bad I almost couldn't see. Which was good, it was just a blur we were dragging to the tracks, not our brother. Jimmy started dry heaving, nothing would come out.

We laid him on the tracks. I turned away quick. Jimmy kept staring down at him. He started sobbing again, hard like it hurt really bad. It hurt my ears to hear it.

"Come on," I said. I felt sick again. The sun was making everything quavery. Jimmy finally limped over to me. He looked around for a bit. Then he kicked the cinder block that had hit Johnny on the head. He kept kicking it lightly, rolling it over and over, until he got it way over by the train cars. Then he picked up the pipe Johnny was going to kill him with—he was really going to kill him—and started whacking at it. Pretty soon the cinder block was all just tiny tiny pieces, and dust. Then he threw the pipe back into the bushes.

"Let's get outta here," he said after that. We started hustling down the tracks, Jimmy limping. We came to an old half-tipped-over trash barrel that had some rainwater in it. We walked by it, then Jimmy turned around. He took his T-shirt which he'd been holding in his hand, dipped it into the water, then cleaned off his leg wound. It didn't look as bad once the blood was cleared away, but already there was a lump on it bigger than an egg.

When we came up to Dwyers' backyard, Jimmy said, "Keep walking. Just say you were down this other end of the tracks. Don't come home until . . . until after the train goes by. Don't walk on the tracks." But we didn't have to wait. Jimmy stopped talking and his eyes darted around. I heard it at the same time. He pulled me into the bushes. The train was about half a mile up the tracks. I kept waiting listening for a loud whistle, a blast of screeching brakes. But all I could hear was my heart beating in my ears. I closed my eyes. Jimmy was holding my wrist tight. We both clenched our eyes and bowed our heads when the train went rumbling by us a few seconds later. It never stopped, or made a sound other than its usual roaring.

They never even asked us questions. Ma was taken to the hospital that night, she was crazy. She hurled one of the living room lamps out through the front window onto the street, where it shattered into a million pieces. It almost hit a little kid on his bike. Then they took her away. Grandma Flynn came and lived with us for a month, until Ma came home again. Grandma Flynn asked me and Jimmy to say the Rosary with her that night before we all went to bed. Dad was still at the hospital where they took Ma.

"Why, Mercy Me, child," Grandma Flynn said, in between the Second and Third Sorrowful Mysteries, "what on earth happened to your leg?" In his kneeling, Jimmy's pant leg had scooted up a bit. You could see a very angry purple blotch. That was just the tip of it.

"I . . . ahh, I whacked it," Jimmy said.

And that's what happened.

It's almost midnight when there's another knock on my door. I probably won't get much sleep this night anyway—tomorrow being the Big Day—and the last thing I need is more visitors. I roll over, but then I think maybe it's Jimmy, saying goodbye. He'll be leaving on the morning train, off to Art School in New York City, thank God, before everything happens. I want him to be way away out of town, even though I'm not sure yet what's going to happen. But I can guess.

I get up and tiptoe over to the door. The old rectory wood floor creaks.

"Jimmy?" I whisper.

"Sister Marie," I hear instead.

Uh-oh.

"May I please come in, Christine?"

"Okay," I said. She came in. I avoided her eyes and snapped on the desk lamp, which is ugly and old fashioned.

"May I sit down, Christine?"

"Sure." Her habit rustled again, like Grandma's tablecloth. I liked that sound. There was a small chair at the desk, and she pulled this out and sat in it.

"I came to say good-bye," she said.

"You're leaving?"

"Yes. My time here is through. There are other places I must go, other tings I must do."

"When?"

"Tomorrow. The early train."

"Oh. That's when Jimmy's going too," I said.

"Yes, I know. I am going wit him as far as New York City. I tink I will see him settled."

I bit my lip so I wouldn't cry, kept looking at the carpet, at my bare feet.

"Thanks," I whispered. It was all worth it. "Thank you thank you thank you. I . . . I did this all for Jimmy. And for you."

"I know dis," Sister Marie said. "I know dis. I am sure you did not know how dis whole crazy world would come slamming down on you . . . but I tink even if you did know, still you would have done dis. For Jimmy. And for me."

I nodded.

"Just when you tink you have seen it all," she said, and she smiled and her eyes were far away.

"So," she said after a minute looking back at me, "how are you?"

"Okay I guess. A little spacy. I'll . . . be glad when this is all over."

"Ah, I must tell you Christine . . . et will never be over, ma chere," she said. She paused. "Now I want to ask you something, Christine."

"Okay. Shoot." She took my hands in hers.

"I was wondering ef you are . . . planning on telling the truth tomorrow?"

She felt my hands tighten.

"I . . . I don't know if I can," I said. The room started getting hotter.

"I will help you," she said. "I will help you now. Look at me, Christine."

She reached out and took my hands. I tried to pull away, but she held on with a tenderness I couldn't break. I sat down on the edge of the bed across from her, and slowly lifted my head. Our eyes met. I tried to look away, but I couldn't.

After a minute I began shaking.

"Don't be afraid," she said, her voice inside me more than outside me, but I was, I couldn't help it, I was more afraid than I'd ever been, more afraid than the day Johnny died.

"Please, please," was all I could say. "I'm sorry, I'm sorry." My heart felt like it was beating under a huge strain, and my tongue flew up to the roof of my mouth. I made a start for the door but she was in front of that too, she was everywhere and light all around—

"You know who I am now," she said. I could only shake. I jammed my eyes shut and fell to the ground, covering my head. If there was anyone I could have called on in this world, I would've screamed their name.

"So you see Christine you weren't entirely lying. Look at me."

I raised my head slowly. I opened my eyes.

There was nothing but light in front of me, blasting light like horns were blowing and I could see the light exploding out of them.

"I wish you could see how beautiful you are," she said.

I burst out sobbing.

"I w-wanted to h-help Jimmy," I gasped. "I wanted to help you, I didn't want them to fire—"

"I know," she said, gently. "I told you, I know. I know. I know everyting. Listen, Christine—tomorrow, they are expecting Jesus to come. To walk down the street maybe. Like someone in a parade. Dis will not happen. The Spirit is Master of the Flesh, but you cannot expect the Spirit to act like the Flesh, no? Christine, look at me. They will look to you for answers. You tell them dis: can you listen?"

I couldn't stop shaking.

"O-okay."

"Dis es what you tell dem. You tell them every time someone call someone else they have the quarrel with, and make peace, Jesus comes to town; you tell them every time someone visits prison, Jesus comes to town; you tell them when a young person sticks up for another young person that everyone else is calling fat, or faggot, or anyting, Jesus comes to town; you tell them every time someone is so full of despair and loneliness that they feel like nothing but ashes and dust inside, Jesus has come to town to suffer wit dem; when you let someone love you, Jesus comes to town; when you invite the homeless into your home, when you work for justice, when you feed the hungry, Jesus comes to town. Whenever you do something for another, something for love that terrifies you, then Jesus comes to town."

There was something warm moving through me and I didn't think I could stand not to faint. My body began shaking frantically.

"Dey will not believe you, tomorrow," she went on in my mind, a voice like water flowing. "Dey will say this is all lies. Dey will laugh at you. Dey will dismiss you. Dey will scorn you. Dey will say terrible tings about you. Even your mother. Dey will turn you into a freak, and the only ones who will believe you are those the world calls freaks, and losers, and the sad crazy people who sometimes see so deeply. And all your life you will be considered as one of dese."

"Oh . . . my p-punishment," I somehow groaned, relieved.

"No punishment," she said. "Dis is no punishment. Dis is a reward. But not the only one. There is anoder . . . " She stood up and pulled me into her arms, and everything started slanting and whirring. "And that is dis: now you know Christine," she said. "Now you know. Now you know." I couldn't handle it anymore and I think I blacked out, spinning and upside down and everything and nothing and light.

When I woke up I was lying on my bed, still dressed. The sun was coming through the window. It was Sunday, December 1. I felt nothing, but then I remembered, and I felt something heavy like ten thousand old books fell on top of me.

But that was okay. No problemo, really.

Sister Marie was right. You see, I knew.

When I came out of the bathroom, a photographer was outside my window, he'd lowered himself from the roof with mountain-climbing ropes. I let him take pictures of me as I numbly sat at my desk, drawing pictures of flowers. Then I think the police saw him, he disappeared kind of quick.

Brenda's Aunt Teresa, who's the cook at the Rectory, brought me Frosted Stars, some juice, a banana, and some toast for my breakfast. But I couldn't really eat.

At nine o'clock, I thought, *they're on the train now, the two of them.* And I knew I could take anything. Plus I knew. There's nothing in this world that can really bother you, once you know.

On the way to the church, it was crazier than I even had imagined, even with what I was used to. There were helicopters right overhead, and a blimp over that, and everywhere I looked, people. People on roofs, people crowded together so tightly they stopped looking like people anymore. It was just all waving hands and stretched arms and blurry faces and police and cameras and signs and posters and bullhorns and police and noise.

By the time I got up to the platform they'd set up for me at the head of the church, I didn't recognize anyone around me anymore, except for Father McCarthy. I'd never seen the church fuller, but they weren't any of the regular parishioners or neighbors. Most of them were outside, where they'd set up huge speakers for the thousands and thousands gathered for blocks around.

"She doesn't look that holy to me," I heard one man say with a laugh. "She looks nervous," someone else said. There was a whole section reserved for the press, and they were all snickering among themselves mostly.

I cleared my throat to silence everybody, and began.

I tried to remember exactly what I'd been told the night before.

"Jesus won't be coming here today," I said. "I mean, not in the way everyone expects." Out of the corner of my eye, I saw Father McCarthy's head jerk back a little, like he'd been slapped. He took a step back, away from me. Every head in the church raised up. Eyes became huge and blank.

"B-but each one of us," I continued, "has the power to make Him present whenever we wish."

There was a vast silence.

"Wh-whenever we're nice to each other," I added. My mouth parched up. I couldn't seem to remember Sister Marie's exact words. I looked out at the crowd again. I tried to find a friendly face, maybe someone that was smiling, if I could find just one friendly face I thought I'd be able to talk.

But I couldn't. I kind of froze.

But I knew this collapse was a gift too. It would throw me up out of the unimportant things of this world and free me.

"When . . . when we f-forgive someone," I stumbled. I froze again. The flashes from the cameras blinded me.

"Liar!" someone called out from the back of the church.

"She's a fake!" someone else cried.

Two waves ran through the crowd—one almost of relief, I think. The other—definitely—was kind of like a satisfied outrage. These waves broke on each other toward the middle of the crowd. They canceled each other out, like negative numbers in math, but a noise rose out from this center area. It was the growl of the crowd.

They were grumbling like lions now. Remembering something, I pulled an onion out of my pocket.

"We are all like onions!" I yelled into the microphone, above the crowd, but way too loud like Mr. Dooley the Nervous Lector. My consonants POPPED. But it didn't matter anyway, the words bounced off the crowd like flat rocks skipping over water.

They didn't want to hear it. There was a surge like a tidal wave in my direction—

But that's okay. Like a good Catholic, it was time for me to do my Penance. If you're not Catholic, that means when you forgive yourself, so you can forgive everyone else.

ABOUT THE AUTHOR

J. G. Hayes, an ex-newspaperman, is a writer and landscaper living in the Boston area.

Order a copy of this book with this form or online at:
http://www.haworthpressinc.com/store/product.asp?sku=4592

THIS THING CALLED COURAGE
South Boston Stories

_____in hardbound at $27.95 (ISBN: 1-56023-380-X)
_____in softbound at $17.95 (ISBN: 1-56023-381-8)

COST OF BOOKS_____

OUTSIDE USA/CANADA/
MEXICO: ADD 20%____

POSTAGE & HANDLING_____
(US: $4.00 for first book & $1.50
for each additional book)
Outside US: $5.00 for first book
& $2.00 for each additional book)

SUBTOTAL_____

in Canada: add 7% GST____

STATE TAX____
(NY, OH & MIN residents, please
add appropriate local sales tax)

FINAL TOTAL____
(If paying in Canadian funds,
convert using the current
exchange rate, UNESCO
coupons welcome.)

BILL ME LATER: ($5 service charge will be added)
(Bill-me option is good on US/Canada/Mexico orders only;
not good to jobbers, wholesalers, or subscription agencies.)

Check here if billing address is different from
shipping address and attach purchase order and
billing address information.

Signature_____

PAYMENT ENCLOSED: $_____

PLEASE CHARGE TO MY CREDIT CARD.

Visa   MasterCard   AmEx   Discover
Diner's Club   Eurocard   JCB

Account # _____

Exp. Date_____

Signature_____

Prices in US dollars and subject to change without notice.

NAME_____
INSTITUTION_____
ADDRESS_____
CITY_____
STATE/ZIP_____
COUNTRY_____ COUNTY (NY residents only)_____
TEL_____ FAX_____
E-MAIL_____

May we use your e-mail address for confirmations and other types of information?   Yes   No
We appreciate receiving your e-mail address and fax number. Haworth would like to e-mail or fax special
discount offers to you, as a preferred customer. **We will never share, rent, or exchange your e-mail address
or fax number.** We regard such actions as an invasion of your privacy.

Order From Your Local Bookstore or Directly From
The Haworth Press, Inc.
10 Alice Street, Binghamton, New York 13904-1580 • USA
TELEPHONE: 1-800-HAWORTH (1-800-429-6784) / Outside US/Canada: (607) 722-5857
FAX: 1-800-895-0582 / Outside US/Canada: (607) 722-6362
E-mail: getinfo@haworthpressinc.com
PLEASE PHOTOCOPY THIS FORM FOR YOUR PERSONAL USE.
www.HaworthPress.com